On Wings of the Morning

Also by Marie Bostwick

River's Edge

Fields of Gold

"A High-Kicking Christmas"
in the anthology
Comfort and Joy

On Wings of the Morning

MARIE BOSTWICK

KENSINGTON BOOKS
http://www.kensingtonbooks.com

To the Women's Air Service Pilots

With Gratitude

I thank God for giving me the opportunity and inspiration to write and for surrounding me with the wonderful mix of friends and family who make writing my joy. Without the encouragement and support of so many, especially my husband, Brad, my dear friend, Pamela Helm, my agent, Jill Grosjean, and my editor, Audrey LaFehr, this book would never have been written. Thank you all.

Additionally, I want to extend a special and heartfelt thanks to my first-round reader, Elizabeth Walsh, whose humor, optimism, attention to detail, patience, and uncanny sense of dramatic timing, make all the difference to her little sister's books and life. Betty, I'm glad you're my sister.

Prologue

Morgan

Knowing who I am, you might think I was born to fly. Probably there is something to that. If the yearning for flight is something you can inherit from your parents like blue eyes or a bad temper, then I suppose I come by it honestly enough. But if that is true, then it might just be the only honest piece of my birthright.

Though it was years before we could talk about my father, Mama says that even as a little boy I sensed the truth, or at least part of it. She still speaks in hushed amazement of the night of my fourth birthday, the night she tucked me in under her present to me, a quilt of the Oklahoma night sky appliquéd with star points over a field of cobalt and midnight, stitched by hand with the three-strand thread that held Mama's whole world together—imagination, determination, and secrets. There was so much we couldn't, or didn't, talk about.

And I wanted to know everything. Things about her. About me. About why, when she thought I wasn't looking, she would fix her eyes on closed doors as though waiting for someone to open them. Who was she waiting for? I wanted to ask, but didn't. Somehow I sensed that if I pulled on the strand that stood for secrets, all of us would unravel at the seams.

Maybe that's why I made up the story I told her that night, about the father I'd imagined for myself, a father who'd died and flown a recon mission to Heaven, just to make sure the coast was clear for me. I knew he was an invention, but an invented father was better than a void. Mama's eyes welled up when I told her my story, but they were happy tears, I could tell. Somehow I'd hit upon something right, something that caused a flickering light of hope to shine through her tears. I rolled my tale out as a bolt of whole cloth, woven with equal parts of plausibility and fabrication, and Mama did what she always did: she embellished it with explanations and appliquéd on a desire for things the way they should have been, and by the time I closed my eyes to sleep we'd stitched a story so sincere and inviting that it could nearly have passed for truth. Nearly.

If the truth is to be told, and I think the time has come, it wasn't my heritage that drove me to the sky. It was the secrets. The first time I pulled the stick back and nosed my plane skyward, breaking through a bank of bleached muslin clouds into a field of edgeless blue, I realized that I'd finally found the place I belonged, the only place where my skin didn't feel as if it were bound too tight around my soul. The longing was always there, but how could I have known what it was I longed for? I was just trying to outrun the secrets.

The family history Mama and I patched together was warm and comfortable and tightly sewn; we wrapped it around ourselves as a shelter from the hard blows of life, but at the end of the day it was just a collection of lies.

There are no secrets in the sky. There is no need for them. When I see the heavens stretched before me, it does not matter where I came from, or where I am going, or who came before me. No one asks me questions, and I don't ask them of myself. That moment is *the* moment for me. There is no time and no regrets, nothing to weigh me down.

The closer you fly to Earth, the more your craft will be rocked and battered by turbulence, and if the tumult is strong it can throw you completely off course. But if you fly high enough, where there isn't oxygen enough to sustain a lie, you'll find bright skies and air so smooth you can cut through the clouds, slippery and free. That is where I live.

I am the eagle's son.

PART ONE

❧ 1 ❧

Morgan

Dillon, Oklahoma—1933

There was a patch of dried blood stuck in the crease where my upper lip met the lower. I squashed my face up and felt the blood crack into a dozen dry little flakes. I rubbed them off with my hand, held my palm open, and watched the wind grab hold of the rusty flecks and suck them into a passing dust cloud. By nightfall those dried-up blood slivers would most likely be blown into the next county, but the rest of the evidence would be harder to conceal.

I'd used the sleeve of my shirt to sop up the blood that had spurted from my nose where Johnny McCurdle's elbow had clipped me as I'd wrestled him to the ground. I knew by tomorrow morning he'd be telling everybody that he'd broken my nose, but I wasn't worried about that. There'd been plenty of witnesses to the fight, and they'd be more than ready to testify to the truth—that Johnny hadn't intentionally been able to land a single punch on my face, that he looked much worse than I did when it was all over, that when he fought he closed his eyes and flailed his arms like a girl, and that, being frustrated in his effort to connect his fists with any vulnerable part of my anatomy, he'd kicked me in the shins with those hard, pointy-toed cowboy boots he always wore, which, in the unwritten rules of schoolyard fisticuffs, is just flat bush-league.

No, I wasn't worried about my reputation suffering after my fight with Johnny, but I was worried about how I was going to keep the news from getting to Mama. The blood from my nose had spread and bloomed into a good-sized stain on the sleeve of my shirt. On the walk home from school, I'd scuttled down the dirty banks of the irrigation ditch that ran parallel to Grandpa's parched wheat fields, hoping to find some water to wash out my shirt. It was spring, and the trench should have been home to a fresh and flowing stream, but this was the Oklahoma panhandle in the third year of what would be a nearly ten-year drought, and there was barely a trickle of water to be found at the bottom of the ditch. The soil rising up from the streambed had dried and cracked into a pattern of uneven diamond shapes, like the skin on an alligator's back, and the stingy rivulet of water that dribbled past my feet was so thick and muddy that washing with it would probably have left my shirt dirtier than it had been to start with. I had no choice; I'd have to walk home and get myself cleaned up at the pump in the barnyard before my mother could spot me and start asking questions.

The pump handle squeaked in protest as I wrenched it up and down, trying to bring forth the flow of water. After some effort the old pump complied, but even so, the stream that poured from the spout was slow, and I knew that our well was getting low. I took off my shirt, squatted down next to the pump, and filled a bucket with water before shutting off the spout. In years past I'd have carelessly let the water run out onto the ground, but even at the age of ten, I knew that water in a drought is precious and mustn't be wasted. I plunged my shirt into the bucket and scrubbed the stain by rubbing one piece of fabric against another, the way I'd seen Mama do, and noted with some satisfaction that the combination of cold water and elbow grease was doing the trick; the bloodstain was fading.

"Now that your shirt's clean, have you thought about how you're going to get it dry before your mother sees it?" The sound of my grandfather's amused Irish brogue startled me, and I jumped.

"Geez, Papaw! You don't need to sneak up on a guy like that. I almost tipped the bucket over."

"Sorry, Morgan." He grinned, and the corners of his eyes drew up like folds in a paper fan. "I whistled to you from the hog pen, but I don't think you heard me. You were pretty intent on doing your laundry." He nodded at my sodden shirt that dripped a trail of water, streaming a dark stripe over the thirsty soil.

Papaw took a step and leaned down to get a closer look at me. His face grew solemn. "That lip is pretty swollen. Your nose doesn't look any too good, either."

For a moment I considered telling him that I'd fallen or been beaned by a wild pitch during a game of baseball, but I didn't want to lie to my grandfather. Papaw was my best friend, even if he was a grown-up. I didn't say anything. His eyes bore into me, questioning.

Finally, he drew his eyebrows up and smiled. "So, how does the other fella look?"

I grinned. "Not too good. Two black eyes and a split lip."

"Well, I don't doubt but he deserved it," Papaw said evenly and paused for a moment. "Did he deserve it?"

I thought about Johnny McCurdle and the things he'd said about me. About me not having a father. That wasn't anything new. I'd endured that kind of schoolyard taunting for as long as I could remember. They could say anything they wanted about me and I'd just shrug it off or turn the joke on them. In Johnny's case that wasn't too hard. He had ears that stuck out like open doors on a car, so all I had to do was call him "fender face" and that would set all the other kids to laughing. Suddenly Johnny himself would be the butt of the joke, surrounded by jeering classmates, coloring with anger and embarrassment to the tips of his car-door ears while I slipped away from the crowd unnoticed. Much as I disliked Johnny, always had, I didn't enjoy doing this. I only picked on him when he started it. He was mean, it was true, but more than that, he was just not too bright. By making fun of me he was trying to get a little attention for himself, and he always seemed a little perplexed when his plans turned around on him. Part of me felt sorry for him. I suppose that's why I'd never fought him—not until that day.

It was one thing to call me names and quite another to bring my mother into it. That day he had. He'd called Mama a name so bad that I didn't really know what it meant, and I bet Johnny didn't, either. Probably he'd heard it from his older brothers, but definitions aside, I got his general drift. The sneer on his ugly face told me of his intent, and the shocked gasps from some of the older girls who stood nearby let me know that this was a word that went far, far beyond the normal range of schoolyard insults. Nobody could talk about my mother like that and get away with it. "He deserved it," I muttered darkly and felt my hand involuntarily ball up into a fist. If Johnny had been standing there I'd have beaten him a second time.

"Said something about your mother, did he?" Papaw's eyes were dark.

"Did what I had to do, Papaw."

He took in a deep breath and nodded. I knew that was all the explanation he required. He wouldn't ask me any more questions.

Living with three women in our house—Mama, Grandma, and Aunt Ruby, who wasn't my aunt at all but Mama's best friend who lived with us—I sometimes felt like I was in danger of drowning in a flood of chintz and feminine fussing. The house was bursting with women, but the barn and barnyard, that was our world, mine and Papaw's—a world of men where people didn't ask endless questions, or go to pieces over the sight of a little blood, where it was understood that sometimes a man had to do what a man had to do, and where sometimes a simple nod of the head was as good as an hour's conversation. What would I have done without Papaw? I knew I could have told him anything, but I also knew I didn't have to—he understood.

"I guess we'd better decide what you're going to tell your mother. Clean shirt or no, she's going to know that something happened. You're a sight, lad." Papaw sucked on his teeth thoughtfully, and then he walked over near the barn door and picked up a rake that was resting against the wall. He brought the rake back to where I was standing and thunked me—squarely, but not too hard—on the head with the wooden handle.

"Hey!" I protested. "What was that for?"

"If your mother asks what happened to you, you can say that you got hit with a rake while you were out helping me, and it won't be a lie."

"You mean like I accidentally stepped on the tines and the handle flew up and whacked me on the face?"

Papaw nodded. "No need to go into details, but, yes, that's the general idea."

"She's not gonna buy that, Papaw. Mama is way too smart to fall for a story like that. We've got to come up with something better."

"Listen to me, Morgan. Don't start telling lies to your mother. If you tell one lie, you're bound to have to start telling others just to cover up the first one. After a while it gets to be a habit."

"But, isn't this the same thing? I might not be exactly lying to her, but I'm trying to keep something from her."

"No." Papaw shook his head. "We're not trying to keep something from her. We're trying to protect her from something that would only cause her worry and grief. She's had enough of that in her life. If you'll just tell her your story without offering too many details, she'll leave you be. You'll see."

Papaw was smart about people, I knew, but I couldn't imagine that Mama would let this slide so easily. Mama wasn't a big talker herself, but she was interested in everything that happened to me.

Almost every afternoon of my life, once I'd finished my chores, was spent sitting on the floor next to Mama while she sat sewing at her quilt frame or tracing around templates for quilt blocks.

When it came to quilt-making, Mama was an artist. She made quilts that looked like paintings, and until the Depression was in full swing and cash was so scarce, people waited months and paid top dollar for the privilege of owning one of Mama's creations. She had more orders than she could handle and was often weeks behind in her work, but those after-school chats were our special time together. She always had time to listen to me jabber away about school, my teachers, my friends, anything that might be on my mind. And the thing is, she didn't just murmur absentmindedly, pretending to listen while rocking her needle up and down through the fabric, making those tiny, absolutely even stitches she was famous for. She truly listened. She asked just the right question at just the right moment. She made me feel important—as though whatever I had to say was worth listening to. Mama knew me inside and out. She wasn't going to fall for any half-baked explanations about the source and nature of my injury. Papaw read the doubt on my face.

"Morgan, your mother is no fool. Deep in her heart, she's going to know there is more to the story than you're sharing, but she's not going to press you about it. She can't change the past. Not hers. Not yours. When you can't fix a problem, sometimes it's easier to pretend there isn't one. Know what I mean?"

I looked at him blankly.

"Never mind. You'll understand when you're older. Your mother is a good woman, son. No matter what anyone says, your mother is a good woman."

"I know that." It was the closest we'd ever come to talking about my mother and, more importantly, my father. Suddenly it dawned on me that Papaw knew who he was—his name, what he looked like, maybe even where he lived and why he wasn't here with me. Papaw knew everything, and I came that close to asking him. My mouth opened, and the question formed on my lips. "Papaw," I began, but that was as far as I got. My grandfather could read the question in my eyes, knew what I wanted to ask before I could ask it, and in his eyes I could read, just as clearly, that he wouldn't give me an answer. He couldn't. That was Mama's secret, and as long as she kept silent, we'd all have to.

Papaw dropped a big, calloused hand on my shoulder. "I've got to finish fixing that wobbly board on the hog pen. The sow worked it loose again rubbing up to scratch her back. You pump some fresh water for your chickens and get them back inside for the night. I saw a big black dog skulking around last night. Probably a stray. Might be the same one that got to Thompson's birds last week, so you make sure you shut those hens in good and tight. We've got about an hour to supper. Should be enough time for your shirt to dry."

"Yes, Papaw." I stooped over the bucket to squeeze the last drops of water from my shirt. The water wasn't clean enough to give to the chickens but I could pour it over Aunt Ruby's tomato plants.

Papaw turned and started walking toward the hog pen, but he only got a few steps before he called to me over his shoulder.

"Morgan!"

"Yes, Papaw?"

"You're a good son." He smiled and kept walking.

I stood up and shook out my shirt. A quick, sharp gust of prairie wind lifted the wet fabric into the air, blowing dust onto the previously clean cloth. I held tight to the sleeves, and the shirt billowed out in front of me like a sail trying to draw me into the breeze, and I wished, for the hundredth time, that I was light enough and free enough to fly.

∞ 2 ∞

Georgia

The 1920s

I've always been a realist. I had to be, because my mother's grip on reality was so tenuous. Someone had to be the grown-up in our family, and by the time I was six years old it was clear to me that Cordelia Carter Boudreaux was not putting in an application for the position.

Cordelia Carter Boudreaux. Lord! How in the world did she ever conjure up a name like that? One thing I'll say for my mother. She had imagination.

Delia had no more claim of descent from New Orleans aristocracy than from the crowned heads of Europe, but it wasn't her style to let something as inconvenient as facts stand in her way. We weren't from anyplace half as romantic as the French Quarter or even the Bayou, just the cracker part of Florida, far from the beach, that humid, bug-infested part tourists never go to unless they accidentally read the map sideways and get themselves lost.

I was the child of a moderately well-to-do, married storekeeper named Earl. He came to visit us on Sundays, bringing bags of groceries. There was always a bit of penny candy tucked in among the oranges, grits, and cans of tuna fish. My mother would give me the sack of lemon drops or sticky caramels and tell me to go outside and play on the tire swing in the yard while she and Uncle Earl talked. She made it clear that I was not to come in the house and bother her until she came to get me or she'd take my candy away. I guess the pull of my sweet tooth was stronger than my curiosity because I never did sneak inside to see what Mama and Uncle Earl were "talking" about. When I was older I pretty well figured it out.

Earl's store was at least three or four miles from our house. I don't know how I figured out the directions, but once I walked there all by myself. How old was I? Four, maybe? Earl gave me an orange Nehi and a ride home in his car. He wasn't mad or anything—in fact, he let me shift the car while he was driving—but he said I shouldn't wander off so far because I might get lost or come across the path of a mean old gator with a hankering for the tender flesh of little girls. When we got to the house he patted me on the head and told Mama to keep a better eye on me next time.

He was always nice to me, and other than cheating on his wife, he didn't seem like a bad man. I'm sure if he'd realized what he was doing before he got himself mixed up with my mother, he'd have thought twice about adultery. Well, he wasn't alone in that. Before Delia was through there were a lot of men who would have said the same thing. They could have formed a club and held meetings.

I don't remember Earl's last name, though I know it wasn't Boudreaux. I do remember that one dry, hot summer day—not a Sunday—he showed up at our house, a little shotgun cottage on the edge of town that was in no better or worse repair than the others on our street, and he was mad as hell. I was sitting cross-legged on chipped-paint floorboards of the front porch, cutting Dolly Dingle paper dolls out of an old copy of the *Pictorial Review*, so intent on my work that I didn't hear him drive up. Earl stomped hard climbing the porch steps, making my scissors wobble so that poor Dolly lost three fingers on her right hand. I looked up and saw a man's trouser legs and a pair of brogans covered with Florida dust. They looked like someone had sprinkled them with Hershey's cocoa powder.

"Hey, Uncle Earl!" I greeted my father by the only title I knew and waited for him to respond with his usual "Hey, yourself, June Bug!" but he didn't see me. He wrenched open the screen door with such power that I thought he'd pull it off the hinges. He started hollering for my mother even before he got in the house and let the screen door slam closed behind him.

"Jean! Jean! Where the hell are you?"

Her heels made a hurried tap-tapping sound across the wooden floor. She had tiny feet, size fours, which she was very proud of. Even before we moved to the city, my mother wore high heels every day of the week.

"Why, hello, Earl. What a nice surprise. I didn't expect to see you until Sunday. I just made some iced tea. Do you have time for a glass?"

"No! I did not come over here for tea. It's a workday, Jean. I should be at the store looking after my business, but instead I had to drive over here to ask you a question—have you lost your mind?"

"I don't know what you're talking about. . . . "

"Don't give me that. You were over at Annabelle's dress shop today, and you were tracking Marlene from one end of the store to the other, whispering little comments, holding dresses up to yourself, and wondering out loud, 'Would Earl like this red better, or the blue?'"

"Well, I *was* at Annabelle's this morning, but I had no idea your wife was there. I was so busy deciding what dress to buy that I must not have noticed her. She's not that hard to miss, is she? I did finally settle on the blue one. Shall I try it on and show you? It's a little low-cut in front, but I didn't think you mind that *too* much." Eavesdropping on the front porch, I couldn't see Mother's face, but I didn't have to. Her voice was breathy, and I knew she'd be looking at Earl with her eyes wide open and her chin tucked down, that she'd reach up to stroke his shoulder and bite her lower lip slowly, in that way that always made him swallow hard so you could see his Adam's apple bob in his throat. It was a move that never failed—until today.

"Knock it off, Jean!" I heard the scuffle of feet and wondered if he'd shaken off her caressing hand or pushed her away. "You humiliated Marlene today, and now everybody in town is talking about it! She came to the store in tears. I feel bad enough about things without you going and making her a laughingstock. She may not be as pretty as you, but that's not her fault. I never wanted to hurt her. Tried to spare her feelings," he mumbled in a voice husky with guilt.

"I told her I'd quit seeing you two years ago and that I'd joined an Elk's Lodge all the way over in Bleak Springs and had to drive over for a meeting every Sunday. She believed me, or at least she wanted to believe me, if only to preserve her dignity. Now you've gone and made that impossible!"

"Well, I am so sorry! Forgive me for bursting Miss Marlene's little bubble of domestic bliss, but you told me some things, too, a lot longer than two years ago. You said you were going to leave her. You promised, Earl!"

"That was a long time ago, Jean. I was in a fever for you—I was delirious. You were the most beautiful thing I'd ever seen. I'd have said anything to have you." His voice softened a little, with remembering, I suppose, or with wanting. Mama was beautiful, with looks that turned men's heads and would for a long, long time to come.

Earl's voice grew firmer, as though he'd rediscovered his resolve. "But you had to know Marlene would never give me a divorce. She's too good a Catholic for that. You knew that, Jean. I knew it, too, and you know something else? I don't want to divorce Marlene. She's been the best wife she knew how to be for thirty years. She's put up with a lot from me, and today, when she came in the store crying like her heart was broke . . . Well, I was never so ashamed of myself." He was quiet for a moment. "Sometimes I wish I'd never laid eyes on you. It's over, Jean."

"I'm sorry, Sugar Bear. Really. Honey, I just love you so much and get so jealous sometimes that I can't help myself." Mama used the wheedling tone and endearments that always broke down Earl's defenses, but when he didn't say anything I could hear an edge of panic creep into her voice. "Now, darlin', don't look at me like that. I said I'm sorry. I'll stay away from Marlene from now on. I promise. I'll never set foot in Annabelle's again if that's what you want."

"Jean, it's not going to work this time. If the June Bug hadn't come along, I'd have called it off years ago, but I was trying to do the right thing by her. I was going to move ya'll over to Bleak Springs in the fall, anyway, before Georgia starts school, but that's still too close. Word is bound to get out, and I don't want kids teasin' her 'bout not havin' a daddy. She's a sweet little thing. No reason she should suffer just because I'm a damned fool."

"But, Earl! Daddy!" Mama pleaded. I heard the sound of paper crumpling and Earl's cold, businesslike voice.

"Take this," he said. "There's two hundred dollars in that envelope and a check for another eight hundred. If you will leave quietly by the end of the week, you can cash that check when you get wherever you're going, but if you make the least bit of fuss I'll stop payment on it. My brother Bob's a lawyer in Alpharetta. Here's his card. You write to let him know your address and your bank account number. As long as you don't contact me, or Marlene, or anyone we know except Bob, I'll send you seventy-five dollars a month for as long as I live and I'll leave a little something for the June Bug in my will. But if you ever, ever try to get in touch with me or embarrass my family in any way, that is the last dollar you'll ever see from me."

"But, Earl. Honey . . ."

"Don't test me on this, Jean. I've made up my mind."

*   *   *

That's how my mother and I wound up on a train to Chicago in the summer of 1926, and somewhere on that journey, while the steady thump of wheels on rail ticked off the miles between Florida and Illinois, Mother made herself up.

She was no longer Jean Carter, petite and pretty cracker, spurned mistress of an aging Florida grocer. Using a handful of French phrases she picked out of a French-English dictionary she'd found abandoned in the parlor car, and her own imagination, she invented Cordelia Carter Boudreaux, a genteel widow in reduced circumstances. Cordelia was the wife of the late Colonel Beauregard Boudreaux, an elderly gentleman of the Big Easy who had met and fallen for the charms of a young Atlanta belle on her post-debut tour of the South. It seems Cordelia admired the colonel but had been shocked when he proposed because she did not love him. However, her parents, people of impeccable southern lineage themselves, pushed for the match. Cordelia had been too malleable to resist, "I was so young, you see. Just sixteen. Mama said I didn't know what love was, which was, of course, quite true. I suppose it still is." She blushed and fluttered her lashes nervously delivering this last. The implication was that the colonel, while devoted to his child-bride, was too elderly to fulfill his matrimonial obligations to her. Cordelia was not only beautiful, she was pure in both body and breeding, an irresistible combination.

"The colonel was a New Orleans Boudreaux, mind you. His family lived in the Quarter for generations. Though I do believe that there was a connection to the low-country Boudreauxes several generations before." Here Delia would pause to take a ladylike sip from a glass of iced tea before continuing in a thick magnolia accent to whatever adoring male was most recently entangled in her web. "Colonel was an honorary title. Given as a courtesy, of course."

"Of course," the man who did not yet know he was destined to be my next uncle would murmur. He was too far from the Mason-Dixon line to realize that Delia's put-on patois and manners wouldn't have passed muster inside the borders of Louisiana and too sense-less with lust to care. Delia may not have had much education, but she was no fool when it came to geography. Chicago was the perfect place for her. She could never have pulled her act off in Atlanta or even in Raleigh.

Our new life in Chicago required my mother to write a new autobiography under a new pen name. On the other hand, I was still Georgia June Carter, but I'd never be known as June Bug again. From the moment we stepped off the train at Union Station in Chicago, I was no longer my mother's daughter, but her baby sister, whom she'd taken in after our parents died suddenly in a car accident, having previously lost their fortune due to the machinations of an un-principled business partner. Living with an orphaned sister rather than an illegitimate daughter gave Delia an air of nobility and self-sacrifice that only added to her charm. And it wasn't a totally un-likely ruse. Delia couldn't have been more than fifteen or sixteen when she gave birth to me, young enough to be my older sister.

Still, I don't completely understand how a Florida cracker with a bastard child and a monthly allowance from her former lover man-aged to pass herself off as the virgin widow of a southern aristocrat, but she did. Her story was embellished with such convincing details that I guess it just seemed like it had to be true, and, of course, her admirers wanted it to be true. They wanted to believe that they were the first to hold and completely possess that lovely creature. Before much time had passed, I think Delia believed the story herself, and that made all the difference. She was so utterly convincing.

There is something I want to make clear here. You might sup-pose that I am bitter toward my mother, that I hate her for living a life of lies. It simply isn't so. Delia wasn't a liar so much as a hope-less romantic. Hopeless was the life she was born into—poor, uned-ucated, with a face and body that made men want her as a woman even while she was still a girl. Romance was what made her take the cards she'd been given and try to bluff her way to a better hand, and it was the part that made her believe her own inventions. Delia had a great and misguided faith in the power of myth.

She truly did believe each new "uncle" was the prince on the white horse she hoped he would be, that this one really was unattached, or at least that he would soon become so, and that he really was going to marry her—just as soon as he could, whenever that was.

No, I didn't hate my mother. If anything, I pitied her a little. She couldn't help herself. She couldn't help believing in the power of love and that it was bound to find her eventually and right all life's wrongs. It might have been better for me if she had been different, but there was no point in wishing that. Fairy tales aside, wishing never changed anything. I figured out young that you had to fend for yourself, but Delia never did. She was who she was, and nothing could change that, but that didn't mean I had to go along with it.

In many ways I'm grateful to Delia. Watching the mess she made of her own life made me determined not to make the same mistakes. I would make my own luck—not invent it, imagine it, yoke it to something as ephemeral as love. I would work for it and rely on myself.

I told you. I am a realist. That's the only way to get on in life. But it doesn't hurt to have some luck. The first taste of mine came in August of 1927.

At least, I'm pretty sure it was August. Delia and I were going on an outing with Bert, a car salesman and the first in a series of Chicago uncles. I know it was summer because I wasn't in school, which was fine with me.

Delia had enrolled me in parochial school. It was a quick three-block walk from the apartment we'd rented in a working-class neighborhood of brownstones. Delia said she'd chosen it so she wouldn't have to worry about me getting home safely on my own if she worked late. There was probably some truth in that, but I think my education and our sudden conversion to Catholicism had as much to do with maintaining her image as a bayou belle as any concerns for my safety. In any case, my first year at St. Margaret's had been a rocky one. During the first mass of the school year, I failed to genuflect before entering the pew. Not from any disrespect, but because I didn't know you were supposed to. Until we arrived in the Windy City we'd been Baptists, when we'd gone to church at all, which wasn't often. I tried to explain, but Sister Mary Patrick didn't believe me.

"Don't give me any of your cheek, Georgia Carter. Shame on you! Telling such lies about your own sister. And her so good to take you into her home, providing for you out of what little she has left from her dear husband's estate after the lawyers cheated her out of the bulk of it. You'll stay inside at recess to say the rosary and after school to clean the blackboards." As you can imagine, things didn't get any better for me when I tried to explain that I didn't know the rosary. It was not an auspicious beginning to my academic career.

So, even though the August heat was thick enough to make the brim on Delia's hat curl and my legs stick sweatily to the leather rumble seat, I was happy—happy to be out of school, happy to be riding in Uncle Bert's new roadster, happy to be headed out to Midway Airport with the rest of the crowds, happy and excited because I was going to see the most famous man in America and maybe the world—Charles Lindbergh, at the Chicago stop on his forty-eight-state victory tour!

After his groundbreaking transatlantic flight from New York to Paris, the papers were full of Lindbergh and aviation. If there was other news in the world, no one cared. Every kid on our block was practically vibrating with anticipation because the Lone Eagle was coming to our city. I had never seen an airplane except in still photographs and newsreels, but that was about to change. I was one of the lucky ones who were actually going to see him because I had access to transportation. Bert had taken the day off work and borrowed a car from the dealership so he could drive us to Midway in style. He seemed a little smarmy to me, but I was willing to overlook that for the time being.

We left early because we wanted to find a good spot where we'd be sure to see Lindbergh. So did everybody else. We were stuck in traffic, with the midwestern sun sweltering down on us. Bert offered to put the top up, but Delia demurred. "That's all right. I imagine it would be even hotter with the sun beating on that black fabric. At least this way we can catch the breeze when it passes. But, of course, you know best, Bert." Delia smiled and laid a gloved hand on Bert's forearm. "If you want to put up the top, I'm sure that will be just fine with me."

"Naw," Bert said. "It's better with the air circulating. I was just worried about you getting too much sun," he grinned agreeably and laid his arm over her shoulder. Bert had only been around a few weeks, and I don't think he'd quite made his way around all the bases yet. She could have asked him to take off the tires and run that car on its rims and he'd have agreed to it.

"Well, that's why I brought my *chapeau*," Delia said, tossing out a little French to further charm her already smitten beau. "My mama always said a lady should never leave the house without a nice big hat. And I always listen to my mama." Delia laughed, showing all her perfect white teeth. Bert joined in, guffawing as if she'd said the funniest thing in the world.

Yech. I rolled my eyes and rested my chin on my hand, disgusted, and wondered if Lindbergh would be gone before we got to the airfield.

I felt the plane a split second before I saw it—felt a vibration come through my elbow where it rested on the metal body of the car, rising up through my forearm, to my chin, to my head, where the humming started in my ears and grew into an echo, a rumble, a roar at once mechanical and alive, more powerful and terrible and wonderful than anything I'd ever heard. I felt a great surge of wind and heat, the stirring of troubled air just before a storm. I looked up.

He was coming in for a landing, flying straight over the line of traffic, not more than a rooftop's height above us. Delia and Bert and all the other people in the stranded cars around us immediately ducked in an instinctive crouch, stooping to protect their heads while covering their ears against the howl of engine noise. And just as instinctively, I leapt onto the back of the rumble seat, shouting, reaching skyward, stretching on tiptoes, unfolding my fingertips high and straight, trying to make myself large enough to touch that wonderful, magical plane, trying to catch hold and fly. The *Spirit of St. Louis* headed straight for me. I imagined that inside Charles Lindbergh saw me, a little girl standing tall with longing while the world around her cowered in fear, and that the wavering dip of his wings as he came in for landing was much more than an answer to a turbulent headwind; it was a private salute between us, an acknowledgement that he recognized me as one of his own. He passed over me, a breaking wave of silver and shadow that felt like a gift of farewell, a remembrance to tide me over until we met again.

The sea surf ringing in my ears condensed and gave way to the sound of my own ringing laughter and the faint echo of Delia's shouting for me to get down, for heaven's sake, get down, Georgia, what were you thinking, you could have gotten yourself killed.

"Did you see it? Did you see it?" I shouted, still laughing. "Delia, did you? He was flying!"

"Georgia! Get down from there this instant! What's got into you? Of course he was flying," Delia barked, her initial fright giving way to exasperation. "Why do you suppose we came down here?"

What was obvious in Delia's mind was astounding in my own. I was silent for a moment, marveling that she failed to sense what I did, to feel in the wind and heat and shadow the opening of doors.

The world never would, never could be the same. Didn't she understand?

Then I remembered, Lindbergh's plane heading toward me, singling me out from the crowd as one who knew, and me rising up to return the salutation. It wasn't for everyone then, this calling to the air. How strange. Looking at Delia, beautiful and desired in ways I could never be, I felt suddenly special, lovely, and more important than I had a moment before. Simultaneously, Delia seemed different in my eyes, smaller and powerless. I was only seven years old, but I knew my mother would never again be as important to me as she had been before I climbed onto the rumble seat and tried to catch hold of a dream revealed. How strange. How wonderful.

3

Morgan

Dillon, Oklahoma—August 1941

It felt funny to be standing on the front stoop of the parsonage at six-thirty in the morning, but I had to come early. I didn't want anyone to see me. If they did, my visit would be the talk of the town, and somehow or other it would certainly get back to Mama. The first knock failed to elicit a response. For a second I thought about just forgetting the whole thing and going home. Maybe I'd come back later. But I couldn't come back later. This time tomorrow I'd be at the University of Oklahoma, getting myself settled in the freshman dorm. It was hard to believe.

And I still had to drop by Virginia Pratt's house to say good-bye to her. *Maybe I should go over there now*, I thought, but then remembered the time. Mr. Pratt would kill me if I showed up at his house at this hour; besides, my visit to Virginia could wait. It didn't matter if anyone saw me walking into her house. Everybody in my class knew we'd been seeing each other for a couple of months. We weren't going steady or anything, but it was understood around town that Virginia was my girl. No, if I was going to see Paul, it had to be now.

One more time, I thought and gave the door three good raps. I waited a moment, listening, and heard movement inside. The door opened.

"Hey, Reverend Van Dyver!" I greeted him formally, teasing him because I knew he really preferred for me to call him Paul.

"Morgan! What a wonderful surprise!" He beamed a wide smile. He was completely dressed, in his black pressed pants, starched black shirt, and clerical collar, but his hair looked like it hadn't been combed yet, and he wasn't wearing shoes. His feet and hair were odd contrasts to the rest of his buttoned-up appearance, as though he had dressed himself from the center out.

"It's kind of early but I wanted to see you before I left." I looked down at his bare feet. "Maybe I should come back later?"

"Don't be silly. Come in! Come in! I am delighted to see you." He opened the door wide, nudging a curious tabby cat out of the way with his foot. "Come on, Maxine," he murmured to the recalcitrant feline. "Stand aside and let Morgan come in."

I came inside and bent down to scratch Maxine between the eyes. She wound around my pant legs and purred a greeting. "I haven't seen you in a while, Maxine. How you doing, girl?"

"That's right. She was just a kitten last time you were here. It has been quite a while, hasn't it? She is full grown now—though between keeping the mice down and eating my cooking, she seems to be carrying a little extra weight. Ah, speaking of cooking," he said as he walked toward the back of the house, beckoning me to follow, "it smells like the bacon is ready. Come. Sit down and have something to eat."

I followed him into the kitchen. "Are you sure I'm not too early? I didn't mean to interrupt your breakfast."

"Don't be silly. You're not interrupting because I haven't started yet. I've finished my morning prayers, my coffee, and my newspaper, and was just getting ready to eat. I made pancakes and bacon, and there is plenty. Maxine and I get tired of eating alone. Don't we, girl?" He addressed the cat, who was sitting at his feet staring hopefully up as he turned sizzling strips of bacon in the pan.

I stood a little awkwardly, not sure if I should sit down or offer to help. The kitchen was small, but orderly and spotlessly clean. I felt in the way. Paul set the cooked bacon to drain on a sheet of brown paper and called over his shoulder, "Take two plates and glasses off that shelf behind you, would you, Morgan? The cutlery is in the drawer by the sink, and there is apple juice in the icebox. Do you want coffee?" He pulled an enormous stack of pancakes from the oven where they'd been warming while he finished frying the bacon.

"No, thanks. I'll just pour myself a glass of milk, if you don't mind." Paul told me to help myself to the milk. We sat down, and after Paul said a short blessing, we dug in. "You sure know your way around the kitchen, Paul. These pancakes are really good," I said sincerely.

"Thank you, but it is not so hard. Necessity being the mother of invention, I had to learn to cook. A single man who can't cook is either going to be very thin or very broke from paying someone to do it for him. Can't afford that on a pastor's salary."

"Still," I mumbled through a mouthful of perfectly crisp bacon, "I'm impressed. I can't boil water."

"You could learn if you wanted to," he answered. "You're a smart young man. Smart enough to be going to university. And smart enough to fly an airplane, I hear." He reached for another stack of pancakes and smothered them with syrup. Paul always had an enormous appetite. Until a year ago he'd been a frequent dinner guest at our house and could always eat twice as much as I did. Once I saw him eat an entire rhubarb pie.

"I can't fly yet. I'm still learning. We bought a used Stearman trainer. Took delivery on it last week."

"I heard," said Paul. "You were the talk of the deacons' meeting.

I could hardly get them to focus enough so we could take a vote on whether or not we should have Vacation Bible School in July or August. Everyone was much more interested in your plane, your imminent departure for college, and your future prospects than in the meeting agenda. Frankly, I felt the same way. We are all so proud of you."

I smiled and shook my head. Of course he knew about my plane. This was Dillon. Up until now it had always bothered me how everyone in town put their nose into my business, but just now, hours away from leaving Dillon, it struck me that there was something nice about a place where people cared enough to gossip about me. And it was nice to know that Paul was keeping tabs on me.

"The word is that you got yourself quite a plane. Mr. Dwyer said that Bud Olinger said it could do two hundred and fifty miles an hour." Paul whistled, pretending to be impressed. He knew enough about aviation to know that Mr. Dwyer's speed report was hugely exaggerated.

"Well," I said, laughing, "that would be about double her maximum speed, but she cruises at about one hundred miles per hour. The paint job is rough, but she's got a sweet little engine. I can't solo yet, so Whitey Henderson will fly me to Oklahoma City and then take a bus back home. I found an airfield near school where I can park the plane and take lessons on weekends. Whitey's been teaching me, but I still have a way to go before I get my pilot's license. You know Whitey, don't you? He works over at the airfield in Liberal."

"Certainly," Paul answered. "Remember, I gave you a ride to the airfield that time your car broke down and I found you hitchhiking on the road. You weren't worried about the car, just about getting to work on time. You were washing planes for Whitey, weren't you?" Paul speared a couple of pancakes with his fork and held them out to me. I nodded and he dropped them onto my plate.

"Washing planes, pumping gas, sweeping floors. Anything to help pay for flight lessons. They sure are expensive."

"And buying an actual airplane must be more so. Even a used Stearman with a rough paint job has to run into some real money."

I nodded and took a gulp of milk from my glass. "Yeah. I feel bad about that. Mama sold off some land to do it. I argued with her about it—said I didn't need to go to college and that we could use the tuition money to buy the plane, but she wouldn't go for it. You know how she is." I cut my pancakes, and the knife grated against the plate. The memory of that conversation still rankled. I still wasn't convinced I needed to go to the University of Oklahoma. I wanted to be a pilot, and all I needed for that was a license. I wanted to spend the rest of my life flying, and I wanted the rest of my life to begin as soon as possible. Spending four years taking a bunch of English and philosophy and who-knew-what-else classes just seemed like a big waste of time.

Paul grinned. "I do know how your mother is, but I'm not sure exactly what you're referring to. Do you mean that I know she's stubborn, or that I know she's smart, or that I know she's right?"

I groaned. Paul was a great guy, but I should have known he'd side with Mama, no matter how close we were. Paul was practically a second father to me, taking me fishing, playing catch with me in the yard, helping me build a radio for the school science fair— things a father would do.

For a time I'd thought Paul would become my father. He used to visit us at least two or three times a week. It was obvious that he cared for Mama, and it seemed she liked Paul pretty well, but then one day he just stopped coming. I wondered if he and Mama had a fight, but she never said anything. Probably she thought it was her own business and she didn't have to explain it to anyone. Well, maybe, but it affected me, too. Next to Papaw, Paul was the most important man in my life. That was why I'd come to see him. He and Mama might not be talking to each other, but that was their problem. I couldn't just leave town without saying good-bye.

I sighed and rolled my eyes. "Oh, brother. Are you on Mama's payroll or something?"

Paul threw back his head and barked out that single, joyous "Haw!" that distinguished his laugh from everyone else's. "Very funny. If I agree with her, it is only because she is right. It's a wonderful thing to be able to get a university degree. I know you want to take up a career as a pilot, but there is no reason you shouldn't be a pilot with an education. From what I've heard about your grandfather, he would have felt the same way."

"Papaw wasn't educated, not that way. What he learned, he taught himself."

"True, but your mother says he put a great store on education. If he'd had the opportunity to go to college he surely would have taken it."

I gave up trying to argue the point. There would be no budging Paul on this position, and, besides, I didn't figure on being in college for long. The papers were full of war news and debates about whether the U.S. should send in troops or sit it out. As far as I was concerned, it was time that somebody went over there and taught Hitler a lesson, and the sooner the better. From what I'd read, it looked like President Roosevelt agreed with me. The war was bound to start any day, and when it did I was going to join up. I wasn't going to ask anyone about it; I was just going to do it. My only worry was in getting my pilot's license before the fighting started. Then I could enlist as a flyer. No way was I going to spend the war on the ground, but there was no need to tell that to Paul or anyone else. One thing I'd learned living in a small town: the best way to keep something secret was to keep it to yourself.

"Well, I still don't feel right about Mama selling off land to pay for college and my flying. I'm old enough that I should be helping her, not adding to her burdens."

"I won't scold you for feeling a sense of duty to your mother,

Morgan, but Eva knows what she is doing. She's a smart woman and a strong one," he said and then added in a softer tone, almost to himself. "I admire her more than any woman I've ever known. I miss her terribly."

He was quiet, looking straight ahead at some indistinct location beyond where I was sitting. It felt odd and a little awkward to see him sitting there, so completely absorbed in memories of my mother. He looked so vulnerable. There was nothing reverend-like about him just then. He was just a man, like other men, with no more re-markable insights or answers than other men, and in some way I sensed that allowing me to see him this way was a mark of trust. At that moment we were no longer teacher and student, parent and child, pastor and penitent. We were two men talking—friends. It gave me courage to speak.

"Paul, what happened between you and Mama?"

He drew in a deep breath and let it out slowly. His eyes were thoughtful and focused, as though he were reading my question off a printed page, an examination question he'd studied and memorized but whose answer was suddenly lost to him. "It's hard to explain."

"But you love her." It was a statement, not a question.

"Yes. I do. From the first moment I met her. It was right before your grandfather's funeral, you remember?" I nodded. I remem-bered everything about that terrible day.

Papaw worked himself to death trying to hold our family to-gether during those starving dust-bowl years, taking a job plowing another man's dry fields to try to keep the topsoil from blowing away, swallowing so much choking dust that it eventually killed him. Dust-bowl pneumonia, they called it. I remembered how Grandma, always the stern and powerful center of our home, suddenly seemed to lose her sense of self and reality and how I spent hours hidden in my room so I could cry without being seen. I remembered how Mama stepped up and took over the reins of the family, how she kept us from falling apart. I remembered how, once he was gone, I realized that Papaw was the best, bravest man I'd ever met and how heartsick I felt because I'd never really told him that he was my hero.

Paul was Dutch. He had been in America for less than a year and had been appointed to the pulpit in Dillon only a few weeks before Papaw's death. Folks in Dillon weren't sure about him. I'd heard some of the men hanging around Dwyer's store say they thought he was too serious, that his sermons were too long, and that they could hardly understand him because of his accent. But it wasn't that bad. Some people just like to complain, and for a few residents of Dillon complaining was practically a profession.

In time, Paul's accent would soften, though he would always speak carefully, enunciating his words the way people do who've been taught a language rather than grown up with it. His manner was a little formal, but sincere. If someone was talking to him he looked right at them and furrowed his brow just a little, concentrating on what the other person was saying instead of thinking about what he was going to say next. I liked him right off. We all did.

When he came to talk to Mama about Papaw's funeral, he said he was willing to say the service, but he thought someone else should give the eulogy, someone who really knew Papaw. Though I was just thirteen, he thought that someone should be me. Mama was hesitant, but Paul convinced her. I didn't say anything about my grandfather that everyone in town didn't already know. He was a good man, and everyone liked him. He was my hero. None of that was news to anyone, but being able to say it out loud was important to me. Paul said he couldn't eulogize a man he didn't know, but I think even if he'd known Papaw for years he would still have let the office fall to me. He knew how much I needed to say good-bye and how giving Papaw the honor in death that should have been his in life helped me let my grandfather rest in peace and move past my grief.

Yes, I remembered it all, and I thanked God that Paul had come into our family at the moment we most needed him.

"That was the first day I met your mother," Paul continued in response to my nod. "It was such a sad day. Your grandfather's death was so sudden, so unexpected. You had this hollow, orphaned look in your eyes, and your grandmother was . . . well, she wasn't herself. Clare was the widow, and by rights I should have been talking to her, but your grandmother was in no condition to see to the funeral arrangements. Eva handled everything.

"She was dressed in black and wore no powder or lipstick. She hadn't bothered much with her hair, and her eyes were puffy from crying. She was still the most beautiful woman I'd ever seen. There was something about her, soft-spoken and thoughtful, utterly feminine. In spite of her own loss, she was taking care of everyone else— her mother, you, even Ruby. It is her nature to give. I could see how much she loved her father, but her mourning went deeper than this one tragedy. There was a lifetime of loss in her eyes, but she refused to speak of it to me, or to anyone. She never allowed herself the option of self-pity and would tolerate none from others. I didn't even notice her crippled leg at first. When I did, when I realized what determination the simple act of walking across the room required of her, I admired her more than ever.

"Even before I saw her quilts, how she uses those little scraps of cast-off fabric to give voice to her dreams, I was amazed. I thought she was the loveliest, strongest woman I'd ever met—and the most alone. I could not help myself. From that moment on, I loved her utterly."

"Did you ever tell her?" I asked.

"I couldn't. Not then. I sought only her friendship because I sensed she would be slow to trust, that one word of love from me would send her running for cover. But I was willing to be patient. From that day forward, I knew there could be no other woman for me. In time, I felt she would reach the same conclusion. I was willing to wait a long time. I did wait a long time." Paul closed his eyes and let his head loll back to rest on top of the tall, ladder-backed kitchen chair.

"But not long enough?" I asked, certain I already knew the answer because I knew Mama.

She was, as Paul had said, a loving and giving person, but she had a hard time believing anyone could love her back. Her crippled leg was part of it. Sometimes I would see her rubbing it when she thought no one was looking, but I wondered—was it bodily hurt that slowed her gait and made her foot drag along behind her like an anchor scraping along a lakebed, or was there more to it? Sometimes I thought Mama was like a wounded animal so severely marked by the memory of pain that it favors an injured limb long after the wound has healed.

Sure, there were people in town that had been mean to her on account of her not being married when she had me, but not everyone felt that way. Still, when anyone got too close she backed away like a spooked horse. That must have been what happened with Paul.

"You told her how you felt, and that scared her off? Paul, you shouldn't let that keep you away forever. It's been months since you've seen each other. In some ways, maybe that wasn't such a bad thing. I know she misses you. After I leave for school you should go see her." I was certain that when she saw him all would be forgiven and they would pick up where they left off. My departure would leave her feeling more alone than ever, and she was already lonely. I could tell. So was Paul. They needed each other, and I would feel better about leaving if I knew Paul was looking out for her. Oklahoma City was a long way away. Germany was even farther.

"Maybe you could bring her some flowers or something," I suggested. "You know, kind of soften her up a little."

Paul lifted his head and opened his eyes. "It isn't quite as simple as that.

"I love Eva, and I know that she is the only woman I ever have loved or ever will love, but her feelings are for someone else."

"Someone else?" I protested. "But there has never been anyone else. . . ."

Then I stopped myself and remembered. It felt odd to be thinking about my own mother's romantic life, but I thought to myself, why should it? She was my mother, but she was still a living, feeling person. I was the proof of that. Mama never spoke of him, not since that night in my bedroom when I was four, so I thought any feelings she'd had for him had been snuffed out long before, but there had been someone else once. My father. And if Paul was right, she loved him as much as ever.

I should have known. Mama would never love lightly. Other girls might have crushes or ill-considered flings, but Mama wasn't like that. She was too cautious. Even as a girl, it would have been impossible for her to succumb to a teenage passion unless she'd really been in love. I should have known.

"Eva cares for me in a way, of course," Paul said. "We understand each other. If I was willing to settle for friendship then I'm sure we could be friends, but I can't. I can't pretend my feelings for her are merely platonic. It would be too painful a charade. I'd show up on her doorstep with a whole florist shop if there were a prayer of her changing her mind, but there isn't. She loves him." The faraway look returned to his eyes, and he shook his head, as if he couldn't quite believe it. "After all he's put her through, she still loves him."

"My father?" I asked. Paul looked startled.

"You know who he is, don't you?"

"Forgive me, Morgan. I've said too much."

"No! You got to tell me who he is, Paul. I have a right to know the name of my own father!"

Paul was quiet, gazing at me steadily, considering. "Yes, I think you do, but it isn't my place to tell you. It's Eva's. I promised her I'd never speak to anyone about it, and that promise extends to you. You'll have to ask her yourself, Morgan. This is something between the two of you. I've no right to butt in. This is a family matter."

I wanted to tell him that he was family. That was what I'd come for in the first place, to thank him for all he'd done for me: for teaching me how to bait a fishhook, for listening to my complaints and questions about God without judging, for helping me with my calculus homework and teaching me how to change the oil in the Ford—for treating me like a son. I began to say just that but didn't get far before Paul interrupted me.

"There is no need, Morgan. Knowing you, seeing you grow from a boy to a man, and being allowed to play some small part in the process is thanks enough," he said and smiled in a way that let me know he meant it.

Breakfast was over. I helped Paul clear the table and stood at the sink drying dishes after he'd washed them. We talked of small things—sports, and airplanes, and what classes I would be taking as a freshman. Paul tried to convince me to take Ancient Greek for my foreign-language requirement, but I just laughed. "No way! I'll be lucky to pass freshman Spanish!"

"Ah, well." Paul shrugged and let out the rubber stopper to drain the water from the sink. "At least I tried."

I looked at the wristwatch Mama had given me for graduation. It was time to go. Paul walked me to the front door to say good-bye. "I won't wish you good luck because you won't need it. You're completely up to this. And don't worry about your mother. She may not be speaking to me, but I'll still keep an eye on her. I'll make sure she's all right while you're at school." He paused a moment and, without me saying anything, addressed the concern that was uppermost in my thoughts—the impending war and who would watch out for Mama when I joined up. "No matter what happens, no matter where you go, I'll always look out for her. You can count on it."

"Thanks, Paul. That means a lot to me." I put out my hand for him to shake, and he gripped it hard.

"Don't mention it."

Later, I said my good-byes to Grandma and Aunt Ruby back at the house. Ruby cried and Grandma tried not to. Mama drove me out to the airfield herself. We didn't say much during the drive—just talked about the weather and about how good the harvest was looking. "Mr. Thompson said he's getting two bushels more per acre than he did last year," Mama said.

Mr. Thompson was our closest neighbor. "Well, that's good," I said. "He must be happy about that."

Mama smiled and threw me a quick glance before training her eyes back on the road. "He said it would probably drive down the price. Said he'd be lucky if he broke even."

I grinned. Some things never changed. Thompson was a full-time farmer who moonlighted as a part-time curmudgeon. He never had a good word to say about anything, but I was going to miss him. I was going to miss everyone. I couldn't think of what to say next, and Mama seemed to have run out of conversation, too, so I turned up the radio and we listened to music for the rest of the drive. Bing Crosby was singing "Only Forever."

> *Do I want to be with you,*
> *As the years come and go?*
> *Only forever,*
> *If you care to know.*

Whitey was waiting at the airfield, standing next to my plane. My plane. I was still amazed to think she was actually mine. Rough paint job or no, the sight of her made me smile.

Whitey had already done a preflight check, so everything was ready. We loaded my gear into the plane. Watching my duffel bag and suitcase get stuffed into the cargo hold, Mama suddenly remembered all the good advice she'd ever forgotten to give me and started peppering me with reminders to eat right and get enough sleep, not to forget to wear my hat, and to remember that she'd put some horehound lozenges in my duffel in case I got a sore throat.

"They're in with your clean socks. Oh! And I put a roll of stamps in there, too. And some stationery and pre-addressed envelopes."

"Mama, you didn't have to do that. I'm eighteen years old. I think I know my own address by now."

"I know. I just thought it would be easier for you that way." Whitey gave the propeller a good crank. The plane stuttered a little before the engine caught hold, but when it did, it roared, and the whole fuselage started to hum and vibrate as if she couldn't wait to get airborne. Mama was startled by the noise. Both her hands flew up to cover her ears.

"Promise you'll write!" She hollered to be heard over the engine.

"Every Tuesday and Saturday," I shouted. "I promise!"

Whitey waved his arm, signaling it was time to go. I gave Mama one last squeeze, lifting her up off her feet, before hustling myself over the plane and climbing into the passenger seat. Mama backed away to stand by the car where she could watch us take off. She smiled and waved as if our parting brought her nothing but pride, but I could see her eyes shining with tears. She looked so small standing next to the battered old Ford. If she'd crooked a finger, or blinked an eye, given me the smallest indication she'd wanted me to stay, I would have. It just didn't feel right leaving Mama all alone, but we'd talked it out a hundred times, and she was determined that I had to go out in the world and make something of myself. It felt wrong to leave her, but not as wrong as it would have felt to let her down.

I threw Whitey a thumbs-up, indicating I was ready, and we started taxiing down the runway. As we picked up speed, the miracle that never would cease to amaze me happened again. Fighting headwinds and gravity, the nose of the plane lifted off the ground, and we were airborne. We took off toward the west, straight into the afternoon sun, and as we gained altitude, worries and contingencies fell away as surely as the earth fell away from our wings. I felt suddenly large and limitless.

Whitey made a wide arc across the sky, looping back to find the southeasterly course that would take us to Oklahoma City, and we passed over the airfield again. Mama stood below, sweeping her arm wide above her head. Thinking that I wouldn't be able to see them from the sky, she let the tears flow freely, but I could see she was smiling through her tears, and I knew that she'd meant what she said. She really was proud of me, and as much as she wanted me to stay, she wanted me to test my wings even more. It was all right to go.

Looking across the horizon, a short mile from where Mama stood, I could see another car parked by the side of the road and another figure standing shadowed against the earth. Paul waved both arms above his head, bidding me farewell. For a moment, I could see Mama and Paul at the same time and somehow I knew that no matter what happened to me, Mama would be all right. In my mind, I thanked God for both of them and prayed that somehow the distance between them would be closed. Then, as quickly as the thought formed in my mind, Whitey pulled back the stick, we climbed higher, and I lost sight of them.

❧ 4 ❧

Georgia

Chicago, Illinois—January 1940

Thirty-three dollars and twenty-eight cents. That was all.

In my heart of hearts I knew that the ten-cent-an-hour raise I'd been given in recognition of faithful service to the housewares department of Marshall Fields wasn't going to make me rich, but as I tore open my pay envelope, I prayed for a miracle of loaves and fishes—a divine intervention that would mystically transform my little raise into a figure that would be enough to pay for flying lessons *and* my bill at the grocer's. It didn't happen.

"So much for the power of positive thinking," I mumbled as I folded the check in half and tucked it into my pocketbook. The truth was, it was a nice raise, but it wasn't enough to finance my dream. I'd tried everything I could think of—working every over-time shift I could, baby-sitting on evenings and weekends, walking to work to save the fare it cost to ride the El, but it wasn't enough. I'd even taken a couple of bookkeeping classes at a nighttime secretarial school, hoping that bookkeeping would pay better than sales did, but the jobs I'd been offered didn't pay any more than what I was making at the department store.

Compared to most girls my age, I was making good money— enough for food, rent, an occasional night on the town, and, thanks to my store discount, a nice wardrobe—if that was what I'd wanted to do with it. None of my old girlfriends from St. Margaret's were making as much as I did, and they were all jealous that I had a generous discount at Chicago's most fashionable department store.

I'd met Frances Ruth Callaghan, Fran, my best friend from St. Margaret's, for lunch in the store coffee shop just the week before, and she'd gone on and on about it. Eating out was a rare treat for me, but we were celebrating our birthdays—we were born in the same month. We went dutch, and with my employee discount, lunch in the café cost only a little more than my usual brown bag in the break room.

"I can't think why you're wearing that same white blouse and the same black pumps you wore to graduation when you've got the latest styles at your feet, and all at a discount! You could have a nice apartment, but instead you live in a one-room garret and cook on a hot plate!"

"True, but it's *my* one-room garret, and that makes all the difference." It would have been cheaper to keep living in Delia's apartment, but that was where I'd drawn the line on frugality. My rented room was only three blocks from her place, and since we worked in the same store, albeit in different departments (thank heaven!) I saw her every day. Having my own place gave me a break from her endless conversations about what I should wear, who I should date, or how pretty I could look if only I'd fix myself up a little. It also meant I could avoid awkward meetings with the latest "uncle" who might be sitting at the kitchen table drinking his morning coffee in the same shirt he'd worn the night before. That alone was worth double the rent I paid for my garret.

"Honestly, Georgia! You never spend a dime on yourself. If I was in your shoes I'd dress like a fashion plate," Fran said through a mouthful of chicken salad. "And I'd have the cutest little place with everything new—a whole matching set of dinnerware, with the serving pieces and everything, and some of those sheets with the scalloped embroidery on the edges, and matching pillows with my monogram. Wouldn't that be elegant? Do you get a discount on monogramming, too?" she asked hopefully.

"No. Just on the things the store buys from vendors. They have to pay people in the store for monogramming and tailoring, so that's full price."

Fran bit her lip thoughtfully. "Well, that's all right. I can live without the monogram," she said before going on. "And a pile of big, fluffy cotton towels—in pink, to match the tile in our new bathroom. Did I tell you about the tile in the house?" I nodded and kept eating. She had, several times, but I knew she was going to tell me again anyway. I didn't mind. Fran was just three weeks away from living her dream life. Soon she'd be married to Richard Morelli, the manager of the movie house where Fran was an usherette, and living in her own home—a new two-bedroom bungalow with a pink-tiled bathroom and an honest-to-heaven picket fence. She was happy, and I was happy for her.

"It is just so darling! Even the toilet is pink! It matches the tile and looks so fresh against the white walls. I'm going to sew a shower curtain out of white eyelet lace and find a pink liner to go underneath so the color will peep out through the eyelet holes." She took another bite of her salad and sighed. "Just darling!" she repeated. "But really, Georgia, I don't understand why you don't put that discount to good use and get yourself a new wardrobe."

"Because Marshall Fields doesn't sell anything I want, that's why."

Fran rolled her eyes. "I know. I know. You're saving every penny for flying lessons. Georgia! If I didn't know better I'd think you were nuts! When are you going to grow up and realize that this is just a crazy dream? I mean, honestly! How many female pilots do you know?"

"Amelia Earhart, Jackie Cochran, Bessie Coleman . . ." I ticked them off on my fingers.

"I mean real people!" she interrupted.

"They are real people. I saw Amelia Earhart give a lecture at Northwestern one day. She talked, and breathed, and drank water, and everything."

"I mean regular people. People like us. Ever since we were kids you've been talking about flying, and you're not any closer to being a pilot now than you were when we were ten."

"That's not true," I answered. "I've already finished my lessons for ground school—"

"Yes, and that took every dime you'd saved. Now you're broke again. Georgia," she said sweetly, as though trying to explain something to a not-too-bright kindergartener, "I used to want to be a ballerina, but since my parents could never afford dance lessons, I realized it was never going to happen, and I moved on. You've spent all your money trying to become a pilot, and you've still never been up in a plane! How crazy is that? How do you even know that is what you want?"

"I just know," I said. We'd had this argument before, and I was trying my best to keep my tone light and dismissive, but Fran's doubts were beginning to grate, mostly because I sometimes asked myself the same questions. And yet, and yet . . . I did know. Without ever having flown, I knew.

"Don't you ever think about getting married and having a family?"

There it was. The exasperating question Delia asked me about three times a week, and now Fran was after me, too. My question was, were there women anywhere who thought about anything else? "Oh, for heaven's sake, Fran. Why should I?" Fran looked positively scandalized, so I reframed my question. "I mean, why now? What's the hurry? I'm only eighteen years old."

"Just turned nineteen," she retorted.

"So what? Frannie, why do I have to get married right away? For that matter, why do I ever have to get married?" I asked as I took a sip of iced tea.

She looked at me blankly. "I don't understand. Are you saying you want to become a nun?"

Involuntary laughter caused some of the tea to go up my nose. I pulled my napkin up to my face, coughing so hard my eyes started to water. "A nun?" I choked. "Me? The girl who had to stay after class to clap erasers every day for three months because she didn't know how to say the rosary? If you hadn't taken pity on me and helped me learn my prayers I'd probably have gotten some lung disease from inhaling so much chalk dust! Even if I wanted to, I'm pretty sure the Church wouldn't have me. But are those the only choices? You either get married or take the veil?"

"Of course not. I'm just trying to understand you," Fran said sincerely. "Do you have something against marriage?"

Her eyes searched me, and I felt bad about having laughed. Fran was my best friend. She was just days away from her own wedding, and here I was casting doubt on the institution of marriage. I chose my words carefully. "It's not that. If I could ever find a man who really cared for and respected me as a person, not just as a potential wife and mother of his children, but really shared my interests and my dreams, then maybe I'd want to get married. Maybe."

"Richard respects me," Fran said a little defensively. "And we both have the same dream. We want a home and a family."

"And that's great! Richard is a wonderful guy, and I know that you two will be happy together. It's just that my dreams are a little different than yours. It might take a long time for me to find someone to share them—if I ever do." Fran furrowed her brow as I went on.

"Look. Delia has spent her whole life wanting one thing—to find a man, any man, and get him to marry her. She's turned herself inside out trying to be what they want her to be, and the more she does that, the quicker they turn and run. That won't do for me, Fran. I've got to be myself first and last. If someone can love me for that—great. If not, I can live with that. What I can't live with is the lie of trying to be something I'm not. Does that make sense to you?"

"No," Fran said and smiled as she picked up her fork and speared a slice of tomato, "but there's nothing new in that. You've always been crazy, Georgia, but I guess that's what I like about you."

"Ditto," I said with a grin and took a bite of my sandwich.

"So this whole convoluted conversation was just to explain why you dress like the ragpicker's child and won't use your store discount?"

"I never said I wouldn't use the discount. I said I *don't* use it—not for me, anyway. But there's no reason I can't use it for you. Let me know how many of those towels you want. I'll order them for you today."

"Really?" Fran's eyes grew wide with delight. "Are you sure? I'll pay for them and everything. Just let me know how much."

"I'll total it up as soon as I get back on the floor." Minus the monogramming fee that I'd decided to pay for myself—that would be my surprise gift. "Speaking of which," I said, glancing at my watch, "I've got to get back to work." I wolfed down a last bite of sandwich and pulled some money out of my purse so Fran could pay the bill.

"Say, Georgia." Fran cleared her throat as I pushed back my chair. "Want to go to the movies with Richard and me on Saturday—and his brother, Martin? He just got a promotion at the factory. Shift supervisor. He's such a nice guy, and he thinks you're cute. C'mon," she pleaded. "It'll be fun."

"I'm sure it would, but I said I'd pull an extra shift this weekend. Thanks anyway. Besides, Martin's just not my type."

Fran sighed. "That's what Richard said you'd say."

"Well, Richard is a smart guy," I said. "That's why he's marrying you. Now, I've got to run. I'm late. I'll call you this weekend." I picked up my pocketbook and started to leave, but Fran tugged at my sleeve.

"Wait! Richard also said to give you this. I didn't want to, but he made me promise." She stuffed a newspaper clipping into my hand. I wondered what in the world it could be, but another glance at my watch showed I was now five minutes late. I shoved it into my purse, waved good-bye, ran for the elevator, and didn't think about the clipping again until I came home from work that night.

Fumbling around in my pocketbook, looking for my keys so I could open the door to my apartment, I pulled out the newspaper clipping. It was a classified ad from the *Waukegan News Record*.

HELP WANTED: Experienced waitress for restaurant located next to busy municipal airport. Good pay. Good tips. Uniform provided. Start immediately. Contact Thurman at the Soaring Wings Café, Waukegan, Illinois

Good pay. Good tips. None of that registered in my mind. The words that kept repeating themselves in my mind were "next to busy municipal airport" and "start immediately." I found my keys, opened the door, pulled the string to illuminate the one bare bulb that lit the room, and started frantically searching under the bed for my suitcase.

Start immediately. How long, I wondered, was the bus ride to Waukegan?

As it turned out, Waukegan was just about forty miles north of Chicago. It was bigger than I'd thought it would be, and pretty. Sitting on the shores of Lake Michigan about ten miles from the Wisconsin border, the town boasted houses in good repair with green lawns and green trees. A nice town, but even if it had been the armpit of the earth, nothing would have stopped me from packing my things, leaving a note for my landlady with what was owed on my rent, and taking a milk-run bus ride to Waukegan in the middle of the night, all in hopes of getting a job I didn't know anything about.

When I reached my destination, a few streaks of daylight were climbing up from the horizon. It was too early to think of finding a hotel room. I went into the bus depot bathroom to brush my teeth and hair and splash a little water on my face, then dropped a nickel into the slot of an empty metal locker so I'd have a safe place to keep my things until I got the job. *You mean* if *you get the job*, a voice of doubt spoke in my mind. I did my best to ignore it but wasn't entirely successful. Maybe Fran was right, I thought. Maybe I was crazy. Who picks up in the middle of the night and moves to take a job they aren't even sure they'll get, that probably pays less than what they were making before, in a town they never heard of just because the job is next to an airfield? I must be crazy.

Who knew how old that newspaper ad was? What if the job was already filled? It had asked for an experienced waitress, and I'd never waited a table in my life. And I had a more immediate problem. It was five o'clock in the morning and I didn't even have an address for the café, let alone a means of getting there. There were a million reasons for me to believe this half-cocked plan of mine would fail and only one reason to think it wouldn't—it was the only plan I had.

I knew I had to fly. I'd run out of ways to make that happen, and this was the only open door I could see. How a waitress job at an airport diner was going to put me on the road to becoming a pilot was beyond me, but something told me that it would. I stuffed my doubts into the locker along with all my other baggage, shut the door tight, and locked the whole mess inside.

5

Georgia

Waukegan, Illinois—June 1940

"Georgia!" Thurman hollered as he slapped two steaming plates onto the counter and then hit the order-up bell with a force that made the clapper ring flat. "Scrambled on two! Let's try to get 'em out there while they're hot."

"All right already!" I said as I handed him another order. "Sheesh! Why are you so grouchy today? What's the matter? Have a fight with your wife or something?"

"Very funny," he growled. Thurman was single. After his girl-friend, Margot Pfeffenhauser, threw him over in the eighth grade he'd decided that all women were more trouble than they were worth and sworn never to marry. He was pushing sixty, and it was beginning to look like he was going to keep his vow. "I don't want customers complaining their eggs is cold and me having to make the order again just because you ain't gettin' the lead out."

In the five months I'd worked at the Soaring Wings I'd never had a customer send back food because it was cold. Undercooked, overcooked, or badly cooked, yes, but never because I hadn't served it quick enough. I was about to remind Thurman of this when he interrupted me.

"He's here again. Table six." Thurman scowled and jerked his head toward a corner table where Roger Welles was sitting, pretending to examine a menu he'd probably memorized weeks before. I didn't blame him. Thurman was glaring daggers at him, and flimsy as it was, that menu was the only shield he had handy.

"I finally get a new waitress trained, and every stray dog in town starts hanging around the place," Thurman grumbled. "Knew it was a mistake to hire you. I shoulda hired Lucille Grant instead. She's got bunions and a bad back, but she's ugly," he said longingly. "Nobody'd be loitering in my restaurant, nursing cups of coffee, taking up space from good paying customers trying to start a conversation with Lucille, that's for sure. This is the last time I hire a pretty waitress, I swear."

"Aw, gee, Thurman. That's the nicest thing you ever said to me."

He muttered something undecipherable and sucked his teeth. "Get his order and then get back to work. We got other customers. *Real* customers."

I delivered the scrambled eggs to the Fosters, an elderly couple that came to the Soaring Wings every Tuesday morning to have their breakfast while they watched the planes take off and land. We had a lot of regulars like that. The planes were as much an attraction as the food. Actually, they were more of an attraction than the food. Truth was, Thurman wasn't much of a cook, but the prices were cheap, the portions were large, and there was plenty of entertainment to be had just by looking out the window. Waukegan wasn't exactly a bustling airfield, but any diner who came into the Soaring Wings was likely to see a couple of takeoffs and landings before the dishes were cleared. A lot of that air traffic came from the flight school.

Roger Welles was the school's owner and principal flight instructor. In fact, he owned the whole airfield. Ever since I'd waited on him, about two weeks after I'd started working at the café, Roger quit bringing his brown bag to work and ate lunch at the Soaring Wings. Some days, like today, he had his breakfast there, too. And he always sat in my section.

He was quite a bit older than me, about thirty, and good-looking in a rugged, outdoorsy kind of way. His face was tanned and lined, but he had a boyish twinkle in his eye, and, like a boy, he blushed when he got flustered. I knew he liked me—that was pretty obvious after he started showing up for lunch every day—but I figured he was just a guy on the make, so I didn't encourage him. But as he sat there day after day without pushing himself on me, I started to think he was all right. One day I returned his smile, and we chatted for a couple of minutes while I took and served his order. The next day we talked again, and pretty soon it got to be a regular thing.

I'd known he was a pilot right off because he always came in wearing his flight jacket, but it was a few days before I learned he was also an instructor. Little by little, I told him my story, how I'd come to live in Waukegan and why. Since then, he'd been after me, pushing me to go flying with him and saying he'd be glad to give me free lessons.

Flight lessons! For free! I was so tempted to say yes, but I couldn't do it. It was too big a gift and too big a debt. I liked Roger, but it was clear that his feelings for me were more than just friendly. Accepting such a generous gift was bound to give him the idea that he could expect something back from me. I'd spent enough time watching Delia to know that any man who shows up at the door with flowers, or candy, or an invitation to dinner is expecting to get more than a smile and a thank-you in return—even when that man was as nice as Roger Welles. And as much as I wanted to learn to fly, there were some prices that were too high to pay, even to catch hold of my dream.

"Coffee, Roger?" I already knew the answer but asked anyway as I filled his cup to three-quarters and checked to make sure there was enough cream in the pitcher. Roger liked plenty of cream in his coffee, no sugar.

"Thanks." He took a sip. "That's good. Can you bring me a number three, Georgia?"

I nodded and wrote on my order pad. "Bacon crisp. Eggs over medium. Wheat toast with extra butter. Is that all?"

"Just one more thing," he said. "Come flying with me. Oh, come on, Georgia. You know you want to! Nobody puts themselves through ground school just to expand their mind. It took you two years to save up enough money just for that.

"I'm a pilot. I know what it's like. You want to get off the ground so bad you can taste it, so bad that you're willing to sling ten thousand plates of hash trying to save up enough money to get your wings. And here I am, offering you the chance because I know what it's like to need to fly, but you keep giving me the brush-off!"

"I can't, Roger."

"Why not?"

"I told you. I just can't," I said firmly, but then, seeing the disappointed look on his face, I softened my tone. "You're sweet to offer, Roger. Really. But I can't let you do it. It's too much."

He was quiet. He knew there was no point in arguing with me.

"Now, is there anything else I can get for you?"

"No. Just keep the coffee coming, please. I need it this morning."

I gave his cup a warm-up. "You look tired. Late night?"

"Yeah. I was up half the night trying to untangle my books." He sighed and rubbed his hand over his face. "I tell you, Georgia. I'm a good pilot and a good teacher, but I'm no businessman. The girl who used to keep my books got married and moved to Carbondale, and I haven't been able to find anybody to replace her. I've been trying to do them myself, but I can't make heads or tails of it. I don't know who I owe or who owes me. And don't even talk about the tax man." He groaned. "If I can't get my books straightened out they'll

audit me for sure." Roger took a deep draught from his coffee cup
and looked up at me.

"What? What are you grinning about?"

"Roger, I've got a business proposition for you."

For every two hours I spent working on his books, Roger would
give me one hour of flying lessons. It was a perfect arrangement for
both of us. Roger wanted to make it a one-to-one trade, arguing that
my time was just as valuable as his, which was sweet, but I wouldn't
go for it. Bookkeepers come a lot cheaper than flight instructors,
and I wanted to be very certain that Roger looked at this as a business deal, not a favor. I didn't want to be beholden to anyone.

After getting off work that night I headed over to Roger's office
and started trying to untangle his books. And, believe me, they were
a tangle.

"How long is it since your old bookkeeper left?" I asked as I
opened yet another shoe box full of loose receipts and began separating them into piles for personal, business, and unknown.

"About six months," Roger answered, a little chagrined. "Pretty
bad, is it?"

"You've got yourself a mess here, for sure." I sighed. "But it
could be worse. Your old girl had a pretty good filing system worked
out before she left. If we can just get all these loose papers orga-
nized, I'll be able to get you straightened out before your taxes are
due. Now, you said you've got an employee?"

"Yeah, Stubbs Peterson. He's my mechanic. Been with me since
I opened. He's not much on looks and is cranky as all get-out, but
he knows more about plane engines than anybody alive. He was a
real find. He worked in California until a couple of years ago. Could
be working anyplace in the country and for more money, but he's
from here originally. When his father died and his mother got sick
he came home to take care of her. There aren't a whole lot of jobs in
aviation around here, so when he came by looking for work I

snapped him up. I couldn't run the place without him. Do you know, he actually met the Wright brothers?"

"Really," I commented as I shuffled through a mountain of papers and manila folders. "He sounds like a find all right. Do you pay him?"

"Pardon?" Roger asked.

"Your mechanic. Stubbs. Do you pay him? Because I can't find any pay stubs for him anywhere, or for you. I can't find the checkbook, either. You have one, don't you?"

"Oh! I should have told you." He jumped up out of the wobbly desk chair he'd been sitting in, crossing the office in three big strides, and opened the lid of a battered old fruit crate that was sitting in the corner. "I keep all that in here." He pulled a check ledger out of the box along with a lidless cigar box overflowing with old pay stubs. "I thought it'd be a good idea to keep them separate from that stuff on the desk."

"It was," I said and took the checkbook from his outstretched hand. Roger grinned, apparently pleased by my approval. *He really is a sweet man*, I thought to myself. He reminded me of a big, gamboling puppy—always cheerful and eager to please.

"Well," I said. "You'd better leave me alone with all this for a while. I'll see what I can make of it."

"Sure you don't need me to stay and help?"

"No, I'm fine. Thanks." He looked a little disappointed but took the hint.

The office door led right into the hangar, and when he opened it the smell of fuel and engine grease filled the room. "Georgia?" He turned back to me as he was leaving. "After you're done—say, in a couple of hours—you want to go flying?"

I put down the folder I was holding, rested my chin in my hand, and smiled at him. "I'd love to."

Roger grinned and raised and lowered his eyebrows a couple of times in a comical expression, and tossed me an enthusiastic thumbs-up signal. Later, I would come to think of it as his "all-systems go" face, a small ritual that he performed whenever we made a date to fly, or just after he'd given the propeller a powerful yank and the engine caught hold, or anytime the exhilaration and anticipation of being airborne again was just too much to contain. The look on his face was pure joy and boyish enthusiasm, and I thought to myself, *Here is a man who will never grow old.* His excitement was contagious, and I couldn't help but laugh.

"All right, then! I'll see you in two hours." He nodded his head. As he left he said, "Big day! Think of it, Georgia!—Your first flight! You'll never forget it."

The door closed behind him. Leaning back in the desk chair as the worn springs creaked in protest, I let his words wrap themselves around my mind like an embrace.

Your first flight. Amazing. Finally, after all these years, I was just two hours from my dream. I'd never been farther off the ground than my own feet could lift me, but I already knew Roger was right. It was a day I'd never forget.

What Roger didn't say, what I learned on my own was this: that the amazement and the yearning never fades. If anything, it becomes stronger. From that first moment I touched the sky, each moment I spent on the ground was a moment spent waiting to leave it again.

Every day I've ever flown is a day I'll never forget.

6

Morgan

Oklahoma City, Oklahoma—December 3, 1941

"Morgan! You're here already," Mr. Wicker said with surprise as he slammed his car door closed. "I wasn't expecting you until nine-thirty. How long have you been waiting?"

"Oh, not long," I lied. The truth was I'd been there since six that morning, hoping Mr. Wicker would show up a little early. I'd waited, crouched down with my back resting against the cold wall of the hangar, so I'd have a good view of the Jenny and could admire the clean lines of her as the sun rose, glinting red and silver against the new paint I'd labored to put on her during every hour I could spare from studying. My calculus grades hadn't been much to write home about, but mine was the best-looking plane on the field and, to me, that was what mattered.

I'd been sitting there so long my legs had cramped up under me. "I just thought I'd get here a little early," I said and heaved myself to my feet, fighting the cramp that suddenly took hold in my left leg.

Mr. Wicker smiled a little as he watched me struggle to get up. "Couldn't sleep?"

I shook my leg to try to get the circulation going and smiled. There was no point in trying to play it cool. "Not a wink," I admitted. "I've been sitting here three solid hours."

Wicker threw back his head and laughed out loud. "Well, I don't blame you. It's a big day. You're not nervous, are you?"

I shook my head.

"Good! You've no reason to be. You're about the best natural pilot I've ever had the pleasure of teaching, and that's a fact. It's an instinct with you."

"Thank you, sir. I appreciate that. But I think I've been pretty lucky to have you as my instructor. You've taught me a lot."

"Well," Mr. Wicker said, casting his eyes up to check the weather as he fished the keys out of his pocket and opened the flight-school door, "if you're ready, I can't see any reason you can't take off a little early. Make sure you stretch out good before you go, though. You don't want your legs cramping on you."

"Yes, sir!"

"And Morgan?"

"Sir?"

"You enjoy yourself up there." I didn't answer him. I didn't have to. We both knew there was no possibility of me doing anything else.

My heart was beating fast as I approached my plane all alone, my body buzzing with adrenaline and anticipation, but my mind was absolutely clear. I went through my preflight check carefully and deliberately, exactly as I'd been taught, but it was almost a surprise to realize I wasn't the least bit afraid, just utterly focused, and that gave me a sense of control I'd never experienced before. I was confident, and unconcerned for my safety because I was aware that it lay so completely in my own hands. I felt powerful.

I reached high to grip the prop and felt the muscles swell and strain in the heavy sleeves of my flight jacket as I gave the propeller one mighty wrench and the engine caught hold on the first try. She roared to life, and the whole plane pulsed and quivered, impatient to be on her way. I scrambled into the cockpit and settled myself inside, looking over my instrument panel one last time.

Mr. Wicker had been in the office all this time, though I doubted he had any pressing business inside. I think he wanted to give me the privacy I needed to savor the moment. But when the engine started up he'd stepped outside to watch, and he raised his hand over his head in salute as we taxied past, the Jenny and me—heading to the airstrip, making a slow right turn to the takeoff point, waiting for the all-clear signal from Jerry, who ran the tower, then picking up speed, following the ribbon of runway that led to the point of no return, pulling back the stick to lift the nose. We lifted off as smoothly and easily as if the Jenny were my own body responding to a sudden, careless idea that it might be nice to head skyward. The Jenny and I were two parts of one being, our desires and actions a perfectly integrated whole, because flying was our whole reason for being.

We cut a path through the wind. And the sound of air splitting across my face and moving past my ears was like the roar of ocean surf, constant and powerful, a force to be met and conquered. I spied a series of clouds off to my left and banked left to bring myself closer. I thought, *I could punch a hole through those clouds if I wanted to,* and then, just to prove it, I did. I pulled the stick back even more, rising steadily, putting even more distance between the earth and myself. The old feeling was there again. I felt limitless, exuberant, and peaceful all at the same time, completely comfortable in my own skin in a way that it's impossible to feel with two feet on the ground.

I was living the moment and living the memory all at once. I thought, *This is what it means to be truly alive.*

I felt invincible. And when the fuel gauge was hovering above empty, and I had to land, the feeling stayed with me. Not forever, but for a while. It was with me on December eighth when I walked into the recruiting center and signed my enlistment papers. I was ready and willing to die flying airplanes, defending my country against the Japanese, who'd bombed us the day before, though I couldn't seriously fathom it coming to that, what with me being invincible and all.

As I said, the feeling stayed with me for quite a while.

7

Morgan

Dillon, Oklahoma—Christmas, 1941

Christmas didn't start off quite the way I'd hoped it would.

"So you see, Mama," I explained, "I've only got a few days before I have to leave. I know you'd counted on me being here until the fourth, but my bus leaves right after Christmas." Her face clouded over with an expression that might have been anger, disappointment, shock, or all three. Maybe it hadn't been a good idea to tell her I'd enlisted just as soon as I landed. Maybe I should have waited until we'd gotten home, or even on the drive from the airfield, but it was too late now. I just kept talking, hoping that if I did she'd collect herself and realize that I was only doing what I had to do, the same as thousands of other mothers' sons across the country.

"I know it only gives me about a week, but don't worry, Mama. I'm going to use every minute. Make me a list of chores. Tell me whatever needs fixing, and I'll get it done before my train leaves. I'm going to give the tractor a tune-up, too. That way it'll be all ready for the spring planting."

Mama was quiet a moment, and then she spoke, in a voice choked with anger. "Is that what you think I'm worried about? About how smooth the tractor will run come spring? You think I'm worried about *me*?" She opened her eyes wide, staring at me, and set her mouth in a straight line, waiting for an answer.

"Mama," I sighed and kicked the ground with the toe of my boot, "why do you have to be like that? Just this once, couldn't you make it easy for me?" I wasn't being fair and I knew it. Mama had always tried to make things easy for me, or as easy as she knew how, but I was angry with her. On the flight over, I'd rehearsed this conversation in my mind several times, and though in my imagination Mama had shed a few tears when she heard the news, she always ended up saying that she was proud of me. Clearly, the reality of a man leaving for war wasn't anything like they made it look in the movies.

"I didn't ask for this war," I continued, "but, after what happened at Pearl Harbor, you know we've got to get into it. Even before I left for school you were saying there was no way we were going to be able to stay out of the war and that somebody had to stop Hitler. I heard you say exactly that to Aunt Ruby."

"I know what I said!" she snapped.

"I'm a pilot, Mama. They need trained pilots. There are thousands of guys signing up who will be learning to fly from scratch, but it'll take months and months before they are ready to take up a plane. With a little combat training I'll be ready to go. They need me! The sergeant at the recruiting office said one trained pilot like me was worth a hundred untrained recruits."

"I'll bet he did." Her eyes flashed for a moment, but then she sighed and it seemed like all the air went out of her.

"I just thought . . . I just . . . You might have talked to me before you went and joined up. That's all." She pulled her coat tighter around herself. She was so small. I felt bad for standing there and arguing with her in the cold. "I just thought maybe you could wait a little while—at least until after Christmas. It would have been nice to have Christmas without all this hanging over us."

"I'm sorry, Mama. Maybe I should have talked to you first, but I guess I didn't want to risk you trying to talk me out of it. All my friends joined up, too. Almost everybody I know. Probably half the guys from my dorm are catching hell from their mothers right this second for joining up without asking permission," I smiled, trying to move past the moment by making a joke of it, but Mama wasn't buying.

"Watch your language," she responded automatically.

"Sorry." I waited for her to say it was all right, but she just stood there, looking at me with an expression I couldn't read.

"Mama, I'm a good pilot. Mr. Wicker, my instructor, said I fly like I was born to it. I'm going to be all right. I promise."

Mama bit her lower lip and nodded. She blinked a couple of times, and I told myself it was just the cold prairie wind that was making her eyes tear up, but I reached out and wrapped my arms around her anyway and hugged her tight as I could. When I let go she sniffed and gave me a smile that didn't quite make it to her eyes.

"Let's go home. There's a good fire in the stove, and Ruby baked you a pie. Grandma can't wait to see you. Is the plane tied down?" I nodded. "Good."

She reached down as if to pick up my grip, but I grabbed it. "I'll carry my own bag, thanks. Do you want me to drive?"

"Are you sure? Aren't you tired after such a long trip?"

"Naw. Besides, I'm starving. You drive so slow, Mama, it'll be morning before I get a piece of Ruby's pie," I teased. "Give me the wheel and I'll have you home in no time. I am a highly motivated individual." Mama smiled, but just a little.

"Not too fast," she cautioned as she handed me the car keys. "I finally had Mr. Cheevers hammer out that dent you put in the bumper two summers ago. No point in putting another one in its place."

"Don't worry, Mama. I told you, I'm a good pilot. Make that a great one!" I threw my bag in the trunk and then ran around the car to open Mama's door. She got in, and I was about to shut the door when she reached out, closing her hand over mine.

"Morgan," she said softly. "You're doing the right thing. I'm proud of you."

We didn't talk about my leaving again. Everyone seemed determined to enjoy the holiday and refused to acknowledge the elephant in the room, my imminent departure. But every now and then when I would look up quickly, I'd catch a glimpse of Mama's face before she had a chance to replace her mask of composure, and I'd read worry in her eyes. Just a few days before, I'd felt invincible, heroic, and absolutely certain of my victorious and rapid return from the field of battle, but the look in Mama's eyes started to rub against my bravado, making it just a little thinner and more brittle. I started to worry a little, too, not about myself so much, but about what would happen to Mama, Grandma, and Ruby if something happened to me. Since Papaw had died, I'd always considered myself the man of the family, responsible for the well-being of these three women who had raised me and cared for me since before I could remember. The weight of responsibility hung on me, and the look on Mama's face in unguarded moments drove me to activity.

I worked as fast as I could to make sure everything on the farm was in perfect repair. I tuned up the tractor, then mucked out the barn, replaced the rotted floorboards on the front porch, put a new blade on the windmill in place of the old one that had split, cleaned out the root cellar, put a new door on the storm cellar and made sure the latches were secure, and split a mountain of logs. Late on Christmas afternoon, the day before I was to leave, I went up on the roof to replace a bunch of shingles that had been pulled loose by the relentless prairie winds. The weather had turned cold and bitter, but I was running out of time and determined to finish the job, especially since I felt so guilty about not getting it done the day before when the weather had been good.

Grandma came outside when I was up on the roof and stood at the bottom of the ladder, shaking her head and scolding.

"You're working yourself to a frazzle! Come down from there and eat something. I just pulled a pecan pie out of the oven, loaded with nuts, just the way you like it."

"Be down in a minute, Grandma," I said through a mouthful of roofing nails.

"It's Christmas, Morgan. And it's too cold to be working out here. There's no point in fussing over those shingles. The wind'll just blow them off again tomorrow."

"Maybe, but at least I'll know they were all nailed down tight today. Besides," I said, laying down the hammer and flexing my right arm so my biceps strained against my sleeve, "it's good exercise. Just think how many push-ups I'll be able to do if I keep this up."

Grandma shook her head and went back inside. I went back to work. I couldn't help myself. I was like a squirrel getting ready for winter who knows there is nothing he can do to stop the bad weather from coming but is driven by instinct to prepare as best he can.

One thing I hadn't had a chance to do was take Mama flying, even though I'd promised I would as soon as I got my license. The weather was unusually nice on Christmas Eve, and I'd said we should go then, but Mama insisted I go into Dillon and see some of my old friends instead. She said we could go flying when I came home on leave. Even so, I wouldn't have agreed to go into town if I hadn't needed to buy roofing nails and tar paper, but I knew I had to get the job done. That roof wouldn't last the winter otherwise.

As I was coming out of the hardware store, there she was, Virginia

Pratt, wearing a dark green sweater that outlined her shape and a matching hat that made her eyes bluer than I remembered.

She seemed genuinely happy to see me and didn't even fuss at me when I explained why I hadn't been over to visit.

Instead she just squeezed my arm and said, "Morgan, that is so sweet! Taking care of your mother like that before you leave. I bet you'll look so handsome in your uniform. And I think you're just so brave to volunteer! I heard that you're a real pilot now. Mr. Dwyer said that you fixed up that old plane so it looks brand-new. I sure wish I could see it before you go, but it sounds like you've got too much to do. Would it be all right if I wrote to you while you're gone?"

Virginia was different than she'd been when I left. She talked more, and her hands kept fluttering like butterflies and then lighting on my arm ever so briefly, but I was acutely aware of every spot she'd touched. Wearing that close-fitting sweater she looked . . . well, let's say she looked a lot more mature than she had just a few months ago. She was flirting with me. I knew that. And I knew there was a mountain of work waiting for me at home, but Virginia was beautiful and the weather was fine and before I knew it I'd asked her if she wanted to go for an airplane ride. She squealed with delight and scrambled into the passenger's seat of the Ford when I held the door open.

For a moment I thought about Mama and Aunt Ruby, who were home baking cookies and trimming the tree. They were expecting me home, but I told myself I'd only be gone a little while.

I ran around to the driver's side and got in the car. Virginia scooted across the seat and sat near me, talking and laughing and lighting on my arm with butterfly hands as I steered the car toward the airfield.

The Jenny set back down on the runway with barely a bump, a textbook-perfect landing. I taxied her toward the hangar, parked near it, and hopped out of the cockpit.

The old invincible feeling had returned as soon as we were airborne. The flight had left me feeling reenergized—that, and the wide smile and compliments Virginia was throwing my way. I stood next to the wing, held up my arms, and she leaned into them, her body sliding close along mine as I lowered her down. Even after she had both feet on the ground, she stayed near me, her arms draped over my shoulders and her eyes looking into mine. She reached up with one hand and pulled off the helmet and goggles I'd lent her. Red-gold hair cascaded down her back in a beautiful tangle.

She let the goggles drop from her hand onto the ground, then reached up and buried her hand deep into her curls and shook her head a little. "I must look a mess," she said, laughing, meaning the opposite.

"No. You're beautiful. You look perfect." And she did.

My head moved lower. She rose up on her toes, and our lips met. I had kissed Virginia a couple of times before when I'd dropped her off at home after our high school dates, but those kisses had been quick and tentative, nothing like this. She opened her mouth and I let my tongue outline the rim of her lips, then pass beyond to explore the perfect ridges of her teeth and the depths of her mouth. Her body was pressed close to mine, but I pulled her even closer, every inch of her feeling every inch of me. Her heart was beating as fast as and frantically as my own. I lowered my hand to the curve of her hip where her sweater met her skirt and she covered it with her own, guiding my hand under the soft fabric of her sweater.

Her head fell back, and her mouth opened in a soft sigh. I felt her hips rock toward me, and, without thinking, I pushed forward to meet her. For a long moment we moved together in an instinctive, ancient rhythm. Virginia reached her hand low and a sound came from me that was part moan, part gasp.

"Where can we go?" she asked and leaned her head into my chest. The airfield was empty. The field was so small and removed that we didn't even have a tower, and the few people who might have been around were home getting ready for their Christmas celebrations. Whitey Henderson had an office at the back of the hangar. He kept an old army cot there so he could catch a few winks when business was slow. I knew where he kept the key.

There was no doubt in my mind what she was asking or exactly what would happen if I took her by the hand, took the key to Whitey's office, brought her inside, and laid her down on top of the rough woolen blanket that covered the cot. I could see it in my mind, the image so clear it made me forget everything else—the roof that was bare of shingles, the bus ticket to boot camp that lay on the kitchen counter at home, and the look in Mama's eyes that made me wonder if my courage would hold out. All I saw, all I wanted, was Virginia, and I knew she wanted me.

Taking a step back, I moved to take her hand. She lifted her head from my chest and looked at me with those wide green eyes. She said, "I love you, Morgan," and waited.

Virginia's eyes were the same shade of green as Mama's, and suddenly I saw my mother twenty years younger, vulnerable, waiting for an answer to the same question Virginia's eyes asked now: do you love me?

Did I? That I wanted her was certain. That I had thought about her many, many times since I'd left Dillon was true, but was that the same as love? Maybe it was. I didn't know. But until I did . . .

"It's getting late, Virginia. I'll take you home."

8

Georgia

Chicago, Illinois—August 1940

On the third knock she finally answered. "Yes?" Delia drawled as she opened the door. Fourteen years in Chicago and she could still make "yes" into a three-syllable word.

"Hello, Delia." I picked up my overnight bag with one hand and opened the screen door with the other.

"Georgia? What are you doing here?"

"I've come for a visit. It's nice to see you, too." Her hair was messy, and she was wearing a robe with no belt that she kept closed by clutching the folds of fabric around her waist. It was three o'clock in the afternoon, but I was suddenly suspicious. I stood on the threshold and craned my neck, squinting through the gloom of the darkened apartment. "You don't have anybody in here, do you?"

"I most certainly do not!" Delia retorted, scandalized. "The very idea! It's the middle of the afternoon, Georgia. Just what do you take me for."

I wasn't touching that one with a ten-foot pole. Instead I asked, "Why do you have all the shades drawn and the windows closed?"

"I was taking a nap."

"Well, it must be ninety-five degrees in here. It's summer in Chicago, Delia. Hadn't you heard?" I dropped my bag next to the entry table, went into the living room, and started opening windows. "Let's get a little breeze in here at least. Don't you have a fan?" Delia pointed silently to the front hall closet. I took out the fan and plugged it in. "There. That's better. That should get some air circulating."

I turned around. Delia was still standing there, clutching her robe even tighter. "Delia, what are you doing napping in the middle of the day? Why aren't you at work?"

She didn't answer.

"Are you all right?"

Delia drew herself up taller and looked as if she was going to speak, but instead her face crumpled. Her mouth opened in a silent cry, and tears seeped out from her closed eyelids. She released her grip on the robe, balled her hands into fists, and covered her face with them. I had never seen her like this.

"Delia! What happened? Are you sick? What is it?"

Her body quivered and was wrenched with tremendous, silent sobs. She tried to speak, but when she opened her mouth nothing came out. For a minute the only sounds that escaped her were the gasping, openmouthed intakes of breath she made when trying to get some air between surges of heaving, silent weeping. Finally her sobbing subsided a little, just enough for her to choke out one word.

"Barney!" she wailed.

"Barney?" For a moment I was confused, but then I understood. "Are you talking about that Fuller Brush salesman you've been seeing? Is that what this is all about? You mean that Barney?"

She nodded in response and burst into a fresh torrent of tears.

I had been patting her on the back, trying to comfort her, but when I realized what she was crying about I let my hand drop. "Let me guess," I said. "It turns out he's married."

"He's dead!" she cried.

"Oh my gosh! That's terrible! I had no idea, Delia. I'm so sorry."

"It was our six-month anniversary. We went dancing to celebrate, and he dropped dead right in the middle of a fox trot! His heart gave out on him, just like that." She snapped her fingers, then reached into the pocket of her robe, fished out an already sodden handkerchief and fruitlessly started trying to dry her eyes with it.

"He was going to ask me to marry him that night," she continued, sniffing.

"He was *going* to ask you? Did he tell you that?" It seemed odd to think of a man announcing his intention to propose without actually doing it. Delia shook her head. "Then how do you know he wanted to propose?"

"Because he had the ring in the breast pocket of his coat. See?" She lifted up her left hand and I saw a small ruby solitaire gleaming dully on her fourth finger. "We were dancing, and he grabbed at his arm and his face turned all red. He dropped to the floor, and when he did, the box with the ring fell out of his pocket." She started wailing again.

"And you took it?" I asked, incredulous. "He hadn't given it to you yet, but you took the ring that fell from a dead man's coat pocket, and you kept it? Delia, have you lost your mind?"

"Well, why shouldn't I have taken it?" Her tears subsiding, she lifted her chin in righteous indignation. "He meant for me to have it. If I'd have left it in his pocket anybody might have taken it—a dishonest policeman, somebody who worked in the coroner's office, his wife . . ."

"His wife? He was married?" I threw up my hands. "What am I saying? Of course he was married. He was dating you.

"Delia, for once in your life couldn't you find an unattached male? How many people live in Chicago? About three million? Surely, in a population of three million people, there are at least one or two single men you could go around with."

Delia's eyes narrowed. "Well, it's not my fault. It's not like I go out looking for married men. We met at the store. I sprayed a little White Shoulders on the inside of my wrist so he could see what it smelled like, and after he did, he wouldn't let go of my hand until I said I'd have dinner with him. It was just one of those things. I couldn't have known he was married."

"Delia, *any* man who is showing up at the Marshall Fields perfume counter is married! They're buying the perfume for their wives. How is it you've never been able to figure that out?"

Delia started sniffing again, and her eyes started tearing up. "Why do you always have to pick on me? What did I ever do to you besides feed you, clothe you, and work my fingers to the bone trying my best to take care of you? And this is how you repay me? My fiancé is dead and all you want to do is stand there and make fun of me."

"Delia," I said, exasperated, "he wasn't your fiancé. That ring might not even have been for you. Don't you think if he'd been planning to give you an engagement ring it would have been a diamond? That's a ruby on your finger. It was probably a gift for his wife."

"Oh! How can you say such an awful thing! He was going to leave her. He promised me. Barney would never have cheated on me. He was an honorable man," she said, gathering her robe and dignity about her again.

I started to point out that any man involved in an adulterous relationship with a woman he's met at the perfume counter while buying a gift for his wife could be called a lot of things, but honorable wasn't one of them, but I kept my opinions to myself. There wasn't any point in arguing with her.

She was crying again, but softly, without the frenzied grief she'd displayed before, and I knew these tears were about more than just losing Barney.

She looked tired and discouraged. The light that poured in

through the opened windows revealed a web of lines around her eyes that hadn't been there the last time I'd seen her. Even in her moments of greatest despair, Delia had always been a stunning beauty, but not today. The light in her eyes was dimmer, and the vibrant bloom in her cheek was muted, like the dulled tones of a painting that has been left too long in a sunny window. The harsh afternoon sun had exposed the truth—Delia's beauty was beginning to fade. Her courage had always been tied to her vanity. Now they were both failing her, and I could see fear in her eyes. I didn't have the heart to argue with her anymore.

"I'm sorry, Delia. Really, I am. Don't cry. Can I do anything for you? Make you a cup of tea?"

"Yes, thank you. That would be nice, but make it iced. It's so hot." She sniffed and touched the end of her nose with her balled-up handkerchief, then drew her eyebrows together as if suddenly remembering something she'd forgotten to do.

"Georgia, what are you doing here? I'm glad to see you, but you didn't say you were coming for a visit. Is something wrong?"

"Yes," I said. "Roger has asked me to marry him."

I sat at the dinette while Delia scurried around the kitchen making the tea, pouring boiling water over a half dozen bags of Luzianne tea and dumping a heaping cup of sugar into the mixture, her energy suddenly renewed. I was never completely sure, but I think Delia had that tea shipped up to her by Earl's brother, the attorney from Alpharetta. It was probably part of her price for keeping quiet. You couldn't get Luzianne in Chicago, but Delia insisted that a Southern lady would never make iced tea with anything else.

I wanted to ask who kept her supplied in tea, but couldn't get a word in edgewise. She peppered me with questions.

"So how did it happen? What did he say? Did he give you a ring? Have you set a date? What about the ceremony? Church wedding or justice of the peace? You know, a church wedding is always so nice, but I wouldn't blame you if you wanted to save the money and go on a nice honeymoon instead. I've always wanted to see Niagara Falls," she reflected dreamily as she ran a little cool water over a tray of ice cubes before lifting the metal lever to crack the cubes loose from the trays.

"If you *do* decide on a church wedding I'm sure you'll want to have your friend Fran as one of the attendants, but it is more traditional to have a close relative as the maid of honor. A sister perhaps?" She smiled brightly as she poured the dark, sweet tea over two glasses of ice. The cubes made cracking sounds as they came into contact with the warm liquid. Delia garnished the glasses with sprigs of mint, brought them to the table, and sat down.

"Yes, I'm sure that would be lovely," I said. Delia's smile spread even wider, and I was sure she was imagining how fetching she'd look holding a bouquet of sweetheart roses and wearing a wide-brimmed picture hat trimmed with ribbons. "If I had a sister. As it is, I'll have to settle for Fran to stand as witness and you as mother of the bride."

Delia frowned. "You shouldn't be so sassy, Georgia. Brides are supposed to be sweet."

I covered my face with my hands, trying to stifle a short squeal of frustration. "Oh! Will you just take a breath for a minute and let me talk! I'm not a bride. Roger asked me to marry him, but I told him I didn't think it was a very good idea. That's why I came here. I told him I needed a couple of days to get away and think."

"And you wanted to talk to me about it?"

"Yes. I guess so," I said reluctantly. "I didn't know where else to go."

"Oh, Georgia! That is just the sweetest thing! But, honey, I don't understand what you need to think about. From everything you've told me, Roger is a lovely man. Why in the world didn't you say yes right off?"

"Because I don't think I love him, that's why. I like him. He's very sweet, and what with our both loving flying so much, we have a lot in common, but I don't think I love him."

Georgia smiled knowingly. "Have you been . . ." She hesitated, searching for a word. "Intimate with him?"

My face flushed as I caught her meaning and remembered Roger's few attempts at romance and how I'd turned my head away after one or two clumsy kisses. "No. Not really."

"Well, there you go!" Delia exclaimed throwing up her hands in a gesture as if my answer had explained everything. "No wonder you aren't sure how you feel about him."

"Because I haven't been . . . You think if I'd been romantic with Roger then I'd feel love for him?" Delia nodded. "But what if you've got it backward? What if the reason I haven't been romantic with him is exactly because I'm not in love with him? Shouldn't love come before romance?"

Delia stirred her tea and sighed. "Georgia, can you give me one good reason you shouldn't love Roger? You told me yourself that he's nice-looking, that you like him, that you have a lot in common. He's been kind to you—taught you to fly and everything. You could never have done that without his help. And even though I think the idea of a woman being a pilot is perfectly silly, he thinks it is just wonderful. There aren't too many men who'd be interested in a girl who has such a . . . well, such an unfeminine hobby. The fact that you fly airplanes would send most men running in the other direction."

"Well, then they can just run." I retorted. "I can do just fine without them."

"Maybe," Delia said doubtfully, "but someday you're going to want to have a man in your life—you'll want to be somebody. It seems to me that Roger is your best bet. He's got a nice little business. He can take care of you, and he loves you. Maybe you don't love him now, but you can learn to love him. It's not like there's anything wrong with him, is there?"

She took a ladylike sip of her tea, staring a question at me over the rim of her glass.

I stayed in my old bedroom that night, but I didn't sleep much, turning over all that Delia had said in my mind.

A lot of what she'd said didn't make sense to me, even though I knew it made perfect sense to Delia and a lot of the rest of the world. Delia had spent her whole life trying to become a wife—anyone's wife—because that was what would turn her from a nobody into a somebody. That just didn't seem right to me. It never had, but I knew most of my girlfriends would have said the same thing, maybe not in those exact words, but that was how they all felt. A woman who wasn't a wife was no woman at all.

Delia said that most men would turn away once they learned I was a pilot. I'd already seen enough to know that was true. Lots of men, even other pilots, looked at me like I was from Mars when they discovered I was learning to fly. Well, that was fine with me. Being a pilot was part of what made me somebody, and anyone who didn't understand that would never understand me. But Roger did understand, and that was one of the reasons I liked him. We spoke the same language, at least when it came to flying.

He'd timed his proposal carefully, asking me on the day of my first solo flight. Oh! It was so exhilarating! I'd never felt so free! And when I'd taxied back in from my landing I was so happy to see Roger waiting for me because I wanted to talk about it, share the experience with someone who would understand. He was grinning from ear to ear as he watched me hop down from the cockpit. I ran toward him, and he scooped me up in his arms. For once, I didn't push myself away from his embrace. I was just so happy! But my happiness faded when he put me back down on the ground, got down on one knee, and pulled a small green velvet jewelry box from his pocket.

A lot of girls, I knew, would have been thrilled with a proposal like that. Why wasn't I?

As Delia had pointed out, there were a lot of perfectly good reasons why I should love Roger. Could it be as simple as she made it sound? If I married Roger and let him love me physically as well as emotionally, would I start loving him back? Delia was right, there was nothing wrong with Roger, but was that reason enough to marry him? Didn't Roger deserve a little more from life and love than that? Didn't I?

The next day, I dropped by to see Fran on my way back to Waukegan. She was five months pregnant and glowing. I hadn't seen her in months, but she was the same old Fran, bright and bubbling and full of energy, but she was different too, calmer and more serene. She didn't ask me for my opinion every ten seconds as she had when we were younger. This more mature Fran was able to make choices on her own and seemed happy with the outcome.

Fran insisted I stay for lunch, so while she was making lemonade and tuna sandwiches, I took myself on a self-guided tour of the bungalow.

She had done a great job making the little house into a home. The whole place was neat as a pin and smelled faintly of lemon oil and candle wax. At the door of the nursery, freshly painted in rubber-duck yellow, I stood admiring the sweet little room that was big enough for the crib and rocker Fran had bought secondhand and lovingly refinished. I wondered how I would feel if this were my house, my nursery, awaiting the birth of my child.

Over lunch I told Fran about Roger's proposal. She reacted just like Delia had—utterly thrilled by the news and utterly confused as to why I had not immediately accepted. I tried to explain but could see that she was confounded by my uncertainty.

We hugged and said good-bye. I ran to catch my bus and made it, but just barely, squeezing between the doors just as the driver was closing them.

I tossed my overnight bag onto the luggage rack, collapsed into an empty seat, and tried to catch my breath. My face turned toward the window that framed the receding Chicago skyline, but the picture of the sun streaming through the window of the nursery, warming the hand-rubbed finish of the wooden crib, stayed with me all during the long ride home.

9

Georgia

Waukegan, Illinois—October 1941

Roger poked his head in the office door and called, "Hey, hon! I've just got this last flight check with the Barnes kid and then we'll go. You ready?"

I nodded and closed the cabinet drawers where I'd just finished filing the month's billing and flight logs. Roger whistled as the drawers slid back to reveal my new black dress with the little white polka dots and wide red belt that made my waist look even more slender than it really was.

"Whew! You look good enough to eat in that!"

"Thank you." I smiled. "But, Roger, you shouldn't have. Real silk! It must have cost a fortune."

"Business has been good, wouldn't you say, Miss Bookeeper? The government keeps hiring me to teach these college kids to fly. And one thing I'll say for the government, they pay well and on time. Our tax dollars at work, don'tcha know. Well, God bless Franklin D. Roosevelt and the Civilian Pilot Training Program. They are the reason I can afford to buy you a nice dress."

"I know, but it's still too expensive, Roger."

"It's the first time I bought an anniversary present. I didn't know there was a spending limit."

"The first year's gift is supposed to be paper. That's why I got you that subscription to *Life* magazine."

"And I love it," he insisted.

"But it makes me look like a cheapskate next to this beautiful dress," I complained. "I should have gotten you something nicer."

Roger stepped into the office and closed the door. "You can give me an extra present after our dinner date," he said, shifting his eyebrows up and down in a playful, mockingly sensual expression. Gathering me in his arms and pressing me close, he kissed me hard on the mouth. After a long minute, he turned me loose. "Mrs. Welles, I'll pick you up in an hour."

"All right," I said as he left. "See you in an hour."

I walked to the office window and watched my husband as he greeted Barnes, the young pilot he was taking up for a flight check. Barnes was one of the scores of college students who had been coming to take lessons as part of the government's Civilian Pilot Training Program, or CPTP. The students only had to pay forty dollars toward their training, even though it cost a lot more. The government hired private instructors like Roger and paid them the difference.

The demand for teachers was so great that Roger had urged me to study to become an instructor myself. It was exciting and demanding, but I loved it. Soon I'd be ready to take on my own students, and not a minute too soon. We had far more than Roger could handle alone.

All talk of neutrality aside, it was becoming more and more apparent that America was going to be drawn into the war in Europe. The CPTP was part of the government's plan to make sure they had enough trained pilots on hand when that day came. It was good for business, that was for sure, but as I peered out the window at my husband and Barnes, who was in his early twenties but looked about fifteen, an involuntary shiver made my shoulders twitch.

Flying is so beautiful, I thought. *What is it about men that can make them take something as magnificent and freeing as an airplane and turn it into a weapon?*

Barnes and all the other students that came streaming through our doors were just as excited about learning to fly as I had been. Ten percent of the CPTP program spaces were reserved for women, so we even had a few girls taking lessons. Had I been in their shoes, I would have taken the government's offer of cheap flight training as eagerly as they did, but I wondered if they ever thought about what would come next? I did.

Roger said his female students were every bit as capable as the men, but it was impossible to imagine they would be allowed to pilot military aircraft, so I wasn't worried about them. But what about the boys? How many of these fresh-faced boys were going to be shot down and killed in combat over foreign soil? And what about Roger? He'd already told me that if the war came, he was going to join up. Now that I had the office running like clockwork and would soon be teaching, he said he knew he could count on me to run things until he got back. He said it was his patriotic duty to serve his country if we went to war and my duty to take care of everything while he was gone. In my heart, I agreed with him, but that didn't mean I liked the idea.

I truly cared for Roger. After a year of marriage, I could say that and know it was true. The passion that Delia had assured me would come with marriage had never materialized, but I'd always suspected she was exaggerating the joys of romance. Although even Fran had shyly intimated that she often found the physical aspect of marriage pleasurable, even exciting. I had nodded at her admission, wanting her to think I understood. I didn't want her to start asking any embarrassing questions and, besides, I was perfectly content with Roger. Our marriage was successful, even if it wasn't romantic.

Romance. After our dinner celebration, Roger would want to go back to the little house we'd rented on Third Street for a romantic end to the evening. Well, why not? I asked myself. He's your husband. It's your anniversary. He has a right to expect a little affection.

I never resisted Roger's advances, but I never made any myself, though he'd hinted vaguely that he wouldn't mind if I sometimes took the lead in lovemaking. But I just couldn't bring myself to do it.

For the first few months I found intimacy painful and awkward. When Roger approached me, I told myself to relax, just as my doctor had advised, but sometimes I inadvertently flinched at Roger's touch. I knew that hurt his feelings, but I couldn't seem to help myself. One night he poured me a glass of wine before we turned in, and though it left me feeling a little detached from what was going on in my own bed, it did help my body relax. After that, the cocktail hour was incorporated into our evening ritual. Gradually, I became accustomed to the intimate side of marriage. And though I never invited Roger's advances, it made me happy to know that by my simple act of acquiescence, I could bring my husband such obvious pleasure. I owed him that, at least.

Roger was so good to me. We were really very happy and well suited to each other in so many ways. We loved flying together. Those were the best times, those hours in the air. For me, they were the most intimate, precious moments of our marriage.

Even grounded, we made a pretty good pair. We were two sides of the coin when it came to running the flight school; I had a good mind for administration, and Roger was the best flight instructor I'd ever seen or ever would see. If I'd amounted to anything as a pilot, the credit went entirely to Roger. And, with a little coaching from me, Roger got to be much better about keeping our affairs in order and making good decisions on the most efficient and profitable places to invest our time and money. We drew on each other's strengths and helped shore up each other's weaknesses. I found a great satisfaction in knowing that I was helping Roger with the business. He had such grand plans for the school. I loved listening to him as he spun out his dreams for the future.

"And thanks to you, Li'l Feller," he'd say, using the nickname he'd given me after we married, "it's all starting to happen. In a few years, we'll have the biggest, best flight school in Illinois. Maybe in all the Midwest."

Yes, even if I hadn't learned to love Roger in the way Delia had promised I would, we were good together. We had almost everything we wanted, but the one thing we didn't have was beginning to loom larger and larger in my mind.

In spite of Roger's frequent and enthusiastic efforts, I still wasn't pregnant.

Fran's little girl, Bonnie, was ten months old. She was a darling baby, with a halo of reddish-blond curls. Whenever she gave me one of her single-toothed grins, I couldn't help but laugh, but during the bus rides back home, I'd think of her sweet, smiling baby face and my heart would hurt. My arms ached to hold a baby of my own. I was beginning to think it might never happen. We never talked about it directly, but I knew Roger was starting to wonder too.

President Roosevelt had signed the Lend Lease Act in the spring, and already American aircraft were being sent to help the Allied war effort; could American pilots be far behind? It could be any day now. I wanted a baby so much. Roger did, too.

After lovemaking, he would lay his hand on the flat of my stomach and rub it gently, not saying anything. I was sure he was wondering if the seed had found its way home and a baby was beginning inside me. Sometimes I thought it had, but month after month I was disappointed. I went to the doctor again. He said I was young and healthy and to just give it time, but time was running short.

Maybe it was my fault. Maybe, because my heart hadn't opened completely to my husband's love, my body had followed suit. Or maybe the invisible possibility of a baby that was hidden inside me refused to plant itself and grow because it wasn't sure it would be born into a family of love. Maybe, if I could find even a little bit of that passion that Fran had hinted at and Roger seemed to want to see in me, I would finally get my child.

Roger finished his flight check with Barnes and came into the office to fill out his flight log. We climbed into our truck, a dark green Ford with WELLES FLIGHT SCHOOL emblazoned in red letters on both doors, and Roger took the wheel.

"Where are we going?" I asked.

"You'll see," Roger said mysteriously. He turned right outside the airfield gate, drove about five hundred feet, and turned into the parking lot of the Soaring Wings Café.

"You've got to be kidding," I laughed. "We're having our anniversary dinner here?"

"Yes, ma'am. This is where I wooed you, wore you down, and finally won you. I couldn't think of a better place to celebrate our anniversary." Roger set the parking brake with a decisive wrench, took the key out of the ignition, and jumped out of the truck.

"But the café is closed for dinner," I protested as Roger opened my door and helped me down. "The only reason people eat here in the first place is so they can see the planes take off and land, and you can't do that at night."

"I heard that!" Thurman growled as he stepped through the front door of the café.

Roger raised his eyebrows in an "uh oh" expression. I wanted to laugh but covered my mouth with my hand, pretending to cough instead. "Sorry, Thurman. I didn't mean anything by it."

"I knew what you meant," Thurman said. He held the door

open wide as Roger and I passed through. An intoxicating aroma met us as we came inside.

"Smells great, Thurman," Roger said, sniffing the air appreciatively. "What is it?"

"Just the best chicken you ever ate," he said. "It's my mother's recipe. There's forty garlic cloves stuffed under the skin. You cook it slow so the meat's real juicy but the skin still comes out crispy. I'm serving it with mashed parsnips perked up with a little nutmeg and some just-picked sweet corn made into a relish with sweet peppers, green onion, and a little dill. I've got a nice fresh tomato and cucumber salad to start and a peach melba for dessert."

"Thurman, it sounds delicious," I said, more than a little surprised. "I can't believe you went to all this trouble."

Thurman barked out one quick, sharp laugh. "You mean you can't believe I know how to cook such fancy grub! You think all these old hands can do is sling hash." He'd absolutely read my mind and there was no denying it, so I just kept my mouth shut and smiled. "Well, I feed people what they want, and around here what people want is a big, greasy plate of hash. But I know how to cook right, if the occasion calls for it. I was an army cook for eighteen years. Started out making vats of oatmeal for enlisted boys and ended up making gourmet meals for generals in Paris. I learned a few things in France, but my mother's forty-garlic chicken still beats them all," he bragged. "Tonight, you're eating at the best restaurant in town."

"Thanks, Thurman," Roger said. "I sure appreciate this."

"Well, we'll see if you still appreciate it when you get the bill. Cooking like this don't come cheap." He cleared his throat. "You're paying for the dinner, but there's a bottle of champagne on your table. That's from me. Happy anniversary."

"Oh, Thurman! That's sweet of you. Thank you." I moved to hug the old man, but he sidestepped me.

"Yeah," he muttered gruffly, "I'd better be getting back to the kitchen. Don't want the chicken to burn. You two can seat your-selves." He jerked his head toward the dining room, turned on his heel, and disappeared into the kitchen.

Roger escorted me to a table in the corner and held out my chair for me. The table was covered with a white cloth. In the center, a pair of pale blue candlesticks in glass holders flanked a small bou-quet of blue violets. A bottle was chilling in a galvanized bucket that looked a lot like the one Thurman used to mop floors with. The table was set with two of the blue plates that lunch specials were served on and the diner's usual silverware, but it had been polished and, in the glow of candlelight, the cheap flatware shone like ster-ling.

Roger sat down across from me. "The place looks a little differ-ent at night, doesn't it?"

I nodded and then, without my quite knowing why, tears pooled in my eyes.

"What's the matter, Li'l Feller?" Roger asked. "Are those happy tears or sad ones?"

I sniffed and wiped my eyes with my paper napkin. "Happy. You're just too good to me, Roger."

"Well, I don't know about that, but I do my best. Why shouldn't I? I love you." He reached across the table to take my hand. "You're the best thing that ever happened to me. You know that?"

I started crying again. "No, I'm not! It's not true! You've been so sweet to me. And so patient and gentle and I . . . I just can't seem to . . . I don't . . ." No matter how hard I tried, I just couldn't con-jure the words to say how sorry I was that I wasn't the lover he de-served.

"Roger, I know you weren't ever married before, but you're ten years older than me and you've . . . you've traveled and seen the world. I'm sure you must have known a lot of women before you met me. Did you . . . ? I mean, did any of those women have trouble with . . ."

Roger's eyes smiled as he lifted my hand to his lips. "Is that what all these tears are about?" He paused a moment to give me a chance to answer, but I didn't respond.

"Georgia, you're just young and inexperienced, that's all. When I met you, I thought you were a tough little thing—funny and bright, but tough. And determined," he whistled low. "I'd never met a woman as determined as you—determined to become a pilot and determined to give me the gate. I knew from the first you were something special, but I was a little intimidated by you. You made it clear that you were doing just fine on your own, thank you.

"But then I got to know you, and I saw that was just a cover-up, a way to protect yourself—especially from men. From what you told me about Delia, I'm not really surprised. Seeing the way she's been used and thrown away time and time again, I'd expect you to be nervous about men. You don't think we're trustworthy. Well, Li'l Feller, I'm determined, too. I'm going to change your mind—at least about me. When you know for certain that you can trust me, it'll be easier. I promise. Give it some time." He kissed my hand again as if sealing the bargain with his lips.

"But it's been a whole year already," I said.

"And it's getting better already. Isn't it?" he asked.

I nodded but couldn't bring myself to look him in the eye. I kept my head down and said, "If the war comes—"

"Don't let's talk about that tonight," he interrupted. "Not on our anniversary."

"But it's been all this time and I'm still not in a family way."

He shrugged, but the expression on his face wasn't as unconcerned as he was trying to appear. "We don't know that. Maybe you are. Maybe you are right now. Maybe that's why you're so emotional. I hear women get weepy when they're having a baby. And even if you're not, you will be soon," he said reassuringly.

I took a deep breath and thought about Roger. How patient he'd been and how well he knew me, maybe even better than I knew myself. With my free hand, I reached under the tablecloth, found Roger's knee, and laid my hand on it. I moved my fingers along the smooth fabric of his trousers, high up to his inseam. I lifted my head and saw the surprise in his eyes.

"Soon," I said softly. "Maybe tonight."

Roger grinned and shifted a little in his seat. "Can I pour you a drink?" he asked as he reached for the bottle of champagne.

I shook my head. "No. I don't need it, Roger. Not tonight."

❧ 10 ❧

Morgan

The Pacific—June 1942

It was my own fault. I'd been standing there, holding my chow tray and scanning the mess tent for an empty spot for a good minute and a half—the sure sign of a recent arrival. Seeing a not too crowded table in the far corner, I made a move toward it, trying to look like I knew where I was going. Too late.

Out of the corner of my eye, I saw a crowd of guys wearing flight jackets laughing, and talking, and checking me out. Pilots. Even sitting down, they possessed the unmistakable swagger of hotshots. The man at the end of the table, a redheaded fellow so tall I wondered how he managed to fold himself into the cramped confines of a cockpit, was looking at me hard. He elbowed the guy next to him and jerked his chin toward me with a sly "watch this" expression on his face.

Their table was directly along my path. As I approached, the red-haired pilot shouted, "Gentlemen! FNG at two o'clock!" With that, the whole bunch of them leaped to their feet accompanied by the clatter of spoons against chow trays and the scuffle of a dozen pairs of boots. Startled by the noise, I didn't see the redhead's boot stuck out directly in my path. I tripped. My tray went flying and I followed. The mess hall rumbled in laughter as I came down for a landing in a pile of mashed potatoes and beef gravy. The pilots laughed hardest of all and offered me advice.

"Better watch where you're going there, FNG."

"Hey! The uniform of the day doesn't include gravy."

"Hope he's not my new navigator. This FNG can't navigate his way through the chow line!"

The guys were enjoying themselves, and fresh ripples of laughter accompanied each witty remark. A new pair of boots moved into my field of vision, and the merriment ebbed as the pilots greeted the newcomer.

"Hey, Fountain! How you doing? Good run?"

I flexed my knee a couple of times to see if the pain in it was anything serious. In an elegant drawl of the Deep South, the voice that belonged to the boots said, "It was A-OK, gentlemen. Another Jap bought the farm."

A murmur of congratulations greeted this information. "Who's this guy on the deck?" he asked, obviously referring to me.

"FNG," the redhead responded.

"An FNG? You sure?" I was already starting to get up, but the speaker, Fountain, reached down, gripped me by the shoulder and helped haul me to my feet. A big, open face topped by a shock of white-blond hair looked into mine. He turned so his back was toward his buddies, brushed invisible dust from my shoulders, and gave me a conspiratorial wink.

"You bunch of yahoos!" he barked. "This is no FNG! This is my cousin."

"Your cousin?" The redhead said, an edge of doubt creeping into his voice. The guy they called Fountain sounded really mad.

"Yeah! My cousin! Wee, what are you doing, tripping my cousin and messin' up his uniform? Give him your handkerchief so he can clean himself up," he ordered. The redhead he'd addressed as Wee quickly complied.

"Thanks," I said as I used the handkerchief to sop up the gravy on my shirt.

Wee furrowed his brow. "He's your cousin? His accent isn't anything like yours."

"Well, that's because my cousin is from the Texas branch of the family, isn't that right, Cousin . . . Cousin . . . ?" He paused a moment, waiting for me to fill in the blank.

"Morgan. Morgan Glennon. And I'm from Oklahoma," I said and handed the gravy-soaked handkerchief back to Wee, who dropped it on the table with a splat.

"That's right," Fountain continued without missing a beat. "Like I said—Cousin Morgan. From the Oklahoma branch of the family. Our grandfathers were brothers. They were both graduates of the Citadel, but that was before Cousin Morgan's grandfather left South Carolina to find and seek his fortune in the oil fields of Oklahoma."

"The Citadel," one of the guys called out. "Wasn't that the college they expelled you from?"

"I wasn't expelled," Fountain explained calmly. "The president merely suggested that a natural-born leader like myself would best serve our country by enlisting immediately rather than wasting two more years in college."

"Was that before or after he found you and his daughter steaming up the windows of his Pontiac?" the other guy asked. Fountain grinned broadly, and all the pilots burst into raucous laughter.

"So, this guy's your cousin. That right, F.W.?" Realizing he'd been duped, annoyance and amusement battled in Wee's face. Amusement won out. He smiled and stuck out his hand. "Nice to meet you, Cuz. Bill Williamson. Also known as Wee Willy Williamson, or just Wee for short."

"It certainly is," Fountain commented.

Wee punched him in the shoulder but without any real malice. He was obviously used to his nickname by now. "Very funny."

"Wee is the section leader of these fine gentlemen," Fountain said. I nodded to the assembled group. "And I will be your section leader, which, naturally, makes you a member of the hottest section on base." He grinned and extended his hand. "Fountain Walker the Third, known to my friends as F.W., of Goose Creek, South Carolina. That's near Charleston."

"Nice to meet you."

"I heard you were coming, but wasn't expecting you until tomorrow."

"There was room on an earlier transport."

"That's good. We've been shorthanded. Could have used your help today. We took out a couple of Zeros but not before they put some holes in our planes. One of my guys kind of limped back home, but everybody made it."

"Where were you stationed before this, Morgan?"

"Lackland," I answered. The other pilots laughed when they heard this. Wee laughed the loudest.

"You just graduated from Lackland? This is your first combat posting?" I nodded. "What'd I tell you, Fountain? Your cousin's an FNG!"

I looked at Fountain, who was laughing with the others. "What's an FNG?" I asked.

"F***ing New Guy," he said and clapped me on the back. "That's all right. I can tell already that you're going to be one hell of a good wing man. You're quiet, and that's what counts. Remember, there's only two things a good wing man needs to say. 'Your tail's on fire,' and, 'I'll take the ugly one.'" The guys guffawed, and I smiled, too. "Trust me. You've got the top section leader in the squadron. With my guidance, you'll be an ace in no time."

"That right?" said Wee. "As of yesterday I had five kills to your four, which officially made me an ace. You got another today, so now you're a member of the club, too, but that still leaves us tied."

"Oh, didn't I tell you?" Fountain said in a voice as smooth as southern loomed cotton. "I took out two Japs today. Two." He held up dual fingers to emphasize his point.

"That right?" Wee smiled and then looked around the table. "Well, gentlemen, I guess that means we'd better finish up here and get to our briefing." Wee and his crew gathered up their gear. As he left, Wee grinned at Fountain.

"Enjoy that title, Ace, because you'll not be at the top heap for long. There's Japs out there today. I can smell 'em, and I'm going to get 'em."

The two pilots shook hands. "See you when you get back," Fountain said seriously.

"See you. Oh, you boys can keep that handkerchief. I've got others." He nodded to me. "Nice to meet you, kid. Welcome to the Thirtieth."

That was the first and last time I saw Bill Williamson. His plane was shot down the same night.

I didn't know about it right away, not until a week later, when I commented that I hadn't seen Wee around and asked Fountain if he was still the top section leader or if the other pilots had caught up to him. Stony-faced, Fountain told me that Wee had bought the farm a few hours after our conversation.

"You're kidding," I said incredulously, but the look on Fountain's face told me he wasn't. "But you never said anything. At breakfast the next day everyone seemed fine. They all just sat there drinking coffee and eating scrambled eggs."

"The Thirtieth Fighting Squadron has a high casualty rate. We're good pilots. The best. So we get sent on the most dangerous missions. Somebody at Lackland must have thought you were some kind of hotshot to send you here with no combat experience. From what I've seen so far, they were right.

"We've lost a lot of guys. Unless we can win the war quick, we'll lose a whole lot more. So we do the job, we fly the tough missions, because winning the war is the best chance we have for getting home alive. When somebody buys the farm we don't talk about it. If we did, it's all we'd ever talk about. We can't do that and still get the job done. Understand?"

I nodded.

"Good," Fountain said. "Now, let's go get some chow."

❦ 11 ❦

Morgan

The Pacific—November 1942

Dear Morgan,

Guess what? Dwyer's got a few cans of real coffee in yesterday and I bought one. I wanted to buy two, but Mrs. Dwyer wouldn't sell them to me. She said that wouldn't be fair, but it seems to me that she should have let me since I was there first. Oh well. Anyway, I'm going to save it for when you come home. Do you think you'll get leave soon?

The weather has been good here. The harvest was good but it was hard getting it in with so many men gone into the service. Vivian Carver and I went to a dance at the Grange in Hadley, but it wasn't any fun. All the boys were kids. I don't think any of them was more than sixteen. We left and went to the picture show instead. We saw KING'S ROW. It was my third time, but I didn't mind. I think that Ronald Reagan is just the best. Have you seen it yet?

I saw your mother driving into Cheevers filling station the other day. I waved to her but don't think she saw me. Have you told her that we're writing?

I hope you can come home for Christmas. It would be so romantic if we could go flying again. I've got a very special present for you when you get here. Will you have something special for me? It seems like I've been waiting for you for such a long time, but you're worth it. I'll wait for you as long as it takes.

I hope you're well. Write soon. I know you must be so busy, but it worries me when I don't hear from you.

Love,
Virginia

"Isn't that sweet," Fountain said as he leaned over my bunk and snatched the piece of pink stationery out of my hand. "She signs her name with little hearts over the 'i's." He lifted the paper to his nose and sniffed. "Doused in perfume. Lavender, I believe. Morgan, this seems serious. Look what it says here—she's got a special present for you. Mmmm-mmm! Sounds like my kind of girl! You told me she was writing, but clearly you left out some of the pertinent details. Did you do this girl before you left home, Glennon? Or is she just hoping you will when you get home? How come you never told me about this? You're my best friend and bunkmate. Are you keeping things from me?" He shook his head and made a tsk-tsk sound.

"Knock it off, F.W. Gimme that," I reached for the letter, but he held it high out of my reach.

"Uh oh." He frowned as he continued reading. "She's asking if you'll have anything special for her. In case you weren't aware of it, in female-speak that translates into 'engagement ring.' Brother, every girl that's been dating a fellow more than three weeks thinks that come Christmastime, he ought to buy her a ring. Why is that?

Well, don't you do it, Morgan. You're a young man yet. Far too young and far too fine a pilot to get yourself entangled with any old ball-and-chain."

I jumped off my bunk and grabbed the letter. "Thanks for the advice, but I've no plans to marry in the immediate future. Virginia's nice enough. When I was in high school I thought she might be the one, but now that I'm older . . . I don't know. She seems kind of goofy. She's crazy over movies. Spends all her spare time and money at the pictures." I opened the door of my locker and looked at the picture of Virginia I'd taped inside the door.

"Well, buddy, she might not be the crispest cracker in the barrel, but who cares? That is one fine-looking flower of womanhood." Fountain whistled low. "If I was you, I'd be figuring out a way to get myself back to Oklahoma for Christmas so I could open *that* present."

"I don't know if I love her," I said, half to myself. "I know she's counting on me asking her to marry her when I get back, but I'm just not sure. It doesn't seem fair to keep her hanging on, waiting for me. I've thought about breaking up, but I can't bring myself to do it."

Fountain was sitting on the edge of my bunk, not kidding me anymore. "Sounds like she's got some kind of hold on you," he said.

"Yeah, but it's not the kind of hold she thinks it is. I know I ought to let her go, but if I do, then I won't have anybody. I look forward to her letters. I like thinking somebody back home is waiting for me, planning for our future. It makes me think there is a future to go home to." I was quiet for a moment, waiting for him to say something.

"Do you think I'm a jerk for leading her on?" I finally asked.

"Hell, no!" Fountain exclaimed. "Just a pilot who is far from home and needs somebody to remind him what home is all about. If Virginia Pratt helps you remember to fly smart so you can get back to Oklahoma in one piece, then I say 'amen' to that." Fountain raised his hands and voice during this last, in a tremulous imitation of the Reverend Warren E. Plowshare, pastor of his home church, the Goose Creek Third Baptist Church, an impersonation he performed frequently and well. I smiled in spite of myself.

"Really, Morgan," Fountain said in his natural voice, "I don't see that you're doing this girl any harm. You read her letter. It's not like she's got a lot of other prospects. All the eligible male residents of Dillon, Oklahoma, have left for the glories of war. You're not keeping her from finding true love or anything. And, as you say, you're not sure how you feel about her. Maybe by the time you get home you'll be sure. Then you'll either marry her and live happily ever after, or let her go so she can take her pick from the crop of returning G.I.s. And believe me, a girl that looks like that is going to have plenty to pick from."

"Maybe. It still doesn't seem fair to her—"

Fountain interrupted, "Now, don't go getting all serious and guilt-ridden on me. Next thing you know you'll be asking her to marry you out of pure remorse, and that's no good. I told you before, a married pilot is a pilot who's either lost his edge or is about to. Makes a guy too cautious. I need you to stay at the top of your game."

Fountain slapped his hands on his thighs, signaling that as far as he was concerned, all issues had been resolved. "Speaking of which, a guy trying to stay on the top of his game needs a little recreation from time to time. To which end, my friend, I have secured us a twenty-four-hour pass beginning on Thursday night. Holmes and Franklin are coming along. We are going to have a steak dinner in a fine restaurant, consume several bottles of well-aged grain alcohol, and enjoy the companionship of some women of breathtaking beauty and easy virtue—not necessarily in that order."

I grinned. One thing I had to say for Fountain, he had style.

Right up until he'd gotten himself expelled from the Citadel, he'd had the finest education that money could buy, and it showed. Fountain Walker III could make twenty-four hours of drinking and debauchery sound as sophisticated and edifying as a grand tour of Europe.

"As appealing as that sounds, F.W., I think I might pass."

"Morgan! You've got to come. I'm not taking no for an answer!"

I thought about it for a minute. It would be nice to get off base, even if it was just for a few hours, but I wasn't quite ready for the kind of evening that Fountain was proposing. "Tell you what, I'll come along to chaperone. We can have dinner and a couple of beers, and then you three can go engage in whatever foolishness you want to. I'll be there to make sure you get back to base before they send the MPs out looking for you."

"Really? You'd do that for me? Are you sure I can't tempt you to sample the favors of some belle of the Pacific? I'm buying."

"No thanks. Besides, I'd have to take the ugly one anyway."

Fountain slapped me on the back. "Morgan! You're the best wing man in the military! I knew it from the first. When I saw you, laying on the mess hall floor facedown in a mound of mashed potatoes, I took one look at you and said to myself, 'F.W., that is a man of exceptional talent.'"

"Thanks, F.W. I appreciate that."

"To Thursday night!" Fountain pretended to hold a glass in his empty hand and raised a toast.

"To Thursday!" I answered as we clinked imaginary glasses.

❦ 12 ❦

Georgia

Waukegan, Illinois—Summer, 1942

At least twice a week, I sat down at a desk piled high with bills to be paid and papers waiting to be filed, with my coffee cup on my right and Roger's enlistment photo on my left and wrote a letter to Roger, just like I did on July 25th.

> *Darling,*
>
> *I got your letter just yesterday and (from what I could tell after the censors had done their worst—it looked like a mouse had gotten to it!) was glad to hear that you're doing fine and that the food and beds at this new base are better than the last.*
>
> *The news reports here say that American bomber pilots have been giving the Germans a big dose of their own medicine. I'm sure the English are grateful for all of you brave pilots, but not too grateful, I hope. In other words, steer clear of any overly appreciative, young Englishwomen! Just kidding, Sweetheart.*
>
> *Business is still slow, even slower now that gasoline ra-*

tioning is in full force. We really don't have any students at this point. We're getting by mostly on fees from pilots who've stored their planes with us for the duration of the war, but sometimes when the men enlist the checks seem to come irregularly or not at all.

Thurman is having a hard time too. With so little private plane traffic, not as many people are coming to the café. We have been doing a little in the way of engine repair. Stubbs has been teaching me and I turn out to be a pretty decent mechanic. Just yesterday I replaced the fuel pump on a beautiful Waco YKS-6. I took her for a spin after I was through and she handled like a dream! What a ride! It was the highlight of my week. I wish you could have been there with me.

Oh, I almost forgot! Given your recent experiences with the efficiency of the military billeting system, you'll love this story.

Recently, I learned that the government was hiring private pilots to ferry some aircraft from factories to bases so they don't have to use military pilots for that kind of work and can save them for combat. Thinking that might help us make ends meet, I showed up at the office to apply, brought my license and my flight logs to show I was qualified. I was shown into the office of a very cranky, self-important captain who made it clear that the government had no intention of entrusting its airplanes over to a female pilot. He wouldn't even look at my logs. Whether I'd logged two hundred hours or two thousand, it made no difference to him. The sign on the clubhouse door read 'No Girls Allowed!' and that captain slammed it in my face but good.

Well, I was pretty sore at being given the brush-off by this guy (not to mention using two gallons of precious gas to drive to his office just so he could ignore me!) but I calmed down some by the time I got home. Anyway, I went into the office the next day and what do I find on my desk? A letter from Jacqueline Cochran, the most famous lady flyer in America! It seems the army is forming an all-female branch of the air force, specifically to ferry planes, fly transports and other noncombat missions to free up men for combat assignments and they were inviting me to put in an application! I guess the higher ups didn't consult with the cranky captain before putting their plan into action.

Really, it was kind of flattering to get the letter. If I wasn't a married woman with a job to do, I think I'd be tempted to accept, but don't worry. I'm still here and taking care of our business. It'll all be ready and waiting for you when you get home. But isn't it great that they are going to use women pilots to help with the war effort? When it comes to winning this war and quickly, I say, all hands on deck!

Of course, now that you're on the scene I'm sure you'll send the Germans packing in no time and we'll be together again! Until then, know that I'm keeping the home fires burning until you get back. One way or another, Stubbs and I will keep things afloat.

I miss you so much, Sweetheart, but I'm so proud of you. Keep flying high!

All my love,
Georgia

P.S. I'm tucking a new picture that Stubbs took of me standing next to that Waco. Just thought you might like to see what a good job we did fixing her up!

I wrote three more times after that but, as far as I know, this was the last one Roger received. Ten days after I sent it, I received a telegram from the War Department informing me that my husband had been killed in action.

In the letter that followed, Roger's squadron commander told me that the B-24 Liberator Roger was flying had been attacked by enemy fighters on a bombing run. The entire crew was lost along with two of the three P-38s that were escorting them. The heavy, lumbering Liberator was a good bomber, but there was no way it could outrun or outmaneuver those fighters.

Because the plane had gone down over the ocean, there were no remains, but I received a box with an American flag and Roger's personal effects. Along with his clothes, I found several snapshots of myself, and a couple of Roger and me together. The white edges of the pictures were bent and worn; I guess he had looked at them often. Only the one with me standing in front of the Waco looked fairly pristine, but there was an unmistakable fingerprint on the upper left-hand corner of the photograph, Roger's fingerprint.

Holding the picture gingerly by one edge, making sure my tears didn't drip on it and wash away the print, I laid it carefully in a velvet-lined jewelry box that had previously held the opal heart pendant Roger sent me when he shipped out to England. Now it held and protected the only physical evidence of Roger's being, his last gift to me. Before closing the lid I examined the imprinted swirls and whorls of his fingertips that shone clearly against the grainy black and white shadows, embossing them with Roger's message to me; in his last days, perhaps his last hours, he'd thought of me. I closed the lid and put the box on my dressing table. I still have it.

Before he died, Roger flew dozens of successful bombing raids. He personally trained scores of private pilots who went on to become some of the best flyers in the military. Would we have won the war without Roger? Yes. But how much longer would it have taken? How many lives did Roger save by putting his on the line? There's no way to tell, but I know he did his part and then some.

And yet there were no monuments to honor his memory, no child to bear his name, but, somehow, I would make sure he was remembered. I owed him that and so much more.

He taught me to trust. He gave me wings. I loved him so.

PART TWO

❧ 13 ❧

Georgia

Sweetwater, Texas—December 1942

I stepped off the train at the Texas and Pacific station and found myself ankle-deep in West Texas mud. As I would soon learn, it didn't rain very often in Sweetwater, but when it did, it poured. There wasn't a porter in sight, so I took off running, lugging my bags. By the time I reached the protection of the station's overhanging eaves, I was drenched. With every step, muddy water squelched from the stitching of my shoes.

Great, I thought. *Four dollars for new pumps and a precious shoe ration right down the drain. That's what I get for trying to make an entrance.*

I looked around, hoping to spot a taxi or even a bus, but the only vehicle in sight was a battered 1932 Dodge pickup. The pickup door opened, and a tall man, made taller by a high-crowned Stetson, got out. He came toward me in big, loping steps, like a kid crossing a creek by leaping from stone to stone. Rain poured a little waterfall over the brim of his hat. "You going to Avenger?"

When I said yes he grabbed my bags, tossed them in the back of the truck, and covered them with a piece of canvas. Supposing that this must be the West Texas version of mass transit, I followed, not even bothering to run through the rain. I couldn't get any wetter than I already was.

The windows of the truck were fogged up. The tall Texan pulled a faded bandanna from his pocket, wiped off a dinner-plate-sized peephole on the window, and started the engine.

He gunned the motor and took off so fast that the rear of the truck fishtailed in the mud. Startled, I grabbed the door handle, but after a second the tires found some traction and the ride evened out. The cowboy was still driving too fast for my taste and for the weather conditions, but he seemed to know where he was going, and it wasn't like I had a whole lot of other options, so I relaxed my grip on the handle, looked out the window, and tried to enjoy the ride.

"Yeah," he said as if answering a question I'd neglected to ask, "we don't get a whole lot of rain here, but when we do . . . whoo-whee," he made a whistling sound through a gap in his front teeth. "It's a gully washer."

"Well, I'm glad you were at the station. It would have been a pretty miserable walk." At that, he made a sound like he was sucking something off his teeth and gave one quick nod of his head. I wasn't sure exactly what that meant, but it seemed a friendly enough response. "So, do you do this for a living? Are you the town taxi driver?"

He grinned. "No, ma'am. I got a regular job. Don't take no money for this. It's kind of my hobby. Wanted to go into the service, but they wouldn't take me on account of my hand. Had a run-in with a buzz saw when I was younger." He raised his arm and for the first time I noticed that his left hand was missing three fingers. "The man at the induction center said I couldn't handle a gun, and I said it was news to me because I'm about the best shot in this county, but he wouldn't listen. So I decided if they wouldn't let me fight, least I could do was help out by meetin' the trains and takin' pilots over to the airfield. 'Course, up until now they was all men. Then I heard tell that they was switchin' to women. Didn't believe it till ya'll started showin' up last month. Girl pilots! Dozens of 'em!" He whistled again. "Makes doing my patriotic duty a whole lot more interestin'.

Reaching forward, I laid my left hand, which still bore my wedding band, conspicuously onto the dashboard.

"Don't worry, ma'am." the driver assured me. "I saw right off that you was married, but there's plenty that ain't. 'Course, they'll keep you girls so busy with trainin' that I don't suppose you'll get to town much. On top of that, I'll have plenty of competition. A beat-up old cowhand like me don't stand much chance against these fly-boys."

Up until now I'd been listening with only half an ear, peering through the fogged up windows and wondering if there were any trees in Texas, but the mention of male pilots got my attention. "I thought you said that Avenger was an all-female training base? That's what I'd been told."

"It is," he assured me, "but word has got out to the other bases. Suddenly every pilot within two hundred miles is havin' engine trouble when they get in range of Avenger. There's been a whole lot of emergency landings since you girls got to town." He grinned even wider and shot me an appraising look from under the brim of his hat. "Well, can't blame a fella for tryin'. Tell the truth, I kinda wondered what a bunch of girl pilots would look like, but I've picked up near every one of you from the station, and, mostly, ya'll are real nice-lookin' girls." He didn't bother to mask the surprise in his voice.

"Well, thanks," I said.

Missing the sarcasm in my tone, he said, "You're welcome," as if he'd just paid me the highest of compliments.

He took a sharp left turn onto a narrow road and said brightly, "Here we are! Avenger Field—home of the Women's Air Service Pilots Training Division. If it all works out, in four months you'll be a WASP, flying airplanes for Uncle Sam. 'Course, about a third of trainees wash out before graduation. Leastways, that's how it was for the men. Who knows? With girls it might be more."

Butterflies with cactus prickles on their wings suddenly started fluttering in my stomach. The magnitude of what I was undertaking hit me full force. I had just left my home and business, bought a train ticket, and traveled all the way to Texas, only to arrive in a blinding rainstorm at what was surely the flattest, most desolate patch of real estate on God's earth. I was tired, hungry, soaked right down to my step-ins, and sitting in a dented pickup truck with a seven-fingered Texan who'd just informed me I had a one-in-three chance of being sent home before I ever got my wings. What had I been thinking?

The truck pulled up in front of the gate, and the tall Texan jammed on the brakes, making a curtain of mud fly up from under the tires. He looked at me expectantly. When I made no move to exit, he said, "Hey. I was just kidding before. You're going to do fine. Just fine. They wouldn't have asked you to come if they thought you'd wash out."

He glanced at my ring and continued, "And your husband. He must think you'll make it or he wouldn't have let you come. I s'pose he's in the service too or you'd be home takin' care of him. Bet he's real proud of you. He'll be prayin' for you, just like you been prayin' for him. Prayer does a powerful lot of good. I been a church goin' man all my life, so I know," he said seriously, "You're going to do just fine."

I took a deep breath and blinked a couple of times. "I'm sure you're right," I said. He nodded, accepting this as a compliment.

"Thanks for the ride, mister. I know you do this as a way to help out the war effort, but can I pay you something? At least let me pay for your gas."

He sucked on his teeth again. "Nope. But if you wanted to buy me a drink, a beer at the Tumbleweed Roadhouse costs two bits."

I pulled a dollar bill out of my purse and held it out to him. "Here. Have four."

"No, ma'am." He waved off the bill. "One beer on Saturday night is all I need or want. I told you. I'm a churchgoin' man."

I gave him a quarter, climbed down from the truck, and grabbed my bags. As he was getting ready to go I tapped on the window and he rolled it down.

"Say, what's your name, anyway?"

"Tex," he said with a "what did you expect" grin on his face. Then he tipped his hat, gunned the engine, and sped down the road, splattering mud all the way.

❦ 14 ❦

Morgan

The Pacific—February 1943

I squared my shoulders and knocked on General Martin's office door.

"Come in!" The grizzled, white-haired general sat at his desk, bent over a pile of papers and chewing on the end of a corncob pipe à la MacArthur. Another officer might have gotten a ribbing using the same pipe as the Supreme Allied Commander in the Pacific, but General Martin was a good egg, and we all respected him. Besides, he'd been smoking corncob pipes since MacArthur was a boy. As far as the men of the Thirtieth were concerned, it was MacArthur who was imitating Martin, not the other way around.

I saluted, and the general gave me my ease. "Sir? You asked to see me?"

"Yes. Take a load off." I pulled up a chair and sat down a little uneasily. It wasn't usual for a lowly lieutenant to sit in the presence of the base commander.

"Relax, son. I didn't bring you in here to bawl you out." My jaw unclenched a little at this, but not much. "Morgan, you've been doing an outstanding job."

"Thank you, sir."

"You're not only a helluva pilot, you've earned the respect of your men. I know you got your field commission because we'd lost so many of our junior officers in combat, but you earned that rank and no mistake about it. You're a natural-born leader. And, as of last week, you lead the squadron in enemy kills. However," he said, taking the pipe from his mouth and tapping the stem against a personnel file that topped the stack of papers sitting in front of him, "your superiors are a little concerned about you."

He picked up the file and began reading from it, underlining the text with the stem of his pipe. "'Lieutenant Glennon possesses outstanding leadership qualities, exemplary character, superior technical skills, and commitment to the mission. From the first, he has displayed an admirable personal courage. However, in recent weeks, Lieutenant Glennon's willingness to undertake personal risk has moved from the realm of the courageous to the reckless and may present an unnecessary danger to himself and others.'"

The room was quiet for a moment while I waited for the general to speak. He took his time before saying anything, his eyes still on the paper as he silently reread the file. "Captain Conroy's quite a wordsmith, isn't he? I've been in the service for twenty-eight years and I still can't write a personnel report with anything like his style. But, all military jargon aside, there's a fine line between bravery and foolhardiness, and Captain Conroy thinks you've crossed it. I tend to agree with him. Twelve kills? And you've only been here since June. That's quite an impressive record, Glennon."

I cleared my throat. "Permission to speak, sir?"

"Of course. I told you, you're not here to get bawled out."

"It is true that I have a high record of enemy kills, but it's been more luck than anything. For whatever reason, my section has come under fire more frequently than some others. When we have, I've tried my best to do my job, engage the enemy, and protect the craft I've been assigned to escort by neutralizing the threat. I haven't gone looking for those Zeros, sir. They've come after me, and when they did, I took them on. That's my job, sir."

"Morgan, when you're assigned to escort a ship, your job is to defend them against the enemy, not go looking for them. Twice last month, when your group came under attack you engaged the enemy and took out one of their planes—very ably, according to this report. But then, after the Japs peeled off and headed for home and the ship you were assigned to protect was no longer in danger, you took off after them. Is that correct?" General Martin peered at me over the top of his black-rimmed glasses.

"Sir, I was concerned that they might come back and attack a second time, so I gave chase to make sure they'd gotten the message."

"But that is not the procedure. When you are on escort duty, your orders are to defensively engage the enemy. This isn't the Wild West, Lieutenant, and you're not the Lone Ranger. You don't go off chasing the bad guys unless you've been told to. Fortunately, it worked out for the best both times. But what if, while you were off hunting Japs that had already decided to call it a day, there had been an attack from another direction? Your section would have been down a man. Your absence could have given the Japs the advantage they need to take out one of our pilots, one of the boys in your own section. The pilots that you are supposed to be leading!" In spite of his assurance not to bawl me out, the general's voice was loud and accusing. I didn't blame him. I deserved it.

"Then we'd be down two pilots, and that, as you know from experience, could be just the opening they'd need to shoot down the rest of the escort craft and then start bombing the hell out of the ship you were assigned to protect! Your little stunt could have caused the failure of the entire mission—not to mention a terrible and un-necessary loss of life! What in the hell were you thinking, son?"

"I . . . I guess I wasn't, sir. It was a stupid mistake. It won't happen again."

The general took a deep breath. "I'm sure it won't, Glennon. But I don't believe it was just a mistake. You're too fine a pilot for that." He picked up his pipe and wedged it between his teeth before fishing a match out of his pocket and relighting it. When he spoke again, his voice was calm. Something in his tone and inflection reminded me of Papaw.

"You were in Walker's section, weren't you?" I nodded. "He was a good man. Captain Conroy tells me you were with him when he was shot down. You were the only one who made it home that night, weren't you? Can you tell me about it?"

It was an order phrased as a request. General Martin waited for me to respond, but it took me a minute. It seemed like my Adam's apple was stuck in the middle of my throat.

The only other time I'd spoken about it was to brief Captain Conroy the day it happened. I'd made my report, answering all the captain's questions and including all the pertinent information, but at that time it hadn't really hit me yet that Fountain Walker, Brian Holman, and Tony Campezzio were really gone.

Later, no one asked about it, and I didn't volunteer. That was the unwritten rule of the Thirtieth. But when I walked into the mess hall and sat alone at a table that had been crowded with my buddies the day before, moving my eggs from one side of my tray to the other and tearing my toast into pieces, I could feel the stares of the other men boring holes into my back. They wondered why I was the only one still alive. So did I.

Now the general was ordering me to tell him about that day. It took all my effort to bring forth a painful trickle of words, but once I started it was almost a relief. Memories roiled to the surface like a flood, so brutal and unyielding that they knocked me off my feet, forcing me to abandon the stoic posture I'd held for so many weeks.

I told him everything. How it had started off as a routine escort of a routine bombing mission, like dozens we'd flown before, and what a clear blue the sky had been that day. How relaxed we'd been after takeoff, joking back and forth on our radios, certain we were too close to the base for the Japs to show themselves. How Fountain had razzed me about brushing off the advances of an old street-walker who'd approached me on Thursday night. How he'd called me Choirboy of the Fighting Thirtieth, and everyone, including Fountain, had laughed. And how, just like that, the sound of our laughter was engulfed by a wave of engine noise. They were on us.

They shouldn't have been there, not that close to the base. I guess there were so many of them they felt like they could risk it. They counted on being able to hit us hard and fast, to finish the job before we could radio for backup. They were right.

They took out Holman first. A Zero came boring down and got off a lucky shot right into his gas tank. The explosion was so fast and fierce that I doubt he ever knew what hit him. I could hear Fountain hollering on the radio, telling the base that we needed more backup. I knew help was on the way, but I also knew there was no way they could get there fast enough. We were going to have to take care of these guys ourselves.

Campezzio was next to go down, but not before he scored some pretty serious hits to one of the Zeros. The crippled Jap plane bugged out and headed for home, but we were still outmanned two to one, and the whole time we were trying to hit those Zeros without getting ourselves killed in the process, they were buzzing in and out, taking turns with the bomber.

I banked hard right, came up behind one of the Japs, and scored a direct hit that sent him into the drink, but Campezzio was hit at almost the same moment. The two planes, one Japanese and one American, spiraled into the sea side by side, streaming smoke. If you could have blocked out the sound of roaring engines, stinging bullets, and Campezzio's screams coming over the radio, it would have looked like some terrible and beautiful aerobatic ballet as they floated toward the blue below, striking the water at the same time, sending up a final wave of white before disappearing under the waters forever.

There was no time to think about the fact that two of my friends had been killed in a little over two minutes. We were weaving in and out between the planes, trying every piloting maneuver we knew and inventing some new ones, fighting to keep the Zeros away from the bomber, to get ourselves into a decent firing position, to stay alive long enough for reinforcements to arrive.

Everything was happening so fast. Two Zeros were after Fountain, stalking him like wolves. In the meantime I had problems of my own. Fountain hollered a warning to me over the radio. Thanks to him, I spotted the Zero just in time and barrel-rolled right to evade a hail of Japanese bullets. I pulled out of the roll and, for a split second, was in a perfect position to hit one of the Japs that was after Fountain. He went straight down.

Then, I'm still not sure what happened, but I think a stray bullet must have hit the pilot of the other Zero, because I saw him slump forward over his controls, either dead or unconscious. I called out a warning to Fountain but I don't think he heard me. He was trailing smoke, and the Zero was closing in on him fast but Fountain didn't see him. Another Jap was after me, but I looped down and lost him, then banked as hard as I could and circled behind, trying to get into a position where I could shoot down the Zero before it collided with Fountain. But I was too late. The unconscious Japanese pilot slammed into him, setting off an explosion that engulfed both planes in a ball of fire.

The blast was so powerful that I could feel the heat of it through the skin of my plane. If I'd have been three seconds quicker, maybe even one, I could have saved him.

I took a deep breath and closed my eyes, trying to compose myself, trying to banish the mental picture of Fountain's plane—strafed with bullets, flames shooting out of the starboard wing—the nightmare picture that invaded my dreams and startled me from sleep every night, the last image I had of Fountain before five of our guys flew in and Japs took off. The bomber was crippled but still in one piece. My tail was so shot full of holes that it was like trying to fly with a cement block tied to my rudder, but we made it. The other planes stayed close until we landed, first the battered bomber and then me—the only fighter out of the original four who made it home that day.

"One second. Just one," I whispered. "I was too slow. That's what killed him."

"No," General Martin said sternly. "It was the Japanese that killed your friend. It was the war that killed him. What you did was try to save him, but you can't save everybody, Morgan. Is that why you're going off, chasing after every Zero you see, trying to kill them before they get another one of your guys?"

"I don't know. Maybe. I just . . . I just don't understand why I'm still here and Walker, Holman, and Campezzio aren't. Especially Walker. Half those maneuvers I used to get myself out of trouble that day was stuff he taught me. He was ten times the pilot I am. It should have been me that died, not him. Why am I still alive?"

Looking up, I could see the sun dipping lower in the sky, beaming shafts of light through the venetian blinds that covered the general's windows. I'd talked longer and said more than I'd intended. *The old man probably thinks I'm a nut job. He'll probably take my wings and bust me down to kitchen steward before the day is out,* I thought.

But he didn't. Instead, he opened a wooden box that sat on his desk, took out a cigarette, and offered it to me. I don't really smoke and was about to tell him so, but all of a sudden, a cigarette seemed like a good idea. I needed something to do with my hands. The general held out a lighter built into an enormous hinged conch shell. I leaned toward it and lit up.

"Ugly-looking thing, isn't it?" he said as he snapped closed the shell lid. "MacArthur sent it to me last Christmas from Manila. I've known Doug since we were cadets at West Point—gave him his first pipe. He's got a brilliant military mind, but not a nickel's worth of taste." He chuckled and leaned back in his chair before continuing.

"Morgan, every soldier who's seen combat—at least, any soldier that's worth his salt—wonders the same thing. I don't think civilians can really understand the bond that exists between soldiers. You go through so much together that the guys in your unit get to be like brothers, even closer. That's what I love about the military. It's also what I hate about it." He took a long pull on his pipe, making the tobacco in the bowl glow orange-red before he spoke again.

"If you're a guy selling insurance in Peoria and your neighbor drops dead of a stroke while mowing his grass, you feel bad about it, but life goes on and you forget about it before too long. After all, it wasn't your fault. It's different for soldiers. We're a unit. When we lose a buddy, we lose a piece of ourselves. And pretty often that brother dies while we're watching, and we can't shake the feeling that it could have been, maybe even should have been, us. But who lives and dies is God's business. There's no 'should have been's in a war, son. There's only 'what is.' Somehow or other, you've got to find a way to live with it.

"On the battlefield, when the man who carries the company flag falls, one of his buddies comes up and carries it in his place. They can't do a thing about their friend who was lost, but they can pick up the ideals he died for and carry on. That's the greatest tribute we can offer a fallen comrade—not to die in his place, but to live in it. And to live well, in a manner that brings honor to his memory. Isn't that what you would have wanted Walker to do if the tables had been turned?"

"I guess so, sir. Yes."

"Well, I don't know who was the better pilot, you or Walker, but Captain Conroy says you were two of the best he's ever seen. Conroy earned his wings before you were born, so that's saying something. He thinks you both rely too much on your instincts, but, thank God, your instincts are good. Nobody but you two could have held off that many Zeros for that long—long enough to save that bomber and her whole crew. You and your buddy saved a lot of lives. Walker is gone, and there is nothing you can do about it, but you can pick up his flag and carry it in his place. That's why I'm sending you home."

"Sir?" I asked, not sure I'd heard him right. I leaned forward and crushed out the butt of my cigarette in the ashtray he pushed in my direction. "I don't understand."

The congenial air of comrades-in-arms suddenly dissipated. The general was a general again, and I was a junior officer with only one pathetic bar on my uniform. The general stood up, and I did the same.

"I'm sending you stateside for a few months. You're going to train to fly P-38s, and then you'll be assigned to a new unit."

"Excuse me, sir, but what about my current unit? The men in my wing are used to me and—"

"Well, they'll have to get used to someone else. We've got a new crop of junior officers coming. One of them will take over for you. They're arriving on a transport tonight, the same transport you'll be taking back, so you'd better get your gear packed and say good-bye to your men. You leave tomorrow morning." He picked up an envelope from the inbox on his desk and handed it to me. I didn't have to open it to know that it contained my orders.

I wanted to argue with him, but there was no point. I took the envelope and said, "Yes, sir," but couldn't keep the edge of bitterness from creeping into my voice.

The old man narrowed his eyes and looked me up and down. "If you were a different kind of man, Glennon, I'd probably ground you for that Jap-chasing stunt you pulled. But you're too good a pilot to lose. If you get yourself rested, retrained, and refocused, you might just turn out to be a great pilot. And I need every great pilot I can get my hands on. Don't disappointment me." He saluted. "That is all."

❧ 15 ❧

Georgia

Avenger Field, Sweetwater, Texas—March 1943

"Dah-da-da-da-duh! It's time to get up in the mornin'!" Pamela Hellman bawled an enthusiastic and off-key version of reveille into my ear. I threw a pillow at her and put my arm over my eyes, trying to block out the light, but it was no good. Pam cheerfully flicked the light switch on and off.

"All right, already! I'm up. Knock it off." I pulled myself into a sitting position on the edge of the cot and rubbed the sleep from my eyes. "Why do you always have to be so happy in the morning?"

"Dunno. I was born this way, I guess. Irritating, isn't it?" she answered cheerily as she opened my footlocker and began rifling through it.

"I'll say. How can you be so perky at five in the morning? I feel like I've been hit by a truck."

"Well, probably it has something to do with the fact that you were up practicing night landings until two a.m. while I was safely tucked up in bed by ten. Here we go!" She pulled a clean flight suit out of my footlocker and tossed it to me. "And one more thing, it isn't five, it's half-past six. You've got fifteen minutes until breakfast."

"Fifteen minutes! Are you kidding? Why'd you let me sleep so long? I've got a flight check with Maytag today!" Panicking, I jumped to my feet and started peeling off my pajamas. Just a few weeks before I would have felt self-conscious about getting undressed in front of Pamela, but three months of communal living with six women in the cramped rooms we called bays had banished all modesty.

When I'd first come to Avenger, I'd been amazed at the number of girls. I knew there were other female pilots, of course. Growing up, I'd poured over newspaper accounts of famous lady flyers like the brave and tragically doomed Amelia Earhart, and the glamorous Jacqueline Cochran, two-time winner of the Harmon Trophy, aviation's most prestigious prize, winner of the 1938 Bendix Transcontinental Race, and now director of the WASP. But I'd rarely met another female pilot face to face, so I was surprised to find sixty-eight of them at Avenger, and that was just in my class! Before the program ended, more than one thousand women pilots would graduate from WASP training.

I was equally surprised to see the variety of our backgrounds and life experiences. We had everything from housewives to college professors and debutantes to movie actresses. My own baymates were a perfect example. We couldn't have been more different. Besides me, former waitress, sometime bookkeeper, airport manager, and recent widow, we had Carol Peck, a high school physics teacher from Pennsylvania and Betty Barry, a golf pro from Florida. Then there was Fanny Champlain, who had a degree in psychology from Mills College in California and had learned to fly through the college's CPT program. She'd been three weeks away from walking down the aisle with an architect from Oakland when she'd gotten her WASP recruitment letter, called off the wedding, and took the first train to Texas. Donna Lee Curtiss was the only daughter of a wealthy Chicago family who owned a chain of carpeting stores. When Donna Lee wasn't riding airplanes, she rode thoroughbred Arabian horses and had won scores of jumping competitions.

Pamela, my favorite, was a blue-blooded Connecticut Yankee from a well-off family in Darien. Her father was a banker and her mother a clubwoman. She was a tall, angelic-looking girl with a heart of gold and a decidedly wicked streak, at least when it came to her attitude toward her mother. After graduating from Vassar she'd moved to New York City's lower east side and taken a job in a settlement house. A position she'd taken because "I couldn't imagine a career that was further from my mother's plans for me. At least, not until I heard that women could fly airplanes. Naturally, I took that up as soon as possible."

We were as different as any six individuals could be, but we had one thing in common: we all loved to fly, and that bound us together as tightly as if we'd been family. I loved those girls. If I hadn't, there would have been no way I could have shared a room and bath with them for all those months.

Actually, it wasn't as crowded now as it had been. Of the original six baymates, only four were left. Carol Peck had come down with appendicitis in the second week and had to leave, but she'd written and said she was going to join another class as soon as her stitches healed. Darling, athletic Betty Barry had washed out just the day before, sent home for failing to pass the same flight check I was going to take today, with the same demanding instructor. We called him "Maytag" because he had washed out so many girls. Betty was a terrific pilot. If Maytag had sent her packing, what hope was there for me?

"Pam," I said, moaning. "How could you let me sleep so late? On today of all days?"

"Calm down," Pamela said, unzipping my flight suit and holding it out for me. "I know you have your flight check today. That's *why* I let you sleep, and that's why I came to help you get ready. Relax.

As long as you don't fool with trying to get made-up or fuss with your hair, you'll have plenty of time."

"Makeup? Hair? Are you kidding? I gave up powder and lipstick the first week—anything to get an extra five minutes' sleep. If I didn't have to share a room with you, Fanny, and Donna Lee, I'd probably have given up on showering."

"Well," she said sweetly, "I'm sure we're all grateful you didn't. Where are your shoes?"

"I think I kicked them under the bunk," I said, closing the zipper on my simply enormous flight suit and trying, unsuccessfully, to cinch it in at the waist. "This is like wearing a tent!" I complained. "Why do they have to make these things so darned big?"

"Because they never thought any women would be wearing them, that's why." Pamela's muffled voice answered as she rummaged around under my bed and finally emerged with a shoe in each hand. "Here! Now what about socks?"

"Already on my feet."

"Okay, you put on the shoes, and I'll make your bed. You've got ten minutes."

"Pam, you don't have to do that, really. I can take it from here."

"Are you sure? I don't mind." I shook my head. "All right, when you make the bed, tuck those sheets in tight enough to bounce a dime on them. We're all going to the Tumbleweed on Saturday to celebrate passing our flight check, and I won't have you wrecking our plans by flunking inspection. Nothing breaks up the Fearless Four!" she declared.

I didn't mention that, until yesterday, we'd been the Fabulous Five. She already knew. There was no making either of us more nervous than we already were. "Thanks, Pam. You're a dear. What's a nice girl like you doing in a place like this, anyway?" I teased.

"My mother, the Immediate Past President of the Darien, Connecticut, Chapter of the Daughters of the American Revolution, asks me the same question every time she writes. She's convinced they switched infants on her at the hospital. My father, on the other hand, thinks I am a chip off the old block and brags about me to all the Masons." She winked as she headed out the door. "Hurry up, Gorgeous! I'll see you in seven minutes."

"I'll be right there," I promised.

I made the bed quickly, tucking in the corners of the blanket until it was tight as a drum. I knew I should hustle down to the mess hall, but instead I sat on the edge of Betty Barry's vacant bunk. In spite of Pamela's reassurances, I was scared.

The last three months had been the most challenging of my life. The academic classes were beyond demanding. Lucky for me, the time I'd spent tinkering on engines with Stubbs gave me a definite edge when it came to the courses in engine operations, maintenance, and electronics. I was also fairly strong in mathematics, navigation, and meteorology. But the courses in physics and aerodynamics almost did me in. Even college graduates, girls like Pamela, who had a biology degree from Vassar, had a hard time with that stuff.

The endless hours of physical fitness training had us all falling into bed every night utterly exhausted. After the first night there was no chatter in our bay at bedtime; when the lights went out, so did we. We spent long hours on the exercise field doing calisthenics in the broiling West Texas sun and swallowing the blowing prairie dust as we counted our way through endless jumping jacks and push-ups. For the first time in my life I had biceps! I wasn't sure I liked the way they looked, but there was no question that my newly muscular arms made it easier to handle the controls of a 450-horsepower aircraft during long flights. Of course, the best part was the actual flying, but even that wasn't exactly a picnic.

Thanks to Roger's patient instruction, I didn't have much trouble passing the first phase of training when we had to fly the little PT-19s, basic open-cockpit trainers. In fact, it had been so easy for me that I was probably a little overconfident. When we graduated to the much larger BT-13s, I was rapidly reacquainted with humility. Our instructors made us push those planes to the limit. We had to be able to perform complicated high- and low-speed turns, spins, climbs, stalls, and every kind of acrobatic maneuver imaginable. The instructors were demanding, and a few were known to yell, but by and large they were fair-minded. Maytag was another story. Even though there was a war on and every WASP who could fly domestic missions freed up a male pilot for vital combat duty, I just don't think he liked the idea of women flying for the military. He'd use the tiniest error as an excuse for sending a girl home, and there was no way to appeal his decision.

Unless I flew perfectly today, come nightfall I'd be dressed in my civvies on a train headed back to Illinois, and all my hard work would have been for nothing. I just couldn't wash out! I was so nervous that for a second I actually thought I was going to throw up.

I moved my hand up to rub my forehead and as I did, heard a crinkling sound coming from the breast pocket of my flight suit. I already knew what it was. My lucky charm, the last letter Roger ever wrote to me, dated the day he died. Mail coming from Europe was slow, so the letter hadn't arrived until nearly a month after I'd learned of his death. When the postman brought that letter and I saw Roger's handwriting on the envelope, I cried and cried.

Now I carried it with me wherever I went. It was my talisman against fear and a reminder of the reason I'd come to Avenger. Though I knew the words by heart, I took the paper out of my pocket and read it again.

Li'l Feller,

> *It was so good to get your letter and especially the new picture. You're right, that Waco is one beautiful little plane,*

but not half as beautiful as you. I put it on the inside of my locker so I can see you every time I open that door and ask myself how I ever got such a gorgeous wife. I miss you so much, Baby.

Don't have much time to write as I'm flying today, but I wanted to get this out in time for mail call. I was thinking about that letter they sent you asking for women pilots. Honey, I think you should do it. I know you want to, so go ahead. From what you've told me, there isn't all that much business anyway. If we don't have any students, we might as well shut down the flight school for now. We can always get it going again after the war. Stubbs can handle everything else.

Georgia, the school has never run better than since you took over the accounts, but I didn't marry you because I needed a bookkeeper. I love you. That means I love who you are as well as who you will be. And, if you get the right kind of training, the kind that only the military can really supply, you've got it in you to be a great pilot. There isn't any reason you can't be as good a pilot as anybody—including me. There is no way I'd ask you to put your dreams aside just to keep house for me and look after a business, particularly one that is foundering anyway.

So, write back and tell them you want to fly for Uncle Sam. I'm behind you one hundred and ten percent. If the training is anything like what I went through, it'll be tough. Some days you'll want to throw in the towel, but I know you can do it. I'm so proud of you. You can do anything you set your mind to, Li'l Feller.

I'll write a longer letter tomorrow so we can work out the details, but talk with Stubbs too. Gotta run now and bomb a German factory so this war can be over and I can come home

to you. I'm counting the days, hours, and minutes until I can
hold you in my arms again.

   I love you, Georgia. I always will.

> *With all my heart,*
> *Roger*

Blinking back tears, I folded the letter. The stationery bore creases as deep and familiar as memory, and the tidy rectangle fit perfectly in the breast pocket of my flight suit, directly over my heart.

I took another deep breath and stood up. I *would* fly perfectly today. I would pass this flight check, and the next, and the one after that. Nothing and no one was going to stop me. I would graduate. I would do all the things that Roger believed I could, all the things he never had a chance to do. I would do it for him, and myself, and us.

And I did. When I took off that day with Maytag in the passenger seat, I felt like Roger was flying with me. Maybe he was.

I was calm and confident. Until then, every time I had walked across the tarmac to approach the BT-13, she looked like some kind of menacing monster-machine, bent on my defeat. Every time I took her up was a contest of wills as I forced the reluctant beast clumsily through her paces. But that day, from the second the propellers began stirring in the hot Texas wind and I took hold of the wheel, vibrating with the power of four hundred and fifty horses, all my uncertainty vanished. I was never again afraid of the BT-13, or any plane for that matter. My anxiety was replaced by respect—respect for the plane and what she could do, and respect for my ability to make her do it better. That day I began to realize that every craft is . . . well, almost alive. Each plane has a personality with unique strengths and weaknesses, and it is up to the pilot to enhance the former and minimize the latter.

That day the BT and I were like perfectly matched dance partners. We practically waltzed across the wide Texas skies as I led her through dips and dives, spins and stalls, with an easy confidence I'd never known was in me. I forgot all about Maytag, sitting in the passenger seat, waiting to pounce on the tiniest error. I focused my mind and heart on knowing this plane, feeling all the possibility within her and drawing it out. I felt brave and peaceful and vast beyond words.

I walked the wind. I found again what I hadn't even realized I'd lost—the joy of flying, of living—the joy I'd buried with Roger because his death had made living unseemly.

I'd been going through the motions, and very convincingly. Once the girls had gotten to know my story, they'd been all admiration for how I'd picked up and honored Roger's sacrifice by fulfilling his last wish for me. They used words like *brave, patriotic, selfless,* and sometimes I told myself the same thing, but it was all a sham. I wasn't brave; I was terrified, and I was hiding my terror beneath a suffocating veil of obligation. I'd been trying to live on Roger's behalf, trying to be what I thought Roger wanted me to be, trying to live the life I thought he'd been cheated out of and that I owed him because I hadn't loved him completely until it was almost too late.

I'd had it all wrong. As many times as I'd read the letter I wore over my heart, I hadn't understood it. But now, somehow, something in the way the sunlight sliced through the clouds, separating light from dark, finally brought it within my grasp.

I had loved Roger, not at first, but at last, and that was enough. There was no debt to pay, no fee owed. I could finally see the sky again. Aloft, there is no beginning and no end, and if you give yourself up to the sky, you see time as the limiting, contrived idea it is. We were not created to live such boundaried lives. No matter for how long or short a time, I loved Roger and he loved me, and because it had been, even for a moment, it always would be. The price of his love exacted no debt.

Without voice, or words, I heard my husband speak to me one last time, words of love, words of forgiveness, words of release.

I love who you are. I love who you will become. I always will.

When we landed, I didn't even stand around waiting for Maytag to fill out my evaluation. I didn't have to. I knew I had passed with a perfect score. Maytag actually chased me down, waving the form and hollering, "Hey! Aren't you forgetting something?"

I turned around but kept walking, backwards, as he trotted up to me. "Don't think so. Seemed like a perfect flight to me, wouldn't you say?" I knew I was being cocky, but I couldn't help myself. This man had put me through the ringer, and I vowed never to be afraid of him again.

"You'll do," he said flatly and shoved the evaluation into my hand, but just the same, I thought I recognized a look of grudging respect on his face.

When I walked into the ready room, Pamela, Fanny, and Donna Lee were waiting for me with anxious faces.

I pulled off my helmet, ran my hand through my hair, fluffing up my flattened curls, and unzipped the neck of my flight suit. "Can you believe this is only March?" I said nonchalantly. "It must be one hundred degrees out there! I miss flying the PTs. It was nice getting a breeze in those open cockpits."

The girls examined me for a moment, trying to decide if I was teasing them or putting up a brave front in the face of failure. I couldn't keep it in any longer.

"Yee-haw!" My triumphant cowboy yell was accompanied by a spontaneous victory dance and the joyous shouts, squeals, and squeezes of my girlfriends.

"You did it! I knew you would!" Fanny yelled as she threw her arms around me.

Donna Lee grabbed the evaluation that was clutched in my fist. "Look at this! She got a perfect score! I didn't know those existed!"

"Tumbleweed, here we come! I'm buying the first round!" Pamela promised.

"And I'll let you," I said, laughing. "Too bad we can't go right now, but I guess we'll just have to hang on until tomorrow night. Right now I'm due at my meteorology class, and after that I think I might celebrate by sneaking off for a nap. Don't look for me at lunch, girls."

I waved good-bye and scurried off to class. Opening the ready-room door, I hit a solid wall of scorching West Texas heat. But I didn't mind it; I welcomed it. I welcomed the feeling of sun on my face and the smell of mesquite that perfumed the air. My eyes feasted on the endless expanse of blue that stretched across the horizon. Everything around me seemed bright and clear, as if it had been outlined in sharp-pointed pencil, demanding my notice, which I gave, wholly and gratefully.

Purposefully walking through the middle of a whirling dust devil, I stretched out my arms and laughed at the insistent wind. And for the first time in a long time, I thought of how good it was to be alive.

Was it coincidence, then, that I met Morgan the very next day? I suppose it's possible, but you'll never get me to believe it.

✖ 16 ✖

Georgia

Sweetwater, Texas—March 1943

I'd just finished a five-hour flight and was coming in for a landing "under the hood." That meant I had to fly with a black curtain drawn across my windshield to block my view, relying completely on my instruments. Since the primary role of the WASP would be to ferry planes from factories and bases to where they were needed, our curriculum placed even more emphasis on this kind of navigation than the training of our male counterparts did. It wasn't easy.

Flying under the hood required complete focus. You had to keep your eyes glued to the instruments at all times—the airspeed indicator to know if you were going too fast or slow, the altimeter to make sure you were climbing or descending properly, the needle-ball to make sure you weren't listing too far to the left or right—all the while listening to the instructor's directions as they were shouted over the earphones and praying that those instruments really were accurate. You had to have great trust in your plane and your own ability, because you really were flying blind. It was exhausting.

I was looking forward to using the bathroom (long flights didn't include pit stops, and, unlike male pilots, we couldn't take care of business in midair—even if we had, our oversized flight suits weren't exactly designed to accommodate the female anatomy), taking a cold shower, and falling into bed. We were all supposed to go to the Tumbleweed that night, but I thought I'd just beg off and get some sleep instead. But once we landed, my instructor, Dave Kalinowski, pulled back the curtain and said, "Nice flight. Couldn't have been better," and I felt a sudden rush of energy.

Maybe just the ladies' room and shower, I thought. I was ready for a night on the town after all.

I taxied up to the hangar and climbed out of the BT just in time to see another plane, a big, twin-engined monster of a ship, come in for a landing right behind me. Dave and I watched as it touched down.

"What is that?" I asked. "I never saw anything like it."

"That's one of those new P-38 fighters," he answered. "They say that's the plane that will win us this war. They're fast and handle like a dream." We watched admiringly as that beautiful airplane taxied toward us, the sun glinting off her silver finish and reflecting bright diamonds of light into our eyes.

"I'd like to stick around and check her out," Dave said, "but I've got another girl going up in half an hour and I've gotta grab some chow. Say, I heard a rumor that the Fantastic Four were going to the Tumbleweed tonight, that right?"

"Umm. Maybe," I vacillated. "I'm not sure."

Instructors and students weren't supposed to socialize, but, of course, a few did off base. Dave had hinted that he'd like to go out with me a couple of times, but I'd sidestepped the question. He was attractive, with a full head of wavy black hair and a sharp-jawed masculinity, and was a good teacher to boot, but I wasn't going to risk my career by fraternizing with an instructor. On top of that, I just wasn't interested. Not in Dave. Not in anybody.

"Well," he said. "Maybe I'll see you later, Georgia. Real nice work today."

"Thanks." I waved as he walked off but kept my eyes fixed on the approaching P-38. It was one hot-looking plane and I couldn't help but wonder what it would be like to fly her myself. She taxied through shimmering waves of ghostly water brought on by the blistering heat rising from the tarmac, looking like a mirage of a plane, too beautiful to be real.

She parked next to me, dwarfing my BT, which seemed suddenly very plain-Jane next to this gorgeous beast. When her engines were cut and the props slowed and ceased their whine, the canopy popped open, and the pilot stepped out, a man with dark eyes and a serious expression. For some reason, it had never crossed my mind that a man would be flying this plane.

Without thinking, I blurted out, "What in the heck are you doing here?"

The pilot pulled off his helmet. "Emergency landing," he said.

"Oh," I replied knowingly. "You're one of those. Well, you'd better get going, Flyboy. Didn't you hear? Avenger is off-limits to male pilots. Even male pilots with 'emergencies.'"

"What are you talking about?" He frowned, a deep crease appearing between his eyebrows.

"Yeah. Don't play so innocent." I smirked. "The first couple of weeks we opened we had dozens of guys like you—fellas who touched down saying they had an emergency when all they were looking for was a chance to check out the girls and chase some skirt. After that, an order went out saying that no more men could land at Avenger—not unless they had real emergencies. Come on. You'd better fire up your engines and get out of here before somebody writes you up."

I heard a noise and looked up to see one of the base mechanics trotting toward us. It was Joe Palka. I recognized him from a distance because, as usual, he had a cigarette clutched between his teeth. I never saw him without one. Joe was a little fresh, but he was a pretty good mechanic. He ran up to the young pilot and, a little out of breath with a lit Lucky bobbing up and down as he spoke, said, "You the one that called in the emergency?"

The pilot nodded, and Joe said, "Yeah, the tower called the shop and said to come over and check it out. She just stalled?"

"That's right. At about fifteen thousand feet. I tried everything I could think of to start her back up, but nothing worked. I'd just passed you a few minutes before, so I radioed in to your tower. Thought maybe I could glide her in. I banked hard right to circle back, and then, when I tried the engines again, they started up. She seems fine now, but it's a long way home. Maybe your boys can check her out for me."

Joe puffed on his cigarette and pulled his nose at the same time, thinking. "Well, there's no way we're going to get to it tonight, that's for sure. I've got six jobs ahead of you and none of 'em can wait. That means you're going to have to stick around until Monday. The shop is closed on Sunday."

The pilot furrowed his brow and said in a voice that was almost desperate, "Look, I've got to get back by nine o'clock on Monday morning. It's important. Can't you just give her a quick once-over? Maybe it's something simple."

Joe lifted both hands and shrugged off the request. "Sorry, pal. No can do. I already told the tower to call your base and let 'em know you'll be here at least until Monday—maybe the day after. Better head over to our commander's office and see if they can't find you a bed and something to eat. Georgia can show you where to go.

"Don't look so gloomy, Lieutenant." Joe grinned. "A lotta guys would give their right propeller to be stranded at Avenger. There's not another base like it in the whole Air Force. It's hotter than Hades, centrally isolated, and—did I mention?—hotter than Hades. But the scenery! Mister, the scenery here is something else. Isn't that right,

Georgia, honey?" He winked and gave me a leering glance. I stuck out my tongue at him.

"Ignore him, Lieutenant. He's been breathing gas fumes all his life. It's affected his brain."

Joe laughed out one side of his mouth, careful not to lose his Lucky in the process. "Boy, you said a mouthful, honey! I was due to muster out next month but I just re-upped for three more years. There's gotta be something wrong with me!

"Well, I gotta run. There's a busted manifold out there with my name on it. I'll get to your plane as soon as I can, Lieutenant." With that he trotted off again in the direction of the mechanical shops, holding his hand up without looking back, extending his fingers in a farewell salute.

The pilot just stood there looking at Joe's receding figure with an expression of irritation on his face. "Great," he muttered to himself and scuffed the toe of his boot hard against the ground like he wished he had something, or someone, to kick. "That's just great."

I cleared my throat to get his attention. "Do you have a flight bag? Why don't you grab it, and I'll take you over to the office."

"I didn't bring anything. I wasn't exactly planning on being here. That's a brand-new P-38," he said, jerking his head toward the plane. "We just got her from the test pilots, and everything checked out fine. There shouldn't be a thing wrong with her. Heck, maybe there isn't. Maybe I should just start her back up and head for home," he mused.

"Let me get this straight," I said. "You want to fly a plane whose engines cut out on you at fifteen thousand feet without having a mechanic find out why? You must be one important lieutenant if you're needed at base so bad that you'll take that kind of risk with your life, not to mention a plane that cost the government thousands. Who are you? General Eisenhower traveling incognito?"

He glared at me. I hadn't meant to come off as sarcastic, but, honestly, I'd never heard of anything so crazy. And the way this guy was grumbling you'd have thought he'd just been sentenced to life in Sing Sing instead of a couple of nights at an all-girl air base. Of course, my initial greeting probably hadn't helped. I hadn't exactly made him feel welcomed.

"Sorry, Lieutenant," I said. "I didn't mean to be so smart. And I apologize for giving you a hard time about landing here. My mouth gets the better of me sometimes. Let me walk you over to the office, and they'll get you fixed up with whatever you need. You'll feel better after a shower and some food. Come on." I motioned with my head and started walking in the direction of the base offices.

He sighed and started following. "Yeah. Guess there's nothing I can do about this tonight."

"You know, a bunch of us are going into town tonight. My roommates and I just passed our flight checks so we're going to go celebrate. It's just a little roadhouse, but the beer is cold and cheap. If you want to come along, we can give you a ride."

"No, thanks," he said, his voice was flat. "I just want to get my plane fixed and get out of here, so if you'll just point the way to the commander's office, I think I can take it from here. I've already got a girlfriend back home. I'm not looking for another one."

What a jerk!

"Well, that's good, because I'm not looking, either! I'm married!" I held up my left hand and waggled my ring finger in his face. "Who do you think you are, anyway? Clark Gable? I was just trying to be nice to you, but—funny thing!"—I smacked my forehead with the flat of my hand—"The urge is gone!

"The office is over by the flagpole," I pointed to the right. "Captain Dean is in charge of billets for visitors." I turned on my heel and stomped off, but not before shouting over my shoulder, "And I hope he puts you in the barracks with the rattlesnake nest under it! I'm sure you'd feel right at home!"

17

Morgan

Sweetwater, Texas—March 1943

The pretty trainee had been right. I felt better after a shower and some food.

I also felt bad about talking to her that way, but I was so frustrated. Getting stranded in Texas meant that I was going to miss my own flight check on Monday morning. Unlike these trainees, a failed or missed check didn't mean I'd be sent home, but it did mean I wouldn't be able to graduate from my training on time. I'd be cycled back to the class that was behind mine. That would tack on a full month to my training. I shouldn't have been so mean to that girl, but you could hardly blame me for being grouchy.

The mechanic had been right, too. It was hot as blazes, like Dillon at the peak of summer. The food they'd served at dinner was good—pork barbeque, potatoes, corn bread, stewed okra, and banana pudding—and I ate heartily, but it did nothing to lift my spirits. I brought a glass of iced tea back to the visitors' barracks. The ice melted before I got halfway there, but the tea was still cool. I sat down on the stoop in front of the barracks to drink it, hoping to catch a breeze, and wondering how I was going to pass the time until morning.

I thought about writing to Virginia. It had been more than a week since I'd done so, but it was too hot and, truthfully, I just didn't feel like it. She'd sent three letters since I'd last written. Each one read pretty much like the one before it, full of details about what she'd done that day and what she'd worn that day, petty gossip about her enemies and petty complaints about her friends, and, always, not very subtle hints about a proposal. In fact, sometimes they weren't even hints. Her last letter had come right out and asked if I ever planned on asking her to marry her and even accused me of having another girlfriend.

I knew I should write her, reassure her, but I didn't know what to say. Probably, when the war was over, I should marry her. She'd been waiting so long. She'd been excited when I'd come back stateside for my P-38 training. She thought I'd be able to get some leave time to come to Oklahoma. Maybe time enough for a quick visit to the justice of the peace. I probably could have if I'd pushed for it, but the truth was, I just didn't want to go home. Lots of guys went off with a weekend pass and came back with a wedding band. Just a couple of months ago, Virginia had written to tell me that Frank Hodges had swept into town, married Ethel Garland, and hopped a train the next day so he could meet up with his battalion and ship out for England. No, even though it would have been nice to see Mama, Grandma, and Ruby, I wasn't ready to ask for a weekend leave to Dillon.

So, for the time being at least, here I was, stranded somewhere west of Abilene, and, having fruitlessly circled my brain around all the problems that I was faced with, I came back to my first question: how was I going to keep myself occupied until morning?

I took a sip of my now lukewarm tea and pondered the issue. Then, as if in answer to my question, a group of girls dressed in matching blue blouses and regulation-looking skirts rounded the corner of my barracks, laughing and talking. A pretty, petite brunette led the group, the same trainee who had blessed me out while showing me to the base offices.

I got up from the stoop and stepped into her path.

"Hi," I said sheepishly. "Remember me?" She glared at me with those huge brandy-brown eyes like she wished she didn't.

"I don't think I ever really introduced myself." I stuck out my hand and hoped she'd take it. "Morgan Glennon. I was stationed with a fighter wing in the Pacific until a few months ago, but they sent me back home to train in P-38s." My hand hovered, unclasped, in empty air. I drew it back awkwardly, feigning the need to push my hair out of my eyes. The trainee just kept glaring at me, but one of her friends, a tall girl with an Eastern accent, stepped in front of the girl and stuck out her hand.

"Nice to meet you, Lieutenant. Or may I call you Morgan?" I said that Morgan would be fine. She said her name was Pamela and then introduced me to the other girls, Fanny and Donna Lee, before continuing.

"And, of course, you've already met my friend, Georgia Welles, Avenger Field's own little Miss Congeniality." She elbowed her friend and said, "Georgia! Don't be rude. Say something to the man."

"That's all right. I can't say as I blame her. We didn't get off on a very good foot this afternoon."

"So we heard." Fanny giggled. "Georgia said she tried to show you a little WASP hospitality and you told her to take a hike!"

"Of course that was right after she'd called him a masher and accused him of faking engine failure just so he could prey on innocent lady pilots," Donna Lee said practically but with a trace of a smile. Then, looking to her friend, she said, "Georgia, you can't blame him for being sore after you were so snippy." Georgia's wide eyes got even wider. She opened her mouth as if she were ready to tell Donna Lee exactly what she could do with her clumsy attempts at diplomacy, but I interrupted before she could utter a word.

"No," I explained to Donna Lee. "It was all my fault. Really. I was upset and took it out on Georgia. You see, I'm due at my base for my final flight check in the morning, but since I'm stuck here, I'm going to miss it. I won't be able to finish with my class. They'll send me back to the next group, and I'll graduate from the program a month late." I glanced over at Georgia and saw a flicker of doubt in her eyes.

"A whole month!" Fanny exclaimed. "If somebody told me I was going to have to spend an extra month here while the rest of you girls went on and got your wings, I'd probably pop somebody right in the kisser! You poor guy!" she said sympathetically.

I nodded my head slowly and tried to look like exactly that—a poor guy: ignored by flight mechanics, friendless, stuck in the middle of nowhere, with nothing to do on a Friday night but sit on the stoop of the visitors' barracks drinking lukewarm tea, nursing my regrets. I sighed melodramatically and gave Georgia a sideways glance.

She tipped her head, showing she was on to me, and laughed. "All right already. All is forgiven. But why didn't you tell me that in the first place? I wouldn't have been so hard on you." Before giving me a chance to answer, her friend Pamela piped in.

"Why don't you come down to the Tumbleweed with us? It's not exactly the Coconut Grove, but it'll be more fun than hanging around here all night."

I looked for permission at the pretty one. "Is that all right with you?"

She considered a moment. "Why not?" she said with a shrug. "The more the merrier."

Pamela wasn't kidding. The Tumbleweed Roadhouse not only wasn't the Coconut Grove, it wasn't even the Hy-Life Tavern, the only bar in Dillon.

The Tumbleweed was way out on a dirt road east of town. The long, low building leaned slightly to the northwest and was topped off by a rust-laden roof of corrugated tin. If the Tumbleweed had ever had known the stroke of a paintbrush, which seemed unlikely, blistering sun and hard Texas winds had peeled off the evidence years before.

We'd come in two battered trucks that the girls borrowed from friends. I rode with Pamela, who took the wheel, and Georgia had the other girls with her. Pamela was a nice-looking girl, tall and blond, with a quick wit. I liked her right off. She asked if I had a girl back home. When I reported that I did, she snapped her fingers and said, "Nuts! No smooching for me tonight! Guess I'll just have to settle for a turn around the dance floor."

The parking lot was crowded. Georgia grabbed a spot near the door, but I had to park on the far end. As we drove in I heard a crunching sound under the tires that I thought was gravel, but when I opened the door of the truck and stepped out, I found the ground was covered, literally, with old beer caps. There were thousands of them. "When the sun goes down and it cools off a little, the cowboys like to buy a brew and drink it outside, standing around the trucks," Pamela explained. "Somebody told me it was an old icehouse, that people used to buy their beer here because it was the only way to get a cold one. We're walking on decades of beer caps—layers and layers of them. In another thousand years some archeologist will dig up this place and write a thesis on the beer-drinking habits of prehistoric man."

We joined the others, who were waiting for us at a spot slightly closer to the door. Pamela gave a loud, and pretty realistic, impression of a wolf howling at the moon as we approached. Like her, the other girls were clearly excited, giddy with relief over passing their flight checks, and energized by the prospect of a night on the town. I knew exactly how they felt. I'd enjoyed many such celebrations with my buddies, especially with Fountain, who could turn any sliver of good news into an excuse for a party, but it was odd for me to think of girls acting like this, getting ready to tie one on just the way my flying buddies did.

Georgia was more subdued than her friends, but she appeared to be enjoying herself, or at least enjoying the fact that the girls were having fun. She walked near the back of the group. I fell into step beside her and leaned down to whisper in her ear, "So, are you the adult in charge of this crew?"

She grinned and nodded. "I guess so. At least, I'm the one that makes sure they all get back on base before roll call and with their garters still attached to their girdles. I'm not really a drinker. Don't like the taste. I usually order one beer, drink half of it, and then switch to Coca-Cola."

"I'm the same way. I don't have anything against drinking; I just don't care for it much myself. Still, it's fun to come out and have a good time with your friends. They seem like real nice girls."

"They are. The best. And they are terrific pilots, too. In another month"—she knocked her head like it was wood for good luck—"we'll all graduate and start ferrying planes for the war effort."

"Good for you!" I said. "We could sure use the help."

Georgia turned to look at me with an expression of surprise. "Really? You think so? A lot of guys think it's a waste of time and money to train women as pilots. They think we won't be able to cut it. Even some of the officers and instructors at Avenger feel that way. We've passed the same classes and gone through almost the exact same training as male flight cadets, but a few of the men who are supposed to be helping us get ready to fly would still like nothing better than to see us wash out."

"Well, that's just stupid," I said, and I meant it. "If a girl can pass the same training as a man, I can't see any reason she shouldn't fly. We need every combat pilot we can lay our hands on, and if women can help win the war by flying stateside so more guys can get into the fight, I can't see why they shouldn't. Heck, I'm grateful for the help!"

Georgia's pace slowed slightly as we approached the door of the roadhouse, and I kept in step with her as the other girls forged ahead, eager to let the party begin.

"Well, you're a breath of fresh air," Georgia said and then puffed in disgust. "I just don't understand the attitude of some of these guys. Here we are, every one of us is already a pilot with a minimum of seventy-five hours in the air, and most with a lot more and—my gosh! Why shouldn't we fly if that will help end the war sooner? Everyone should do their part, and the way I see it, my part is flying airplanes because that's what I know how to do and that's what needs to be done.

"Would they be happier if I stayed home and knit socks? Of course"—she laughed and raised her hands in front of her "—one look at my knitting and they'd probably be just as happy to let me pilot airplanes. The nuns tried their best with me for ten long years and I still can't darn a sock or sew on a button."

I looked at her and couldn't help but smile. At first glance, I'd thought she was hard and standoffish, but underneath she really was a sweet girl and a very pretty one. Even in the middle of frustrated attempts to get off this air base, I'd noticed that right off. Now, with the moonlight shining on her hair and her eyes sparkling in laughter, I decided she just might be beautiful.

"Well, maybe you weren't the problem. Maybe it was the nuns. I've never met any myself—my hometown is so small that we don't even have a Catholic church—but my old buddy Tony Campezzio, used to tell some horror stories about the ruler-wielding sisters in his elementary school."

"Oh, the sisters are like any teachers, I suppose—some good and some not so good. My guess is your friend Tony deserved whatever he got," she said with a chuckle. "I had some good teachers growing up, but Sister Agatha taught sewing, and she never liked me, not from the first day."

"Well, there you have it!" I smacked my hand against my leg to emphasize my point. "Sister Agatha never liked you, so you never liked sewing. The right teacher makes all the difference. Bet my Mama could teach you. She makes quilts, but not like anything you've ever seen before. Her quilts are like paintings."

"Wow." Georgia replied, but flatly. I could tell she wasn't convinced.

"I'm not kidding. My mother is an artist. And she's patient. She could teach you for certain." A little smile tugged at the corner of her mouth.

"What?" I asked. "You don't think I'm telling the truth."

Georgia shook her head. "No, not exactly. It's just that every boy thinks his mother is the greatest."

"Well, why shouldn't I?" I teased, mocking indignation. "That's what we're fighting for, isn't it? Mom, apple pie, and the American way?"

Our conversation was interrupted as Pamela shouted, "Hey!" from the porch of the roadhouse where she and the others were waiting. "Could you two walk any slower? Come on already! I need a drink!"

Georgia sighed. "My master's voice," she said with a tolerant smile. "Come on."

Bottle caps crunching metallically under our feet, we trotted up to the porch of the roadhouse where the rest of the group was waiting. Pamela pulled open the heavy door, and when she did, a wall of sound—guitars, fiddles, and the stomping of dozens of pairs of boot-shod feet dancing the Cotton-Eyed Joe—hit me square in the face. The floor, except the dance area, was carpeted with a blend of sawdust and peanut shells. A neon sign over the bar that said LONE STAR: THE NATIONAL BEER OF TEXAS and a single yellow spotlight trained on the band provided most of the illumination. The place smelled like beer, bacon grease, and cigarette smoke. It was a real dive, but, judging from the number of patrons that crowded the dance floor and lined up at the bar, a popular one.

Donna Lee spotted an empty table, littered with empty beer bottles left behind by the previous occupants, and waved us over to it. Fanny and Pamela started clearing the debris from the table while Georgia and I went in search of three extra chairs. Shouting to be heard over the noise, Georgia leaned toward me and said, "I wouldn't order any food if I were you, but if you do, make sure it's deep fried!"

In spite of Georgia's warning, I did order food but stuck to the chicken-fried steak, which was pretty good. I took turns dancing with the girls. I'm not exactly light on my feet, but it was fun. Before long, local boys, some in uniform and some not, found their way to our table and asked the girls to dance—all except Georgia, who indicated her refusal by a quick wave of her wedding ring. Other than one quick turn with me, and that was only because the other girls urged her to, Georgia didn't dance all night—not until a grinning, gap-toothed cowboy with a battered Stetson in his hand approached.

Georgia smiled and said, "Love to, Tex," and went off to join the other couples dancing to a sentimental country waltz.

Fanny and Donna Lee were still on the floor. Pamela sat next to me, resting between dances and downing her fourth Lone Star of the evening. "Who is that guy?" I asked.

Pamela gulped down a swallow of beer. "Him? Oh, that's Tex. Nobody says no to a dance with Tex."

"Really?" I took a second look at the lanky, not especially handsome cowboy, who I'd just realized only had two fingers on his left hand, and wondered what the attraction could be.

"Jealous?" Pamela asked but broke into laughter before I could respond. "Don't be. Tex is just a harmless old farmhand, but a patriotic one. He meets all the trains in Sweetwater and drives the girls out to the base. It's his contribution to the war effort. He's a sweet old thing. Doesn't hardly even drink, except his one beer on Saturday night, but he sure does like to dance. He's pretty good at it, too!"

Pamela was right. I watched as Tex guided Georgia around the floor with all the style and confidence of an Arthur Murray teacher, "He's got me beat, that's for sure. I'd just wondered about him since Georgia turned down everybody else. It's sweet the way she won't dance because she's married, but I don't see where a couple of dances would hurt anything. Her husband must be the jealous type. Where's he stationed, anyway?"

Pamela's persistently present smile faded. "She didn't tell you?"

"Tell me what?"

"Georgia's not married; she's a widow. Don't tell her I told you, but her husband was a bomber pilot. He was shot down over the Atlantic. She was crazy about him. They owned a little airfield and flight school in Illinois, and Roger—that was his name, Roger Welles—was the one who taught her to fly. He did a good job, too; she's one heck of a pilot.

"She joined the WASP just a couple of months after he was killed. If it had been me, I think I'd have stayed home and cried and felt sorry for myself, but not Georgia. She joined up and took her husband's place. She's something. She doesn't talk about Roger much, but I know she misses him. She still wears his ring; it helps keep the wolves at bay. If they knew she wasn't married, half the instructors on base would be after her. But I wish she would start dating a little bit. Sometimes she seems so sad. She almost never goes out with us, and when she does, it's out of loyalty—somebody has got to make sure we all get home without disgracing ourselves." Pamela's smiled returned. "She's a good friend."

The waltz ended, and Tex dropped Georgia back at our table and excused himself. A little out of breath, Georgia smiled and said,

"That Tex is some dancer!" as she flopped into her chair and took a drink from a half-empty bottle of Coke.

A tall man, who I'd learned was a flight instructor by the name of Dave Kalinowski, came up and asked Pamela to dance. "I'll be right with you," Pamela said. "I've just got to run powder my nose first."

Dave grinned and said he'd meet her at the bar, then excused himself. "Dave must really have a thing for you," Georgia said to Pamela, shouting to make herself heard over the music. "Isn't this the fourth time he's asked you to dance tonight?"

"Fifth," Pamela reported, "but who's counting? I think he's a doll."

"You'd better watch it," Georgia advised. "If you get caught dating an instructor there'll be hell to pay."

Pamela dug a lipstick out of her purse and stood up. "We're not dating. We're just dancing. But it would be kind of fun if we were. And he's Polish! That would drive my mother simply crazy!"

I couldn't help but laugh. "Well, that doesn't exactly seem like the foundation for a lifetime of bliss."

Pamela winked wickedly over her shoulder as she headed off to the ladies' room. "Maybe not, but it's a start!"

Georgia laughed and shook her head. "She's something else, isn't she?"

I nodded agreement. We sat in silence, listening to the band, and I tried to think of a topic of conversation. I almost asked her about her husband but thought better of it. If she'd wanted me to know about him she'd have said something; and, besides, Pam asked me not to.

Georgia suddenly said, "Hey, Morgan. I've been thinking about your plane. You say the motor cut out, but when you turned so you could land at Avenger, it started again?"

"Yeah," I said slowly, wondering what she was getting at. "I banked her hard, and when I tried to start her again, she fired up right off."

Georgia rested her chin in her hand, covering her mouth, her eyes glittering with calculations. She stayed in that position for a long minute, and then, grinning from ear to ear, jumped to her feet, swallowed the dregs of her Coca-Cola, and started looking for her purse and keys.

"You going somewhere?" I asked.

"Yes," she answered. "And you're coming with me. I've got an idea, and if I'm right, we just might be able to get you home in time to take that flight check after all!"

∽ 18 ∽

Morgan

Avenger Field—March 1943

The night sky was dark, strewn with white-bright stars on a field of black velvet. It reminded me of home. For a moment I stood motionless, remembering boyhood nights in Dillon spent staring at the stars and dreaming of being a pilot—and now I was one. Amazing.

"Found it!" Georgia yelled from somewhere inside the open hangar and flipped a switch, unleashing a flood of light from three spots mounted on the exterior wall. She emerged from the hangar pulling on a laddered scaffold. I ran over to help her wheel it into place next to the plane.

"Explain to me again what we're doing?" I asked.

"Trying to fix your airplane," she said flatly, as though speaking to a none too bright child. "You would like to get back to your base before you miss your flight check, wouldn't you?"

"Sure. Yeah." I hesitated, pretty sure my next sentence would rub her the wrong way. "But, I mean . . . how do you think you're going to fix her? You're a pilot, and I'm sure you're a good one, but that doesn't exactly make you a mechanic, does it? I mean, we've all had a few engine maintenance courses, but . . ."

She rolled up the sleeve on her blouse and started unscrewing the wing-tank bolts as she said in an annoyed tone, "I've had more than a few maintenance courses. Back home in Illinois, at the airfield my husband and I ran, I used to help our mechanic, Stubbs Peterson, all the time. Stubbs knows everything there is to know about airplanes. He worked with Claude Ryan, the man who built the *Spirit of St. Louis*. Stubbs and I have worked on all kind of planes.

"Here. Hold these bolts," she commanded, then stuck her head down inside the dark mechanical recesses of the plane. "It's too dark. I can't see. Can you dig a flashlight out of that toolbox and hand it to me?"

I rummaged around and found the flashlight. "Georgia—and understand that I mean no disrespect—I'm sure your mechanic friend taught you a lot, but what kind of airplanes could you really have been working on at a little private field in the middle of nowhere? Sixty-horsepower Cessnas? These P-38s are the latest, twin-engine fighters! I'm sure your friend, Stubbs, was a first-rate mechanic in his day, but to compare the *Spirit of St. Louis* with a P-38 is like comparing a Sherman tank to a Model-T!" I didn't even bother to mention the fact that she was fussing around with the gas tanks even though I was pretty sure this was an engine problem.

She wasn't listening. "The valves all look good and tight," she mused. "Hand me a wrench." While I rifled through the toolbox, she continued.

"Don't be such a worrywart. I know this is a complicated machine. I've never seen anything quite like it. But I kept thinking about what you said to Joe, about it maybe being something simple—something obvious that would be easy to fix. That gave me an idea. If I'm wrong about it . . . well, we'll just close her back up and no harm done. But, if I'm right . . ." She shrugged her shoulders. "What have you got to lose?"

She peered down into darkness, trying to see past the complicated tangle of hoses and wires that connected the wing tanks to the
engine. "I still can't see," she complained. "Can you hold the flashlight? Shine it right there on that drainage valve."

While I beamed the flashlight onto the spot she'd indicated, she
loosened the valve, then reached in and triumphantly pulled out a
grimy ball that turned out to be a wad of paper.

"Here's the culprit!" she exclaimed. "It was keeping the gas from
feeding out evenly. That's why your motor cut out. The engine wasn't
getting enough fuel." She smoothed out the gasoline-soaked paper.
"It's somebody's grocery list! Look at this—eggs, milk, pears. . . .
Whoever was working on the tank must have put this down for a
second, turned their back, and accidentally knocked it into the
tank. Probably they went to the market, turned their pockets inside
out looking for the list, and then got in trouble when they came
home because they forgot the milk!" She laughed, and I was reminded again of just how beautiful she was.

"Georgia, you are something else," I said admiringly. "Forgive
me for ever doubting you. But how did you know it was a piece of
paper stuck in the valve? I mean, what are the chances of something
like that happening?"

"Oh. Well, I didn't know for sure," she admitted. "I didn't think
it was the engine itself because I heard you come in, and I stood
right next to her when you taxied in. The engine sounded great; it
was running like a top. But when you said that it started up again
after you'd banked right, I wondered if maybe something wasn't
keeping the fuel from draining out of the right tank. See, it wasn't
completely blocked. If it had been, that would have been the end of
you for sure. But, when you banked, you tipped the wing up enough
so gravity started working for you and draining the gas down where
it belonged. At least, I thought that could be it. It could have been a
dozen other things, but I got lucky."

"So did I. Thanks."

"You're welcome. Looks like you won't miss your flight check after all. Of course, you'll have to pass it to graduate with your class, but somehow I don't think that'll be a problem for you." She smiled. "So, you'll take off first thing tomorrow morning?"

"Yes. I suppose so," I was surprised to realize that even though a few hours before I'd have given anything to leave, I really wouldn't mind sticking around Avenger a little longer. "Best to get back before dark if I can."

Georgia nodded but didn't say anything. I stood there awkwardly for a moment before finally saying, "Well, thanks again for everything."

Georgia said not to mention it and that she guessed we'd better head on back. I wheeled the scaffold back into the hangar while she put away the toolbox and doused the lights. We walked, side by side, down the path that led back to the barracks. We were quiet for a long time, but then I said, "Sorry if I ended up wrecking your evening, but I sure appreciate everything you did. You know, it's only just a little past eleven. If you wanted, we could go back over to the Tumbleweed for a while. I hate thinking you missed the party on account of me."

Georgia shook her head and waved off my apology. "No, that's all right. The Tumbleweed really isn't my cup of tea anyway. I think I'll probably just turn in." She added, almost sheepishly, "The other girls mostly sleep in on Sunday, but I've been getting up early and going over to this little church in Sweetwater. It's kind of silly, I know, but . . ." Her voice trailed off, and her eyes darted away from mine, as though she expected me to burst out laughing.

"I've always gone to church. I was raised on it," I said. "I don't think it's silly at all."

Georgia's eyes narrowed, and she bit her lip, thinking. "No? You don't think God seems kind of irrelevant in today's world? That's what Pamela says. She took some religion classes in college, and the professor said it's all just superstition. She makes fun of me for wasting my Sunday morning in church when I could be catching up on my sleep. The truth is, I feel kind of dumb for doing it myself. I don't know what it is I think I'll get out of it." She rolled her eyes, as if apologizing for her own foolishness before going on.

"When I was little I went to church but only because the nuns made me. Probably it would have been easier to believe back then—life was so much less complicated. Now I'd like to believe in God, but I'm just not sure if I can. I mean, if God is out there and in charge of everything, why does He let so many bad things happen? Why did He let this war happen? Why does He let so many good, decent men, get killed?" Her eyes filmed a little at the last. Probably she was thinking about her husband, but I wasn't supposed to know about that, and I didn't want to give away Pamela's confidence, so I didn't say anything.

"Oh! Look at me! You must think I'm crazy spending my time worrying about God and the universe!" She laughed and reached up to lay her hands on her cheeks that had grown pink with emotion. Her eyes were tearing.

I smiled, dug a handkerchief out of my pocket and handed it to her. "Not for a minute. Those are good questions. I think you'd be crazy if you didn't ask. In my book, the only thing crazier than not asking would be letting somebody else dismiss the whole thing just because they've got Ph.D. behind their name. No offense to Pamela, she seems like a bright girl, but I don't think I'd believe or not believe something just so my opinion could match up with some professor's. I went to college for a while, and I can tell you, some of my teachers were brilliant, but some I wouldn't trust to guide me across the street, let alone tell me the meaning of God and the universe!" I chuckled, and Georgia joined in, rubbing the end of her nose with my handkerchief.

"Seriously," I continued, "it seems to me like this is the kind of a thing a person has to decide for themselves. I used to have the same kinds of questions you did. When I was little I'd ask my mama about that and later, our pastor, who was almost like a father to me. They gave me some things to think about, but I really had to figure it out on my own."

"And did you?"

"Well, I still have moments of doubt, if that's what you mean. I think everyone does. But I just started thinking how it all must look from God's perspective."

Georgia let out a little puff of exasperation. "You mean like one great big mess?"

"Sure, sometimes, but that's not what I'm talking about. You're a pilot. You know how completely different everything looks from the air? How individual people, and buildings, and trees all get smaller, but somehow they become bigger because they are melded into this amazing, limitless landscape that has more beauty and more meaning than any of those things possesses separately? I think that's maybe a little bit of how God sees the world. Sometimes we get so focused on the small pains and tragedies of life, and even on the enormous ones, that we forget to see the larger goodness and beauty in life. For us, death is the ultimate punishment, but it must be different from God's perspective. Maybe God sees it more like a gift. Who knows?" Georgia's face grew dark and angry when I said this.

"And for the people who get left behind? What about them? Where's their gift?"

"No," I agreed. "Not for them. I don't have a father. He died when I was little," I said. It wasn't true, but explaining my parentage would be too complicated, and, besides, I reasoned, I was probably never going to see this girl again. She didn't need to know every detail of my life. "But my grandpa was like my father. He died when I was eleven. It was so hard on Mama and me. He was the one who'd held us all together, and when he died I felt like I'd just fallen into this big hole and couldn't climb out. He was my best friend, and I think Mama felt the same way. They were real close. On top of that, it was the middle of the Depression. Young as I was, I knew we were in real danger of losing our home."

"And you weren't angry with God for taking your grandfather just when you needed him most?" Georgia asked, the challenge in her voice apparent.

"Of course I was. Who wouldn't be? But that's my point. I could only see things from my own perspective, and as far as I could see, we were all going to fall apart without Grandpa. But we didn't. We were stronger than we realized. Maybe it was part of the plan for helping me to be able to stand on my own two feet—and my mother, too. She's as shy and quiet as anything, but when Grandpa died, she had to kind of hitch herself up and get on with it. Mama is so strong, but if Grandpa had lived another twenty years, would she have known that? Would she have figured out how to take her talent for quilting and turn it into a means of supporting us? Would I have found the guts to leave the farm and become a pilot? Maybe. Maybe not. I think Mama feels about quilting the way I feel about flying. It's like oxygen to us; we need it to live. But if our lives had turned out even a little bit differently than they did, taking a few turns we felt were the better at the time, we could have missed the things that bring us our greatest happiness."

We reached the door of the visitors' barracks and stopped near the front stoop. "Don't you ever think it's funny that we all question and complain about why God lets bad things happen to us that we don't deserve, but we never think to ask the same questions about the good that comes our way that we don't deserve?" Without the accompanying beat of our feet crunching gravel as we walked, my voice sounded louder, embarrassingly so. I suddenly realized that I'd been talking for a long time.

"Anyway," I mumbled. "Sorry for going on like that. But it's like I said at first, Georgia, you've got to think it out on your own. I don't think there's any other way. If going to this church is helping you find some answers, then don't let anybody talk you out of it."

She just looked at me, and I couldn't tell if she was thinking about what I'd said, or feeling grateful I'd finally shut up, or waiting for me to kiss her good night. I was pretty certain it wasn't the last, but with the moon behind her, spilling light over her hair and shoulders like a halo, just an arm's breadth away from me, I wanted to do just that. And even though a vision of Virginia Pratt lurked accusingly on the edge of my mind, if I'd spied the least hint of an invitation in her eyes, I would have. As it was, I stood my ground and waited.

Finally she said, "Well, it's pretty late. I guess I should let you get some sleep. You've got a long trip tomorrow." She lifted her hand in farewell and started to walk away, but I reached out a hand to stop her.

"It's pretty dark out here. Can I walk you back to your room?" She smiled.

"No, I'm all right. Other than you, there isn't a man within five miles. I'll be fine walking alone. Thanks for offering, though. Good night."

"Good night. Thanks again for all your help. I'd have been in a jam without you."

"That's all right. I enjoyed getting a closer look at your plane. She's a beauty. It was nice to meet you, Morgan. Really. Maybe we'll run into each other again sometime."

"Maybe," I answered and watched as she walked away.

As soon as I finished my training they'd be assigning me to a new unit. It might be in Europe, or it might be in the Pacific, but one thing was for sure, it wasn't going to be within a thousand miles of Sweetwater, Texas, or any other place Georgia might be stationed.

If you've got any brains at all, I said to myself, *you won't waste any time or energy thinking about her.*

She disappeared around the corner. I stood for a long time, staring at the spot where she'd been a moment before, waiting for the imprinted memory of the kiss I hadn't dared to take to fade from my mind. It was no good. When I took off the next morning the memory of her followed.

~ 19 ~

Georgia

Avenger Field—April 1943

"Georgia! Fanny! Look what just came in the mail!" Pamela, with Donna Lee close on her heels, burst into the room holding up a brand-new Brownie camera. I left my half-packed suitcase and came over to check it out.

"Graduation present from dear old Dad," Pamela explained. "He made me promise to take a picture of the whole gang of us so he can put it on his office wall at the bank. Say cheese!" she commanded cheerily.

Fanny complied, sticking out her chest and putting a hand on her hips in a mocking Betty Grable pose. "Here I am, Mr. Hellman! The First Bank of Darien's own personal pinup!" Pamela snapped the picture as we all giggled.

"Here," Donna Lee said and reached for the camera, "Let me take one of the three of you."

"No! We all have to be in the picture. I'm going to run next door and see if Doris will come take one for us." Pamela tossed the camera to me and started to leave in search of one of our neighbors.

"Wait a minute," I said. "We should wait until tomorrow, after graduation. You don't want to waste the film. Think how much better the picture will look when we're all dressed up in our uniforms, with our new wings and our hair fixed. Right now, we all look a mess."

"Speak for yourself!" Donna Lee protested.

"Oh, don't be so frugal!" Pamela said. "I've got lots of film. We'll take one today and some more tomorrow after the ceremony."

"No! Wait!" I cried and grabbed Pamela's arm.

She turned around and gave me a look. "Gosh, Georgia! What's got into you?"

I wasn't sure myself. "Nothing. I just think we ought to wait until we actually graduate. It's silly, I know. Donna Lee has finished everything, but I've got a last meteorology test today, and you and Fanny still have your final flight checks to pass. I just don't want to jinx anything by celebrating too early, that's all. Besides, Doris left about ten minutes ago. She's got the flight check right before yours. She dropped by and asked if she could rub my lucky penny before she took off."

Pamela laughed, and the other girls joined in. "Boy! You really are superstitious! I always knew it."

I chuckled gamely, but no matter what Pamela said, it really wasn't like me to give in to superstition. Maybe I was just worried about passing meteorology, but something inside me felt uneasy, as if we were dangerously close to tempting fate. "I know, but just humor me, all right? The second graduation is over I'll pose for as many pictures as you want."

They teased me about it but agreed. I finished my packing and sat down to do some last-minute cramming before my test. Donna Lee said she was going to do her laundry. Pamela and Fanny hurried off to the ready room to meet up with their instructors and go up for their final flight checks.

About an hour later, as I was trying to memorize various mathematical formulas for predicting atmospheric circulation, I heard my name being called. Donna Lee ran in the door, out of breath and sobbing, on the verge of hysterics. I grabbed her by the shoulders and begged her to calm down, but the only intelligible word she uttered was "crash." It felt like all the blood had drained from my body, and I was afraid I might faint. All I could think of was Pamela and Fanny.

I grabbed Donna Lee and shook her, trying to get more information from her, but she was beside herself. "Come on!" I commanded and clapped my hand around her wrist, dragging her with me.

Whatever it was that had happened, word had already sped through the base. Scores of girls were streaming to the ready room, some with tears running down their faces, others dry-eyed but wearing expressions of panic and disbelief.

Don't let it be true, I thought as I ran up to the door of the ready room, but I already knew it was true. There had been a crash, a bad one.

I opened the door, and the look on the faces of the girls who were whispering together in groups or comforting their crying classmates told me at least part of what I needed to know. There would be an empty chair at our graduation tomorrow. The crash had been fatal. Still dragging the sobbing Donna Lee behind me, I started going from group to group, searching. Where were they? *Please God,* I begged, *don't let it be Pamela or Fanny. Please!*

Finally, across the room I spotted the back of Fanny's head. She was standing in a circle of girls, and from the way her shoulders were shaking I knew she was crying. I pushed through the crowd to make my way to her. Grabbing her by the arm, I pulled her around to face me. "Where is Pamela?" I demanded.

"I'm here." Pamela was coming toward us through a side door and smoking a cigarette. Her hands were shaking, and her face was drained of color, but her eyes were dry.

"Oh! Thank God!" I cried and threw my arms around her. Relief flooded my mind, but only for a moment. The image of the empty chair flashed in my mind. "Who was it?" I asked, releasing Pamela from my grasp.

She inhaled deeply and blew out a sighing column of smoke. "Doris," she said, and her eyes began to tear. "Nobody knows what happened yet, but they went down about twenty miles from base. There was a fire. Dave was with her. No survivors."

"Oh, Pam!" She had never talked about it openly, not even to me, but I knew that she and Dave had been seeing each other in secret. One afternoon she had showed up at dinner wearing a new gold locket and a smile. I was sure it was a gift from Dave and figured a ring wouldn't be long in coming.

"Oh, honey! I'm so sorry." I reached to put my arms around her.

To my surprise, Pamela pushed me away. "Don't," she said coldly and then softened a little. "I'm sorry, Georgia, but I just can't. I can't afford to fall apart right now. None of us can. Most of these girls still have tests and flight checks to finish. Me included."

"What are you saying? You think they're still going to make us keep flying today? Even after this?"

"If this was a base full of men and there was an accident, training would continue on schedule no matter what happened. This is the army, not a sorority. We've got to go on just like the men would. We could still wash out—the whole lot of us. If that happens, it would be more serious than just us not getting our wings. Some of the higher-ups might use it as an excuse to say women are too sensitive to fly. It could jeopardize the whole program. We can't let that happen, Georgia. Stop crying. We've got to help these girls—and Doris, too."

I started to ask what she meant by "Doris, too," but Pam wasn't listening. She dropped her cigarette to the floor and crushed it under the toe of her shoe, then breathed in deeply, trying to collect herself. "Come on, Georgia. I need your help."

Grabbing me by the arm, she pushed her way through the crowd of girls. The sobbing was growing louder and more intense with every minute and threatened to burst into a deluge of uncontrollable keening and grief as the news of our classmate's crash and horrific death by fire spread through the mob.

Using a chair for a stool, Pamela climbed on top of the nearest table and motioned for me to follow. "Help me get their attention," she commanded. I started clapping my hands along with her, and we both shouted, "Ladies!" over and over again. Finally, the room quieted. More than one hundred pairs of eyes looked at us, waiting. Pamela, her voice strong and steady, spoke.

"Girls, I know we are all devastated by the news about Doris Fredlund and Dave Kalinowski. It was a terrible accident and a terrible loss for everyone here." She paused for a moment and let her eyes pass slowly over the sea of faces. While the news of Pamela's relationship to Dave wasn't exactly public knowledge, there were certainly rumors. The hush that had started among the girls became a respectful silence as they listened to Pamela speak, knowing that she had more reason for tears than anyone.

"We are here because there is a war on. And just like thousands of other units stationed at bases in Europe, in the Pacific, and all over the world, today we lost a friend in the fight. We're feeling sad, and lonely, and scared. That's natural. But just like the men who are flying combat missions overseas, we are at war, and wars have casualties. We all knew this day would come. We are sad, and we grieve the loss of Doris and Dave. But it won't be the last time we grieve.

"No matter what happened today, we are still at war, and we still have a job to do. If Doris were here, she'd be the first to tell you that. Her death is a tragedy, but it would be an even greater tragedy if we let ourselves be so overcome by our grief that we don't finish the job all of us, Doris included, came here to do—earn our wings, and do our part to end this war quickly and victoriously."

As Pamela spoke, I was watching the faces of the listening girls.

The few who were still crying were trying to dry their eyes. They were calmer and, suddenly, determined. I sensed that all through that room, women were making silent vows to pull themselves together, to fly better and more courageously than they ever had, as a testament to Doris, our first fallen heroine, and to all those that would come after her. I was so proud of them. It was everything I could do not to start crying again.

But I was caught off guard when Pamela said, "Before we dismiss and get back to our work, I think we should all be silent for a minute. Then Georgia is going to lead us all in a prayer." She turned her back to the girls and nodded to me.

"Pamela!" I leaned toward her and hissed urgently. "I can't say a prayer in front of all these girls! I don't know the first thing about it!"

Pamela hissed back. "You've been to church every Sunday for the last four months. You must have picked up something! Besides, you have to do it. I already said you would."

She jammed an elbow into my ribs and shoved me forward. Facing the rows and rows of solemn, waiting women left me feeling absolutely tongue-tied, but I knew I had to do something. I cleared my throat, asked them all to close their eyes and bow their heads for a moment of silence and did likewise.

With my eyes screwed shut I silently said, *Please God, I'm not sure that you're there or if you can hear me, but if you can, let me know it. Help me. Give me something, anything that would give some peace to these women. If you give me a message for them, I'll share it. Anything. Just a word. They're all torn to pieces inside, and I don't know how to help.*

I stood there with my eyes closed for a long minute, waiting, hoping, wanting but not quite believing, and suddenly there it was.

I hadn't seen Morgan for a month, not since that night when we'd walked from the hangar to the barracks and I'd listened as he'd explained his understanding of God. He had suffered terrible losses, not one father but two, and yet he came to believe that everything, the good and the bad together, was part of the same majestic, ultimately liberating landscape, even if we didn't have the heart or perspective to recognize it from inside the envelope of grief.

I'd probably never see him again, yet I'd thought of Morgan every day since we'd parted. But not, I reasoned, because I was attracted to him personally. Meeting Morgan so soon after that life-changing flight of resurrection was more than chance, I was sure. It was a confirmation that I was on the right path, that it was time to put off the suffocating cloak of mourning I had worn for so long, and that in doing so, I wasn't forsaking my husband but keeping his memory alive. I would never love anyone like I had Roger; I was sure of that. But the memory of that night with Morgan, the picture of his eyes as they burned with a steady, certain flame of conviction, stayed with me. When he'd talked about seeing the world as coherent and replete with meaning when viewed from the heavens, my heart had burned inside me. My mind and soul had whispered, *Yes, there is something to this. There must be.*

I was reaching upward. It was like when I was a little girl and Charles Lindbergh flew over, only feet above my outstretched, yearning grasp. I didn't really know that famous aviator, he was not part of my world, but somehow I knew we were joined by risks, longing, and visions that other people didn't even try to imagine. It was like that with Morgan. Though we were strangers, I recognized him. His words spoke to some undefined longing inside me, helping me lay a fingertip hold on things beyond me.

Raising my head to look over a reverent field of bowed heads, I realized that I understood more than I knew. So did they.

"Dear God," I began. "Thank you for the lives of our friends, Doris and Dave. Thank you for bringing us together. Just as it is hard to understand why you have allowed this terrible war, it is hard for us to understand why you would allow Doris and Dave to be taken from us. We know that sometimes what is good is salvaged from what is bad. We know that with our heads, but our hearts still ache as we struggle to understand the reason for death.

"But you see things differently than we do, God. We know that better than most. Help us to rise up from the plain of grief, anger, and fear that we stand on today. Allow our souls to ascend above, to the place where we can see death and life with eyes more like yours. Give us courage to press on, to search out and fulfill our purpose in life.

"Today we say good-bye to Doris and Dave. Tomorrow, as we graduate and go out to fulfill the duty to which we were called, we will say good-bye again. Life is filled with so many good-byes. Everyone we love, everyone who loves us, eventually leaves us—everyone but you, God. You are with us today, and tomorrow, and forever, just as you are with Doris and Dave. Their souls are at peace. Grant us peace even in sorrow. Help us understand that they and we are never out of your sight." And as I was about to pronounce the amen, Marjie Kellog, Doris's roommate and best friend, looked up at me, her brown eyes filled with sorrow but her voice strong as she repeated the words of a psalm I had never heard before.

Wither shall I go from thy spirit? Or wither shall I flee from thy presence?
If I ascend up into heaven, thou art there;
if I make my bed in hell, behold, thou art there.
If I take the wings of the morning and dwell in the uttermost parts of the sea,
Even there, thy hand shall lead me and thy right hand shall hold me.

Only minutes before, Pamela had asked me to lead a prayer to a God I wasn't even certain I believed in. But somehow, between that

moment when I had asked for help from a source whose very existence I doubted and uttering the final "Amen," belief had come.
Not answers, not justifications, but belief, faith. The faith I'd been
seeking since Roger died and, I realized, long before.

Why did it come then? Why not when I had been under the
guidance and teaching of the good sisters, or during the countless,
more practical expositions Frannie had delivered on saints and
sacraments when we were children? Why not when I was standing
under a full moon listening to Morgan's story, or during those Sundays I spent sitting on hard pews in the First Baptist Church of
Sweetwater?

Maybe I wasn't ready before. Like Morgan said, some things you
have to think through for yourself. I don't know why, after such a
long search, God chose that moment to be revealed to me. I probably never will. But in my heart, I think it happened because of that
first, uncertain, and wholly honest pledge I laid before God: *I don't
know if you are real, but if you will speak, I will listen. And listening,
I will speak.* It had been a prayer for belief, made while in a state of
unbelief. And it had been answered.

It wasn't until breakfast the next day, graduation, that I realized
what Pamela had meant about Doris still needing our help.

We'd been looking forward to this day for so many months, but
the accident cast a pall over what we'd all thought would be a joyous occasion. In the mess hall, conversations were few and whispered.

The room became silent when Donna Lee clinked a glass to get
everyone's attention and Pam stood up to speak.

"Girls, as you know, even though we operate under a militarized
system of discipline and training, and will work as uniformed employees of the Army Air Force, the WASP is not a fully militarized
unit. That was the agreement you made with the government when

you signed up for the program. We aren't paid as much as militarized, male pilots who do the same job, and we receive no military benefits. Every one of you had to come to Sweetwater under your own steam and at your own expense, and if you had washed out during training you would have had to go home the same way. That same rule still holds, even in the event of death."

The room, which was already quiet, became absolutely stony silent as the girls heard this last sentence and realized what Pamela was saying. "Georgia has contacted the pastor of the First Baptist Church of Sweetwater, and the church has kindly agreed to hold a memorial service for Doris and Dave at eight o'clock tomorrow morning so you'll all be able to attend before you have to leave for your new assignments.

"Lieutenant Dave Kalinowski's family has already been notified of his death. After the service, his remains will be sent to his family in Idaho. I hope we will be able to do the same for Doris.

"Doris was from Little Rock, Arkansas. She was unmarried. Her father was a high school math teacher who died several years ago. Her only family is her mother and two younger sisters. The family isn't especially well off, and it will cost at least three hundred dollars to send Doris's remains home to Arkansas."

Pamela turned and nodded a signal. When she did, Fanny, Donna Lee, and I got up and started passing around three bread baskets we'd borrowed from the kitchen, like a trio of church ushers gathering the collection. Pamela continued.

"I know I won't have to urge you to dig deep, but I do want to ask you to give as much as you can. Beyond the cost of the train, I'd like to send Doris's mother enough to help with funeral expenses and as much as we can to help the family. Doris sent almost every cent of her paycheck home to her mother. Those will stop coming now, so if we could help out her mother and little sisters, I'm sure they would appreciate it."

She was right. She didn't have to ask for generosity. Every girl present emptied her pockets. The baskets were so full they had to be emptied three times. After all, it could have been any one of us, and, though it wasn't something we wouldn't discuss, we knew Doris's funeral might be the first, but it wouldn't be the last.

✤ 20 ✤

Morgan

At home or abroad, mail call is the highlight of the day on any military base. It wasn't any different at Baxter, where I was undergoing my training. And I got more mail than just about anyone on base.

Growing up in a small town like Dillon, Oklahoma, where everybody treats you like family—with all the good and the bad that the word implies—I received letters almost every day, if not from Mama, Grandma, Aunt Ruby, or Virginia, then from somebody in Dillon. Everyone from Mr. Dwyer, the head of the deacons' board, to the entire second-grade class of Dillon Elementary, whose teacher made me a homework assignment, wrote to me. I appreciated every letter they sent, but there was never one that gave me more joy than the one I received from Paul telling me that he and Mama were hoping to marry—that is, Paul said, if I would give them my blessing.

I didn't have to think long about saying yes, that's for sure. I knew that Mama and Paul would be very happy together. I'd thought so for a long, long time. That they really did love each other, I had no doubt, but more than that, I think they genuinely liked each other. I didn't know much about love, but I was sure that was a pretty good base to build a marriage on.

I dashed off a note and sent it to them right away, saying,

Dear Mama and Paul,

You have my blessing, my approval, and my sincere congratulations. I've always believed you were meant for each other. Why did it take you two so long to figure out what I've known for years?

Really, this is great news. I am so happy for you. My only regret is that I can't be there for the ceremony; I think I'd have been a great best man. Well, you know I'll be there in spirit. I'm going to go over to the PX and buy you a wedding present as soon as I mail this.

I'm expecting my new orders any time now and I imagine I'll have to ship out as soon as they come. Make sure you take some pictures. I'll let you know where you can send them. I'll write more later, but have to close now so I can get this sent today. Congratulations!!

Your loving son,
Morgan

After my initial excitement over the news about Mama and Paul, I felt a little blue. Of all the things that are hard about soldiering, being far from your family during holidays and big celebrations is the hardest. Especially when you're about to ship into a combat zone you're not sure you'll return from alive.

I was nearing the end of my P-38 training, and I should have had my orders already, but they'd been delayed by bureaucratic bungling. I'd gotten used to that. It seemed to be part of the military culture. There was a joke about "military intelligence" being an oxymoron, and as far as I was concerned, that was no joke, just a statement of fact. My training was a perfect example.

I only lacked one flight check before I could graduate and ship out to my new unit. But just before my graduation, some moron sent half of our instructors off to a brand-new base in New Mexico, which didn't have nearly as many guys as Baxter did, even though our base was packed to the gills. There weren't enough instructors to handle the backlog of pilots waiting for flight checks. Until I could get my final flight check and finish my training, there wasn't much I could do besides wait.

Of course, you'd have thought that, under the circumstances, they might have let me take leave, go home and see my family. That would have been the logical thing, but again, that would have fallen under the heading of "military intelligence," so there I sat, polishing my shoes, playing pickup basketball, reading and rereading letters from home, answering letters, and daydreaming about Georgia Welles.

Just the day before, I'd started writing her a letter—just a friendly note, I told myself, but I tore it up after I finished the first paragraph. There was a lot more than friendship in my intentions toward Georgia. But I already had a girlfriend, Virginia. The girl who had been waiting for me all these months, writing me two and three times a week, the girl who had pressed herself close and asked if I loved her, the girl I had almost . . . No, there was no point in starting something with Georgia. I already had a girlfriend. Virginia knew everything about me, just like everyone else in Dillon. She knew about my mother and my father, or lack of one, and she cared for me anyway. I didn't have to explain things to Virginia.

Taking out a clean sheet of paper, I began writing an answer to Virginia's most recent letter, assuring her for the umpteenth time that I wasn't seeing anybody else, but I ended up throwing that out, too. Frustrated, homesick, and stuck, I stood up and kicked my footlocker so hard that the handle flew off. My roommate, Jake Patterson, was just walking in the door. The flying handle hit him square in the face.

"Hey! Watch it!" Patterson rubbed the spot above his right eye where he'd been hit. "Sheesh, Morgan! Save it for the Japs, will ya?"

"Sorry, Jake. It was an accident. I just kicked it and it went flying."

"What's the matter?" he asked, motioning toward the pile of mail on my bunk. "Bad news from home? Did your girl dump you?"

"Naw. I'm just bored. Sick of hanging around here with nothing to do," I complained.

"Yeah, I hear you. That's why I came in here looking for you. We're getting a basketball game together, and we still need somebody on defense. Wanna play?"

I shook my head. "No, thanks. I already played two games before lunch. I don't want to have to take another shower before dinner."

"Suit yourself." Patterson shrugged. "But until your orders come in, it's the best offer you're gonna get."

He was probably right, but I begged off anyway. As anxious as I was to receive my orders, another part of me was dreading the moment of their arrival. I didn't know where I'd be stationed, but wherever it was, I knew I'd be back in the thick of combat. That's what the P-38 was designed for, and that's what my training had been all about—getting back into the fight.

When General Martin told me I was being sent stateside for training, I'd resented it. I felt like I was being sidelined. But as time went on, I started to think that my training would pay off after all. Up until the P-38 came on the scene, America didn't have a fighter that could match the enemy's. But the P-38 changed all that. She was fast, powerful, and agile. If Holman, Campezzio, and Walker had been flying P-38s, I was convinced they would still be alive. I was anxious to get back into the fight and even up the score. And waiting around base with nothing to do was making me more anxious, but in a different way.

Recently I'd started having dreams. It was almost always the same thing. I was back in the Pacific, flying an escort mission with Fountain. We were the only two planes covering a whole fleet of bombers. The weather was perfect, the skies a clear, bright blue. Suddenly, on my left, I saw an enormous bank of clouds, moving faster than any cloud formation I'd ever seen. Fountain was flying about a thousand feet below me. I called him on the radio saying, "Hey! Look at this cloud! Did you ever see anything like it?"

Before he could answer, the cloud split in half like a curtain, a deceitful Trojan horse of a cloud, and out of the gash spilled an angry swarm of Zeros, hundreds of them. Emerging from the vapors they broke into separate attack groups, eight or ten planes flying together to concentrate on a single bomber, vicious wolf packs destroying their prey with terrible and bloody efficiency. The biggest pack went after Fountain, riddling his tail with bullets, injuring his plane, but not badly enough to down him, not yet. It was as though they wanted to prolong the kill, to toy with him before finishing the job—to torture him. I was the only target they chose to ignore, inflicting me with a different kind of torture, taunting me with my own helplessness.

A thousand cries of terror howled into the radio, begging me for cover, for help, for salvation I couldn't supply. There were too many voices. Fountain's was the loudest of all. He called to me, pleaded with me, and finally cursed me. I tried to come. I wanted to rescue him. I wanted to rescue them all. But when I tried to push the engines, the throttle wouldn't answer, and when I grabbed it, the stick broke off, crumbling in my hands. Frantically, I peered out the windows and realized that I was in the wrong aircraft. I should have been in a fighter, but this was a glider. There were no engines on the wings, and when I looked back at the control panel, all the instruments were gone. The panel was a black void and the only piece of equipment I had left was the radio that kept emitting a stream of piteous, anguished cries for help. Listening to them was agony, and I tried to rip the headphones from off my ears, shutting out the keening cries of dying men, but they were stuck tight to my head.

The glider kept to her path, flying a constant thousand feet above the carnage, a tolerant witness to the butchery below. And there was nothing I could do to stop it. No matter what I tried, the plane refused to answer. Helplessness made me frantic. Though I knew it would down the craft, I tried kicking out the windshield—better to share a comrade's death than to watch it happen and do nothing— but no matter how hard I kicked, the glass remained unmarked. I was trapped behind it, powerless to do anything but ride escort, watching the bombers and their crews disappear into the sea as they were picked off, listening as one by one the desperate cries for help decreased, then stopped altogether, and finally only Fountain's voice was left, and he cursed me, shouting, "Morgan! Do something! Help me! They are killing me! For God's sake, why don't you do something? Help me, you impotent bastard!"

Until finally, bored with the game, the Zeros turned on him with savage precision, strafing his plane with a percussive hail of gunfire. I heard the sound of it through the earphones, the rattle of Fountain's last breath, and the explosive roar of metal and glass as his plane slammed into the waiting sepulchre of the sea and vanished.

The job done, the Zeros departed, dismissing me for the innocuous threat I was, disappearing into the cover of the cloud, hidden, until the next time.

Night after night, I dreamed that dream. I came to dread sleep because I knew the minute I closed my eyes, the nightmare would return.

The same thing happened that night, but before I got to the end I was mercifully interrupted. Jake Patterson shook me awake. "Morgan! Hey, Morgan! Wake up, buddy."

I opened my eyes and saw Patterson, dressed in an undershirt and skivvies, peering down and assuring me that everything was fine. It had just been a bad dream. My heart was beating like a drum, and my breath came in short, gasping bursts, like I'd been running from something. It took a while to remember where I was.

"Sorry if I woke you, Jake. It's just a dream I have sometimes." Patterson was a good guy, but he'd come straight from flight training. He hadn't seen combat yet, and I didn't feel the need to bother him with details.

Patterson sat down on the edge of the bunk, pulled a pack of cigarettes out from under the mattress, and lit one up. "Sometimes?" He made a wry face and shook the match to extinguish the flame. "You've been mumbling and groaning in your sleep every night for a week."

"I have? Sorry."

He exhaled and shrugged dismissively. "That's okay. Doesn't bother me. Never have any trouble getting back to sleep. I was just kind of worried about you. Something's bothering you, that's for sure. Maybe you should talk to somebody. The chaplain or something."

"No. I'm all right."

Patterson looked at me doubtfully. "You sure about that? Three nights running you've been thrashing around, punching the air, and telling whoever you're mad at to come back and give you a fair fight."

"Oh, that. It's nothing. Just a dream I have sometimes. I played football in high school and we lost the biggest game of the year because their ref was a hometown boy. Sometimes, if I'm keyed up I kind of replay the game in my sleep. It's nothing. Just all this sitting around and waiting has me on edge, you know?"

"Yeah, I hear you there," he agreed and puffed sagely on his cigarette. "I wish they'd just make up their minds and send me somewhere. Anywhere. At this point I'd be happy to get posted to

Siberia. Anything's got to be better than sitting around here and waiting."

I nodded agreement, and we sat in the dark for a minute, thinking our own thoughts while Patterson finished his smoke. "Well, if you're sure you're all right," he said, crushing his cigarette butt into the pickle-jar lid he used as an ashtray, "I'm going back to sleep. 'Night, Morgan."

"Good night."

Patterson wasn't lying about his sleep habits. Within three minutes he was out and snoring. I lay awake for the rest of the night, fending off sleep and the camouflaged cloud of dreams that lurked on the other side of consciousness.

When morning finally came I got dressed and carried on with the mind-numbing routine of a pilot without orders or airplane. I did some push-ups, ate, reorganized my footlocker, finished the letter to Virginia, and then headed over to the Post Exchange to see if I could find a wedding present for Mama and Paul, finally deciding on a cut-glass flower vase.

There wasn't much to choose from. The vase was a little fussy for my taste, but I knew Mama would like it. She's always loved flowers and grew a small cutting garden next to the big one that was just for corn and vegetables, so we had bouquets on the table all summer long. But, like most everybody else in Dillon, she put her flowers in quart mason jars left over from the canned goods we'd consumed over the winter. Mama would think this vase was positively elegant. But Paul? Well, if Mama was excited about the present, I was sure Paul would be, too. What he wanted most was for her to be happy.

I walked back to the barracks. As I was coming into our room, Jake was coming out, grinning and waving a very official-looking sheet of paper. "Hot damn! They're here, Morgan! We've got orders at last!"

I ran inside and ripped open the envelope that was lying on my bunk. The more I read, the happier I felt—no, overjoyed was more like it. I dug my wallet out of my pants pocket and opened it to see how much money was left. "That'll do," I said, satisfied that I had sufficient funds for my rapidly hatching plan. I stuffed the wallet back into my pocket, grabbed my orders, and headed out the door.

"Hey, look at this!" Jake demanded excitedly, pointing to his orders. "They're sending me to London! I'm going to Europe! Where are you going?"

"If it all works out the way I'm hoping, to the commander's office, a long-distance phone booth, San Diego, and New Guinea—in exactly that order! See you later!" I ran out the door, leaving my bewildered roommate behind.

Less than an hour later, I was making good on the second proposed leg of my journey. Mama didn't have a telephone, but the church did. I placed a long-distance, person-to-person call from Lieutenant Morgan Glennon to Reverend Paul Van Dyver. It only took a few minutes, but it seemed like forever before the operator came back on the line saying, "I have the Reverend Van Dyver on the line, Lieutenant. You have three minutes. Go ahead."

"Hello? Morgan, is that you?" The line crackled with static, and the voice on the other end sounded tinny, like we were calling through cans connected by miles of string, but I would have recognized that Dutch accent and carefully pronounced English if I'd been calling from the bottom of the ocean. It was definitely Paul.

It was so good to hear his voice that I just about jumped for joy right inside the phone booth. "Are you all right?" He sounded worried.

"I'm fine! Don't worry, nothing bad has happened. I just wanted to call you and say congratulations. About the wedding, I mean. I think it's wonderful, Paul."

"Oh, I'm so pleased you approve, Morgan. Your mother has made me the happiest man on earth. But," he said, his delight suddenly tempered by Dutch practicality, "you should have just written us a letter. Long-distance is so expensive! This must be costing you a fortune."

"Don't worry about that. Listen, I don't have much time. I just got my orders. They are sending me back to the Pacific, to New Guinea, but the troopship that's taking me there won't leave until the twentieth. I've got to hang around here for a few days so they can go through the medical routine—you know, physicals and shots and all that, but I just talked to my C.O. He is going to give me a three-day pass so I can go to San Diego a little early. I've been saving up some money. I was going to send it to Mama, but there's enough here for me to buy train tickets for the two of you to come out here! I'd love to have a chance to see you before I ship out. What do you say?"

"That is a wonderful idea, Morgan. But don't use up your money on train fare for us. I was thinking of taking your mother on a trip after the wedding. This will be perfect." I started to protest, but Paul interrupted. "No, Morgan. It's a very generous offer, but I insist. Eva is going to be my wife. I can take care of her. However, if you would like to buy us dinner in San Diego, I will be happy to accept."

"Fair enough," I said. "It's a deal. I can't wait to see you and Mama together! But, Paul. Just one thing . . ." I hesitated, thinking how to phrase my question. "Are you sure you want me tagging along on your trip? I mean . . . well, it is your honeymoon and everything."

On the other end of the phone, Paul laughed a big, booming laugh. "Oh, yes, Morgan. I know I can speak for your mother when I say that she would be thrilled and delighted to have you tag along on our honeymoon. And I feel exactly the same way."

21

Morgan

I'd passed my last flight check with no problems. My papers were in order. My gear was packed. Mama and Paul's train was due to pull into San Diego on the morning of the twentieth. I'd bought a bus ticket that would get me to San Diego in plenty of time to meet them. At least, that was the plan.

Three days before I was set to leave, I went in for my final physical. The doctor poked and prodded and listened, then scribbled down a few notes on a chart without ever asking me a question or even murmuring a quizzical "Hmmm." He had about as much bedside manner as a meat inspector looking over a side of beef. I sat on the exam table wearing nothing but my shorts and shivering while he took his time writing up his notes. I tried looking over the clipboard and reading his notes upside down, but it was no use. He wrote in such chicken scratch, I probably couldn't have read them even if they'd been right side up. I sure felt sorry for whatever nurse had to read his writing. Finally, he put down the pencil and said, "That's it, then."

"All through? Thanks, Doc. You were making me nervous there for a minute." I hopped off the table and pulled on my undershirt.

"Nothing to be nervous about, just an ear infection. I'm putting you in the hospital until it clears up."

I was thunderstruck. For a minute, I honestly thought he was joking, but when I looked at his face, I realized he was dead serious. "An ear infection? You're going to put me in the hospital for an ear infection? What are you talking about? My ear doesn't even hurt."

The doctor shrugged and scratched his nose. "Maybe not now, but it will. It's red and filled with fluid. I can't clear you to fly until it's healed. A thing like that could affect your equilibrium, you know."

"Come on, Doc," I said. "You're not really going to put me in the hospital over this, are you? My mother is coming all the way from Oklahoma to meet up with me in San Diego. You've gotta let me go!"

The doctor shook his head. "Can't do it, Lieutenant. You'd better call your mother and see if she can't come here instead. When are you supposed to meet her?"

"Thursday. I'm leaving to meet up with her on Tuesday. I've got a ten o'clock bus."

The doctor said, "Well . . ." slowly, like he was considering something, and for a second I thought he was going to relent. Instead he said, "You might be over it by then. No guarantees, but it's possible. I'll see you again at nine on Tuesday, and if it's better, then I'll discharge you in time to make your bus."

"But," I argued, "there's no way it'll clear up by then. Not in three days! I used to get ear infections all the time when I was little, and they never got better in less than a week. Doc," I pleaded, "you've got to let me go! I won't be doing any flying until I get to my new post, anyway. It'll be nearly a week until I leave San Diego and at least another week on a navy troopship until I get to New Guinea. It should be better by then, and I'll have the doctor at my new base check me out before I get within a mile of a cockpit. I swear!" I held up my right hand, Boy Scout style, as a pledge of my good faith.

"Calm down, Lieutenant. I'm going to put you on penicillin." He smiled, as if he had just handed me a Christmas present and was waiting for a thank-you note, but when I didn't say anything, he frowned, "Penicillin. The new wonder drug. You haven't heard of it?"

I shook my head, and he looked at me as if I'd been living under a rock.

"It can clear up all kinds of infections—and fast. I don't know if it'll take care of that ear of yours by Wednesday, but it might. We'll just have to see." I started to argue again, but he wasn't listening to me anymore. He stood up, handed me a prescription and an order, and opened the door to the examining room.

"Report to the hospital, Lieutenant. The faster you get started on this, the faster you'll get out of there."

"Yes, sir," I mumbled morosely.

Before closing the door, he said, "Lieutenant, don't look so depressed. You'll either make your bus to San Diego or not." With a fatalistic shrug, he added, "If you don't, it's probably because you were meant to be someplace else."

At that moment, I could have smacked him with pleasure, but it turned out there was something to what he said.

Doyle McMillan was the officer in charge of the control tower at Baxter Field. On Tuesday I burst into his office, furious and frantic.

"Hey! Watch it, Glennon! What are you trying to do? Kick down my door?"

"Doyle," I said, without taking time to apologize, "you've got to help me! You got to let me have a plane!"

"Whoa!" He held up both hands in a halting gesture, a touch of irritation in his voice. "I don't gotta do anything. Especially when it comes to lending out government property. What's the big problem?"

I took a deep breath and tried to speak slowly and patiently. The last thing I wanted to do was tick off Doyle, but I had to convince him. He was my last chance for getting to San Diego in time to meet up with Mama and Paul. "I was supposed to catch a bus to San Diego this morning to meet my family. The doc wouldn't let me go unless this ear infection cleared up. He said he'd check it out this morning, and if it was better he'd let me leave—"

"Hey," Doyle interrupted, "if you don't have medical authorization to take up a plane, there's nothing I can do about that."

"No! You don't understand! I got to the infirmary, and they left me sitting in the waiting room for an hour. The doc cleared me, but he was so late that I had just enough time to run all the way to the bus stop and see the bus pull out without me. You've got to let me have a plane. My mom's train is pulling into the station in twenty-two hours. Cut me a break, Doyle! I haven't seen her in two years!"

Doyle sighed and tapped his pencil on the desk, thinking. "Gee, that's rough," he said, and for the first time during that frustrating morning, I felt a surge of hope. Though Doyle was only one step ahead of me in rank, he wielded considerable power. If anyone could get me a plane, he could—that is, if he was willing to help. The sympathetic look on his face told me that just might be the case.

"You're shipping out to the Pacific soon, right?" he asked and then, without waiting for an answer, mused, "A guy ought to be able to see his own mother before he goes off to fight for his country." He bit his lip, still considering, and reached for a clipboard that was sitting on the edge of his wooden, government-issue desk.

He flipped through a few pages, mumbling to himself as he did. I just stood very still, watching him, praying that my ticket to San Diego lay somewhere in that pile of paper. Three minutes felt like three hours. Finally, he put down the clipboard, but even before he spoke I could tell that the news wasn't good.

"I'm sorry, Glennon, but honestly, there's nothing here I can let you have. Everything with wings is spoken for. If I gave you a plane that was meant for somebody else they'd bust me down to airman by lunch."

"Please, Doyle! You've got to help me!"

"I'd like to," he said. "Really I would but . . ." He broke off and suddenly his face lit up, looking for all the world like there was a big lightbulb of an idea floating over his head.

"Wait a minute!" He grabbed the phone and started dialing. "There's a factory that makes cargo planes about thirty minutes from here. Lots of them end up in San Diego. I'll see if they've got any being delivered today. It's a little irregular, but if they've got a ferry pilot that wouldn't mind bringing a passenger along, you might just be set! I've got a friend over there," but before he could finish the sentence, someone picked up on the other end. McMillan's face brightened. "John? Hey, buddy! It's Doyle. Listen, I need a favor . . ."

In less than an hour, Doyle himself was dropping me off at the factory. We were met by his friend John, who rushed me quickly through the factory gates, then to the runway.

"Thanks, John!" I hollered gratefully over the sound of engine noise and closed the door behind me, ready for takeoff.

The pilot, who was busy giving the instruments a final once-over, didn't look up when I came on board, but waved me forward. I stowed my gear and collapsed gratefully into the copilot's seat. "Thanks, buddy. I can't tell you how much this means to me."

"No trouble at all," said a voice from my dreams. The pilot looked up from the control panel. My eyes met Georgia's, and when they did, I'm sure the surprise on my face matched her own.

22

Georgia

San Diego is a navy town, so the residents were used to seeing men in uniform, but when Morgan and I walked into the Gaslight Steak House, all eyes were upon us.

The waitress handed us menus and left. I opened mine, peered over the top of it, and whispered to Morgan, "So, you think they don't get a lot of lady pilots wearing flight suits four sizes too big for them in here? I told you I should have changed before we went to dinner. They're going to be staring at us all night!"

"You think it's you they're looking at? Naw. I think it's me. We're so close to where the movie stars live, they've probably mistaken me for Errol Flynn. Happens all the time," he said with a world-weary sigh.

"Errol Flynn? More like Groucho Mark," I teased, returning the jab. "But, seriously, we should have gotten cleaned up before going out to eat. I feel self-conscious with all these people staring at us. Maybe we should have just gone to the U.S.O."

"What? And have donuts for dinner instead of a nice, juicy

steak? And if we were at the U.S.O. I'd have to spend my whole evening chasing off all the flyboys who would be fighting for a dance with you," Morgan said. "Especially once they got an eyeful of you in that swell outfit."

I made a face and clunked Morgan on the head with my menu. "Very funny."

"Ouch! Is that any way to treat a guy who's trying to give you a compliment? Not to mention taking you out to dinner—"

I interrupted him. "Morgan, this isn't a date, and you're not taking me out to dinner, remember? We're just eating together because we don't know anyone else in San Diego. When the check comes we are splitting it right down the middle. That's what you agreed to."

Morgan held up his hands in surrender. "I know. I know. It's not a date."

The waitress returned to take our order. Morgan ordered a T-bone, but I just asked for a hamburger. Since it was a special occasion, we each decided to try a glass of red wine.

"If we're splitting the check down the middle, it looks like I'm going to be getting a deal. Are you sure you don't want a steak?" Morgan asked.

I shook my head and took a sip of water. "I'm not that hungry."

"Really? You should be, after flying all the way here. I've got to tell you the truth, Georgia, I wasn't sure a little slip of a thing like you would be able to handle that bomber. What do you weigh? Maybe a hundred and ten pounds?"

"Hundred and seventeen," I corrected. "Probably a hundred and fifty if you count the flight suit."

"And now you're flying twin-engine cargo planes?" Morgan whistled admiringly. "You've learned a few things since last I saw you." I couldn't help but blush a little. It felt good to earn another pilot's respect, especially one as good as Morgan. During our flight, he'd told me about his experiences in the Pacific, but only after I prodded him. Twelve combat kills was an impressive record; most pilots would have let you know about that before they even said hello, but not Morgan. I liked him more because of it.

"Well, you may only weigh one hundred and seventeen pounds," Morgan continued, "but the first hundred must be pure muscle. If I'd had to manhandle that monster all the way to San Diego, my arms would be feeling like spaghetti right now."

"Who says they don't?" I laughed and reached for a hot roll from the basket the waitress had left on the table. "When we were at Avenger they must have made us do a million push-ups, and now I know why. I only graduated a month ago, but I've already flown more different planes than most pilots handle in a lifetime—fighters, dive bombers, pursuit planes, you name it." I knew I was bragging, but I couldn't help feeling a little proud. Sometimes, when I'd walk up to some big behemoth of an airplane and realize that I was going to get behind the wheel and actually take her off the ground, I could scarcely believe it myself.

"That is something," Morgan replied sincerely. "They sent me to school for almost as long as you went, and I only came out knowing how to fly P-38s."

"Well, it's a little different. You've got to fly them in combat, so you've got to know that plane inside and out. All I have to do is get them up in the air and land them again. Nobody's shooting at me while I'm trying to do it."

The waitress brought our dinners. I took a bite of my hamburger and let out a groan of pleasure. "Mmm. I am in heaven! This is the best hamburger I've ever had."

Morgan was enjoying his steak, too. "This is great! You've got to have a bite, Georgia," he insisted, and before I could protest he cut off a big piece of meat and put it on my plate. He was right. That steak was delicious. I shared half of my burger with him, and we kept talking while we ate. I'd never had red wine before. At first I didn't care for the taste, but after a couple of sips it didn't seem as harsh, I liked the way it felt, warm and rich as it went down my throat. I relaxed a little and stopped worrying about how out of place I must look among all the white tablecloths and fancy silverware.

Morgan picked up the conversation where we'd left off. "You might not be flying combat, Georgia, but you really are a terrific pilot. After you rescued me at Avenger, I already knew you're a better mechanic than I am, but I'm thinking you've got me beat when it comes to navigation, too. You did a heck of a job getting us here today."

"Oh, but that's the training again," I said honestly. "The whole idea behind the WASP was to use women as ferrying pilots, so they spent a lot of time working on our navigational skills. Any WASP worth her wings can get you from Allentown to Albuquerque on the beam, flying in the middle of one radio tower signal to another, and if that fails, we just follow the railroad tracks. It might not be quite how the crows do it, but tell a WASP where you want to go, and, one way or another, she'll get you there."

Morgan sat there for a minute without saying anything, just smiling at me. I started to feel a little funny and wished I hadn't gone on so. After all, I didn't want him to think I was flirting with him. I picked up my fork and took another bite of the steak. "This really is good," I said.

"You really do love flying, don't you?" Morgan asked without a trace of flattery in his voice. The honesty of his tone put me at ease again.

"The planes are either boiling hot or freezing cold. They keep me so busy that I almost never get eight hours sleep at a stretch. When I do sleep, it's never in the same place two nights running. This is the first hot meal I've had in four days. Then, of course, there are the joys of being a woman in a man's world in the ultimate male occupation—with grouchy officers and other pilots who think that a girl pilot is some kind of affront to nature, air bases with no facilities for women, not to mention"—I continued in a slight whisper that I hoped no other diners would hear, holding out my arms to show my flight suit in its full masculine glory—"the challenge of completing long, solo flights wearing this stylish number, which wasn't exactly designed with the female figure in mind."

Morgan cracked up at this last. "Yes, I can see where that would be a problem."

"I'm not kidding," I said with a smile. "I can't tell you how many times I've gotten to the end of a long flight and called into the tower just praying I'd get priority in the landing pattern. You can't exactly radio in saying you're declaring a powder room emergency."

Morgan laughed even harder, and I joined in, enjoying the sound of our combined mirth. A few of our fellow diners began looking at us with renewed curiosity. *Gosh,* I thought as I wiped tears of mirth from my eyes, *it feels so good to laugh with someone. I haven't done that in so long.*

"But, yes," I said, getting back to his original question. "Even with all that, this is the best job I've ever had. I wake up every day and almost have to pinch myself so I can believe it's true! Heck, if I had to, I'd probably pay the government to let me be a WASP. Don't get me wrong: I'm sorry it took a war so all this could happen. I'd hand in my wings tomorrow if it would mean bringing our boys home, but as long as there is a war, I'm just glad to be able to do a little something to help."

"Well," Morgan said, "I'm sure your husband is proud of you. It must feel good to know you're helping him to get home that much quicker." He looked at me, waiting, I was sure, for me to tell him all about Roger.

I popped a piece of steak into my mouth, chewing slowly and trying to keep my face blank while buying myself some time to think.

When it came to men as a whole, my opinion of them hadn't changed much since I was a little girl, watching in disgust as, one after another, Delia's swains declared their lust to be love and, once they'd gotten their fill of what they came for, walking out the door, leaving Delia clutching handfuls of broken promises with no path before her but the one which led to the next bed and the next heartbreak. It was Delia's own fault. She let them take advantage of her, I knew, but she just couldn't help herself. Delia needed to believe the fairy tale, but the men knew exactly what they were doing. I'd learned from my mother's mistakes, and, subconsciously at least, I'd made a pact never to let myself entirely trust men—not until Roger came along.

Now, sitting across the table from Morgan, I wondered if maybe, just maybe, God might have made at least two men worth trusting.

I could tell Morgan liked me, too—that he more than liked me. If he knew that I wasn't, as he believed, a married woman, I was pretty sure that he would allow his feeling for me to go beyond friendship. And how did I feel about him? My mind lit up with snapshots of our brief time together, standing outside the barracks in a starlit night as he shared his faith; his frank admiration and collegial respect for me as a pilot; the memory of his playful humor; his confidence and complete lack of self-consciousness as he strode into a fancy restaurant in the company of a woman wearing a lumpy flight suit; our hours of conversation as we'd flown today; and, even better, the quiet appreciation as we sat side by side in companionable silence sharing the fulfilling, indescribable joy of flight.

Yes, I liked Morgan. I liked him very much. I looked across the table again, warming myself in the steady glow of those amazing eyes and feeling the warmth spread from my face to a place in my heart that had been cold for so long.

I swallowed and started to speak, forming the words in my mind as I prepared to tell him the truth about Roger, but as I did, another picture flashed in my memory. It wasn't a memory in the true sense of the word, but an invented one, the picture I'd formed in my mind of Roger, sitting alone on the edge of his bunk, holding my picture in his hand, leaving a print of love for me to find, putting his last letter into an envelope, holding it close for a moment before getting up and walking out to meet death. Roger. He had loved me.

It had taken months of courtship and even more months of marriage before I had truly loved him back. The amount of time I'd spent with Morgan didn't even add up to a day.

The words that had been forming in my mind crumbled at this touch of reality. I barely knew Morgan. However much I liked him and despite how serendipitous our meeting might have seemed, the truth was that in three days Morgan would be on a ship headed for the Pacific. In all probability, I'd never see him again. It was ridiculous and disloyal of me to let wine and loneliness seduce me into saying things I'd regret tomorrow.

I looked Morgan in the eye and told him the truth. "Roger is the love of my life."

Disappointment flickered in Morgan's face. He started to say something, but before he could, the waitress came to the table and apologized for bothering us. She was holding a rolled-up magazine in her hand and wanted to know if she could ask me something.

"Sure," I answered, relieved at her interruption.

"Are you one of those lady fliers? One of those . . . what do you call them?" she mused, screwing up her face and trying to remember.

"WASP? Women's Air Service Pilots?"

"That's it!" she cried, her face lighting up. "Are you one of them?" I nodded, and she grinned.

"I thought so!" she exclaimed and unrolled the magazine she'd been holding. It was a copy of *Life,* and there was a picture of a young woman with her hair in pigtails sitting on the wing of an airplane, wearing a flight suit just like mine.

"May I see that?" I asked. The waitress happily complied. "Look at this, Morgan! It's all about the WASP. That's Shirley Slade on the cover! I know her. She was in a couple of classes behind mine." I flipped through the pages, scanning the photos for familiar faces. "Where did you get this?"

"It just came out today. Would you mind signing it for me?" She pulled a pen out of her apron pocket and held it out to me. I looked at Morgan, not quite certain of what I should do, but he just grinned.

"But I'm not in any of the pictures," I said. She shoved the pen into my hand just the same.

"That doesn't matter! Sign it anyway." The waitress, who wore a name tag reading JUDY pinned to her blue and white uniform, chattered on enthusiastically while I did as she asked. "When you walked in wearing that outfit I told Harry—he's the manager—" She jerked her head over toward the front counter where Harry was standing. He raised his hand in a sheepish introduction. "Anyway," Judy said, "I told Harry that you must be one of those WASPs, but he didn't believe me. He said there was no way the government would let girls fly their airplanes."

Morgan jumped into the conversation. "Not only that, they fly all kinds of different planes and deliver them from factories to bases all over the country. They do other jobs, too, dangerous ones, like towing targets for artillery practice and even testing planes that have undergone repairs to make sure they're combat-ready. These girls are heroes."

It was kind of sweet to see the starry-eyed excitement of the young waitress. I thought this must be a little like how it feels to be a movie star, but I was starting to feel a little embarrassed, too, by all the adulation. I gave Morgan a look that meant "enough already," but he didn't take the hint.

"Georgia here has flown more different kinds of aircraft in the last month than I have in my entire military career. Just this morning she flew a big cargo plane in from Arizona. No man could have flown it better. I just sat back and enjoyed the ride."

"There! You hear that? You owe me a dollar, Harry!" Judy slapped her hand against her thigh triumphantly and shot the hapless Harry a victorious glance.

Harry sidled apologetically to our table. "Sorry," he mumbled. "No offense intended. I just couldn't quite believe it was true, Miss . . . Miss . . ."

"Just call me Georgia," I said, and gripped his outstretched hand. "And this is Morgan. He's a combat pilot. He's shipping out to a new post in just a couple of days."

"Is that right?" Harry asked. He beamed and extended his hand to Morgan. "It's nice to meet you, Lieutenant. It's nice to meet both of you.

"So you're shipping out in a couple of days? Listen, there's no check for you two this evening. Your dinner is on the house. In fact"—he turned to the waitress—"Judy, why don't you run into the kitchen and see if we've got any of the apple pie left. Bring them a couple of pieces, will you? And make sure you have Charlie melt some cheddar on top."

"Will do!" Judy answered eagerly and scurried to the kitchen.

"You don't have to do that," Morgan assured him, and I agreed, but Harry wouldn't be dissuaded.

"Don't mention it," he said, waving off our protests with a magnanimous gesture. A sudden clatter of noise from the kitchen interrupted his train of thought.

He sighed wearily and started off toward the kitchen. "Sounds like I'd better get in there. You two just have a good time and don't give another thought to the bill. It's the least I can do. It's terrible, the way this war is splitting up so many nice young couples like you." He shook his head regretfully and, as a second clatter of dropped dishes rang out, he trotted off.

"Thank you!" Morgan called to the manager's retreating figure and then chuckled as he turned to me. "Can you beat that? He thinks we're engaged!"

I started gathering up my things. "Morgan, I've got to go."

The smile faded from his face. "Why? Just because of that? It was just an honest mistake, Georgia."

"No, no. It's just that . . ." I glanced at my watch. "I didn't realize how late it was. I've got to fly in the morning, and I need some sleep. That wine went right to my head." I slid across the seat of the booth and started to get up, but Morgan grabbed my arm.

"Georgia, don't run off. Sit down. At least stay and have dessert. Think how disappointed Judy and Harry will be if you don't—especially after they made Charlie go to all the trouble of melting cheese on your pie." Morgan smiled.

I told him again that I really had to leave. Morgan dropped his lighthearted tone and said seriously, "Georgia, you don't need to be so nervous. I'm not going to try anything, really. It's just nice spending time together. I like you. Why can't you just stay for ten more minutes?"

I couldn't answer that question because I wasn't really sure myself. I just knew I had to go. I stood up. "Morgan, I had a great time. I hope everything goes great with your mom and all. Make sure you take her to the zoo. They say it's one of the best in the world. Maybe you can write me when you get settled in at your new base."

Seeing that I wasn't going to be dissuaded from leaving, Morgan got up to say good-bye. He leaned forward, as if to kiss me on the cheek, but I stuck out my hand before he could get closer.

"Yeah. Sure. I'll write you," he said in a disappointed voice. We shook hands a little awkwardly. "It was nice to see you again, Georgia. Thanks again for the lift. Maybe I can see you again before I ship out?"

"Probably not. I'm flying all week, but I won't be coming back to San Diego for a while," I said. It wasn't true, but the lie popped out of my mouth anyway. I was scheduled to return to San Diego on Saturday, the day before he left. Seeing the look of disappointment and confusion etched on Morgan's face made me feel guilty. "But if

I'm around," I backtracked, not wanting to leave him feeling utterly rejected, "then, sure. Yes. Maybe we could have a cup of coffee or something."

Morgan looked at me, and I knew he knew I was lying. I said good-bye. Walking across the dining room toward the door, I could feel the heat of his gaze on my back, but I didn't turn around. I couldn't.

The telephone rang and rang. *Pick up!* I commanded silently.

There was a woman outside the phone booth, impatiently waiting her turn. She was a big, matronly lady. She wore scuffed tie-up shoes and a shapeless gray overcoat that seemed strangely at odds with her headgear, a black felt confection that dripped with clusters of cherries and red ribbon. I stood facing the telephone so I could pretend I didn't see the woman, who tapped her foot impatiently as she waited, making the clusters of cherries bounce with every tap.

"I'm sorry, miss," the operator said in a bored voice, "no one is answering. You can try again later."

"Please, Operator! Just let it ring a few more times. It's an emergency!"

The operator started to protest just as the receiver clicked and a tired, somewhat confused voice on the other end said, "Hello?"

"Long distance calling," the operator twanged. "I have a collect call for Miss Cordelia Carter Boudreaux from Mrs. Georgia Welles. Will you accept the charges?"

"Yes," Delia said, and even as the operator informed us that we could go ahead, Delia interrupted her with a worried, "Georgia? Is that you? Is everything all right? Where are you?"

"I'm in a phone booth." I answered. "Everything is fine. I just . . . I just wanted to call you. I wanted to hear your voice."

Not unkindly, Delia said, "Georgia, it's two in the morning here. Are you sure you're all right?"

"I'm sorry, Delia. I was out walking, and I just wanted to talk to you. I didn't think about what time it was in Chicago," I apologized. Then, without quite understanding why, I started to cry. "I'm sorry, Delia. I'm sorry I woke you. I just . . ." but I couldn't finish the sentence. The tears caught in my throat and mind and washed away everything I'd thought I wanted to say.

"Georgia!" Delia said, the alarm in her voice trumping the usual studied calm of her drawl. "Georgia? What's the matter? What is it?"

I couldn't answer. I couldn't do anything but sob. My head dropped and rested against the wall of the phone booth, the rough grain of the wood scratching the skin of my forehead. My knees were weak, it was all I could do to keep them under me. Delia's voice, insistent and anxious, radiated worry through the phone line, repeating the question, pleading for an answer. "What is it, Georgia? Tell me what's wrong."

"Delia!" I sobbed desperately, incoherently. "Delia! Mama! I . . . I want." But that was as far as I could go. That was all I knew.

Outside, the woman who had been waiting for the phone booth, started tapping on the glass panels of the door, asking if I was all right in there. I didn't answer. I couldn't do anything but cry.

"I want! Mama, I want!" I said again and again, helpless and despairing, begging her for an explanation, pleading for a word that would define and fill the emptiness that enveloped me. "I want . . ."

"Hush, Georgia. Hush," Delia's voice, soothing and deep, breathed comfort long-distance. "I know you do, baby girl. I know. Believe me, I know."

23

Morgan

San Diego, California—May 1943

The train arrived on time. San Diego was the last stop, and there were so many people getting off that I didn't see Mama and Paul at first. I kept scanning the faces of the passengers as the conductors helped them descend the steps and file onto the platform, where a gaggle of anxious Red Caps stood by with ready smiles and well-oiled dollies, ready to help cart away the luggage of anyone who looked like they could tip. One after another, smartly dressed travelers streamed out of the carriages. As the minutes passed, I started to get a little worried. Had they missed a connection?

The platform was noisy with shouted greetings between friends, the calls of passengers summoning Red Caps, the hissing of the engine as it exhaled an exhausted breath of steam, and the unintelligible garble of train departures announced over the public address system, echoing over the heads of the disinterested crowd.

Finally, down at the far end of the platform, I spotted a petite woman with hair the exact shade of Mama's. A conductor helped her disembark from the last car, but the woman was wearing a stylish, navy blue traveling suit and hat—not the sort of thing people wore in Dillon. My heart sank, and I started anxiously looking around again. But then the stylish woman turned her head. She looked just like Mama, except younger.

No, I thought, *not younger. Mama is young, only thirty-eight years old. Happy. She's happy. This is how Mama looks in love.*

We recognized each other in the same instant, and I started to run toward her, waving and shouting. Paul, looking as renewed as Mama, stepped off the car right behind her. Grinning, I pushed through the crowd and scooped Mama up into my arms, lifting her off her feet and swinging her around in a big joyous circle. And when I finally put her down, Paul came over, and I wrapped my arms around both of them. I just couldn't help myself. I was so happy.

"Look," I heard a woman say to the Red Cap who was loading her luggage onto his cart. "Isn't that sweet? They're all together again."

"Yes, ma'am," the Red Cap agreed. "That's one happy family."

We took a cab over to the motel I'd booked for Mama and Paul. Mama was animated. I'd never heard her talk so much. She was excited about everything she saw outside the taxi window, from her first glimpse of the ocean to the size of the buildings, to the trees that lined the streets. Her nose was practically glued to the window of the car. Paul and I just smiled and listened to her talk. She finally turned, and when she saw us grinning, she blushed.

"Oh, you must think I'm so silly going on like this. I'm sorry. I just never thought it would be so beautiful!"

"That's all right," I said, laughing. The truth was, it made me feel good to see her enjoying herself, and a little proud. Mama's wonder at the world outside Dillon reminded me of how far I'd come. When I was a little boy I'd poured over atlases of the world, dreaming of the places I'd go and the things I'd see when I grew up to be a pilot. Now here I was, all grown up, and my dreams had come true. I'd gone to places and seen things that most folks in Dillon could never even have imagined. Virginia told me that her mother and father had taken a trip to see relatives in New Orleans once, and when they got back, all they did was complain about the heat and the people's strange accents and the even stranger food. I was proud that Mama was so enthusiastic and open-minded enough to appreciate new experiences.

"Don't apologize," I said. "This must all seem pretty strange after spending your whole life in Dillon. I did exactly the same thing the first time I went to a big city."

"Well, goodness, Morgan! I'm not a complete hick. I've been to big cities before. I've been to Oklahoma City and to Des Moines."

This was news to me. "Des Moines? When did you go there?"

For just a moment, Mama's eyes flashed surprise. "Oh," she said. "Didn't I tell you about that? I went there for a few days after you went off to college."

"You did? Why?"

"Well, I just decided to take a trip, I guess," Mama said. "There's nothing wrong with that, is there?"

"No." I shrugged. "But why Des Moines? Why not Dallas or Chicago?"

Paul interrupted. "Morgan, tell me more about this new airplane you're flying. It has twin engines? That must be something. How fast can it go?"

Paul was really interested in the P-38. He kept asking questions all the way to the motel while Mama just kept looking out the cab window at the sights of San Diego, lost in her own thoughts.

Over the next two days, I took Mama and Paul to visit every attraction San Diego had to offer. When I laid out the itinerary I had planned, Mama said that we didn't need to go running all over San Diego, that getting to spend time with me, talking and catching up, was treat enough for her, and Paul agreed. But I insisted there was no reason we couldn't do both, and I'm glad I did. We had a great time.

Mama loved everything, but I think the zoo was her favorite. We spent almost an entire day there. When the other tourists approached the cages, they hung around for a couple of minutes, laughing and gawking, before growing restless and moving on, but not Mama. She stood in front of each animal and, fascinated, watched until Paul or I suggested we take a look at the next exhibit.

When we got to the lions' exhibit, which was set up like it would have been in the wild with the lions all living together as a family in a grassy enclosure with trees, instead of separately in cages, Mama's hand flew to her mouth. "Oh! Look at them!" She breathed, more to herself than me. "I never imagined they would be so beautiful!"

Mama walked slowly forward toward the glass wall that separated people from animals. Paul and I hung back a bit. Paul was clearly having as much fun watching Mama as she was having watching the lions.

"She's really enjoying herself," I said. "If we let her, I bet she'd still be standing there come morning."

Paul nodded and smiled. "She sees things that the rest of us miss. If she had been born in another time and place, I think she might have been a poet, or a great painter."

"Well, in a way she is a great painter. Her quilts are her canvases. Did you see the quilt she gave me for Christmas before I left for boot camp?" Paul shook his head.

"It's incredible. The background is an aerial view of the landscape right over the farm. It's perfect—the scale, the sense of space, the angle of the sun setting on the horizon—perfect!" I said wonderingly. "She's never been off the ground, but in her mind she can fly! It's the most beautiful quilt I've ever seen.

"On the ground there are two figures in silhouette, Mama and me, looking up to the sky. Then, at the bottom corner of the quilt, an airplane wing cuts across the fabric field. It's an old biplane wing, complete with wing supports and cables strung between, like the pilot is looking out over the edge of the cockpit to see the little boy and the woman standing on the ground looking up at him. You can't see the pilot, just the wing and a flutter of fringe from the edge of the pilot's scarf, just like they wore back in the old barnstorming days, but you know he's there. And somehow you just feel what that pilot is feeling, how he is sending down a blessing on the little boy who is standing below, dreaming of flying, remembering what it was like when he was that little boy, looking up and dreaming, and how that's who he still is. Every time he lands his plane and sets his foot on the ground, he is still looking upward, dreaming of flying again."

Paul's eyes were solemn as he listened. With anyone but Paul, I would have been embarrassed at going on and on like that, but I knew he understood. Paul listened the way Mama saw—patiently and completely, taking in more than what lay on the surface. I smiled to myself, thinking how perfect they were for each other.

"I wish I had seen it. It sounds remarkable."

"It is," I said.

His gaze returned to Mama. He bit his lower lip, thinking. "It's never been easy for your mother to talk about her feelings. It still isn't."

It was true, but that was all changing for Mama, and Paul was the reason.

Though it seemed like a lifetime ago, only two years had passed since I'd sat across from Paul at the table of his orderly and solitary bachelor kitchen, looking into his face and seeing hopelessness. He couldn't give up on loving, but had given up all hope that his love would ever be returned. I wanted to ask him what had happened, what he had said to change Mama's mind, what prayers he had uttered to surmount circumstances that had seemed insurmountable. I wanted to tell him about Georgia, but I couldn't find the words;

and, besides, what was the point? I was leaving soon, and, even if I hadn't been, she had made it clear she wasn't interested. It was best to forget all about her.

But I couldn't.

During dinner, Georgia had taken a sip of wine, and, without her knowing it, a tiny droplet of wine beaded and clung to the soft curve of her lower lip. It had been everything I could do not to reach across the table and touch her lip with my finger, taking that delicate ruby bead from her lip and placing it between my own. Now, whenever I closed my eyes, I was there again, but in my dreams I didn't restrain my hand, I couldn't. I reached out and took the wine off her lips, tasted her on my tongue. Then I reached out again, pulling her toward me, wrapping myself in her, closing my ears to reason, eclipsing her protests with my desire.

I wanted her. I wanted her body joined with mine, and for her to want me the same way. I wanted to hear the sound of her voice, to know what she was thinking when she pulled her brows together and that little fold of concentration appeared between them. I wanted to know all about her past and tell her all about mine, the things I'd never told anyone else. I wanted to walk with her, fly with her, lie heart to heart, to talk to her, and to sit silent next to her.

You've got to stop this, I told myself. *By this time tomorrow you'll be sailing to Australia. It'll be easier then. You'll be able to forget. You just have to get through this day.*

Though I didn't speak, Paul must have sensed something was bothering me. "Morgan, are you all right?"

I assured him that I was fine, just hungry. Just then, a security guard came up and reminded us it was five minutes to closing time.

Paul looked at Mama and smiled. "Morgan, would you tell her? I don't have the heart."

I came behind her and leaning down, rested my chin on her shoulder. "Mama, the zookeepers say we have to go or they'll lock us in here for the night."

Mama reached her hand up, cool and soft as always, and laid it flat on my cheek. "Hmmm," she sighed. "That wouldn't be so bad, would it? I could watch them for hours. Just look at them, Morgan. They are just so alive! Everything about them is vital and honest. They are what they are and make no apologies for it. Beautiful."

I stepped to her side and put my arm around her. "They really are something, especially that big guy over there," I said, pointing to a large, powerful-looking male lion with an enormous mane wreathing his regal face. "I wouldn't want to meet him in a dark alley."

Mama nodded, "He's a big, handsome fellow," she agreed. "But did you know that it's really the female that takes care of the family? Look at her." Mama gestured toward the much smaller, less muscular female sitting a few feet apart from the male. "She's half his size, but it's the mother who does the hunting. She has the babies, and protects them from predators, and makes sure they all have enough to eat. Without her, the family couldn't survive. She is smaller than her partner, maybe weaker in some ways, but inside, at the core, she is driven by a powerful instinct, some fierce resolution that gives her twice his strength. She knows what she has to do," Mama said in a voice hushed with respect.

I started to say something about Mama being part lioness but instead I just leaned down and kissed her on top of the head. Mama looked up at me and smiled.

"What was that for?"

"It's a coded message. It means 'thanks for being you.'"

"Come on." I took her hand. "Let's get some dinner."

❧ 24 ❧

Georgia

San Diego, California—May 1943

After I'd finally calmed down enough to say good night to Delia, promising her that I was going to be all right, I put down the receiver, dug a handkerchief from my pocket, blew my nose, then squeezed through the door of the phone booth, murmuring apologies to the cherry-hatted matron who was still waiting outside.

"Excuse me," I mumbled, keeping my eyes from meeting hers. "I'm sorry."

"That's all right, honey," she clucked and patted me awkwardly on the arm. "Is there anything I can do for you? Do you need a ride somewhere?"

Everyone in the restaurant was staring. I shrank back from her touch, embarrassed to find myself the object of pity and interest to so many strangers. "No. I'm fine. Thanks." I pulled my jacket close and pushed my way quickly through the staring gauntlet of diners, singles on one side perched on counter stools like birds huddled on a telephone wire, and a sprinkling of couples on the other side, clustered together in booths, hunched over cups of coffee and half-eaten pieces of pie that they'd abandoned in favor of something more interesting—me, the central character in a drama they understood not at all but whose plot appeared satisfyingly sad and familiarly sentimental, like one of those B-grade war movies that Hollywood churned out as a means of touching the national heart and romanticizing the reality of war.

As I neared the exit I heard one of the pink-aproned waitresses stage-whisper a question to the woman. "What's wrong with her? What happened?"

"She was calling her mother. Must have gotten bad news, the poor thing. Probably lost her sweetheart or her husband."

"Poor thing," the waitress echoed. "It's terrible, this war. Ain't it?"

"Terrible," the other woman said, wiping a tear from the corner of her eye. She sniffed, and the cherry clusters bobbed up and down, nodding agreement.

I spent most of that night walking, crying, and thinking. When I finally went back to the boardinghouse near the base where I stayed whenever I was in San Diego, it was hard to sleep. I only dozed off for a couple of hours before the alarm jangled in my ear, and I jumped out of bed and splashed some water on my face before reporting for duty.

I had a passenger for my first hop, a captain who was heading out to a new post, but he must have been out celebrating the night before because he fell dead asleep about two minutes after we took off, breathing out beer fumes with each snore and not waking up until we touched down. For the next couple of days I did nothing but deliver single-seat fighters, so I had plenty of time by myself.

There is no better place to think than behind the controls of an airplane, where the constant hum of the engine blocks out all distraction and the beckoning lure of the horizon pulls the mind out of the trap of self-absorption and into the calm center of the universe, where it is easy to name the truth, easy to live with it. When I'm flying, my problems fall away, suddenly seeming as small and insignificant as the miniaturized landscape I'm flying over—tiny cars, tiny buildings, tiny problems with obvious solutions. At least that's how it seems when I'm in the air.

When I returned to San Diego late on Saturday night, I had a plan.

After I landed, I ran over to the boardinghouse to clean up a little. It was nearly eleven o'clock by the time I got to the base. Twenty thousand feet above sea level, my plan had seemed foolproof, but the closer I got to the visitors' barracks, the more nervous I felt. Half of me was afraid of finding him already asleep while the other half was afraid he wouldn't be.

Morgan's blinds were closed, but the door was open. It was a warm night. He'd left the screen closed to keep out the bugs. Lamplight shafted through the screen door, throwing a rectangle of light onto the sidewalk and scrubby brown grass that led to the door of his quarters.

For a moment, I thought about turning back. I stepped up to the door and looked through the screen. There was a half-packed duffel sitting on the dresser but no sign of Morgan. He was gone. Maybe it was just as well, I thought to myself, relieved and disappointed all at once. I turned to leave, but he must have heard me.

"Yeah?" he called, his voice muffled behind the closed bathroom door. "Who is it?"

I took a deep breath. "Morgan? It's me. It's Georgia."

The bathroom door opened, and he stepped out. He wore only his shorts, undershirt, and a disbelieving expression. His hair was wet, and he held a damp towel in his hand. "Georgia?" He walked toward the screen, squinting as if peering at a mirage, trying to sort out what was real and what was false.

I had rehearsed a long introduction, something about going for a cup of coffee and a talk, about honesty and forthrightness, about being fair to him and myself. But standing on the front stoop, watching him come toward me, smelling of soap and shaving cream, his body backlit by lamplight, spilling over the chiseled muscles of his shoulders like a sun rising over a mountain landscape, I forgot how the speech began. All I could manage to say was hello.

He closed the distance between us in four long strides, opened the screen door, and pulled me into his embrace. Without releasing his hold on me, Morgan pushed the door closed with his foot.

I hadn't planned on coming into his room. My only thought had been to go someplace quiet to talk and to tell him the truth about myself, that I was a bastard, a mistake of a child born to a woman whose entire life was consumed by wanting, who went from bed to bed pretending to be something she wasn't, just so someone, anyone, would love her. It didn't matter to Delia if it was true or not. She was willing to be whatever they wanted. It didn't matter if she was loved for a lie. She expected it; she was that certain no one could love the truth of her.

I had planned on telling him how I'd rejected her and pushed her away, inventing a new life for myself and denying she was my mother as surely as she had denied I was her child. That night as I wailed my want through the phone line was the first time I understood how closely Delia and I were related. We were both searching for the love we had to have and didn't know how to get, both hiding behind walls of secrets because we were so afraid of revealing our true selves and being cast out yet again. I was going to tell him it had to stop, that I had decided it would stop with me. Then I would tell him that I had married a man I didn't deserve and didn't love until it was too late, that I was still afraid I didn't know how to love. That was why I'd lied and let him believe I was married.

Working it through in my mind three thousand feet aloft, it had all seemed so easy. I would roll the truth out at Morgan's feet like a scroll so he could read it for himself. And somehow it would all work out from there. I'd be in his arms, forgiven, understood, wanted. Everything would be all right.

But everything had gotten jumbled. In his arms I couldn't remember what I had wanted to say. All I knew was Morgan. His name was the word that came after "I want."

His arms around me were taut and strong as iron bands, but they moved with me, shielding and releasing all at once, and there was nowhere else I wanted to be. It was not like any lovemaking I'd ever known. There was no questioning hesitancy in the pressure of his lips on mine, no considered, tentative surrender in my response, only the need to yield and, for the first time in my life, to demand.

Reaching my arms high over my head, I pulled his mouth closer to mine. He arced his body over mine. I pushed myself toward him, reaching on tiptoe and arching my back into an answering curve of desire until our bodies met at every point.

I lowered my arms, wrapping them over his shoulders like a covering shawl and took a single step backward, leading the dance. He moved with me, and we were on the bed, lying face to face, matching breath for breath and kiss for kiss.

Morgan pushed himself half up, leaning his weight on one arm and gently pressing my shoulder with the other so I lay down next to him. I guided his hand to my blouse buttons. I wanted him to hurry up. I wanted him to slow down. I wanted my body joined with Morgan's, possessed and possessing, but that wasn't all.

My hand fluttered above his for a moment, a shy bird hesitant to light, before covering his, stopping him at the last button. His hand lay warm against the flat of my stomach, and it was everything I could do not to arch toward him, silently pressing him to carry on. I knew I had to say something and hear something before I let myself go further.

I opened my eyes. "I love you, Morgan."

His eyes, deep and questioning, looked down at me, focused on my lips as they spoke, then moved to trace the curve of my brow, and the bone of my cheek, examining one part of my face and then another as if determined to memorize each feature individually. He was silent so long, and I couldn't read his expression. A cold anxiety gripped me. Finally, his eyes returned to mine.

"I love you, too, Georgia. I really do." My heart warmed as he said it, and I rolled toward him, but he pushed me away. "That's why I have to stop."

It felt like I'd forgotten to breathe, like my heart had skipped a beat. "I don't understand."

"We can't do this, Georgia. I love you too much to go any further. You'll hate yourself if you do, and you'll hate me for letting you."

"But, Morgan, if we love each other, then how can we just . . ."

He pulled himself away from me and lifted himself up to sit on the edge of the bed, groaning as if in real physical pain. "Georgia, you've got to go. I have to report to my ship in eight hours. I'm headed to the other side of the world. I'll probably never see you again. Not to mention the fact that I'm a fighter pilot. The chances of me surviving the war are slim. Nearly every guy I started out flying with is dead. This one night is all we'd ever have together. Tomorrow I'll be gone, and all you'll have to remember me by is a guilty conscience." He stood up and walked across the room, picked up a shirt from where he'd hung it on the back of a chair, and put it on. "I do love you, Georgia. I love you too much to let you betray yourself for a one-night stand."

I was flooded with relief. I understood. He looked so pained, so ashamed, but why wouldn't he? He thought I was another man's wife. I shouldn't have let either of us get so carried away. I should have stuck to my plan, told him the truth before ever doing so much as shake his hand.

"Morgan," I began, "you don't understand. I have to tell you something. In fact, that's why I came here in the first place. I'm not married, Morgan. My husband is dead. I should have told you before."

"I know, Georgia. I knew that from the first. Your friend Pamela told me," he said quietly. He stood up, towering over me with his shirt buttoned up tight and tucked evenly into the waist of his trousers.

Suddenly I saw myself the way he did. My discarded shoes lay piled next to the bed where I'd kicked them off. My skirt was wrinkled and hitched halfway up my thighs, and my blouse was completely open, showing my brassiere and the flesh that spilled from the top of it, mottled and reddened with fading passion and embarrassment at finding myself so exposed. I sat up and tried to smooth my hair with one hand while pulling the edges of my blouse together with the other, trying to cover myself. I was so ashamed. I looked exactly like what he'd said I was—a one-night stand after the night is over.

He could never love me. I should have known it from the first. I was Delia's daughter.

I slid my skirt back down below my knees. "I have to go," I said, looking down as I fastened the buttons on my blouse and tucked it tight inside my skirt. I couldn't look at him. "I'm sorry, Morgan. I should never have come here tonight. It was a mistake." I slipped on my shoes, then picked up the pocketbook I'd let drop to the floor when Morgan first pulled me into his room. Clutching it close to my breast like a shield, I reached for the doorknob. Morgan put his hand on my shoulder.

"Wait a minute," he said. "It's not what you think. Don't run off like this. Let's talk."

I pulled away from his grasp and opened the door. "There's nothing to talk about, Morgan. It's my fault. I have to go." I ran outside, stepping into the harsh shaft of lamplight that spilled through the door, beaming a wedge of light into the black night. The sound of my high heels hitting the pavement was loud in my ears, nearly drowning out the sound of Morgan's voice calling my name as he stood in the doorway. I listened hard as the distance between us lengthened and his shouts faded in the night, half-dreading, half-hoping to hear the sound of footsteps behind me, pursuing me, demanding an explanation, and offering another chance. But none came.

It couldn't work. You knew it, an inner voice said accusingly. *You knew it all along.*

❧ 25 ❧

Morgan

San Diego, California—May 1943

I'd set my alarm for five, but I didn't need it. I'd lain awake all night, thinking about Georgia. One minute I wished I'd run after her, and the next I wished I'd just followed my instincts, told her I loved her, too, made love to her then and there, and waited until morning to figure out if it had been right or not.

Fountain always used to say, "You know what your problem is, Morgan? You think too damn much. You got to let yourself live a little, son, while you still got life left in you."

Maybe he was right, but it was too late to do anything about it now. I was due to meet Mama at the all-night diner for breakfast in forty-five minutes. An hour after that I would have to tell her good-bye and report to the base, ready to ship out later in that day. For the next few hours the only thing that mattered was Mama. I had to perk up and put on a happy face. It might be another two years before I saw her again. Or I might never see her again. There was no way of knowing.

Until today I had been able to shove my imminent return to the battlefield into a shadowy, closed-off compartment of my mind. Now I had to face the truth.

When General Martin had transferred me back to the States, I hadn't wanted to go home. Now I didn't want to go back, but I knew I had to. There was no way out of it and no way to ignore it, not anymore. It was beyond my control. I needed help.

For the first time in a long time, I got down on my knees and prayed.

> *God, I don't know if this war was part of your plan or if we brought it on ourselves, but I know it's no surprise to you. I don't know if I'll make it home this time or not, but unless you've got a better idea, I'd like to come home in one piece—if not for me then at least for Mama. Watch out for her while I'm gone. And thank you, God, for Paul. He'll take care of her no matter what happens to me. Thank you that I don't have to worry about what will happen to her if I don't come back.*
>
> *And Georgia . . . I don't know what to say about her, God. When it comes to Georgia, I don't know if I should say I'm sorry for being weak or thank you for helping me to be strong. Just take care of her. Help her have a good life.*
>
> *Amen.*

I got to the diner a couple of minutes before Mama arrived and slid into a booth near the door. The waitress was yawning and took her time delivering the menus. I drummed my fingers on the table-top, looked out the window to see if Mama was coming around the corner, and wondered why anyone would decide to cover every booth and stool in a whole restaurant with upholstery that was the same color red as those hard candied apples they sold at county fair-grounds. It was too jarring a color for this early in the morning; just looking at it made me antsy. But, then, maybe that was the idea—to keep people pepped up so they'd eat, leave, and make room for more paying customers instead of putting up their feet and lingering over five-cent cups of coffee.

I was actually thinking of asking the waitress her opinion on the subject when I heard bells jangle as the door was pushed open and looked up to see Mama. I jumped out of my seat to give her a big hug and a smile. I wanted our last hour together to be happy. There was no point in allowing the gloom of impending farewell to spoil what might be our last meal together for a long time—or ever. We both understood the situation. It was pointless to dwell on it.

We settled ourselves back into the booth and took a look at the menu. I ordered three over-easy with bacon and two donuts. Mama got scrambled eggs and toast. The waitress filled our coffee cups and took the order back to the kitchen.

Pretend you're just going away for a little while, I told myself, *like when you went away to college.*

It worked. I started off asking Mama to fill me in on a little of Dillon's gossip, especially about Bud and Jolene Olinger's baby boy. Aunt Ruby, who was always in the know when it came to the details of Dillon's sordid and seamy underbelly, had hinted that the Olinger baby, who was reported to be only nine months old, was already walking. Ruby's intimation was that Jolene, who had shocked the town by entering into a May-December marriage with the gray-beard Bud, was already a few months in the family way before the wedding ceremony and the couple's subsequent extended honeymoon in Texas. I couldn't have asked Mama about it with Paul sitting there; there are some things a minister in a small town simply can't know about—or if he does know about them, he has to pretend that he doesn't.

Blushing and whispering, even though I told her she didn't have to keep her voice down—there was no one in the diner but the two of us—Mama confirmed the story. I laughed out loud. "Well, good old Bud! Who'd have thought it!"

Mama hushed me and drew her brows together disapprovingly,

but I could see her working to compress the smile that played on her lips. I teased her, and we talked some more, and for a few minutes it was just like the old days back in Dillon, but better because I was older and we could share stories and jokes in a way that wouldn't have been possible when I was still a boy. It was just like old times, but different because I was different and so was Mama. She was still my mother, but now she was my friend as well. It was nice.

Her eyes twinkled as she told me how she'd sweet-talked Mr. Cheevers, who'd run the filling station ever since I was a little kid, into selling her an extra gallon of gas beyond her ration so she could take Grandma on a birthday picnic at the lake.

"Mama the Black Marketer!" I laughed, and Mama joined me, but then I caught a glimpse of the clock on the wall and my heart sank. For a few minutes I'd forgotten that we were running on borrowed time. In fifteen minutes I'd have to go. Mama knew it, too.

Mama pushed her eggs from one side of her plate to the other; she'd hardly touched her breakfast. I dunked my donut into my coffee and took a bite, trying to buy some time while I figured out what I could say that would lighten the mood. Suddenly, without really thinking, I cleared my throat and blurted out, "Mama, have you seen Virginia Pratt lately?" I gave my donut another dunk into my cup, trying to act casual, but my mind was racing. Virginia Pratt? What made me ask about her? I'd sent her a letter just before I left for San Diego, but just that morning I'd decided to write another telling her I didn't think we had a future together and she should look for someone else. *I should have done it months ago,* I thought guiltily.

"Why no," Mama answered with a trace of surprise in her voice. "Not recently. I guess she's about ready to graduate, isn't she?"

"Yeah. Next month. She made salutatorian," I said and immediately wondered what in the world had made me volunteer that bit of information. Now, just when I was getting ready to break it off, Mama would get all kinds of crazy ideas about Virginia and me.

Just then a soggy piece of donut broke off and dropped onto my uniform, staining it with coffee. "Oh, damn it!" I said, plucking the mess off my shirt.

"Don't curse," Mama said primly and handed me her napkin so I could blot the coffee stain.

We might have taken a brief detour into the landscape of adult friendship, but she was still my mother. "Still trying to turn me into a gentleman, Mama?"

"No. Trying to remind you that you already *are* a gentleman." Frustrated by my inability to eradicate the coffee stain, Mama took the napkin from me, dipped it in her water glass and handed it back. "See if that works any better." It did.

Mama's nonchalant attitude wasn't fooling me. It didn't take two shakes for her to turn the conversation back to Virginia Pratt. Though the stain was all gone, I kept blotting my shirt with the wet napkin.

"She seems a sweet girl. Must be smart to stand second in her class. Always had nice manners, I remember." She paused, waiting for me to volunteer more information, and when I didn't, she cleared her throat and asked, "Anything you want to tell me?"

Not about Virginia, there wasn't.

But there were things I wanted to ask. So many things. I wanted to ask Mama about my feelings for Georgia. I wanted to ask her about everything, about girls and women, life and living, about love and lust, and how to tell one from the other. I wanted to ask how I came to be. Had she loved him like I loved Georgia? Like Georgia said she loved me? If so, where was he now? Where had he been all these years? If he loved her, how could he have left her? Left us? What kind of man does that to a woman he loves?

The look in Georgia's eyes last night—it was the same look I'd seen in Mama's face when I was a little boy and the clucking, self-satisfied wives of Dillon would whisper as we walked down the sidewalk, just loud enough so we could hear. A picture of Georgia flashed in my mind, of Georgia crouched on the bed, undone and suddenly small, refusing to look at me, clutching shirt buttons and shame to her breast, trying to cover herself and get away. She ran away, and I let her. What kind of man does that to the woman he loves? What kind of man was I?

I took a drink of coffee. "Virginia and I have talked about . . . you know, things. But she's awfully young. She wants to go to college. Maybe be a teacher. It'd be a shame if she didn't go while she has the chance and . . ."

What's wrong with me? This might be the last time I saw my mother on earth. I wanted to say at least one thing that was true before I left. Something. Where should I start?

I looked into her eyes. I didn't smile or pretend to smile. "Mama, I'm a pilot. You know the odds aren't good for me."

She bit her lip and whispered, "I know." For a moment I thought she was going to cry, but then she said, "So many times I've thought I should have insisted that you stay in college. Maybe I shouldn't have let you learn to fly in the first place."

"You couldn't have stopped me, Mama. No one could have. It's part of who I am." It was true. That was one thing I knew for certain. "When I joined up, all I thought about was flying, just me and the plane and the blue sky that doesn't end. I never really thought about *why* I would be flying." There it was again—that need to divide things up and shove them in separate boxes, to think only about the things I wanted to think about, the things I thought mattered. What I was starting to realize was that everything mattered. That was the difference between being a boy and a man: facing the truth and naming it.

"It's not that I didn't understand there was a war on and that I would be in it, but I really didn't know what war was. The newspapers clean it up and make it seem so simple and straight, but there's no color in those pictures. There's no spewing of red blood, or ravenous orange flames eating at tail sections, or blue-black ocean that sucks downed planes into the depths and closes over them. A battle reported in black and white is just an outline of the real thing."

"You've grown up fast, haven't you?" It was a question that, in another context, might have been flattering. As it was, it was just a statement of fact, one that seemed to make Mama a little sad.

"Eighteen months are like ten years when there's a war on," I said. "I thought I'd ship out, wrap a white scarf around my neck, shoot down a few Zeros from far enough away so I wouldn't have to see the pilots' faces, win a medal or two. Maybe dance with a few fast girls from the U.S.O. in my spare time." I couldn't help but smile because it had all been so true. Less than two years ago I'd been a baby, a wide-eyed kid who thought heroism was as bloodless and straightforward as a *Lone Ranger* script. When I hopped into the cockpit of my old Stearman trainer and took off for college, I had no idea what I was getting myself into. "I never pictured myself being afraid."

Mama eyes were glued to my face, but she didn't say anything. I couldn't tell what she was thinking.

"Mama, do you remember Mrs. Hutchinson from church?" Mrs. Hutchinson had been my fourth-grade Sunday school teacher, and Mama's and even Grandma's before that. "She wrote me a letter after I made lieutenant, congratulating me and saying how everybody was so proud to have a real live war hero come from Dillon."

Mama nodded. "Mrs. Hutchinson is right. Everybody in town is proud of you. You're Dillon's first pilot."

I shook my head. They were wrong. I could bear that, but I couldn't bear the idea that Mama would think I was something I wasn't. Even if it meant she'd think less of me, she had to know the truth. "Mama, I'm no hero. I just love to fly, that's all. When I climb into the cockpit and feel the engine hum, it's like feeling my own heart beating. And when I lift off from the runway and rise up toward the sun, it's like reaching out to touch the door of heaven."

And it was, every single time. Just for a moment. Just until I remembered that somehow, some time in the past, someone had decided to make flying a way to wage war. What kind of a man was I?

"As soon as I look down and see the airfield fading off in the distance, I'm afraid, because I know there's a good chance of me or one of my friends not making it back. With all my heart I want to turn back at that moment, but I keep the plane on course because I know I have to. Somebody has to."

"Morgan! I think maybe I let you read too many books when you were little." Mama's tone was lighthearted and teasing. My heart sank. I thought she was going to make a joke out of it, start trying to sweep the truth under the rug like we always did, her holding the broom and me lifting the edge of the carpet to make sure it was well covered and out of sight. But she didn't. Not this time.

"Morgan, books are the only places where people aren't afraid. Real people are scared every day. Some of them climb under a rock and hide, and others, the good ones like you, stuff their fears into a sack and do what they have to do. That may not be too courageous, but it's enough to get the job done, and it takes a lot of heart. So, you just let Mrs. Hutchinson send her letters, all right?" And she smiled, smiled all the way to her eyes. She meant it. She knew I was afraid. She'd known it all along.

I wished she'd said so before. I wished we could have learned to talk this way years ago, but at least we'd had this. It was a start.

"Mama, I've got to go."

She nodded and reached across the table and took my hand. "Morgan, how do you suppose that out of the whole world, I got the best young man on the planet as my son?"

I pulled her hand toward me and gave it a big kiss. "I'm glad you came, Mama."

"Nothing in the world could have kept me from it."

We hugged and said good-bye on the sidewalk. I held on to Mama for a long time, squeezing her as tight as I could. There were tears in her eyes and mine, but I didn't try to keep them back. I kissed her through my tears and said, "I love you, Mama."

In the end, that was what it all came down to. Neither of us, not Mama and not me, was as brave as we wished we were. Maybe no one was. We loved each other anyway. That was the one thing that always had been and always would be true.

A few hours later my gear was stowed beneath the cramped bunk that would be my quarters until we docked. I stood on the deck of a destroyer, watching the fast receding shadow of the California coastline and thinking about what Mama had said.

Sometimes you had to stuff your fears in a sack and do what you had to do. That might not be courage, but it was as close to it as I was going to get today.

The sea was getting rough, and the wind blew cold across the deck. I cupped my hands and blew into them trying to warm them, but it was no good. I shoved my hands in my pockets and lifted my head. The coastline was gone. The only thing I could see, front, behind, and on every side, was the swelling and cresting of the blue-black ocean tide.

PART THREE

PART THREE

26

Georgia

Chicago, Illinois—July 1944

"Georgia! Get in here! You've got to see this!"

"Coming!" I promised as I put the last two punch cups on the silver-plated serving tray and carried it into the living room.

"What do you think?" I looked up to see Pamela with her head tilted back, cheeks sucked in so the bones stood out, arms extended gracefully in a cover-girl pose, wearing a paper-plate hat covered with mounds of mismatched gift bows and tied under the chin with a garish lime green ribbon.

Pamela batted her eyes seductively and shook her head ever so slightly, making the pile of bows quiver. "Irresistible, aren't I?"

"Definitely," I said blandly as I set the tray on the coffee table. "I think you should wear that to church instead of a veil." At this the entire group—Pamela, Fanny, Donna Lee, and two more of our old friends from Avenger Field, Jeannie Billings, and Becky Teeters, who had shared Doris's bay—collapsed into gales of laughter. They laughed so hard they were literally crying.

Suspicious, I leaned down and sniffed one of the punch cups.

The ladylike pink liquid had a definite odor of grain alcohol. "Pam!" I scolded. "Did you spike the punch at your own bridal shower?"

Pamela, too choked with laughter to answer, just shook her head.

Donna Lee grinned and waved her hand above her head. "Of course she didn't! What kind of a bride would do that? It was me," Proud of herself even if her speech was a little slurred, she continued, "It's just a little Jack Daniels, Georgie . . . I mean, Georgia. I only put in half the bottle. Don't be such a party pooper."

Smiling, I bent down, picked up the tray, and started back toward the kitchen.

"Hey!" Pamela protested, "Where are you going with that? I'm thirsty!"

"I'll be right back," I promised. "Why don't you finish opening your presents? The big one in the corner is from me."

I left behind a wake of giggling protests and went back into the kitchen. Fran was standing at the sink, filling the coffeepot with water. "You read my mind," I said. "Definitely time for some coffee. Make it strong."

"Will do," Fran said as she put the pot on the stove and turned up the flame.

"Frannie, thanks for letting me have Pam's shower here. It was really nice of you, and they're all having such a good time. I'm sorry about the punch."

Fran shrugged off my apology. "What's to be sorry about? They're just girls kicking up their heels a little. There's nothing wrong with that. If it were up to me, I'd take the punch back in there and let them have at it. They're having such fun."

"Yes, but they won't be in the morning. Every one of those girls is due on the flight line tomorrow. Trust me. An airplane is no place to have a hangover. They may call me a party pooper today, but they'll thank me tomorrow.

"Anyway, thanks for letting me have them here. I thought about having the shower in Waukegan, but it would have been too hard for everyone to get to. As it was, it practically took an act of Congress to figure out how to get everybody to Chicago on the same day between assignments. If it weren't for you, I could never have pulled it off."

"Really, it was no trouble," Fran said as she washed cake crumbs off a plate. I picked up a dish towel and started drying. "Besides, I like your friends."

A shriek of delight erupted in the living room. Pamela's voice called out, "Oh! They are just beautiful! Oh, Georgia! You shouldn't have!"

Fran looked a question at me. "Towels," I reported. "Pink, and edged with eyelet lace. From Marshall Fields. Monogrammed."

Fran smiled. "Georgia, you always did know how to choose the perfect gift." She put down the plate she was holding and wiped her hands on a nearby towel.

"Come on. We can finish these later. Let's go back to the party."

The presents had been opened, the cake eaten, the coffee drunk, and the whisky buzz had worn off, but nobody wanted to leave. Fran didn't seem in a hurry to get rid of us, so we all stayed put. It was nice just to sit and talk. We talked about clothes we wanted but couldn't afford, movie stars we'd never met, shoes, men, face cream, and diets—the same subjects that came up anytime girlfriends got to gossiping. But, also, as it did anytime a group of pilots gathered, whether they be male or female, the conversation soon turned to flying.

All pilots enjoy hearing and telling war stories, but I think we WASP were even a little more eager in this regard. We really were doing something special, jobs that just a couple of years previously would have been utterly off-limits to women, and we were doing them as well as any man—sometimes even better. Originally we were only supposed to be assigned to ferry aircraft. But as time went by, the WASP were pulling all kinds of duty. Donna Lee and I were ferrying planes, though in just a few weeks I would get a new assignment. Pamela was a test pilot, taking up aircraft that had been recently repaired or rebuilt after accidents and making sure everything was in good working order. Sometimes it was and sometimes it wasn't, so test piloting could be particularly hazardous. After our graduation from Avenger, Fanny, who was the tallest and strongest of us, went to four-engine school and learned to fly the huge B-17 bombers that pilots affectionately nicknamed the "Big Friend."

We took as much pride in the accomplishments of our sister WASP, even those we'd never met, as we did in our own. Fanny told us about Dora Dougherty and Dorothea Johnson, two WASP who'd been trained to fly the newest class of very heavy bombers, the enormous B-29 Superfortress. The Superfortress had been rushed into production without the kind of thorough testing and modifications that its predecessors had received. Consequently, its engine had a nasty habit of overheating and catching fire even before takeoff. Understandably, pilots were not too enthusiastic about getting behind the wheel of the B-29.

"So," Fanny said, "some bright-eyed colonel gets the idea of teaching a couple of girls to fly that big monster and then take them around the country on a little dog-and-pony show. You know, to kind of show the boys what they were missing. Maybe tweak them on the nose a little for being afraid to fly a plane that two little girls were handling with no problem."

"Did it work?" Fran asked.

"You bet. One look at Dora and Dorothea and they were lining up around the block just waiting for a turn. They were not about to be shown up by a couple of girls. The girls didn't get to fly them for long, though. After a couple of days the brass called from Washington and pulled the plug on the whole thing because they said it wasn't right for them to be 'putting the big football players to shame.'" Fanny made a sympathetic "poor baby" face, and we all cracked up.

"Just like the words to the old song!" Donna launched into a lusty, if slightly off-key version of the WASP theme song, and every-body joined in.

Zoot suits and parachutes
And wings of silver, too.
He'll ferry planes
Like his mama used to do!

Becky and Jeannie were best friends and had some good stories of their own. They'd been stationed to a base in North Carolina and flew A-24s. They were assigned to tow targets back and forth across gunnery ranges, giving anti-aircraft artillery gunners a chance to im-prove their aim. "The gunners are supposed to aim at the targets, and, mostly, they hit them," Becky said. "But Jeannie had a real close call last week. Somebody aimed right at her!"

We gasped at this information, but Jeannie rolled her eyes. "They didn't aim at me. Not on purpose, anyway. Becky, if you're going to tell the story, then tell it right."

Becky looked offended and said, "Well, fine, then. You tell it."

"Fine. I will," Jeannie said, giving Becky a good-natured elbow in the ribs. "The gunnery officers are supposed to fire tracer bullets to show the gunners where to aim. So the other day I was flying through the pattern, and I hear this noise—Crack! Crack! Crack!—like something was smacking against the fuselage. I radioed down that I think they might be hitting me. Then the gunnery officer comes back and he says, yeah, they had a new guy on the range who thought he was supposed to shoot the tracers right at the plane!"

Jeannie started to laugh, and everybody else joined in. "Can you beat that?" she howled. "I can't imagine what he thought that big white target I was towing behind me was for. Maybe he thought I was flying around up there hauling my laundry behind me so it would dry faster!"

We laughed even harder, and Becky piped in proudly, "Yeah,

and when she landed there were five big bullet holes in the fuselage. Just about this far from where her head had been!" Becky held up her thumb and forefinger to show us exactly how many inches her best friend had been from danger.

Donna Lee whistled, impressed. "That was a close one!"

"Oh, that's nothing," Becky said. "Stuff like that happens all the time. Target towing is dangerous, but somebody has to do it. Otherwise, we'll never win this war and our boys will never get home." Becky had a husband stationed in France. He was in the artillery.

"Well," I said, trying to lighten the mood a little. "For some of us, the war is nearly over. Isn't that right, soon-to-be Mrs. MacAllister?" I turned to Pamela. "What do you think? Are you going to miss it? The three-hundred-mile hop that turns into a weeklong, cross-country marathon with no clean clothes to change into? The run-ins with crabby base commanders who hate all women, and especially women who fly airplanes? Coming in on final approach only to find that the landing gear sticks but nobody bothered to list that on the maintenance sheet?"

The girls laughed. We'd all been through that one.

"Are you sure you're willing to give all that up, just for a lifetime of eternal wedded bliss with the handsomest pilot in this man's army who also happens to worship the ground upon which your dainty feet walk?" I teased, fluttering my eyelashes. "Hmmm?"

Fanny chimed in sarcastically. "Gosh, Georgia! You make it sound like so much fun. Come on. You're not fooling anyone. You love every minute of it. Everybody knows you'd rather fly the dawn patrol over the Dakotas in the dead of winter than make love."

I rolled my eyes at Fanny. "Oh sure," I scoffed.

"Well, it's true," Fanny insisted. "You are the original career girl. You're the Rosalind Russell of the air—untouchable and all business. Every single pilot on the base has tried to date you—"

"And half the married ones!" Donna Lee interrupted, and the girls howled, but Fanny ignored them all and continued.

"And you give them all the brush-off. What's the matter with you? Don't you ever think about getting married again?"

The girls got a little quieter. They all knew about Roger, but they almost never mentioned him. Fanny had a habit of blurting things out sometimes. Probably the lingering effects of the punch weren't helping her to temper that trait. By this time Fanny realized she'd said the wrong thing. Donna Lee elbowed her, and Fanny mumbled an indistinct apology.

It was an awkward moment, and it was up to me to get us past it. "Well, I would think about it if I could find a beau as good-looking as Captain John MacAllister," I said brightly. "But, this isn't about me. It's about the bride elect. So, come on, Pamela. I demand an answer to my question. Will you miss it? Cold chow served on mess trays? Sleeping in a barracks with ten other girls? The adventure? The glamour? The predawn wake-up calls?"

Pamela lifted her shoulders toward her ears, took in a big, deep breath, and held it for a moment before exhaling dramatically and releasing her shoulders. "Yes."

The girls chuckled.

"It's true," Pam smiled, but her voice was wistful. "I will miss it. How could I not? But what can I do? I love John, and I want to be with him. It wasn't so bad before, when we were both assigned to Kansas. But he got this promotion, and it was just too good to pass up. But there's no assignment for me. And if he marries an activated WASP, they'll probably give the job to someone else. You know how the military feels about 'fraternization.'" She held up her fingers, making quotation-mark movements around the forbidden term. "It's a great opportunity for John. When we move to Alabama, he'll be in charge of the whole training program. We've already rented a house, just a mile from the base. John will be able to come home for lunch," she finished cheerfully.

"That will be nice," Fanny said, and Pamela nodded agreement. We were all quiet.

"Oh, well." Pamela shrugged nonchalantly. "But there is some good news. Did you hear? Georgia will be taking John's old job. She's going to Liberal, Kansas, to be a flight instructor."

The other girls murmured excited congratulations, and I happily accepted them. I'd always wanted to be an instructor; now I was finally going to get my chance. I'd only be teaching instrument instruction and navigation, but it was still exciting. I lifted my coffee cup in a toast. "Here's to John! I'd never have gotten the assignment if he hadn't recommended me. He's a great guy, Pammie," I said in all sincerity.

"Well, he'd never have recommended you if he didn't think you were the best pilot for the job, but, yes"—she sighed happily—"he is a great guy. I'm crazy in love with him. I must be. That's the only thing that would make me give up flying."

"But," I protested, "it's not like you're giving up flying. You're just giving up flying for the WASP. Once the war is over and there's enough fuel for private use, you'll be able to go up anytime you want. I thought your dad was going to buy you and John a little Piper Cub for a wedding present."

"He is," Pamela confirmed, "but, like you say, I'll have to wait until the war is over to be able to fly. Even Daddy won't be able to pull enough strings to keep me in fuel before gas rationing ends."

"Well, Pam might be temporarily grounded, but I think she's going to have lots of company before too long. The way things are looking, the WASP are going to get their wings clipped. Maybe sooner than you think." Donna Lee reached into the pocket of her jacket and pulled what looked like a newspaper clipping out of her pocket.

"Why is that?" Fran asked.

"There's been a lot of rumbling and grumbling from the male members of the flying fraternity lately. We're winning the war, ladies. We didn't lose as many pilots or aircraft as the generals in Washington thought we would. They don't need to build or deliver as many planes as they used to. And they don't need as many new pilots to fly those planes. Georgia and John were lucky to land those instructor's jobs because a lot of the training bases are being closed. And they are shutting down the Civil Aeronautics Administration training programs, too. What it all adds up to is a whole bunch of pilots without anything to do. Of course, the war isn't over yet. There is still plenty of fighting to do in the air, but even more on land. All those out-of-work civilian pilots are afraid they're going to be drafted and sent into combat. They'd much rather have our jobs, delivering planes stateside, than do bombing runs over Berlin. Or, worse yet, end up in Japan in the infantry.

"The civilian flyboys are starting to band together to put a bug in Washington's ear. And it couldn't come at a worse time—just when General Arnold and Jackie Cochran are trying to get Congress to militarize the WASP."

In a voice thick with bitterness, Pamela said. "And it's darned well about time! We should have been militarized from the first, with the same benefits and same pay they'd give to a man. We do the same job, and it's just as dangerous for us as it is for a man. If we have to pass the hat to bury one more girl . . ." Pamela muttered darkly. I knew she was thinking about Doris, but there had been many more funerals since then. Our safety record was comparable to that of male pilots, but flying was dangerous; there was no way around it. More than twenty WASP pilots had been killed since the program began. That year we lost a girl every month. We now had a permanent fund that was just to help with the final expenses of any girl who was killed in the line of duty.

"It's just not right!" Pamela declared.

Donna Lee rolled her eyes, acknowledging the obvious. "Well, don't count on it getting any better. A few months ago, *Life* magazine had a picture of a WASP on the cover and was telling the whole world that we were brave, patriotic, and self-sacrificing, a band of Yankee Doodle girls who could ferry pilots as well as any man."

"And so we are!" Becky yelled out gamely and turned to her friend, Jeannie. The two girls exchanged a self-congratulatory handshake.

"Not anymore you're not," Donna Lee said ominously. "Lately the papers have been starting to run all kinds of stories about the WASP, and they don't paint a very flattering picture."

"What do you mean?" I asked.

"I mean they are starting to print stories saying we are bad pilots, just a bunch of glamour pusses that are playing at being pilots. They're saying our accident and fatality rates are much higher than they are for men. They say that we're too expensive, that it costs much more to train us than it does men. They even say that our uniforms are expensive. One paper reported that the government spent five hundred and five dollars to outfit each WASP and that our uniforms are custom-tailored by a shop on Fifth Avenue."

Fanny laughed. "Our uniforms? They've got to be kidding! We didn't even have uniforms at first. Remember? When we first got to Sweetwater, we all had to drive into town to buy ourselves some dungarees so we'd have something comfortable to work in. We wore men's flying suits that were ten sizes too big for us and belted them just so they wouldn't drag on the ground. What are they talking about?"

"That's crazy," I said. "Where are they getting this stuff about us? None of that is true."

Donna Lee shook her head sagely. "Doesn't have to be true. They just have to make people believe it's true."

"But why would they want to do that?" Pamela asked.

"I told you," Donna Lee said impatiently. "Because they want our jobs. Here. Listen to this." She unfolded the newspaper clipping she'd pulled from her pocket. "It's a letter to the editor from a Mr. Emmett Foley." Donna cleared her throat and started reading.

Dear Sirs,

*I found your article about the women flying planes for the
Army very interesting. I couldn't agree with you more. It was
all very well and good for these girls to fly when we were short
of pilots, but now that there are plenty of men to do the work,
I think it is time the WASP hung up their wings and returned
to roles they are more naturally suited to fill. If the government
needs pilots, why not give the "washed out" cadets a chance to
take over these ferrying jobs? The men may not be cut out for
combat flying, but surely they could take over the job of ferrying, target towing and the other easier flying jobs that these
girls are doing.*

Very truly yours,
Emmett P. Foley

Donna Lee concluded and put down the clipping. The room was
silent as we took in the contents of the letter. I was the first to speak up.

"Well, that's just ridiculous! Emmett P. Foley doesn't know what
he's talking about. There's no such thing as an easy flying job. You've
got to know what you're doing. You've got to be able to handle all
kinds of aircraft, in all kinds of weather, and keep a cool head during
emergencies. I had two tires blow out on me last week, a frozen flap,
and an engine fire." I paused and took a sip of coffee. Then, peering
over the rim of the cup, I joked, "It was a slow week." Pamela grinned.

"Really, Donna Lee" Pam said, "you can't make me believe that
any sane person would rather see a washed-out male flight cadet,
somebody who couldn't even get through basic training, flying military aircraft than an experienced, fully trained female pilot. This
guy is just a crackpot. Nobody's going to listen to that nonsense."

Donna Lee shrugged again. "Maybe not. The militarization issue
is supposed to be coming up before Congress soon. Maybe it'll pass,
and then all this will blow over. But I wouldn't bet on it."

27

Georgia

Chicago, Illinois—July 1944

Donna Lee's speech kind of took the wind out of our sails, and the party broke up. The girls hugged each other, congratulated Pamela again and again, thanked Fran, and said their good nights.

Fran and I started picking up the empty cups and dirty plates and Pamela stayed behind to help with the washing up. She scraped plates and cleaned the countertops while Fran and I resumed our respective roles as dishwasher and wiper.

I hummed as I worked, thinking how good it was to be in the kitchen with my two best friends. Pamela and Fran had never met before tonight, but after washing dishes together for five minutes they were chatting like they'd known each other for years. Fran gave Pam her special recipe for chicken croquettes.

"Really," Fran assured the bride-to-be, "they couldn't be easier. You just need to make sure the oil is good and hot before you put them in the pan. Richard loves them."

"Hey," I interrupted, "where is that husband of yours, anyway? Did you stash him in a closet or something?"

"No, he took the girls to his mother's for dinner. They'll be back any minute. Anyway, Pam, try making those croquettes for your John. They are absolutely foolproof."

"Well, they'll have to be if I'm going to make them," Pam said doubtfully. "I think I'd rather be asked to parachute out of a burning plane at two thousand feet than to cook a dinner. I can't even scramble an egg."

"It's true," I confirmed. "Pamela was raised by her father's butler and her mother's cook. She's barely housebroken." Pamela looked at me and made a face.

"Don't listen to her, Pam. She's just giving you a hard time. All you need to be a good cook is willingness and practice. If you're smart enough to fly airplanes, you're certainly smart enough to keep house. Trust me," she said with a sigh, "there's not that much to it. You don't have to be a genius to be a wife. I'm the proof of that."

I glanced at Fran. She looked so sad. Now that I thought of it, she'd hardly said a word during the whole party, just listened to everyone's stories and kept the coffee cups filled.

"What are you talking about, Fran? Your home runs like clockwork. I've stayed here enough times to see all that you have to do around here, and it makes my head spin, but you make it look easy. You're smart. You've always been smart. I'd have never passed sophomore English if it wasn't for you, remember? Remember? With Sister Bernice? We had to read *Moby Dick,* and I didn't have a clue. I just thought it was a story about fishing."

Fran smiled a little but said dismissively, "Well, sure. But that was easy. I've always liked to read. But flying an airplane! When we were girls, I used to make fun of Georgia for wanting to be a pilot. Now, after hearing about all the things you girls have done and all the places you've been! My life is so dull by comparison. Anybody can cook dinner or scrub a bathtub, but flying! That's just . . ." Fran looked up, as though the word she was searching for might be floating above her head. "Well, that takes real talent."

"True, flying is not something you pick up overnight, but, really," Pamela said, "it's not that different from learning to cook. It takes desire and a lot of practice, but with enough of each—and maybe a dash of recklessness—you could learn to fly."

Fran exhaled a disbelieving puff of air and rolled her eyes.

I jumped into the conversation. "Pam is right. You could learn to fly if you really wanted to, Frannie." Pamela nodded confirmation, and suddenly I had an idea. "You know what? We could do it. When the war is over, I'll be reopening the flight school. You can be my first student!"

"Uh huh," Fran said sarcastically, "I'm just going to leave my husband and two daughters and run away to Waukegan so I can learn to fly airplanes?"

"Well, of course not," I retorted. "You can all come—you and Richard and the girls. You can stay at my house for a couple of weeks, like a vacation. Richard can take the kids out during the day while you're taking lessons. Then at night we can all have dinner together." The idea had popped into my head just that moment, but the more I thought about it, the better it seemed.

"Sounds like a good plan to me," Pamela added, but Fran dismissed us with a wave of her hand.

"Oh, you two are crazy," she said. "Richard would never go for that."

"Why not?" I asked, and just as I did, the knob on the back door rattled and Richard walked in carrying sleeping ten-month-old Emily in his arms. She was so beautiful—the image of her mother in miniature.

Then three-and-a-half-year-old Bonnie came in the door, dragging her favorite stuffed toy, a battered feline named Miss Kit, behind her. "Auntie Georgia! I din't know you was here!" she cried when she saw me. She dropped Miss Kit on the floor and ran into my arms. I scooped her up and covered her face with kisses while Fran greeted Richard and introduced him to Pamela.

"Mmm-wah!" I said to the child. "Yes, I'm here! I could never, ever come to Chicago without dropping in to see my favorite girl! How are you? Where have you been?"

"I was at Grandma's for dinner. Din't like it." Bonnie made a face. "Fish. Yech! She let me have cake instead. Two pieces!" She held up two fingers in triumph.

Fran shot Richard a look, and he said, "Well, what did you expect me to do about it? Grandmas are supposed to spoil their grandchildren. It's in their contract."

Smiling, Fran shook her head and reached out to take Bonnie from me. "You've just got Grandma wrapped around your little finger, don't you Bonnie-Boo? Come on, little girl. It's late. Let's get you to bed."

"That's all right," Richard said. "You stay and talk to your friends. I'll put the girls to bed."

"Are you sure you don't mind?" Fran asked.

"It's fine. I can do it."

Fran kissed the girls and then Richard. "Thanks."

"My pleasure," he said. "Come on, Bonnie. Let's get your pajamas on." Bonnie protested that she wanted to stay at the party. But when I promised to send her a postcard from Kansas for her collection—I sent her cards from every new city I visited, and she kept them all pinned to her bedroom wall—she went off without any fuss.

"Good night, Bonnie."

"Good night, Auntie Georgia."

"Oh! Richard! I almost forgot. After the war, I'm going to teach your wife to fly airplanes. Okay?"

"Okay," Richard said as he ushered Bonnie out of the kitchen.

"Ha. Ha. Very funny, Richard. Like I'd be able to learn how to fly." Fran said as she turned back to the sink and started washing dishes again.

"Well, why not?" Richard responded, pausing at the doorway.

"If Georgia can do it, how hard can it be?" He winked at me. "Seriously, hon. If you want to learn how to fly, then go ahead and do it."

"Really?" Fran asked, her voice suddenly bright with excitement. She left the dishes and walked up to him.

He kissed her on the top of the head. "Sure. Why not?" He picked up Bonnie and headed for her bedroom. "But, Georgia, about this flying school of yours," he called over his shoulder as he went, "I expect to get the brother-in-law discount."

"You've got it, Rich. Good night!"

"Good night, Georgia. Nice meeting you, Pam."

"Likewise!" Pam called after him, and then turned to Fran. "That is one swell guy you've got there, Fran. What a sweetheart! I hope John and I will be as happy as you two. Two kids, and you still seem so in love."

"We have our moments, any couple does, but yes . . ." Fran sighed and turned back to the sink, plunging her hands into the soapy water. Pam and I returned to our posts as scraper and dryer. "I love Richard as much as the day I married him. More. I'm sure it will be the same for you. That is, if he's even one-half the dreamboat that Georgia says he is."

"He is!" I promised. Pamela rolled her eyes at me but couldn't keep the smile from her face.

"He is pretty special," she admitted as she picked up a sponge and started wiping down the countertops. "Georgia was actually the one who introduced us."

"I met John when I was delivering some new trainers to Liberal, Kansas, and I thought they'd be perfect for each other. So I called in sick for my next Kansas delivery and asked Pam to fill in. She and John had dinner, and the next thing I knew, she put in for a transfer to Liberal and I was shopping for a bridesmaid's dress."

Pamela said, "And the rest, as they say, is history. Or it will be in two more months. And speaking of love and romance, what about you, Georgia? Any swains on the horizon?"

I shot her a "mind your own business" look and said, "None worth mentioning, Miss Matchmaker."

Pam held up her hands in surrender. "Sheesh! You don't have to get so snippy. I was just asking." She laid a tea towel on the edge of the sink to dry.

"Now that we've finished cleaning up, what do you say we use up whatever's left of the whisky that Donna Lee poured into the punch? Where'd you stash the bottle?" Pamela started opening cupboards until she found the bottle hidden behind a loaf of bread and a jar of sweet pickles. She pulled it out of the cupboard and held it out.

"Here we are! What do you say, ladies? Anybody besides me want a nightcap?"

"Fran?" I asked.

Fran shrugged. "Sure. Why not?"

"That's the spirit! Georgia, find me some glasses."

The glasses found, Pam poured a generous shot of amber whiskey into each.

"Wait a minute," Fran said. "We've got to have a toast. Let me think. I know! To love!" She raised her glass. "And to brides—past, present, and future."

We clinked our glasses together and took a drink. Fran started coughing.

"Good, isn't it?" Pamela said in a hoarse voice. "You all right?" Fran nodded and tried to catch her breath. I pounded her on the back.

"Hey, Georgia," Pam said, as though she'd innocently forgotten my earlier warning to butt out of my personal life. "Remember, that cute lieutenant we met at Avenger? The only real emergency landing in the history of Avenger Field? What was his name?" She winced her face into a mocking model of concentration. "Glennon! That's it! Morgan Glennon. He was a cutie. Whatever happened to him?" She looked at me innocently over the rim of her glass as she took another sip.

"Pam, knock it off already. Just give me a break, will you?"

"Well, I was just wondering. He seemed like a nice guy, and he sure liked you. Did you ever see him again?"

I sighed. "Not that it's any of your business, but yes. I saw him one other time. We had dinner. He shipped out the next day, and I haven't heard from him since."

"Really?" Pam asked a little surprised. "Where'd they send him?"

"I have no idea," I lied. "Somewhere in the Pacific."

28

Morgan

New Guinea—July 1944

"Good morning, gentlemen!" Major Hatch boomed as he strode into the briefing room. We jumped to our feet.

"At ease," he said.

Chairs scuffled and squeaked amid a murmur of quiet laughter and commentary as the pilots of McDonald's 475th Flying Squadron regained their seats. When the room was quiet, the major cleared his throat and looked at his clipboard.

"Just a few announcements. Things are looking pretty quiet today, but there have been reports of enemy activity in the area. We're sending some of you out to do a little recon. Lieutenants Glebe, Glennon, and Sundell, have your men ready to go immediately after we finish. Nash and Grisholm, you and your men will be heading over the Jefman Island."

The major squinted at the clipboard and smiled. "Let's see. For all you bookworms, I've got a note here from the morale officer. We have recently received a complete set of the *Hardy Boys Mystery* series, a donation from the Ladies Benevolent Committee of the First

Presbyterian Church of Warren, Ohio, which is the hometown of our own Airman William Jennings." A wave of laughter swelled in the room as the major nodded to acknowledge Airman Jennings, the newest and youngest pilot of the 475th, who sat blushing on the front row.

A taunting voice from the back of the room yelled out, "What? They didn't send any *Nancy Drew*?" and drew a fresh rumble of convivial mirth.

"All right. All right, you clowns. Settle down. And Jennings," the major said to the embarrassed airman, "when you write home, please thank your mother and the ladies of the church for their generous donation. And let them know that Collingsworth back there would appreciate it if they could send some copies of *Nancy Drew* as soon as possible." Hatch smirked and waited a minute as the jokester, Collingsworth, endured a round of raucous whistles and catcalls.

"Also!" he boomed again, in a voice that demanded and received the full attention of the squadron, "we will be entertaining a special guest for the next few days. Mr. Charles A. Lindbergh." As soon as he said this, the room started buzzing with a ripple of whispered comments. Keeping his eyes on the clipboard, Major Hatch raised his hand to demand quiet and continued reading.

"In addition to being a retired colonel in the Army Air Corps, Mr. Lindbergh was the first man to fly across the Atlantic Ocean and holds countless other records and firsts in aviation. He has been making a tour of bases in the Pacific in his capacity as a civilian technical assistant. He will be accorded officer's privileges. However, you will refer to him as Mr. Lindbergh. He will be here for the next few days, to give you gentlemen some valuable instruction and insights on flying the P-38."

The murmuring resumed, but this time murmurs were liberally sprinkled with griping. Next to me, an airman whispered to his buddy, "He's going to tell *us* how to fly the P-38 better? I've got one hundred and sixty hours in my plane so some old codger who used to fly biplanes in the olden days is going to tell me how to fly my aircraft? What's he going to tell me about my ship that I don't already know. He must be forty years old!" The major shouted the men back to order.

"Hey! Listen up!" The men settled back down. "As I was saying, Mr. Lindbergh will be speaking to us about this subject of vital interest in this room tomorrow at nineteen hundred hours. I have no doubt that you will all give him your complete attention and utmost respect. Your attendance is mandatory." The room was silent as the major looked around the room, scanning the faces of the crowd to make sure he had been understood. He was.

"Thank you, gentlemen. That is all." Hatch lowered his clipboard. The room erupted with the sound of chairs scraping on floors as the squadron rose respectfully to their feet again, but the second the major was out of earshot, the gripe session resumed.

"So whose bright idea do you think it was to bring some old codger in to lecture us on the latest in aviation technology? What a waste of time!"

"Yeah. What's Lindbergh supposed to know about aerial warfare that we don't? When's the last time he was in a dogfight?"

"He's got some nerve coming here after all that America First business, traipsing around the country and going on the radio to tell everybody we should stay out of the war because if we didn't, we'd get our butts kicked by the Germans!"

"You got that right! Why should I listen to some guy who thought the Krauts were better pilots than the boys in his own country? You know, he lived over there for a while, too. The German government even gave him some kind of medal. Whose side is he on, anyway?"

"Yeah. My old man said that Lindbergh was just a coward, and that's why he wanted to stay out of the war."

The rumble of complaints continued. Somebody finally said, "What do you think, Morgan?"

I shrugged. "I don't know. Maybe he's got something worth saying and maybe not. But since it's a mandatory meeting, my opinion doesn't matter a whole lot one way or the other. I figure I'll give him a chance. The man flew across the ocean alone, with no radio, in a plane that, today, you and I wouldn't want to rely on to get us to Port Mooresby and back. And he did it after he'd seen scores of other pilots die trying to do the same thing. Whatever he is, he's no coward. And I'll bet half of you decided to become pilots because of Lindbergh. I know I did."

The guys were quiet. Maybe they were remembering sitting in a darkened theater as they watched the Movietone newsreel of a small, lonely plane with *Spirit of St. Louis* emblazoned on the nose, loaded so heavy with gasoline that it bounced as it lumbered down the runway, lifting unsteadily from the ground, barely clearing the telephone wires before flying off to a future that was very uncertain at the time. Maybe they remembered the anxious waiting for word of the young flier's fate or reading Will Rogers' column while they waited: "No attempt at jokes today. A . . . slim, tall, bashful, smiling American boy is somewhere over the Atlantic Ocean, where no lone human being has ever ventured before. He is being prayed for to every kind of Supreme Being that has a following. If he is lost, it will be the most universally regretted loss we've ever had." Maybe after reading that, they'd knelt down next to their beds that night and asked God to take care of Charles Lindbergh. Maybe they remembered the conclusion of those nail-biting thirty-three-and-a-half-hours, lying on their stomachs in front of the radio with chins resting in their hands as they stared at the glowing dial of the Zenith and heard the ecstatic reporters telling the world that the Lone Eagle had landed, or the solemn conversations of grown-ups as they discussed the wonder of it and how the world would never be the same, or seeing the morning editions with a three-banner headline trumpeting "Lindbergh Does It!"

Maybe they'd even gotten to see him in person as he rode through the streets of New York City, sitting tall in the back of an open car, showered by ticker tape and adulation. Maybe they had been part of the crowds that came to greet "Lucky Lindy" during his eighty-two-city victory tour, sitting on a strong pair of adult shoulders so they could catch a glimpse of their hero in the middle of the throng. Or maybe, like me, they'd actually been lucky enough to meet him in person, even if it was only for a few minutes.

But one thing was certain, in one way or another, every pilot in that room was connected to Charles Lindbergh. He'd filled our dreams and our imaginations and inspired us with visions of what a man could achieve if he was willing to put everything on the line. He might be against the war. He might be over the hill, but he was still the Lone Eagle, the hero we'd all dreamed about when we were kids, and in a few hours we would be sitting in the same room with him.

We stood there with our hands in our pockets, the atmosphere silent and thick with memory until finally one of the guys blew out a long, low whistle and said what we were all thinking. "Damn! Can you believe it? Lindbergh is coming here! Ain't that something?"

It sure was.

My wing had to fly recon that day, so I wasn't around when Lindbergh landed, but by the time we returned from our mission, the base was buzzing with news. Lindbergh had actually flown a mission to Jefman Island. They didn't see any action on the island, but on the return trip they had shot up a few Japanese barges. Jefman had uneven terrain, which made good cover for the boats. Spotting a barge hidden between two hills near the coastline, Lindbergh skimmed over the top of the first ridge, clearing it by only a dozen feet, strafed the unfortunate enemy vessel, and then banked hard left to clear the other hill, all at 250 miles per hour, leaving a burning barge in his wake. It was an impressive performance, and before long everybody was talking about it. Clearly, the old boy still had it.

The next day I had a chance to see him in action for myself. This late in the war, with Japanese resources dwindling rapidly and the battle for air superiority going so well that we rarely faced much opposition, the higher-ups had decided to start loading our P-38s with thousand-pound bombs, trying to put some extra pressure on the enemy.

Our mission that day was to fly to Noemfoor Island, drop our bombs, and get home, engaging in a few strafing runs along the way. This was only the second bombing mission for the 475th and my first, so I was a little anxious to begin with. When I was informed that Mr. Lindbergh would be flying with us, that feeling intensified. I think the other guys felt the same.

He was waiting in the ready room when we arrived. I stepped forward and introduced my men.

"Nice to meet you," Lindbergh said. "Since we're going to be flying together, maybe you'll want to drop the mister. Call me Charlie." His casual manner put everyone at ease.

"Thanks, that'll be fine. Glad to have you with us. I'm the section leader, Lieutenant Glennon. Morgan Glennon." His smile faded, his eyes widened slightly, and he looked at me without saying anything. The silence was awkward.

I cleared my throat. "You probably don't remember, but we've met before. It was in Oklahoma City during your victory tour. I was only about four years old. My grandparents drove all the way over from the panhandle, where I'm from, just so I could see you. Grandpa pushed us all the way to the front of the crowd. You actually waved me forward and talked to me for a while. You even let me climb into the cockpit of the *Spirit of St. Louis,* and then you autographed a picture for me." Lindbergh was still quiet, looking at me, and now the men were looking at me, too.

I didn't know what else to do, so I laughed uneasily and said, "If I hadn't already been set on becoming a pilot, that would have clinched the deal for sure. I still have the picture. Probably you did the same thing at every stop, picked out some lucky kid to talk with, but it meant the world to me." Lindbergh smiled, but said nothing. I cleared my throat and shrugged. "Like I said, you probably don't remember it, but I sure do."

He spoke, and when he did, his voice was a little hoarse. "Actually, I remember that day very well. It's nice to see you again, Morgan." He shook my hand with a firm grip. I felt stupid. I was sure I'd just made the biggest fool of myself, going on and on like some star-struck fan, but Lindbergh was gracious about it.

"Well," I said sheepishly, "it's an honor to have you flying with us today, sir." He gave me a look. "I mean, Charlie. I'll be on your wing. We'll be coming in right behind a bunch of A-20s, trying to finish off any targets they miss. On the way home, we'll do some barge hunting. This is our first bombing run, so I hope we don't embarrass ourselves too much."

"Same here," Lindbergh said modestly.

"All right, then," I said, nodding to my crew. "If you're ready, gentlemen? Let's hit the trail."

The day was fine and bright, but there was a wind coming out of the east. We were covering a dozen A-20 bombers. They buzzed into Noemfoor like a pack of clumsy, fat bumblebees, dropping their loads and inflicting serious damage, leaving the enemy runway that was their target cratered and useless.

Our targets were the hangars next to the airstrip. We circled above, waiting for the smoke from the A-20 bombs to clear so we could see the target. Jessup went in first, but he miscalculated, and his load dropped into the jungle, far from the mark. Garrison, was next and he didn't fare any better. There was a lot of cursing traveling back and forth over the airways. I broke in and tried to settle things down.

"All right, guys, cut the chatter. You both waited too long to release. Garrison, you've to get in there lower and then power out quick. You'll get it next time," I assured them, though I was as frustrated by their performance as they were. If none of us hit our targets, it would mean a whole six-hour mission wasted, not to mention that we'd look like a bunch of rookies in front of one of the greatest pilots of all time, who would undoubtedly report our incompetence to the brass. "All right, Charlie, you're next."

"Roger," Lindbergh answered calmly, then rolled off the edge of the formation, dove down to twenty-five hundred feet, dropped his bomb, and pulled out of the dive before the thousand-pounder's ten-second delay was completed. The resultant explosion was furious and directly on target. The radio chatter picked up again as the men whooped in excitement and shouted encouragement to our guest. I was impressed. Lindbergh's run had been the picture of accuracy and coolheaded piloting. Watching him showed me where the other boys had gone wrong—at least, I hoped it had. I was next.

Taking a page from Lindbergh's book, I peeled off from the rest of the wing, evening out over the target and coming in low. There was an intact hangar right next to the burning one that Lindbergh had hit. That was my target, and it was coming up fast. I let my bomb fly a split second before I thought I should, and then pulled up out of the dive as hard as I could to get clear of the percussion that would follow the blast. Ten seconds later the hangar exploded into a ball of flame. A direct hit! Lindbergh had been right. In these windy conditions, you had to release just a little early to compensate. The boys learned from his example, and three out of the four of the remaining bombs were delivered in the target area.

"All right, boys, that was a good day's work," I called over the radio. "Nice job, everyone, especially for a first try. Let's buzz Jefman on the way home and see if we can't find ourselves a few boats to strafe."

We'd been flying for hours, but the boys were running on adrenaline, excited over the success of the mission. They responded with a chorus of enthusiastic whoops. I smiled under my mask, pleased that everything had gone so well, but I quickly put a lid on the celebration.

"All right. Can the chatter. We haven't seen any Jap fighters out here for a while, but that doesn't mean we won't today. Keep your eyes open and your heads in the game." We hadn't faced any real enemy opposition for weeks, but I wasn't going to get complacent. No matter how well things were going, the memory of my final flight with Walker, Campezzio, and Holman was never far from my mind. It was my job to keep the men focused and get them home alive.

By the time we got to Jefman Island, most of the boys were running low on fuel. We saw six boats below but only had time to attack before Jessup radioed in that he was running low on gas. "I think I'd better head back to base, Lieutenant, or I might end up swimming home."

The rest of the men confirmed that they, too, were low on fuel, so I gave them permission to head for home. I was ready to go as well, but Lindbergh said, "I've still plenty of gas, Lieutenant. Mind if I stick around and see if I can't take out a couple more of those barges?"

I looked down at my fuel gauge. I wouldn't have minded heading back to base, but I still had enough gas for a few more minutes. No matter how good a pilot Lindbergh was, there was no way I was going to leave him out here alone. Nor did I want him to think that we were the kind of outfit that leaves a job half done. "That's fine. Jessup, you lead the boys back to base. Charlie and I will be right behind you," I said.

There was a moment's hesitation before Jessup answered, "Roger. See you at home, Lieutenant." I knew he was questioning the wisdom of my decision. Frankly, so was I, but I figured I still had fifteen minutes' worth of gas before I'd be in trouble.

The rest of the boys headed back to the base while Lindbergh and I circled back over the island. It was worth the trip. Between us, we picked off three of the four remaining enemy boats. The rumors had been true. Lindbergh might be forty-three, which in pilot years is ancient, but he still had his stuff. It was everything I could do to keep up with him, but I did.

This has got to be some kind of dream, I thought. *I can't believe I'm Charles Lindbergh's wingman.*

We made a couple more passes over the island, and I kind of forgot about the time, but reality set in when I finally thought to check my fuel gauge. There was barely enough fuel to make it back to base. How could I have been so careless? If any of my guys had pulled a stunt like that, I'd have chewed them up one side and down the other.

I called Lindbergh on my radio. "Hey, Charlie," I said nervously. "I've got myself into a little bit of a situation here. My gas is running low. I'm not sure I can make it."

Lindbergh's voice was calm on the other end. "Don't worry, Morgan. I'll be with you the whole time. We're both going to get back. Try reducing your rpm and lean out your fuel mixture and throttle back a little. It'll get you some extra mileage."

"All right," I answered doubtfully. I didn't quite see how this would help, but I wasn't in a position to argue at that point, so I did as he asked.

We turned our ships around and flew back to the base. Lindbergh was by my side for the whole trip, and though we didn't talk much, I felt more confident knowing he was there. At least if I had to bail out, he'd be able to report my position to the rescue planes. But as we got closer to home, I could see he was right. My gas was being consumed at a much slower rate. I was going to make it after all.

When we landed I still had fuel left in my tank, but not much. Lindbergh still had seventy gallons to spare. Walking to the briefing room, I shook his hand. "Thanks a million, Charlie. I don't know exactly what you did or why it worked, but I'd have been in real trouble if you hadn't helped me out up there."

"It's just a little trick I learned years ago," he said modestly. "That's what I'm going to speak about during my talk tonight. In fact, I'd appreciate it if you'd come and tell the rest of the men about how it worked for you today. Seeing is believing, after all."

"Sure," I said. "I'll be there."

It was only quarter to seven, but the recreation hall was packed. Every seat was taken, and the walls were ringed with latecomers relegated to standing room. I pushed my way to the front of the room and found a place to stand near a side door where I thought I might catch a little bit of a breeze, but it didn't help much. The room was stuffy with the heat of closely packed bodies and buzzing with conversation. Somebody had set up a small platform and a blackboard near the front of the hall. At precisely seven o'clock, the commander of the 475th, Colonel MacDonald, mounted the platform. MacDonald was a good leader, well liked and, more importantly, well respected by his men. When he spoke, the room was silent.

"Good evening, gentlemen. It's hot in here, and I don't want to keep you any longer than necessary, so I'll get right to the point. As you know, Mr. Charles Lindbergh has been visiting with us for the last couple of days. He has come up with a few techniques for increasing the range on the P-38, and I asked him to share those with you this evening. Mr. Lindbergh?" Colonel MacDonald nodded to Lindbergh and took his seat as the famous Lone Eagle stepped forward.

"Thank you, Colonel. I've only been here two days, but I've already had a chance to see the 475th in action, and it's clear to me that you are as fine a group of pilots as I've ever seen. Thank you for the privilege of flying with you, gentlemen. I've already learned a lot from you.

"As Colonel MacDonald said, over the years I've developed a few fuel-saving techniques that, if applied to the P-38, could stretch your range by as much as four hundred miles." Lindbergh took a piece of chalk and started making notes on the blackboard. He explained that by reducing our rpm from twenty-two hundred to sixteen hundred, setting the fuel mixture to auto-lean, and slightly increasing the manifold pressure, a P-38 could stay aloft for as much as nine hours instead of the current six to six and a half. Putting down the chalk and turning to face his audience, Lindbergh concluded, "Obviously, this additional flight time could allow your planes to show up in places the enemy would never expect you, giving you the advantage of surprise."

The room was dead silent as the men tried to take this in, but I could tell by the looks on their faces that they weren't convinced. I took a step forward and raised my hand. "Mr. Lindbergh, do you mind if I say something?" He nodded his permission, and the guys all turned to look at me.

"Mr. Lindbergh is right about this. During our mission today, I found myself a little short on fuel and a long way from home. But Mr. Lindbergh was with me, and I tried out the techniques he's outlined tonight. I landed safely with gas to spare."

The murmuring resumed, the tones not quite as skeptical as before. Lindbergh was right. The boys were more convinced by evidence that came from one of their own. Still, not everyone was sold on Lindbergh's plan.

An airman in the fifth row grumbled, "Have you ever spent nine hours in the cockpit of a P-38? There isn't enough room in there to change your mind. By the time we land we'll be so cramped up they'll have to pry us out with a crowbar." The crowd rumbled their agreement.

Another voice called out, "And what about the mechanical wear and tear of flying such long missions? You'll grind the engines down if you overwork them like that." The noise level increased as more men voiced their doubts.

Lindbergh held up one hand, asking for quiet, and the guys settled down a bit. "You're right, a nine-hour mission is going to be hard on you and your aircraft. If surprising the enemy, winning this war, and getting you all home to your families as soon as possible weren't so important, I'd never even dream of asking you to do such a thing. I've spent a lot of time in the cockpit of the P-38. Nothing like you men, of course, but you're right. A pilot feels and looks a lot like a pretzel after a long mission. But as far as the engines, I've been working with the aircraft engineers for quite some time now, and I can tell you one thing. These are military engines, and they are designed to take a lot of punishment. So punish them. I promise you, they can take it.

"Just one more thing. If any of you feel uncertain about employing the techniques I've outlined here tonight, you shouldn't use them. You are the captains of your own ships. You have to make the decision for yourself. After all, you know more about flying your planes than I do."

The room was quiet when he finished. Dismissed, their faces were serious as they discussed the evening's events among themselves and left the hall. I was getting ready to leave myself when Lindbergh called me over.

"Thanks, Morgan. I don't know how it went over with the men, but I appreciate your help."

"Don't mention it. I was only telling them the truth. I'd have been in big trouble out there today without your help."

Lindbergh smiled. "But if I hadn't shown up, you wouldn't have been out there running down your fuel in the first place."

"It was well worth it to inflict a little more damage on the enemy. Every mission like that helps us wrap up the war that much sooner. Give the boys a little time to think about what you said. They'll see you're right. They're good men."

Lindbergh nodded, but his face revealed his doubts. "Time will tell," he said before changing the subject. "I was wondering if I couldn't buy you a beer. I've got a meeting right now, but maybe to-morrow night? There's something I wanted to talk to you about."

"Sure," I said. "That would be fine."

"Good. I'm going out on another mission in the morning, but I'll drop by your quarters around nineteen hundred and then we can walk over to the officers' club."

"See you then." We shook hands, and I walked out of the hall, flattered and more than a little amazed to think that Charles A. Lindbergh, the Lone Eagle, the hero whose picture still hung on the wall of my childhood bedroom, wanted to discuss something with me. I was trying my best to be cool about the whole thing, but it was no use. As soon as I was out of sight of the recreation hall, I broke into a run and started composing a letter in my head. Mama would never believe this!

❧ 29 ❧

Morgan

New Guinea—July 1944

Lindbergh stuck his head in the door. "Mind if I come in?" he asked and stepped inside without waiting for an answer. With temperatures in the nineties and humidity levels to match, doors in New Guinea are rarely closed.

"Good to see you," I said and shook his hand quickly before returning to the task of putting on a clean shirt. That was another challenge of living in the tropics; I changed my shirt about three times a day. I nodded toward a desk chair, and Lindbergh took a seat. "How did everything go today? Good mission?" I asked, making conversation while I hurried to get dressed.

"Yes. We saw a little action," he said casually.

"No kidding? We haven't seen hide nor hair of the Japs for a couple of weeks. What happened?"

"It wasn't much, just a Japanese Sonia. There were a couple of P-38s after him, but they'd run out of ammunition. We surprised him. There were four of us. I'm sure he knew he was done for, so he came right at me, hoping to take somebody with him, I suppose. I fired and pulled up at the last second, but he was hit and went into a dive."

His manner was so modest, so relaxed, that I wasn't quite sure I understood him. "So you got him? You took out a Japanese plane?"

"I had to." He shrugged. "It was self-defense."

I couldn't stop myself from grinning. Getting a kill in combat— at his age! No one on earth could convince me that the tall, middle-aged man sitting in my room wasn't the greatest pilot the world had ever seen or would ever see. "Self-defense or no," I said, buttoning the top button of my shirt, "it was still a pretty good day's work. Congratulations. I'm buying the beer." I started toward the door, but Lindbergh kept his seat.

"Morgan, hold on a minute. There's something I want to talk to you about. It's personal, so I'd rather we talked here than in the officers' club, where we might be overheard."

I was surprised. What sort of personal matter could Lindbergh have to discuss with me? "All right," I said and pulled up another chair. He was nervous. His eyes darted around the room, finally coming to rest on the quilt that covered my bed, on the dream quilt Mama had given me when I left for the service. Lindbergh seemed fascinated by it.

"My mother made that, back in Oklahoma." I scooted my chair out of the way so he could see it more easily. "Mama is more artist than seamstress. She's never been in a plane, not yet, anyway—I'm going to take her the second I get home. I don't know how she knew it, but this is exactly how our hometown looks from the air. There is the river," I said, pointing to a winding skein of silver embroidery that cut through the fields, "and all those different squares of yellow and gold are just exactly how the wheat fields look right before harvest. And down there is our farm. The silhouetted figures are Mama and me, when I was a kid."

I lifted my hand, drawing his eye to the upper right-hand corner of the quilt. "And see? Over here she's put the airplane wing with the scarf fluttering out, like the pilot is looking down at the people on the ground and waving back at them. Of course, she doesn't show a face, but the pilot is—"

"Me," he interrupted. Finally looking at me, his gaze piercing and serious, he said, "Morgan, I'm the pilot in that plane. The face you can't see is mine."

I didn't understand what he was getting at, not at first. And even as his meaning became clearer in my mind, understanding his words was one thing; believing them was another.

I looked at him, remembering that day in Oklahoma City so many years before, when I was a boy, practically vibrating with excitement at the prospect of seeing my hero in person. Even if I had only caught a glimpse of him over the heads of the throng, just like the thousand other kids in the crowd, I would have remembered it for the rest of my life. Just like those other thousand kids. That would have been enough. But when he picked me out of the crowd, leaned down to my eye level, shook my hand, and said, "It's nice to meet you, Morgan," as seriously as he'd been talking to a grown-up, I was overjoyed. But it never occurred to me, not until this moment, to wonder why I was the lucky one, why Lindbergh had plucked me, ripe and ready to believe, out of the sea of devotees.

I remember now that we stayed after the rest of the crowd had dispersed. Where did we wait? Did someone shuttle Papaw, Grandma, and me to a back room so the reporters and hangers-on wouldn't notice us? I don't know. I don't remember how that was accomplished, all I remember was a big hand boosting me up into the cockpit of the *Spirit of St. Louis,* sitting in the pilot's seat while Lindbergh carefully explained the function of each control, dial, and indicator as if I would understand exactly what they were for. And I remember feeling as if I did. Four years old. If you had asked me then and there to taxi down the runway and take the *Spirit* for a spin, I would have said, "Sure," and started going through my preflight checklist. No one had ever hurt me or lied to me. Not yet. At that moment, in the belief, bravado, and innocence of a child, I was certain I could do anything. That was a long time ago.

Lindbergh was looking at me, waiting and wary.

"When you said you remembered meeting me in Oklahoma City, you were telling the truth."

"Yes," he said quietly, and he looked at the ground, his eyes avoiding mine. "That was the first time I met you, the only time— until now. I'd only learned you existed a couple of days before.

"I worked out a plan to disappear on my way to Oklahoma City. I'd tell everybody I'd had mechanical problems, then land in Dillon after dark, hide the *Spirit* in an abandoned barn, and walk over to the farm to see your mother. I missed her so much. It had been so long."

"Five years. That's how long it must have been if you didn't know about me. I guess you couldn't have missed her that much." I couldn't keep the bitter edge from my voice. He looked up as I spoke, and his eyes were flat and gray, the spark gone from them. Was that how he looked when someone hurt him? I hoped so. Whatever hurt I could inflict on him, he surely deserved.

"That's when she told me that you . . ." he continued. "that she and I . . . that I . . ." He hesitated. I couldn't help but wonder if he hesitated because he still didn't quite believe it or because he still didn't want to believe it.

"That you had a son?"

He bit his lower lip and nodded. "I wanted to see you, Morgan. I wanted to see you right away, but you'd left for Oklahoma City with your grandparents. They'd taken you to see me. I looked for them in the audience, and when I spotted you, I made sure someone pulled them out of the crowd and asked them to wait. I did my bit for the crowds and then waved good-bye, saying I had to give an interview. Then I hid out in one of the hangars until most everyone had left so I could spend time with you. I wanted to," he said earnestly.

"Really? How much time was that? An hour? Two? Whatever it was, I guess your curiosity must have been satisfied because I certainly never saw you again."

"Morgan, I don't blame you for being angry. It couldn't have been easy for you," he said, and I could tell he was trying to keep his voice calm, determined to keep his emotions in check. "Believe me, I understand.

"I almost never saw my father. He was a congressman. He and my mother never got along. They had terrible fights. They couldn't divorce because of his position, but they didn't live together. Mother and I lived like gypsies, moving from one apartment or rooming house to another."

He spoke with a strange detachment as he reported the facts of his bleak childhood, as if relating a story he'd heard third-hand, a story that didn't have much to do with him personally. But then, as he continued, his voice softened and his eyes misted, focusing past me to some distant point visible only in memory. And for a moment, just a moment, I thought I saw him as he was, rather than as he wished to be seen.

"He died many years ago. But lately, I've been dreaming about him. In my dream, I am the age I am now, but he looks like he did when I was a boy. He comes to see me, but he just stands there and doesn't say anything. I can feel that he's come to tell me something, but he can't get the words out. Finally, I ask him, 'Why didn't we spend more time together when you were alive? Why didn't you ever send for me?'" Lindbergh's eyes had turned dark and angry. "I wait for an answer, but he just looks at me. Then he picks up his hat and leaves the room, and I feel so terribly sad because I know it is too late now. He won't be back." Quietly, he repeated the statement once more, more to himself than me. Then, as if being abruptly woken, he took in a sharp, clean breath and looked at me, aware of my presence once again.

"So you see, Morgan. I understand how you feel."

For a moment, I had been tempted to feel sorry for him, but the mask of cool self-control was there again so neatly that I wondered if he had ever really dropped it in the first place.

"No, I don't think you do. You don't know what it was like to grow up hearing the word 'bastard' whispered behind your back when you walked through town. You don't know what it was like hearing your mother called worse than that by the boys at school, having to black their eyes and getting your own blacked in return defending her honor. You don't know what it was like having to lie to her about it because you couldn't bear to see the pain in her eyes one more time. So don't tell me you understand!"

I jumped to my feet, shouting, unable to control myself any longer. "You can't even begin to imagine how it feels. And if you could, that would make it ten times worse. Because if you'd known, if you'd had the slightest idea of what she was going through and you let her face it anyway, you'd be the worst kind of monster." I looked at him and shook my head disgusted. "And maybe you are.

"What kind of man does that? What kind of man makes a young girl fall in love with him, steals her innocence, and runs off? And when he shows up five years later and is confronted with the truth, what kind of man just disappears again? What kind of man kicks his mistakes under the rug and just leaves everyone else to deal with the mess? What kind of man are you?" I practically spat the question, pouring as much venom into my accusations as possible, wanting to inflict a mortal wound, but he didn't flinch. His conscience was clad in armor.

"Morgan, that's not fair. It isn't as easy as you make it sound. If I had known about you before I'd made the flight to Paris and reporters started hounding me at every step, I would have married Eva. But I didn't find out until it was too late. When I did, I was heartsick. I hated myself for letting your mother go through all that alone. I did the best I could. I tried to make things easier for both of you. I made sure she had enough money, but she wouldn't take much from me. And I kept tabs on you, too, Morgan. My attorneys made discreet inquiries, and I got a report every few months on how you were doing, but there was so little I could really do. It was an impossible—"

That was enough. I wasn't going to listen to any more. "That's a lie! It wasn't impossible!" I shouted. "You just made it that way! I was born in nineteen twenty-three. You flew to Paris in nineteen twenty-seven. You had four years to come back, to find out about me and do right by my mother. She loved you! She waited for you! All those years, she was waiting for you!"

I covered my face with my hands, trying to rub away the pictures in my mind, pictures of Mama waiting. Standing at the window and scanning a clear blue sky, a tiny wrinkle of worry imprinted between her brows. Leaning forward whenever a door opened with expectant, hopeful eyes. But no matter who entered, or tried to enter, it was never the one she'd hoped to see. Her lips were smiling and her words were welcoming, but her eyes gave her away. None of us was the one. Not Grandma or Ruby. Not Paul. Not me.

"You selfish, heartless bastard! She waited for you! Every day for years and years! And every day she was disappointed, but I never knew why. I thought it was me. I tried so hard to be good enough. All I wanted was for her to be happy. I'd have given anything for that. So don't you dare stand there and tell me it was impossible, that you did the best you could, because it's a lie."

I shook my head, disgusted. "Look at you. The Lone Eagle. The great American hero. It's a lie. You're a lie."

All this time he sat there, his face impassive and his eyes flat gray disks of steel, determined to keep his emotions in check and his thoughts to himself. But at this last, I could see the muscles in his jaw tighten ever so slightly, making the vein on his neck stand out. He exhaled a slow, determined breath through his nose, making his chest rise and fall again, like the breath you let out when the doctor is applying a cold stethoscope to your back trying to assess the existence and condition of your heart. He got to his feet.

"You're right," he said. "I'm not a hero. I never said I was. God knows, I'm guilty of many things, Morgan, but that isn't one of them. I never claimed to be that heroic character the press invented. Charles A. Lindbergh, the Lone Eagle, is a mythological creature that happens to share my name and face. But that's where the resemblance ends. I can't live up to that image. No one could, Morgan."

I'd heard enough of his excuses. "Why did you come here? Why did you track me down?"

"I didn't go looking for you," he said. "I knew you'd joined the service and that you were a pilot, and I was proud to hear it, but that was all I knew. My contacts in Washington aren't what they used to be. When we shook hands and you introduced yourself as Morgan Glennon, I was in shock. To tell you the truth, even coming here tonight, I couldn't quite believe I'd found you, not until I saw that quilt on your bed. She made it for me. Did you know that?" I didn't answer.

"She came to see me in Detroit. It was my last radio address for America First, my last feeble gasp on behalf of a cause that was already lost. America was going to enter the war and I knew it. Nothing I could say was going to change anyone's mind, but I went ahead with the speech anyway, knowing I was driving nails into my own coffin. I felt so awful that night, so completely alone. When I looked out into the crowd and saw Eva, I was really shaken. I couldn't imagine why she'd come, but a part of me felt glad to see her, too. After all those years, it was good to know she still cared. I think, maybe, that's what I'd been holding onto. In my heart, I knew she was waiting for me. Maybe I was waiting for her, too, a little, waiting for the life I'd left behind when I landed in Paris. Part of me always thought I could go back, that things would get simpler. Seeing your mother that night helped me realize it could never happen. I'd changed too much.

"She made that quilt for me. It was her way of saying she was still waiting, that you both were. We argued. I think she finally realized that she'd been living with her eyes closed, refusing to wake from a dream that had already passed. We both had. I sent back the quilt without a return address or a note. It would hurt her, I knew, but I had to do it that way. I had to make her believe once and for all that we could never go back."

"You haven't answered my question," I said coldly. "Why did you come here?"

He took a deep breath. "Because the dream of my father and the questions he never answered has been plaguing me for months. I kept thinking about you, what your questions were. I didn't come looking for you, but I would have before long. We met because we were meant to, and I came here just to say this: I'm sorry. I've done a few things that were good, but many more that weren't. I've made my share of mistakes but, Morgan, you weren't one of them. I never once thought of you as such. That's what I came to tell you. I thought you should know."

I looked him in the eye. "Get out."

30

Morgan

The Pacific—July 1944

Thunderheads were forming to the west, and the radio crackled with static. "Brewster to Glennon. Hey? How was your big date with Lindbergh last night?"

Caldwell cut in, eager to toss out a quip of his own. "Yeah. Did he still respect you in the morning?"

Brewster was back and clearly resentful of the interruption. "Knock it off, Caldwell. I was talking. Seriously, Morgan, how was it? What did he want to talk to you about?"

I hit the radio button and yelled, "How many times do I have to tell you morons! No unnecessary chatter! The radio is to be used for communicating important information that relates to our mission, and that is all it is to be used for! It's a piece of vital military equipment, not a party line. Now, get your heads back in the game and stay on the lookout for Japs! Especially you, Brewster! If I have to tell you again, you'll be peeling potatoes for the rest of the war! Do I make myself clear?"

There was a long pause before Brewster responded, "Yes, sir."

After that, the chatter ceased, but I knew that they were all wondering what the hell was eating me.

It was a fair question. My outburst relieved a little of the tension that had been building up inside me all morning, but the minute it was over, I felt bad. Brewster knew I didn't like excess chatter over the radio, but we'd already been in the air more than three hours. It was hard to keep one hundred percent focus on these long missions. There was bound to be a little joking around now and then, and Brewster was a good kid. There'd been no need for me to go off on him like that. I promised myself I'd apologize to him and the rest of the boys after we landed. I never got the chance.

Not three minutes later, Caldwell broke in again. "Caldwell to Glennon. Sir! At two o' clock! There's a pack of Sonias coming for us! Looks like five . . . no, make that six of them!"

But he didn't have to count them. In less than a minute I could see them for myself. Lindbergh and his group had encountered only one of the planes, but we were outnumbered two to one, facing an enemy that was desperate to strike one more blow in a cause that was already lost.

My boys did their best. We took out three of the Sonias before they got Brewster. A fourth flew his ship straight for Caldwell, purposely ramming his Sonia into Caldwell's P-38 and killing them. The flash of flame was blinding. One minute the Sonia was coming for Caldwell, and the next minute he was gone and I was the only one left. It was happening again. Just like the day Fountain had died.

I don't remember everything that happened after—just the feeling of intense panic. I couldn't outrun the Sonias. They made pass after pass at me, and I did my best to dodge the bullets, but they were scoring some hits. The way things were going, it was just a matter of time.

Certain I was a heartbeat from death, I was suddenly and sharply aware of all the mistakes I'd made and the hurts I'd inflicted. Conversations replayed themselves in my mind like recordings played double-time, and faces floated just out of my reach—Mama, Paul, Georgia. Too late. I knew that short of a miracle I was just seconds from death, and I was scared, but more than that, I was sorry—sorry for all the wrongs I would never have a chance to right. "Dear God!" I cried out. "Don't let me die!"

There was a loud, rumbling boom followed by an ear-splitting crack. I thought I'd been hit, but a bolt of lightning sparked and disappeared to the west, like some broken, celestial neon sign, and I remembered. The thunderheads. I banked hard and came around on one of the enemy ships, firing my guns for all they were worth, using the last of my ammunition.

I'd have killed the Sonia if I could have, but that still would have left one more enemy plane to deal with, and me without any bullets. My real goal was to somehow, by luck, surprise, or sheer audacity, get past the Sonia and fly right into the middle of the thunderstorm. It was a long shot. If I made it into the storm, I'd probably die, but if I stayed out in clear air my death moved from the realm of the probable to the certain. It was an easy decision to make.

I think the sheer foolhardiness of my move caught the Japanese pilot off guard. For a split second, he hesitated, and that was the break I needed. It seemed to take him a second to figure out what I was doing, that I was actually crazy enough to be flying toward the center of a raging thunderstorm, but as soon as he did, he was after me. The second plane came roaring after both of us.

"Come on, baby!" I said aloud, urging the wounded P-38 forward. "Give it all you've got!" My ship was damaged, and I could see a thin column of smoke trailing off my starboard wing, but she was maintaining speed and altitude. The thunderheads were close now. Ninety seconds more and I'd reach my destination, but the Sonias were closing. Of course, even if I reached the storm there was a good chance my plan wouldn't work. If the two Japanese pilots were as devoted to the emperor as their friend who had collided with Caldwell, and followed me despite the danger, I would be in big trouble. It all depended on how much they liked living. Thirty seconds.

Please God, I prayed, *let there be at least two traitors in the Land of the Rising Sun.*

There were. They fired another round as I flew into the eye of the storm, but they pulled away and missed. Their hearts weren't in it. I didn't blame them. They probably figured there was no point in wasting bullets on a plane that was going to be hit by lightning or downed by gale-force winds any second. They didn't have to kill me. Nature was trying her best to do it for them.

The wind was blasting, making the plane shudder and shake, buffeting me from all directions. The turbulent winds tossed my ship around like a toy. The clouds were thick, and it was hard to see, hard to know if I was flying straight, or even right side up. I kept my eyes glued to the indicators, trying to maintain a semi-level attitude, but it felt like I was trapped inside one of those snow globes that kids get for Christmas and somebody kept shaking it up. Lightning bolts struck on every side of me. Half my instruments were fried, and I couldn't tell what direction I was going. I couldn't turn back. The Japanese would surely be waiting for me, hoping to finish me off in case God didn't. I kept flying in the direction I hoped was west and prayed that the storm wasn't as big as it looked.

And, thank God, it wasn't. I hung on for what seemed like hours, but it was probably more like twenty minutes. Gradually, the cloud cover thinned and the winds lost some of their fury. Then, suddenly, I was out of it, passing from black storm clouds to bright late-afternoon sun as quickly as if I'd been leaving one room and entering another. My hands were shaking with exhaustion and relief.

I whispered a quick and very sincere prayer of thanks, but when I opened my eyes and looked at my controls, I realized my problems were far from over. I had barely a hundred gallons of fuel left in my tank. What's more, I didn't know where I was, and, with my navigational equipment damaged, there was no way for me to figure that out. Wherever I was, it was a long, long way from base.

A look out my window showed nothing but endless miles of ocean. The sun was low in the sky. I only had a couple more hours of daylight left in which to find a place to land my ship. Otherwise, I'd have to bail out in the open ocean and hope a passing ship picked me up before I drowned, died of exposure, or became shark bait.

I glanced down at my fuel gauge again. The needle now hovered just under the hundred-gallon mark. During the altercation with the Sonias, saving gas had been the least of my worries, and I'd gone through a lot of it escaping them. Now I had to concentrate on stretching out my fuel and finding land. I adjusted the manifold pressure, reduced my rpm, and hoped for the best.

It was a race to see what I'd run out of first, fuel or daylight. The minutes ticked by, and fuel was winning, but not by much. There was still no sign of land. My most optimistic calculations said I had maybe fifteen minutes of flight time before I would be completely out of gas. It was time to start thinking about ditching into the ocean. While keeping one eye on the horizon I checked my survival vest. It had some basic survival gear—knife, flashlight, flares, and so on. I had a couple of Hershey bars, so I tucked those into the vest pockets along with the canteen of water that I always took with me for long flights. I found some rubber bands, so I shoved them in, too. I wasn't sure what good they'd be, but you never knew.

I took another look around me. This was it. There was nothing left to do but wait to run out of gas and pray. As the fuel needle dipped lower and lower, I was feeling increasingly edgy. I half wanted to bail out right then, just to get it over with, but I knew I should stay with the plane as long as possible.

I took a deep breath. It was time to decrease my altitude. That was when I saw something on the horizon, or at least I thought I did. Evening shadows were starting to fall, so I couldn't be sure, but there was a dark spot off to the southwest. I maintained my altitude and hung on, keeping my eyes glued to the horizon, watching the spot. But it wasn't a spot, it was an island—not much of an island, but at that moment I couldn't afford to be choosy. It was still a good way off. Was it too far for me to reach on the gas I had left? Probably, but getting there was my best chance of staying alive.

According to my gas gauge, the P-38 was close to fumes. I decreased my airspeed, hoping that might buy me another minute or two. With every second, the island loomed larger in my field of vision. Maybe, just maybe, I was going to make it. I could hardly believe it. It was a miracle.

Suddenly, a small voice in my mind whispered, *You know, if not for Lindbergh, you'd have run out of gas long ago and had to ditch in the middle of the ocean. Right now, some shark would be picking you out of his teeth—if not for Lindbergh. If not for your father.*

As the thought entered my mind and refused to leave, I felt my jaw tighten. Just then, the plane started to jerk and sputter. *Not quite a miracle,* I thought.

The engines shut down, and everything around me was eerily quiet; the only noise in the world was the whoosh of air pushing past my rapidly descending aircraft and the adrenaline-pumped beat of my heart. My gas was gone. I would have to get as close as I could to the island, bail out, and, assuming my parachute opened and I wasn't knocked unconscious from the impact of hitting the water, swim for land and hope someone found me.

It was time. My finger hovered over the ejection button. In spite of the desperate situation I found myself in, I hadn't lost my sense of irony. Wouldn't it be something if the advice of the person that, at the moment, I hated most in the world turned out to be what saved me?

"Well," I said with a laugh, "there isn't a bookmaker in the world who'd give odds on my chance of living through the day. So don't go taking any bows just yet, Mr. Lindbergh. The day's a long way from over."

31

Georgia

Liberal, Kansas—July 1944

It was the height of summer, but when my alarm went off, it was still dark. I groaned and, with my eyes still closed, pulled my arm out from under the blanket and groped the nightstand in search of the clock. Finding it at last, I punched a button to stop the irritating, metallic clang of the bell and held the clock face close, squinting to see the time.

Three-thirty in the morning? Why in the world had I set the alarm for such an ungodly hour? Then I remembered. There was a new batch of trainees on base and Hemingway, who liked to let people think he was related to the famous author but wasn't, liked to roust the trainees from bed extra early on the first day. "Just to remind these hotshot flyboys that this is a military operation," he'd say with a swagger and laugh, which his toadying junior officers would quickly echo.

It was ridiculous, I thought. These boys had already been through their boot camp. They'd proven their mettle; there was no need to treat them like a bunch of raw recruits. But that was the way

Hemingway wanted it, and since he was the base commander, that was the way it would be.

I snapped on the bedside lamp and groaned again. My eyes felt like they were glued shut. I heaved myself into a sitting position on the edge of my bed. But somehow, in my blind search for the alarm clock, the lamp cord must have gotten wrapped around my arm because when I sat up I accidentally tugged on the cord, and the lamp crashed to the floor and broke into about fifty pieces. Great. That lamp probably cost three bucks, but as soon as my landlady saw the damage, it would undoubtedly become a cherished family heirloom that would cost me half a week's pay to replace. I sighed, got up to find a broom, and stepped on a shard of the broken lamp. The gash in my foot wasn't deep, but it hurt like the dickens. I limped to the bathroom, leaving a trail of bloody left footprints behind.

Snapping on the bathroom light, I peered into the mirror and said to my reflection, "Georgia June, this is not going to be a good day."

Things looked brighter after I bandaged my foot and had a cup of coffee. I made it extra strong, using up the last of the precious can of real coffee that Delia had somehow gotten hold of and sent me for Christmas. I think that was back when she'd been dating a supply officer. It tasted so good, and I knew I was going to need it today, not just to get myself moving on this early day but to give myself the energy to face a new group of students.

Don't get me wrong; I loved my job. Because I spent so much time in the classroom, only taking up students for their occasional flights to check their navigation skills, I didn't get as much flying time as I would have liked. But I'd found a little private airfield just over the Oklahoma state line run by a fellow named Whitey Henderson that had a couple of old biplanes for rent, and on Sundays I'd hitch a ride out to the airfield and take one up for a spin. Flying in an open cockpit was wonderful. I really *felt* like I was flying, like

I had wings of my own, like an angel peering down on a worry-worn world from the edge of heaven and wondering what all the silly fuss was about. Still, I didn't fly frequently. Between teaching, correcting tests, tutoring students who needed extra help, and planning for upcoming lessons, I didn't have the time. And even if I had, I suspect I still wouldn't have gone very often. Flying, as I'd discovered during those months when I'd been ferrying planes, gave me too much time by myself, too much time to think. And I didn't want to think. I didn't want time to feel lonely, or sad, or anything else. I just wanted to do my job and live my life as it was, not wondering what I was missing or why.

By that standard, my instructor's job at Liberal Army Airfield was nearly perfect. Of course, dealing with Hemingway wasn't always a walk in the park, but I'd met his kind before, and, one way or another, I dealt with them. But the job itself was great. There was always something interesting to do, and I relished the challenge. The trainees weren't used to the idea of a female instructor, and while most of them tended to be merely skeptical, there were always one or two who were openly hostile, challenging my authority and trying their best to disrupt the class. But once they realized that I really did know my stuff, the men would buckle down and get to work. Most of them were good, hard-working guys who'd come to Kansas for one reason: to become better pilots, get into combat, and help win the war. And if a female instructor could help them reach that goal as thoroughly and quickly as a man, it made no difference to them.

Of course, there were exceptions. I'll never forget Mick Deering, a real charming piece of work with the personality of a rabid wolverine and an I.Q. to match. He marched into the C.O.'s office and said he flat refused to be taught by a woman. And can you believe it? The colonel patted him on the shoulder, said he understood, and assigned him to another instructor!

Then the old man called me into his office and hollered at me, saying that he'd seen it coming, that he'd known from the first that having a girl teach "his men" was a recipe for disaster, and that if it had been up to him, he'd never have allowed me to set foot on his base. "I don't care what load of road apples the brass in Washington are trying to sell!" he barked, his red face a scant three inches from mine. "A United States military base is no place for a female unless she's cleaning something, bandaging something, or typing something! I am making a note in your personnel file, Mrs. Welles. I've got my eye on you. You are clearly unfit for this job, and the sooner I can prove that to those fools at headquarters who sent you here in the first place, the better it will be for me, for my men, and for the U.S. Army Air Corps!"

It took every ounce of self-control I had not to tell that old coot of a colonel just what I thought of him, but I knew if I did, that would be just the excuse he'd need to transfer me, or maybe even have me drummed out of the WASP for good. I stood there at attention in front of his desk and took everything he had to dish out, but it wasn't easy. I was furious.

Two weeks later I took no small satisfaction in hearing the news that Deering had washed out because he'd failed both a flight check and a test in navigation. He ended up in the infantry.

It still made me smile to think about it. I took another sip of coffee and spied the pile of envelopes that my landlady had shoved under the door—my mail. The room I was renting wasn't really a legal apartment, just a bedroom over my landlady's garage. It was expensive and drafty, but within walking distance of the base. I didn't have a mailing address of my own, so the postman left everything at the main house. Whenever she got around to it, the landlady climbed the rickety wooden stairs to my room and stuffed the mail under the door, the crack underneath being wide enough to admit letters, blasts of cold air, and the occasional rodent.

I picked up the pile of mail and flipped through the envelopes. There was a flyer from the local dry goods store about a sale that had been over three days ago, letters from Delia and Pamela that I decided to read after work, and a strange-looking envelope from Waukegan Oil covered with stamps and notes for forwarding addresses. Clearly, it had been tracking me for some time. Curious, I tore open the envelope and pulled out the notice inside.

"What the heck?" I asked myself. It was a bill for the airfield's heating oil from the previous winter. I frowned as I saw the angry red stamp that said "NINETY DAYS PAST DUE. REMIT PAYMENT IMMEDIATELY. Why hadn't Stubbs paid the oil bill? In his last letter, he'd said everything was fine, that business continued to be slow but we were keeping up. I bit my lower lip as I read the statement again. There must have been some sort of misunderstanding, I decided. Besides, this bill had been chasing me around for so long that Stubbs would surely have paid it by now.

In the background I heard the gentle tick-tick of the clock and looked up. Four-thirteen. I had to be on base in seventeen minutes. Hemingway insisted that all the instructors be present, standing in a respectful line behind him when he gave his "welcome to hell" speech to the incoming trainees. Later, I'd drop Stubbs a line and ask about the oil bill, but right now I had to get to work. I left the mail on the table, took a final gulp of coffee, wedged a piece of stale donut between my teeth to eat on the way, and buttoned my blue battle jacket as I ran out the door.

Ah, I thought, *the glamorous life of a lady pilot.*

❦ 32 ❦

Georgia

Liberal, Kansas—July 1944

My first instincts were correct. It hadn't been a good day. I'd gotten to work three minutes early, but that still made me the last instructor to arrive for Hemingway's speech. He glared as I stepped onto the platform and took my place alongside the others. Then he neglected to introduce me, just let me stand up there looking like a fool, walking right past me as if I didn't exist while he announced the names and positions of everyone else who was standing up front. Afterwards, he'd walked over, sneering, and said that he expected every member of the staff to be on time, and that if I was too busy primping and fussing to arrive to the meeting on time, then I'd best not come at all.

Fine, I thought as I stood there. *You want to play it that way? Next time I'll set my alarm clock for two-thirty, arrive an hour early, and be standing on the platform checking my wristwatch when you walk in the door.*

On top of that, there was a blond troublemaker from Alabama

in my class, Carlton Pickett, who had the potential to be a first-class Deering. And later, unable to get that oil bill off my mind, I'd tried to use the pay phone at the base to call Stubbs only to have the operator tell me that the number had been disconnected. I insisted that she must be wrong, that the number couldn't have been disconnected because it was a business, and I was the owner, but the operator just kept repeating, "I'm sorry, ma'am. The number is no longer in service," in that annoying, nasal twang that seemed to be a job requirement for women who wanted to work for the American Telephone and Telegraph Company.

"Thank you, Operator. You've been so helpful," I said sarcastically before banging down the receiver.

What in the world could be going on in Waukegan, I wondered. Then, I'd had one more class with the new trainees, plus a three-hour navigation flight check with a pilot who hadn't passed the first time and was having a second and final chance to move on to the next phase of training. For the next few hours, I'd have to put worries about Stubbs and my business back in Illinois out of my mind. However, the second I landed and signed off on my student's evaluation form (he'd passed with flying colors), I headed back to my apartment. It had been a long day, and it wasn't over yet.

I brought a big pile of paperwork home with me, thinking I'd get to it right after I wrote a letter to Stubbs asking about the oil bill. After that, my plan was to heat up a can of soup for dinner and climb into a hot bath before bed.

The walk home was short, but the fresh air did me a lot of good. It would have been cheaper, not to mention warmer and cleaner, if the WASP had been militarized and I could have lived on base, but sometimes it was nice to be able to walk away from the job at the end of a long day, even if only for a few hours.

It was a warm day, so when I got home I mixed up the cold coffee I had left from the morning with a little milk and sugar and poured it over ice. I peeled off my battle jacket and sat down at the table with my glass, thinking that sipping iced coffee would help me keep a cool head while I figured out a diplomatic way of asking Stubbs if things were falling apart in my absence.

The stack of mail lay on the table where I'd left it that morning. I picked up the pile, hoping to find a clean sheet of stationery, and one envelope slipped and dropped to the table—the letter from Pamela.

I was hot and tired. Pamela's letter was a welcome distraction, so I decided to read it first and write Stubbs later. My dining table/ kitchen counter/work desk didn't come supplied with anything as elegant as a proper letter opener, but a butter knife did the job just as well.

Dear Georgia,

How are you? I haven't heard from you in a while, but I know you've been busy with your new duties. Still, send up a signal flare every once in a while, so I know you're still alive.

I'm not sure how to ask you this or if it's any of my business, but I was wondering if you've been in contact with Morgan Glennon? I got the feeling that there was more going on between you two than you were willing to admit. You know, he and John knew each other from basic and they keep in touch from time to time. I didn't know if you'd heard anything, but Morgan is missing in action. John just heard about it so I wanted to make sure you knew. If I hear anything more, I'll keep you posted.

John will be home for dinner any minute. I've got to dash. I'll write again soon. You do the same, all right?

Love,
Pamela

My hands shook as I reached for the glass of iced coffee and took a drink, hoping to swallow back the lump in my throat. I read the letter again, searching for more information about what might have happened or details about the search, but there was nothing, nothing but the cold, hard fact that Morgan was missing and the surprising anguish brought on by the news.

"Why are you so upset about this?" I asked myself aloud, wiping tears from my cheeks with the back of my hands. "You barely know him! It's not like you're in love with him!"

I stood up and took a couple of deep breaths, determined to get hold of myself. It was ridiculous, letting myself fall apart like this over someone I didn't love and who had made it very clear he didn't love me. What in the world was wrong with me? I was acting just like when I'd heard about Roger. That was it, I decided. This had brought back the pain of losing Roger, the shock of opening the letter you never expected or wanted to receive, the feeling of utter helplessness, of not knowing but fearing the worst. That was it. It was because of Roger. But that wasn't all it was.

Anxiety clutched at me, and for a moment, I thought I was going to be sick. I took several more slow, deep breaths trying to calm myself, but it didn't work. I started pacing, ten steps from one side of the room to the other and back, but that just made me feel more apprehensive, like a tiger pacing back and forth in a cage. I'd never taken up smoking, but at that moment, I wished I had. At least that would have given me something to do with my hands, some way to smother my thoughts and suffocate my fears.

I couldn't bear it anymore. I had to find something to do. Without bothering to grab my purse or put on my jacket, I opened the apartment door, ran down the wobbly wooden steps that led to the street, and started walking, not knowing where I was headed and not caring.

Liberal is a nice town with pretty tree-lined streets and tidy homes boasting even tidier gardens. Usually I enjoyed walking through my neighborhood in the evening, watching children playing games of kick-the-can in the twilight while their mothers enjoyed a few moments of rest sitting on the front steps, occasionally being called upon to settle some disagreement about the rules or who had reached base first. But I didn't notice any of that tonight. I just walked, without looking right or left or considering where I should go or what I would do when I got there. I don't know how long it took, but eventually I found myself downtown.

Walking had helped me calm down a little, but my stomach was still churning with anxiety and, I realized as I spied a sign for the Midway Café, hunger. Other than coffee, that stale donut was the only thing I'd put in my stomach all day. I decided to go inside and get something to eat.

It was a busy place. The air was filled with the smell of frying beef and bacon, the hum of conversation, and the clatter of cutlery on ceramic plates. But when I came in, everyone stopped what they were doing and stared at me for a moment before finally returning to the business of eating. Clearly, this was a café that thrived on the business of regulars. I felt very conspicuous. I was just about to leave and walk home with an empty stomach when a waitress wearing a white uniform and thick glasses yelled in my direction, "Booths are all full, hon. Grab a place there at the counter. I'll be right with you."

I complied, knowing that my sudden exit would occasion even more interest than my entrance. Besides, I really was hungry. There were three empty stools together, so I took the one in the middle, not wanting to sit next to a stranger. After a couple of minutes, the waitress returned and handed me a menu.

"Sorry for the wait. I had to go in the back and find one. Most folks around here already have it memorized, but you're not from around here, are you?" she asked, peering at me over the top of her black-rimmed glasses. It was more a statement than a question, but I answered anyway.

"No, I moved here just a few months ago. I work at the airfield."

"Oh," she nodded, curiosity satisfied. "You're a secretary." Normally, I would have corrected her. One of the things I enjoyed about being a pilot was the reaction the news of my profession elicited, especially from other women, but I wasn't in the mood for any of that tonight. Wearing a simple pair of slacks with a white blouse, I could remain incognito, and tonight that was exactly what I wanted.

I looked over the menu, wondering what I should order. As if reading my mind, the waitress said, "Cheeseburger's good. Fries, too. They changed the grease in the fryer this afternoon."

"That's fine." I handed back the menu.

"Coke or Dr. Pepper?" she asked, as if those were the only beverages worth considering.

"Coke. And a glass of water, too, if you don't mind."

"I'll put your order in and be right back." She smiled and scurried off. Behind me, I heard the door open. The hum of diners' conversations continued without interruption, so I figured whoever entered must have been one of the Midway's regular customers.

Flashing a smile and waving as she disappeared into the kitchen, the waitress called out, "Hello, Pastor! Good to see you! Take a seat at the counter and I'll bring out your coffee and pie in two shakes."

Behind me, a low voice with a trace of a foreign accent rumbled, "Thank you, Irma." There were only two seats available at the counter, both of them flanking me. The gentleman sat down to my left. He was, as Irma had said, a pastor, and he wore a black shirt and clerical collar under his jacket. I nodded as he sat down but didn't speak to him.

I rested my chin in one hand and drummed my fingers on the counter with the other, hoping that Irma would hurry up with my Coke.

"Here you go," she said, taking the drinks from the tray she balanced expertly on one hand. "A Coke and a glass of water. Shouldn't be too long for the rest of your order." Then, turning to my neighbor, she continued, "And here you go, Pastor Van Dyver. Coffee and a piece of apple pie a lá mode. I cut you a nice big piece and gave you an extra scoop of ice cream." She smiled as she put the food in front of him.

"Irma, you didn't have to do that."

"I know, but you've got a big appetite. Though you'd never know it to look at you." Irma was right; the minister was tall and skinny as a rail. "Don't worry," she said with a wave of her hand, then looked over at me as if I were part of the conversation. "The boss doesn't mind. Ernie's always been grateful for the way you visited him every day when he had his gallbladder out."

The pastor seemed a little embarrassed by the special consideration he was receiving. "Irma, that was over a year ago. Ernie's thanked me ten times over. I didn't mind. It was a pleasure talking with him."

I wouldn't want to accuse a minister of lying, but that was a little hard to believe. How much of a pleasure could it be to visit with someone who was in the throws of a gallbladder attack? Irma grinned as if she was thinking the same thing.

"Just the same, Pastor, Ernie said I'm supposed to take good care of you, and that's what I'm going to do. Now eat that before the ice cream starts to melt," she ordered cheerily before turning to me. "I'll go see where your cheeseburger is at."

She called over her shoulder as she left, "Say, Pastor, this lady's new in town. You should invite her to your church." I opened my eyes wide and glared at Irma, hoping she realized that her tip had just been cut in half. All I wanted was to eat my dinner in peace, not have some local preacher pressuring me to join his congregation.

As if reading my mind, the minister said, "Don't worry. I won't push you to come to our church—unless, of course, you'd like to. You'd be very welcome." He smiled and stuck out his hand for me to shake, "I'm Paul Van Dyver."

"Georgia Welles."

"I pastor a small church over in Dillon."

"Oh," I said, relieved that he'd just given me an out. "That's quite a way from here, isn't it?"

"About ten miles south, across the state line into Oklahoma."

"That's too bad, then. I don't have a car."

Reverend Van Dyver's lips stretched into an amused smile, knowing an excuse when he heard one. "So, you're new in town? What brings you here?"

"I work at the airfield," I answered without volunteering more. Like Irma, he'd probably assume I was doing some sort of administrative work. But he turned out to be more curious than the waitress.

"Really? That must be interesting. What is it you do there?"

"I'm a member of the Women's Air Service Pilots, a WASP."

"So you fly for the military?"

I took a sip of my Coke before answering. "Not as much as I used to. Before this, I was a ferrying pilot. But now I'm a flight instructor, so most of my air time is spent in the passenger seat."

"With white knuckles, no doubt, hanging on for dear life and hoping your students were paying attention to their lessons." He raised his eyebrows and made a face of mock terror.

"Not too often," I smiled. "They are pretty well versed in the basics before I get them. I teach navigation, mostly. I'm not as worried about them crashing as getting lost and having to talk them through the finer points of cow-pasture landings," I joked, thinking how nice it was to have someone to talk to. I'd been working so hard for so long, I'd nearly forgotten how pleasant it was just to sit and chat with another person.

I was about to tell him the story of the student who, unlike Bugs Bunny, actually had taken that left turn at Albuquerque and was ten minutes from entering Mexican airspace before he realized his mistake when Irma showed up with my cheeseburger and French fries. She gave me my food, topped off the pastor's coffee, and scurried off to tend to her other customers.

"Looks good," the Reverend Van Dyver said, nodding toward my plate.

"Well, Irma assured me that the grease in the fryer was fresh, so I bet it is." I took a bite. "Mmmm. Irma was telling the truth," I confirmed. "It's been so long since I've had a hamburger. What about you?" I asked, glancing at his plate. "That's a big piece of pie, but surely that's not all you're having for dinner."

"Oh, no." He shook his head and took a swallow of coffee. "I was over at the hospital for visitation. One of our church members just had a baby and another is in with a case of gout. I'll have dinner at home with my family. This is sort of an appetizer, just to tide me over." He took another bite of pie, which he was clearly enjoying.

"And you?" he asked. "Do you have dinner here very often?"

"No. In fact, this is the first time I've been here. Tonight, I just . . ." I hesitated, not sure how much of my personal life I wanted to share with a stranger. Besides, he'd already put in a full day's work listening to other people's problems. I ate a French fry and let the subject drop.

"Is something wrong? Is there some way I can help you?" He tilted his head slightly as he spoke and leaned closer. It was a question he'd asked a thousand times, I was sure, with just the same sympathetic inflection in his voice, but his eyes were kind and sincere.

I couldn't help but compare him to the pastor of the little church I'd so briefly attended in Texas, where the minister stood at the door after the service, waiting to collect compliments on the sermon and glad-hand the congregation as they exited. He'd said, "Good morning. How are you today?" with just the same tilt to his head as Reverend Van Dyver had, but his eyes, though bright and smiling, were already looking past you to the next congregant as you grasped his outstretched hand and murmured the required "Fine. Thank you." No matter how untrue that was, you'd answer, "Fine. Thank you," because that was the expected answer. It was your line, and you delivered it automatically. Saying anything else would have confused everyone.

Still, the hours I'd spent on my knees searching for answers to questions I wasn't even sure how to ask, singing the hymns that always brought tears to my eyes though I didn't know why, reading the heavy, black Bible with those soaring words that made me want to keep reading, had convinced me that there was something to God. When it came to religion, I was less persuaded. But the man sitting in front of me, with the steady gaze and honest face, patiently waiting for an answer, made me wonder if I'd been too hasty in my judgment. The minister in Texas had been playing the part of pastor. This man was different—he *was* a pastor; he wasn't playacting. Suddenly the words I'd read in the book, words that described what I'd thought church ought to be, came to my mind, "Bear ye one another's burdens, and so fulfill the law of Christ."

I put down the French fry I'd been holding and turned to the minister. I did want to talk. "I had some bad news today. A friend of mine, another pilot, is missing." For a moment, I thought I saw a flash of pain in his eyes, as if he knew exactly what I was going through and laboring under the same load of worry I carried, but he cleared his throat and spoke before I could say anything.

"One of your girlfriends?"

"No." I shook my head. "He's a combat pilot. I really haven't known him for very long. We quarreled when I last saw him, and I haven't heard from him since. I told myself that was fine with me, that I didn't really care for him and that even if I had, I was much too busy to get myself entangled in something as silly as a . . ." I paused a minute, not certain I wanted to discuss matters of the heart with a clergyman, but he didn't seem fazed or embarrassed, so I went on. "Wartime romance, is the way people put it, I guess. But today I got a letter saying my friend was missing, and I realized that I really do care for him. I've tried so hard to push him out of my mind, but it hasn't worked. He's always there." I swallowed hard and dabbed my eyes with a paper napkin. The last thing I wanted to do was start crying, not in front of a restaurant full of people.

"I wish I'd written to him or . . . something. I don't know. But it's too late now. No one knows where he is or what has happened to him, and even though I try to tell myself that he's fine and they'll find him, I can't help but imagine the worst." My eyes started to well up again, and, to my surprise, so did Reverend Van Dyver's.

"And you feel so helpless," the minister said, as if he could read my mind. "You want to do something, anything, but all you can really do is wait."

"Yes."

"I understand," he said quietly. "But there is something you can do. Two things, really." I blinked back tears and looked at him, interested to hear his suggestion. "You can resolve that, if he is found, you will be honest with him and with yourself, that you will tell him the truth about your feelings." I nodded ever so slightly as he spoke, agreeing even though I knew it wouldn't be as easy as he made it sound. "And you can pray. We can pray. Right now."

"You mean here? Right now, with all these people around?"

A hint of a smile played at his lips. "There's no time like the present," he said. "Our Lord said that where two or three are gathered together in his name, he would be in the midst of them. So you see, we shall be in the very best of company." Seeing my hesitancy, he went on, "Trust me, everyone is much too absorbed in their burgers and tuna melts to notice. Even if they do, there's a war on; people pray a lot more than they used to, and in some of the most unlikely places." Without waiting for my assent, he bowed his head and started praying quietly in the middle of the noisy café with the clatter of silverware and the shouted announcements of orders up for accompaniment. I did likewise.

"Dear Lord, one of your sheep is hidden from our eyes, but not from yours. You know where he is, and we are grateful. Please, remain with him, protect him, and return him to his family and loved ones unharmed. And for ourselves, we ask for strength and courage to bear up under the heavy load of worry that we are carrying today. We pray this full of confidence in your power and your mercy and according to your will. Amen."

"Amen," I echoed. Looking up, I asked him, "Do you think it worked?"

This time he didn't bother trying to conceal his smile. "Oh, yes," he assured me. "It worked. We prayed sincerely, and God heard us. Does that mean that your friend will be found? I don't know that."

I frowned, dissatisfied with the answer.

"Georgia," the minister said kindly, "prayer isn't some magical means of getting what we want, when we want it. God isn't a kind of celestial Santa Claus, handing out presents to the nice and lumps of coal to the naughty. God says that we are to pray confidently and according to His will. Prayer is how we begin to align our will with God's. If it is within God's will for your friend to be found, then I promise that he will be."

"And if it isn't?"

"Then, if you rely on Him, God will give you the strength to bear the loss."

I looked away, trying to understand everything the pastor was saying, but I knew there was truth in it. After Roger died, there'd been a time when I thought I would die, too—when I almost wanted to. Yet, slowly, I had rediscovered moments of joy and sweetness in life. But it hadn't been easy or painless. Life isn't like that, and I knew it. Even if I didn't like the pastor's message, I appreciated his honesty.

"Thank you. It's kind of you to take the time to talk with a stranger. I feel a lot better. When I read that letter, I was frantic. I ran out of my apartment without any idea where I was going, without my coat or my . . . Oh my gosh!" I cried.

"What's wrong?" he asked.

"My purse! I left it at home, and I didn't bring any money with me. I don't have a way to pay for this!"

I searched my pockets frantically, hoping to find a spare dollar, but Reverend Van Dyver just laughed.

In the end he not only paid for my dinner, he drove me home. He said to forget about it, that it was his pleasure to buy my dinner, but I insisted that he wait while I ran upstairs to find the money I owed him.

Before I went to sleep that night I said a little prayer thanking God for sending me an angel in the form of the kindly minister and asking Him again to take care of Morgan, wherever he was.

∽ 33 ∽

Morgan

The Pacific—July 1944

The light of dawn shone warm through the thin fabric of my parachute shelter, waking me from a night that had been far too short. I laid my arm over my eyes to block out the light, hoping to be able to go back to sleep, but it was no good. Every muscle in my body was aching, but the searing pain that radiated from my foot was nearly unbearable. I'd injured it when I bailed out.

A couple of bones were broken, and I'd gotten a pretty deep cut, but it hadn't seemed that bad at first. Before wrapping the foot with strips I'd torn from my undershirt, I'd washed the wound out with seawater. The salt water stung so badly that I'd cried out, but I hoped that it would clean out the gash and fight off infection. By the fourth day it was clear that my attempts at first aid hadn't worked. The foot was swollen, flaming red, pulsing with pain, and the fever that raged through my body made the tropical heat feel even more intense.

Seven days before, when I running out of daylight, fuel, and hope, this island had looked like paradise, but in truth, I could hardly have chosen a less hospitable spot in which to find myself marooned. The island was small and had almost no vegetation, just a few scrubby bushes that provided little shade or protection from the elements. There was no fresh water and nothing to eat.

Initially, in spite of the pain from my foot, I'd tried to keep my spirits up and my mind busy by using the survival techniques I'd learned during basic training. Tying one side of the parachute to some of the taller bushes and then piling rocks on the other side to secure it, I'd built a lean-to, spreading my parachute out as wide as possible to make it easier for rescue planes to spot from the air. Out here, wherever that was, an enemy aircraft could spot me as easily as an ally, but it was a risk I had to take. The gear I'd grabbed before ditching had a few rations, but they weren't going to last for long. I made a crude spear by lashing my survival knife to the end of a branch I'd stripped from one of the bushes and securing the ends of the lashing with the rubber bands I'd taken from the cockpit. It actually made a fairly formidable weapon. But there was no wildlife on the island, and the burning pain of salt water on my open wound made it impossible to stand in the water long enough to spear any fish. Fortunately, the fever diminished my appetite. Too bad it hadn't done the same for my thirst. Water was my big problem.

My canteens were nearly empty, though I'd tried my best to limit my water ration. But it wasn't easy. The ravaging fever doubled my thirst. My tongue was swollen, and when I swallowed it felt like my throat was lined with sandpaper.

The day before I'd seen clouds on the horizon. Desperate to capture a little rainwater, I'd laid out my helmet, my canteen, my waterproof map, even my boots, anything I could think of that might serve as a catch basin, then sat for hours watching the horizon, willing the storm clouds to come my way, only to see them blow off to the south. Since the moment I'd crawled up on the beach and surveyed the unforgiving landscape of the island, fear had been crouching at the edge of my consciousness. But when that quenching veil of clouds teased me with hope and then passed me by, fear moved to center stage in my mind.

What is it going to be like, I wondered, *to die of thirst, alone on an island somewhere in the Pacific? Why is this happening? I want to go home—to make things right. What a waste.*

When you're stranded on a desert island, you've got plenty of time, time to think, regret, resolve, to make plans for the future and bargains with God. In those seven days, I thought more about my life and how I'd lived it than I ever had before. And I didn't like what I saw.

When I'd told Charles Lindbergh, my father . . . it was still hard to get my mind around that . . . when I'd told my father to get out of my quarters, I was angrier than I'd ever been in my life. How could he have done it? Left my mother to raise me alone, to face the hardships and shame of living as the mother of a bastard in a town as small as Dillon, where there was nowhere to hide and everyone sticks their nose in everybody's business? And then, having done it, how could he find the nerve to just show up out of nowhere and say, "Hello. I'm your father. Nice to meet you"? What had he expected me to say? Was I supposed to be happy? Grateful that to learn, after a lifetime of fending for myself, that I was the son of the famous Charles Lindbergh? Well, to hell with him!

But at least he *had* told me the truth—a lot later than I'd deserved to hear it, but he'd done it. I hadn't spent much time with him, hardly knew him, but I could see that he wasn't the cowardly, egocentric jerk I was making him out to be. But what kind of man was my father? Maybe just exactly what he'd said, a man who'd made mistakes and was trying to make up for them as best he could. But surely he'd known that there was no way, no way in the world to make up for it. And then I realized that, yes, he had known it. He'd known he couldn't wipe out the past, that there was no apology eloquent enough, no penance harsh enough to make up for all that he'd done and not done. He hadn't tried to pretend there was, hadn't demanded forgiveness or understanding. He'd just decided to tell the truth and let the chips fall where they may. He'd done what he could. He'd been honest. That was more than I could say for a lot of people.

How many people, people I loved and who said they loved me, had been in on the secret? Ruby and Grandma probably. Paul possibly. And my grandfather. On that day when he caught me at the pump, washing the blood from my shirt, I realized that Papaw knew who my father was, but he wouldn't tell me. It was too big a secret. It was *the* secret, and we'd all played our part in keeping it that way, even me. I hadn't pushed for an answer, or been courageous enough to demand the truth. I'd made up my own truth, stories that, if not more believable, were at least more palatable—a legitimate pilot father who'd died bravely and was waiting for us in heaven, an unwary step onto a farm rake that innocently blacked my eye, a perfect son—happy, studious, obedient, pure of body and mind—who'd flown off to college and then to war, not to escape the secrets but to make his family proud and his country safe. What a cool liar I was. What a skilled and trustworthy keeper of secrets. And why wouldn't I be? I'd learned from the best—Mama.

Sitting on the beach waiting for a rescue that seemed increasingly unlikely, it seemed the time for honesty had finally come. I had unleashed my rage on Lindbergh, but Mama was the one I was truly angry with. Biology aside, Lindbergh was a stranger to me, but Mama had my trust and my heart. She should have been the one to tell me, years ago. Why didn't she? It wasn't from lack of love. I knew that. However angry I might be with her, however she had disappointed me or hurt me, I knew that Mama loved me. And I loved her. Whatever she had done, and however wrongly she had done it, her motivation had been love.

On that last day in San Diego, we'd pretended, like we always did, that everything was fine. With all my heart, I had wanted to say something true, something honest to her before I left, and I did, but it wasn't easy. I was so practiced at hiding the truth. I had learned that from Mama. And where had she learned it? From Grandma? From Papaw? Both? And them—who had instructed them in the fine art of secrecy?

Years ago, when I was just a teenager, I remembered Paul preaching a sermon that no one had liked. He talked about King David and how, even though he was beloved of God and had been showered with everything he needed for life and happiness, David had coveted another man's wife, taken her into his bed, and then had the woman's husband murdered. And when David's son, Solomon, had come to the throne, he too had been foolish about women, and it had cost him dearly, and the same with his sons and their sons for generations.

"The sins of the fathers shall be visited on the sons for four generations," Paul intoned ominously from the pulpit, while farmers shifted uncomfortably in their pews, reflecting, no doubt, on their own failings and wondering why they'd polished their shoes and gotten themselves into town early just to be made to feel bad by some foreign preacher who'd never sown an acre of wheat in his life. Paul went on to posit that perhaps the text wasn't warning as much about divine punishment as the need for us to be on guard about the legacy of sin we could be passing onto the next generation, that the individual choices of one person could easily become the habitual, ingrained character flaws that pass through an entire family line. However, he stated, ending on a more hopeful note, it was possible for every person present to break the chains of generational sin. He urged those assembled to examine their own lives carefully, to see what errant inheritance they might have received from their ancestors, and to firmly resolve to break the cycle of sin in their lifetime, thereby rescuing future generations. "It will not be easy," Paul said. "It will require honesty, daily resolve, as well as powerful and divine intervention. But do not be afraid, for with God all things are possible." When he finished, the church was quieter than usual and people seemed to struggle to their feet for the closing hymn. After the service, in the vestibule, I could hear them whispering complaints to one another.

"Why does he have to make everything so complicated?"

"I wish Pastor Wilder was still here. There was a man who knew how to preach! A nice message on forgiveness and the love of God, something on stewardship once a year at pledge time, and you could go home and enjoy a nice Sunday dinner. Now I not only can't digest my supper, but I'm awake half the night trying to figure out what he said. Makes me feel unsettled, and that's not why I come to church, I can tell you."

"Well, I just don't understand a word of it."

And at the time, neither had I, but now I was beginning to.

Sitting under the thin protection of my parachute shelter just a fiery sun was setting on the horizon, I raised my hand in a pledge, reaching toward the sky, trying to grasp with my fingertips that place in which I was most truly myself, and declared aloud to God and the empty world, "With your help, it will stop with me. I promise. If I get off this island, I'm not going to hide anymore. It's going to stop with me."

I watched the last fingers of light fade from the sky before I crawled to the center of the lean-to and lay down on the sand. I slept peacefully, my mind more at ease than it had been in a long time.

Just before dropping off I thought, *Tomorrow. I've accomplished what I was sent here to do. The lesson is learned. Surely my rescue will come tomorrow.*

That was four days ago.

There were two aspirin left in my survival kit. I'd saved them and the last of my water for as long as I could. Now, with the sun almost directly overhead, I couldn't wait any longer. I rolled on to my side, twisted open the metal lid of the canteen, and put the aspirin in my mouth. I swallowed once, twice, and finished the last of the warm water with the third swallow. I tipped the canteen as high as I could and was rewarded with a few more precious drops of liquid, but that was all. My water was gone. I was burning with fever, and the pain radiating from my foot up my leg was excruciating. Unless a rescue plane came soon, I'd be dead by morning.

"And since you haven't seen a single aircraft, neither friend or foe, in a week, I wouldn't start holding your breath on that score, Morgan. They've given up looking by now. And wherever the hell it is you are, it's way out of the area where they'd expect to find you," I said. Talking out loud helped take my mind off the agony of my foot, at least a little, but the effort was draining.

I thought about Mama. When I'd last seen her, that morning in San Diego, I'd admitted my fear of dying, as my friends had, in combat. Now that kind of death, fast and final, seemed ultimately preferable to the slow, dripping away of life that I was facing. Mama. I was glad she'd come. Glad I'd been able to see her again, to see her with Paul, both happy at last. But it had taken so long. Why should that be?

And I thought of Georgia. Georgia laughing, her eyes liquid, dark and delicious like melted chocolate. Georgia concentrating and strong-minded, leaning over the open fuselage of an airplane, whistling a sharp breath through pursed lips, blowing stray strands of hair out of her eyes, her hands busy and determined, searching the depths of the blocked wing tank. Georgia confident and vibrant, her gaze focused straight ahead as she looked over the instrument panel, poised and calm as she prepared to land, setting that big cargo plane down on the runway as gently as if it had been a sparrow coming to rest on a tree branch. Georgia lovely in every light, unforgettable even in my moment of deepest despair. Why had I waited?

I was tired, but I couldn't sleep; the pain was too much. I thought about crawling to the edge of the beach so I could dip my discarded shirt into the surf and then lay it on my burning skin, to get a little relief from the heat, but I couldn't summon the energy to move. I had nothing left.

I closed my eyes and listened to the constant roar of the waves, waiting for it to be over, praying it wouldn't be long. Strange images floated in and out of my fevered, delirious mind, a disconnected jumble of memories and imaginings.

I saw myself sitting on the tractor, the first time Papaw had let me drive it alone, waving to Mama as she stood on the porch beaming, watching me plow a crooked furrow.

I saw Georgia. Georgia lying on my bed, flushed and beautiful and tearful. Saw myself walking across the room, closing the distance between us and lying down next to her, pressing myself as close as breathing, reaching out to trace her cheek with my finger and capturing one sparkling teardrop on the tip, regretting everything and promising everything, and meaning it, holding my breath, waiting to hear her speak.

Then I was back at the farm again, home in Dillon. Leaning on a fence, looking at a green field of unripe wheat, waiting, anxious, uncertain about what I was to do. Then hearing the hum in the distance, feeling it first in my fingertips, then through my whole body as the hum expanded and swirled around me, making the ground shake and the wire strands stretched between the fenceposts vibrate like strummed guitar strings. The roar of a plane filled my ears and mouth and eyes, pouring into every empty cavern of my soul, a salve against uncertainty. I looked up to see a magnificent biplane, painted candy-apple red, with a complex web of wire stretched between wings four times as long as a man, descending from the clouds like an enormous and elegant bird of prey. Lindbergh was at the controls. The green stalks of wheat bowed as he came lower, lying prostrate at his approach. He circled the field, leaning over the side of the open cockpit and waving to me. "Sorry, I'm late!" he shouted over the howl of the engine. "Are you ready? Morgan? Morgan, are you ready? Look up! Let's go!"

"Yes," I croaked through cracked, bleeding lips. "I'm ready."

"Then look up, Morgan! Open your eyes!"

I did, and the wind blew hard, pushing against the billowing fabric of the red parachute, exposing my face and eyes to the open sky and the circling ballet of the search plane flying overhead.

34

Morgan

Port Mooresby, New Guinea—July 1944

I'm in the hospital. Impressions of reality, disparate perceptions of consciousness pierce the walls of delirium and then retreat, never quite melding into full awareness; slanting columns of dust-moted light shafting through venetian blinds, cool sheets, the steady whoosh of an electric fan, efficient padding of rubber-soled shoes on linoleum as a white-capped nurse checks the tubes running into my arm, throbbing pain coming from the fat gauze bandage on my foot, sharp smells of rubbing alcohol and disinfectant, and finally, a pair of eyes that I've seen before, but where? Oh, yes. I remember now—in my own mirror. Eyes exactly like my own, but not my own, more cautious than mine, more acquainted with loss, watching me with raw concern, moving closer, flickering relief when I stir under the ironed sheet.

Getting up from his vigil on the straight-backed, metal visitors' chair, he stands by the bed and leans over the metal rail. He smiles, but barely, and laying his hand on top of the sheet, he whispers hoarsely, "Well done, son. Well done. Everything's going to be all right now."

I can't summon the strength to say I believe him. Instead, I lift my hand to cover my father's and drift back into sleep.

He comes again the next day, when I'm fully awake. He enters my room on Colonel MacDonald's right flank, a disinterested step behind the officer, making sure I see him hanging back so I'll know not to give our relationship away to the colonel. He is Charles Lindbergh again, a kind friend visiting a fellow member of the flying fraternity

I'm a little disappointed when I see how nervously his eyes dart around the room, wondering if I'll give him away, but of course I knew it would be this way. He can't go around shouting news of his bastard son to the world, and I really wouldn't want him to. Coming to see me at all, signaling his personal interest in one injured pilot among the many, was risky, but he'd come. It was good to see him. I wanted to say so, but I just nodded, waiting for the colonel to speak first.

"How are you feeling, Lieutenant? I brought you a visitor."

"I'm fine. Thank you, sir. Mr. Lindbergh," I acknowledge him formally, "it's nice of you to drop by."

"My pleasure. Glad to see you're feeling better."

"Glennon, you owe your life to Mr. Lindbergh, do you know that? We sent search planes to fly over every island we thought you could possibly have made it to, but with no luck. After a couple of days I was ready to call off the search, but Mr. Lindbergh talked me out of it. He assured me that using the new fuel-stretching techniques he'd taught you, you could be hundreds of miles farther out than we'd figured. He was very persuasive and very persistent. In fact"—the colonel chuckled—"he basically refused to leave my office until I agreed to widen the search area and try again. Hell! I only did it to get him out of my hair! Didn't think we'd have a chance in the world of finding you, but I'm sure glad I was wrong."

"Me too, sir. And thank you, Mr. Lindbergh, not just for keeping after the colonel, but also for teaching me how to get those extra miles out of my fuel tank. I'd have died about four times that day if you hadn't."

Lindbergh shrugged off my thanks. "You're a fine pilot—the kind of fellow that keeps a cool head in every situation. I knew you'd remember what you'd learned and use it. All I did was remind the colonel of that."

"Very forcefully. Well, I'm just glad everything worked out in the end. You're a good man, Glennon. I'd have hated to lose you."

"Yes, sir. Thank you, sir. Excuse me, Colonel, but do you have any idea how long it will be before I can report for duty? I'd like to get out of here as soon as possible."

The colonel's smile faded. Clearly, he was discomforted by my question. "Morgan, didn't you . . . hasn't the doctor spoken to you yet?"

"Yes," I answered slowly, wondering what the colonel was getting at. "He came to see me this morning and told me all about the operation, that they'd had to amputate two of the toes on my infected foot." The doctor had smiled and complimented me on taking the news so well, but why wouldn't I? Only a few days before I'd been lying on a beach, delirious, dehydrated, and resigned to the fact of my own death. Losing a couple of toes seemed a small price to pay for waking in the land of the living. "Why? What's wrong, sir? I asked the doctor if I could fly again, and he said yes, that I'd need to have some physical therapy and such, but after that I'd definitely be able to fly again."

The colonel took a breath and let it out slowly. "But not for the military, I'm afraid." He looked at Lindbergh, then back to me. "I'm sorry, Morgan, but without a whole limb, you're categorized as 4-F. That's what we came to tell you. You're going home, son."

❧ 35 ❧

Georgia

Liberal, Kansas—October 1944

It took every ounce of self-control I had to gently close the door to Hemingway's office and exit with my head held high and my dignity intact. What I really wanted to do was tell him, in the kind of language generally reserved for loading docks and locker rooms, exactly what I thought of him, then spit in his eyes and slam the door on my way out. But I didn't. I wouldn't give him the satisfaction of knowing just how hurt I was. And no matter what, I wasn't going to cry. At least not where anyone could see me.

Instead, I walked into the outer office and nodded to Anders, Hemingway's lapdog aide, before going back to my classroom. The smug look on his face told me that he already knew why his boss had called me into the office.

I was fired. And not just me—all the WASP. The program was being dismantled. Smiling, Hemingway read me a letter from headquarters stating that as of December 20th the WASP would cease to exist. Finished, he slid his reading glasses down to the end of his nose and peered at me over the rims.

"The war is nearly won, and there are plenty of more suitable pilots, *male* pilots," he said archly, "to fill these positions. This should have happened months ago. It was just ridiculous, you girls taking away jobs from the men! If you'd had an ounce of decency or patriotism, you'd have resigned and stepped aside long ago." He shook his head in disgust. "I can't imagine what General Arnold was thinking of starting this nonsense in the first place. If it had been me in charge, the first memo hitting my desk suggesting women be allowed to fly for the military would have been tossed into the wastebasket before you could say Jack Robinson."

Squaring my shoulders and keeping my eyes focused on a spot just over the colonel's head, I said, "Given the fact that more than twelve thousand aircraft have been safely delivered by WASP pilots over the last couple of years, I suppose it is fortunate for the country that you weren't in charge." It was folly to speak, I knew that, but I couldn't help it. I had put up with this wingless wonder of a base commander for as long as I could.

His already thin lips became even thinner. "Your replacement will arrive in a few weeks. You'll stay on to train him until the twentieth. I want you off my base on that date by seventeen hundred hours." He pushed his glasses back up off his nose and started pretending to read a memorandum, not deigning to look up as he dismissed me. "That is all."

✁ 36 ✁

Morgan

Dillon, Oklahoma—October 1944

Mama was watching, and so was Paul, but I didn't care. I opened my arms and embraced the Jenny, laying my arms and cheek against the smooth body of my sleek little plane, whispering to her like she was a living thing. "You look good, old girl. I missed you." And it was true, I'd flown a dozen other planes since I'd left three years before, bigger planes with more horsepower, speed, and range, but none of them had ever looked as fine to me as the Jenny did that day. She might not have all the fancy gadgetry and gizmos of a modern military flying machine, but those planes were just that—machines, cold collections of metal and motor designed to do a job. The Jenny was so much more. She was my poem to freedom, designed for delight, to help mortals do what the ancients imagined only the gods could—walk the wind and touch the bounds of heaven.

Behind me, I could hear a scrape-thump, scrape-thump as Mama limped along with the more even sound of Paul's footsteps. They stopped a respectful distance behind me, wanting to give me a moment. I think they understood what this meant to me.

I'd been in the States, recovering at the hospital in San Diego for weeks but had only gotten back to Dillon three days before. My train was met by Mama, Paul, Grandma, Ruby, and about half the town, all of them waving little American flags. There was to be an official "welcome home" reception in the church basement after Sunday services, but even so the house had been so filled with visitors and well-wishers that Mama and I had hardly found a minute to talk. It was all very touching, but I couldn't wait to get away. This was the moment I'd been waiting for. I was truly, finally home.

Collecting myself, I patted the Jenny like she was a good horse and said to no one in particular, "Whitey did a good job taking care of her, don't you think? She looks as good as the day I left."

"He did," Paul agreed. He helped me crank the propeller and get the engine started. She turned over so easily that I could probably have done it on my own, but I still needed the one crutch to get around, more for balance than anything, so I welcomed Paul's assistance.

Mama was worried. I had a crate set up that would act as a step for her, and Paul would give her a boost into the cockpit. Even with the bum foot, I could get in on my own if she'd let me steady myself on her shoulder so I could climb up.

The whirl of the propeller was loud, and Mama had to yell to make herself heard over the noise. "Are you sure you're up to this, Morgan? We've hardly got one good set of legs between us. Maybe we should wait until you're stronger."

"Mama, I've waited three years, and I'm not waiting any longer! I feel better than ever!" I shouted as I settled myself in the cockpit, and it was true. "I'm young, I'm strong, and the wind's behind me! Look up there, Mama!" I shouted joyously, raising my arm high over my head. "This is my sky! I own it! Now get up here, old woman, or I'm taking off without you!"

* * *

It is the strangest thing. Every time I taxi down that runway, I'm half hopeful and half doubtful. I ask myself, Will it work this time? Will we really take off?—and then, when we actually do, I am amazed. I've done it hundreds of times, but it is always a miracle, astonishing and utterly new. And yet, as I rise higher and higher, then finally level off to gaze out over the generous, breathtakingly beautiful land below, the scene below is just as I knew it would be, constant and comforting as it always is, always was. Waiting silently, like a painting commissioned for me and my familiars at the beginning of days. Flying, I am newborn and ancient all at once. I remember the promise that someday there will be a new heaven and a new earth, and I wonder if the words mean what people think they do. Will there indeed be a new heaven and earth or instead, will we finally have new eyes so we can see it all properly, as it was meant to be seen from the first? I wonder.

But today it is enough for me to be here, back where I belong, and to share it with Mama. I have wanted her to see it for so long, to know by sight that which her mind imagined and her fingers fashioned. She is in front of me, sitting in the passenger seat, the wind toying with the stray ends of hair that escape from under her leather flight helmet. Fearless, she lifts her hand out straight and spreads her fingers wide, trying to catch hold of the wind.

And suddenly, in that one simple, familiar, self-possessed gesture—I know. This is not just my homecoming. It is hers, too. She has been here before, with him. And I smile. There is not much all three of us have shared, Mama, Lindbergh, and I. Not home, or bread, or even name—but this! This undeniable calling, these hungry eyes that have seen and long to see again the new heaven and new earth, this is our common blood. This is what bound us from the very beginning.

That night, after the house was quiet and everyone but Mama and I had gone to bed, we sat at the kitchen table with the lights low, drinking tea, I finally asked. "You went up before, didn't you? With him. Before I was born."

"Yes," she said. "And you saw him." It was a statement, but there was a question behind it.

I nodded. "A couple of times. Our first meeting wasn't very pleasant. I heaped a pile of burning coals on his head and then told him to get out." Mama didn't flinch, but her eyes gave away her inward wince. "But then, when I was stranded on the island, I started thinking. He could have handled things differently—he should have, for all our sakes—but he was trying, as best he knew how, to make things right. I respected that. And then, when I woke up in the hospital, he was there sitting by my bed."

"He was?"

I nodded. "And then he came twice more. Once with Colonel MacDonald, when they told me I was being discharged, and then again on his own, just before he had to leave New Guinea. He didn't stay long, but I think he just wanted to say good-bye, to make sure things were all right between us."

"And are they?" Mama asked.

I thought for a minute before answering. "Yes, in a way. At least as all right as they can be. I'm not angry anymore, if that's what you mean, but I don't expect to see him again. He has a family and children. There's no point in adding their hurt to ours, is there?"

Mama's eyes were thoughtful, but she didn't answer me.

"And you know, I'm grateful to him. If it hadn't been for him, they never would have found me. And, I can't be sure, but I think that new instructor's job that's waiting for me is his doing, too. There are plenty of able bodied military pilots lined up around the block for those jobs. It's a cushy assignment compared to combat. Somebody must have pulled some strings to get it for me, and I think he was the one."

"Well, it's about time," Mama said bitterly. She poured more tea into her cup and stared into it as she stirred the brew, making the spoon clink hard against the china surface. "You're his son. I guess you deserve a little something from him. You deserved . . ."

I just shrugged and traced my finger around the rim of my cup, waiting for her to go on. She was upset, that was clear, but I wasn't sure who she was upset with or why.

"Did he tell you about it? About . . . when he took me flying?" She glanced up at me and then quickly fixed her eyes back to the bottom of her teacup.

"No."

"You know, I only flew with him that one time, and it was so brief. If . . ." She paused, blushing a little. "If you hadn't come along, it might have been easy to think I'd imagined the whole thing, but in some ways it was the truest moment of my entire life. I've never forgotten it." She pressed the edge of the blue willow cup, part of the treasured set the church gave Mama and Paul as a wedding present, flat against her lip without drinking, remembering. After a moment she looked up at me and said plainly, "I should have told you about your father before."

That was it, then. She was angry with herself. Well, maybe that was all right.

I took a breath. "I wish you had, Mama. It wouldn't necessarily have made things easier, but I think it would have made me feel less distant from you. Growing up, I felt you were always looking for something, waiting for someone, that there was this hole in your life and that I was the cause of it."

Her eyes teared as she reached across the table and took my hand. "Morgan, don't ever think that. I did wait for him for so many, many years. I was so young. We both were. I didn't understand that when Slim, the boy I fell in love with more than twenty years ago, flew off that day, I'd never see him again. How could we have known? Slim was swallowed up by Charles Lindbergh, a man more cautious, more calculated and cynical than Slim. He had to be. When Slim climbed into the cockpit of the *Spirit of St. Louis* and flew across the Atlantic, the world changed, and he was the one who changed it. He landed in Paris, into an era that hadn't existed until he touched down at LeBouget Airfield." She looked off into a distant place, remembering.

"I saw the pictures of him, surrounded by the mobs that screamed for him everywhere he went, always wanting more of him. But whatever he did or was, it was never enough. Every time I saw those photographs of him with this stiff, nervous smile pasted to his lips, and him surrounded by the crowds of clamoring strangers, I became more determined to be the one person who didn't demand anything from him. That was how I thought I'd prove my love and how I'd bring him back to us, eventually. I didn't understand—not for a long, long time—that Slim was gone forever. Now I think it happened that first day. When he stepped out of the *Spirit* and into the clutch of the crowds, they suffocated him. Slim was too innocent, too trusting to survive, so someone stronger and harder took his place, Charles Lindbergh. And no one noticed. Not even me."

Mama wiped away a tear with the heel of her hand and sniffed before going on. "No, that's not really so. Part of me knew, but I didn't want to believe it. I just wanted so much for the dream to be true. But, Morgan," she said, gazing at me squarely, her voice suddenly deeper and more serious, "you were the part of the dream that was true and the best thing that ever, ever happened to me. If I have suffered any slights in my life, any disappointments, or hardships, they were worth it ten times over because of you. I have been foolish and fearful, and you've suffered because of it. I'm sorry. I thought I was protecting you, but maybe I was just protecting myself."

She started to apologize again, but I stopped her. She'd said all she needed to. "It's all right, Mama. I know. You loved him so. I've always known that."

"I did," she affirmed. "At that moment I did, but it couldn't last.

Your grandpa used to say that real love was with someone who'd be there when the crop fails and your sight grows weak, that you could count on it like the earth under your feet."

In my mind, I could see just how he would make this pronouncement to Mama, his love-struck daughter, his finger a bare inch from her face as he labored, unsuccessfully, to make her hear him.

"Oh," Mama said with a sigh, "I didn't know how right he was."

"Until Paul?"

"Until Paul," she answered. "I love him so. When I think of all the years I wasted, pushing him away, I could kick myself. That might have been the most foolish thing of all."

I couldn't deny it, so I didn't say anything. Mama looked at me and smiled, knowing what I was thinking.

"Well, as Grandma would say, there's no use crying over spilt milk. But, how about you?" she asked casually, in the tone she used when she wanted it to look like she wasn't prying even though she was. "After our breakfast in San Diego, I figured we'd be seeing a lot of Virginia Pratt once you came home, but . . ." She shrugged, holding out empty hands.

I shook my head, "No, Mama. We had a . . . well . . . an interest in each other for a while. But it wasn't love, not for either of us. I knew that right from the beginning, and she did too, but I think we both wanted to be wanted, so we let it go on a lot longer than we should have. I liked the idea of having someone waiting for me, but I wrote her and broke it off right after I left San Diego. I was wrong to keep her waiting so long."

Mama lifted her eyebrows "Well, from what I heard, she wasn't exactly waiting. Ruby told me she'd been writing to six different servicemen, trying to wrangle a proposal out of one of them."

I smiled. "And did it work?"

She nodded, "She's going to marry George Sanderson when he

comes home for his Christmas leave. I'm just glad you already ended it with her. I was worried that I was going to have to tell you all about it and break your heart."

Mama was obviously scandalized, but I just laughed. After all those love letters, all those months, all the anguish and guilt I'd gone through, worried that I was keeping Virginia from finding love . . . Fountain was right, a girl that looked like Virginia wasn't going to be lonely for long.

"Nope. You're off the hook, Mama. Besides, when it comes to heartbreak, it's too late. Somebody beat Virginia to it." I was still smiling, but I'd surprised myself. I hadn't intended to tell Mama about Georgia, but it was too late now. I had to let her in on my secret. Maybe I'd wanted to all along.

"I met a girl during my training. Her name is Georgia. She's a pilot, and she's . . ." I pushed back the kitchen chair, jumped to my feet, and started pacing, too unsettled to sit. "Mama, she's just the most wonderful girl! I never met anyone like her. No one has ever made me feel this way, and it's not just something physical, Mama. With Virginia, she was so beautiful that it took every ounce of self-control I had . . ." I stopped, suddenly remembering that it was my mother I was speaking to, but when I looked at her, she seemed unperturbed, just inclined her head a little, encouraging me to go on. And I wanted to tell her. I had to, because Mama was the only one in the world who would understand.

"What I mean is, Mama, I know the difference between love and lust. And I love Georgia! I know that now. But we'd spent so little time together, and I was worried. I didn't want to tell her anything that wasn't true. I'd already been through that with Virginia. I didn't want to do anything that might end up hurting her later, but that's what happened anyway.

"She came to see me before I shipped out. Things got pretty passionate, and I ended up pushing her away. Not because I didn't want her, but because I did want her, so badly. But I didn't want to end up hurting her. I was trying to protect her!" I cried.

I stopped my pacing and grabbed on to the top rung of the wooden chair, facing my mother. "I kept thinking about you, Mama. I didn't know about Lindbergh then, but I did know that someone a long time ago must have made you fall in love and then left you."

"Oh, Morgan," Mama whispered.

"I thought I loved her, Mama, but I wasn't sure. Everything was happening so fast! And if I did love her, that was all the more reason to hold back. I was only hours from shipping out. I just couldn't take the risk. I didn't want what happened to you to happen to Georgia, but she ran off before I could explain. I should have gone after her, but I was so mixed up." I loosened my grip on the chair and held open my empty hands. "I let her go.

"I told myself that it was for the best, that it was no good falling in love with a girl who was thousands of miles away, especially when I was about to go back into combat. I tried to forget about her, but I just couldn't."

"Morgan," Mama chided gently, "if that's how you feel about her, you should tell her. The war is over for you. There's nothing holding you back from falling in love now, if there ever was."

"I know, Mama," I said. "Believe me, I know."

Frustrated, I rubbed my face with my hands. "When I was stuck on the island I thought about her so much. I realized I loved her. I did from the first minute I saw her."

Mama smiled. "Seems like you did a lot of thinking out on that island."

"There wasn't much else to do. I promised myself that if I ever got out of there, I would tell her the whole truth. And I did. As soon as I was well enough to hold a pen, even before I got back to the States, I wrote her a letter, explained everything, and told her I loved her. That was months ago, but I've never heard a word from her."

Mama got up from the table and came to put a comforting arm around me. "Well, you should write her again. Morgan, you were halfway across the world when you sent that. Anything could have happened to that letter. Maybe she never received it."

I shook my head. "I thought of that. I wrote again from the hospital in San Diego. That was weeks ago, and nothing." I shrugged hopelessly. "No answer. Or rather, that is her answer—nothing. She wants nothing to do with me. She doesn't love me."

Mama wrapped both her arms around me. And I let her. "Oh, Morgan," she said. "Morgan."

37

Georgia

Liberal, Kansas—November 1944

How did I get myself into this? I asked myself as I peered in the mirror and I wiped the color off my lips with a tissue before applying a different, hopefully more suitable shade of lipstick. I pressed another tissue between my lips to blot the color, peered at my reflection again, and groaned. Too orange. How had I gotten to be twenty-three years old and still not own a tube of nice, pink lipstick?

If Fran were here to witness my frantic and clumsy attempts at cosmetic application, she'd have teased me mercilessly. "See?" she'd say. "All those times I tried to teach you about makeup and fashion, you made fun of me, but now I'll bet you wish you would have listened." Yes, Fran would have had lots of fun at my expense, but in the end, she'd have pulled a pink lipstick from the depths of her purse and saved the day. Too bad she wasn't here.

I heard the crackle of rubber tires pulling into the gravel driveway of my landlord's house. I'd have to wear the orange lipstick. At least my new dress looked nice. It had been a splurge, but I couldn't very well eat Thanksgiving dinner in a flight suit; and, besides, in just a few more weeks I wouldn't be able to wear uniforms all the time. I was going to have to get some civilian clothes. I buttoned, unbuttoned, and rebuttoned the top button of my dress, deciding that modesty was the best policy, then donned the hat that the woman in the shop had assured me looked perfectly elegant with the dress. A quick look in the glass convinced me to take it off again. The big pheasant feather pinned to the side made me look like a relative of the main course. Maybe I should wear my WASP beret? Nope. Wrong color.

I heard a car door slam. Panicked, I ran to the window and pulled back the curtain to confirm my worst fears. I was hatless, petrified, and out of time. Morgan was here to pick me up for Thanksgiving dinner with his family.

How did I get myself into this?

Ten days before, I'd been pacing back and forth in my empty classroom, waiting to meet the man who was to take my job. All morning I'd felt like a pot simmering on a stove, just on the edge of boiling, and as afternoon and the introduction to my replacement approached, I became even more agitated. Ever since I'd let loose with that "Good thing you aren't in charge" barb in Hemingway's office, he'd made my last days as a flight instructor as miserable as possible, assigning every dimwit or malcontent on base to my class, suddenly deciding that my classroom should be made into a conference room and moving me to the smallest, mostly poorly lit and poorly heated space on base, then denying my supply requisition when I asked for a portable heater! And though I couldn't prove Hemingway was behind it, I certainly had my suspicions when my paycheck was mysteriously "lost" by the accounting department and it took them three weeks and thirty pounds of paperwork to issue a replacement check.

The more I thought about it, the angrier I became. What had I ever done to deserve this besides leave my home and business behind to serve my country?

Donna Lee had called it right: the days when newspapers ran glowing, glamorized stories about selfless, patriotic WASP pilots ably pitching in to help in the war were long gone. In its place were nasty letters to the editor and derisive newspaper stories that referred to the WASP as "powder puff pilots" and claimed female pilots were less qualified, cost more to train, and had higher accident and fatality rates than the men, all of which were outright lies. And the closer we got to a vote on the militarization of the WASP, the worse it got.

Shortly after Pamela's bridal shower, Donna Lee sent me a newspaper article from the *Galveston Gazette* that summed up the situation perfectly.

Ground Those Glamour Girls! Say Jobless He-Man Pilots

Today, the fiercest campaign in the historic battle of the sexes is being fought in the air. Thousands of well-trained male pilots complain that they are jobless, while the WASP continue ferrying planes, towing targets, tracking and doing courier work for the Army at $250 a month.

Members of Congress have received mountains of mail from unhappy male pilots, most of them former instructors with the now defunct Civilian Pilot Training Program. Reports from the Capitol say that few Congressmen are willing to take up the cause of the WASP, especially in light of the campaign mounted by male pilots' associations call-

ing Jacqueline Cochran's WASP "glamour girls"
that are more expensive, less well-trained, and less
experienced than the men.

Some of the masculine comments are far from
gallant. "Thirty-five-hour wonders" is one tag
they've pinned on the lady fliers.

"This program is just bleeding the taxpayers
dry," said one disgruntled male. "Costs $7000 to
train every female. It's the most expensive way to
ferry planes."

Another said, "If these girls had a shred of patriotism, they'd resign."

"It just doesn't make sense," sighed one baffled
pilot. "Not when we have so many qualified men
who are grounded."

Those in the know on Capitol Hill say that the
men won't go down without a fight and will keep on
the pressure until the ladies holler "uncle."

I wrote a letter to Jacqueline Cochran, asking how long we were
going to sit there and take this, and why didn't she counter with
some press releases and interviews of her own that would let the
public know the truth? Eventually I got back an officially worded
letter advising me that as head of the program, she felt it was best
for the WASP to take the high road, that the accomplishments of
the program spoke for themselves, and that it would be best to wait
for the furor to die down. I knew that she and General Arnold had
been pushing for a bill that would finally militarize the WASP, giving us the military pay and benefits that our male counterparts enjoyed, and between the lines, I felt she was saying that we couldn't
afford to rock the boat and irritate Congress just as the legislation
was coming to the floor. Wait it out; that was her strategy. It was the
ladylike strategy, and it was wrong. The boys were playing hardball,

and we should have done the same, but we didn't, and now it was too late. The WASP had been shown the door. I was infuriated by our summary dismissal, but I was even more infuriated by the unanswered attack upon our record. The women of the WASP had helped win the war with the same attitude of sacrifice, dedication, and patriotism as any combat soldier, and thirty-eight brave and skilled women had selflessly paid the ultimate sacrifice in the effort, but no one would ever know it. Unless someone corrected the record, the public would forever think of the WASP as the "glamour girl" pilots who did little more than joy-ride around in Piper Cubs wearing pink lipstick and five-hundred-dollar custom-tailored uniforms while looking for marriage material in the form of officers and good-looking male fliers.

Even now, just thinking about it made me want to throw something. Without thinking, I grabbed the P-38 model that was sitting on my desk and furiously launched it across the room and toward the door, which opened just before the model crashed into it.

"What the . . . ?" Instinctively, my replacement lifted his hand to shield himself from the tiny P-38 attack and closed his fist around the body of the little plane as deftly as if he'd been catching a ball on the fly. "Is this some new kind of combat simulation?"

My hand flew up to cover my mouth, and my voice was muffled, blocked by my outstretched fingers. "Morgan?" I squeaked in disbelief. "What are you doing here?"

Previously distracted by the Lilliputian onslaught, Morgan now focused his attention on me. He looked just as surprised as I felt. "Georgia? I'm the new navigation and instruments instructor. They told me to come here and meet up with the instructor I'll be replacing." His furrowed brow smoothed out as a smile spread slowly across his face. "I'm awfully glad to see you, Georgia. I didn't think I'd ever see you again. But"—he shrugged, confused—"what are you doing here?"

I'd heard from Pamela that he'd been found, and I'd thanked

God for it, but Pam's letter hadn't said anything about Morgan being sent home. I'd assumed he was still in the Pacific. What was going on? "Morgan, is this some kind of a joke? Did Hemingway put you up to this?"

"Pardon me?"

I didn't answer. I was still trying to get my mind around this whole situation. But the confusion Morgan's face told me that, no indeed, he wasn't kidding. He glanced around the room, craning his neck as if the person he was supposed to meet might be hiding under a desk or behind the American flag that stood next to the blackboard.

"They told me I'd find the old instructor in here. I guess he must have stepped out for a minute. Have you seen him?"

"Yeah," I said in a voice brittle with irritation. "I have. You're looking at him."

Suffice it to say, we didn't start off on a very good note. Certainly Morgan wasn't the first pilot I'd met who had been so unable to conceive of a female flight instructor that he mistook me for the secretary, file clerk, cleaning woman, or girlfriend of the "real" instructor—far from it—but somehow I'd expected more from him. We quarreled, and by the time it was over, I'd stormed out of my office and walked home without even showing him around.

By the time I reached my apartment, I'd walked off a good bit of my mad and actually felt ashamed of myself. After all, it wasn't his fault. All he'd done was taken a job; he didn't know it was my job. But, still, of all the people to have replace me! The man who'd wooed me one minute, rejected me the next, and then sailed off to the Pacific without ever sending me so much as a postcard. Of all the humiliations I'd suffered since Hemingway had triumphantly given me notice, this had to be the worst. For a minute, I thought of just going back to the base, turning in my wings, and going home.

After all, it was just a matter of days until they'd force me to do exactly that. Why prolong the agony?

I spent the rest of the day and evening pacing, thinking, and riding the roller coaster of my emotions, but by nightfall I'd come to a conclusion. No matter what, I wasn't going to let them get to me. Uncle Sam, and Colonel Hemingway, and the reporter from the *Galveston Gazette,* and every man on the face of the earth who'd ever told me I should trade in my wings for an apron and a wire whisk could just kiss my backside. And if Morgan Glennon felt that way, well, then, he could pucker up and get in line! They could be as ungrateful and mean-spirited as they wanted, but I wasn't going to stoop to their level. I was going to do my job and do it well until the minute they said I couldn't. In the end, they'd force me out, but when they did, I'd leave with my head held high and my dignity intact.

Before I went to bed that night, I brushed my uniform and dragged out my ironing board, carefully pressing a knife-edge crease into my slacks and made sure my battle jacket was spotless and free of even the thought of a wrinkle. Come hell or high water, I was going to be the sharpest-looking, most professional instructor on base. Even so, I knew a well-pressed uniform could only mask so much. At least until December 20th, I was still a WASP, and if Morgan was smart, he'd best watch out for my sting!

Of course, that was before I heard about the stunt he'd pulled with Lieutenant Anders. When I got wind of that . . . Well, let's just say that my opinion of Morgan Glennon was considerably altered.

38

Morgan

Dillon, Oklahoma—November 1944

Crossing the border from Kansas into Oklahoma, I glanced at Georgia for what must have been the tenth time since we'd left Liberal, but I couldn't help myself; I just had to make sure she really was there, sitting in the front seat of the Packard I'd borrowed from Paul, on the way to Thanksgiving dinner with my family.

Less than two weeks before, she'd hurled a model plane in my direction, along with a variety of names and accusations, and then stormed off. Well, I hadn't taken too kindly to that. I'd stormed off myself, to the watering hole nearest the base, ordered a beer, and waited for the desire to punch something to fade. Before long Anders, the base commander's toadying aide, showed up and parked himself on the bar stool next to me, getting drunk and giving his opinion on women, the WASP, and the world in general.

When I sat down, I'd felt bitter, twisted, and misunderstood, but after five minutes of listening to the obnoxious aide, my attitude had altered considerably. If this jerk's posture in any way reflected that of his boss (and I was pretty sure that was the case; Lieutenant Anders clearly didn't have the smarts to come out with an opinion that hadn't been issued to him by whatever superior he was currently fawning upon), then I didn't blame Georgia one bit for her outburst. If I'd been in her shoes, I'd have probably thrown a grenade, not just a toy airplane.

"Of course," Anders remarked knowingly before taking another drink of his Lucky Stripe, "it was all a publicity stunt from the start." He put down his glass, leaving a long streak of beer foam, like a child's milk mustache, on his upper lip.

"Uh," I said, lowering my head and tapping my lip with my finger. Anders looked confused for a minute but then caught on, wiping the foam from his face with the back of his hand.

"A publicity stunt? How do you figure?"

"Well, sure it was! This whole idea of letting women fly airplanes was just publicity, something to make the folks at home feel good, a nice little human-interest story to distract people from the horrors of war. Keep up morale, don'tcha know. It's not like these little girls do any serious flying. I mean, ferrying planes is just a cakewalk."

"Oh, yeah? Is that what you think?" I thought about Georgia and our flight from Arizona to San Diego, how she'd handled that big cargo plane like she'd been doing it all her life, and about the stories we'd shared of stalled engines, frozen wing flaps, and landing blind on runways so thick with fog you couldn't see five feet in front of you. A cakewalk. Right.

The drunken aide nodded. "I mean, you're a pilot, you know what I'm talking about. An airplane is no place for a woman. Am I right?"

"So, you're not a pilot yourself?"

He shook his head and belched. "I went to Langley, but after a couple of weeks the brass decided I was too valuable as an administrator to risk losing me in combat."

Meaning you washed out, I thought.

"That's when they made me Colonel Hemingway's aide. It's a plum assignment. The colonel's going places. Very well thought of in Washington," he whispered conspiratorially. "And I'm going with him. Of course, I had a little advantage getting the job. My uncle George is at the Pentagon. He and Hemingway were at West Point, so Uncle George put in a good word for me." Anders winked as he gripped the handle of his beer mug and took another drink.

"That's always the way. Am I right? And not just in the army. It's not what you know, it's who you know. I mean, you must have had somebody pulling for you, or you wouldn't be here, would you?" A flush of heat and anger rose on my flesh, knowing what he said was probably true but hating him for saying it.

"And that girl you're replacing," he declared, holding up one finger and wagging it at me. "She must have pulled something or someone to get here, if you know what I mean." He guffawed, pleased with himself. I felt my hand close into a fist. With a lascivious sneer, Anders cupped his two hands in front of his chest. "I mean, did you get a load of the personalities on her? I'd like to get me some of that, I can tell you. Half the guys on base have tried it on with her, but she gives 'em all the brush-off. Yeah"—he snorted—"like you can make me believe she's not putting it out for somebody. If she wasn't, she'd never have gotten within five hundred miles of this job. Am I right? She don't give the time of day to a lower rank, but you can't tell me she doesn't have round heels for the fella that's got enough bars on his shoulders. Am I—"

But before he could finish, I stood up, grabbed him by the scrawny collar that circled his scrawny neck, and answered his question with a single haymaker directly to the bridge of his nose. It broke with a dull but satisfying crack, and Anders flew backward and fell to the floor unconscious.

Hearing the noise, the bartender shouted and ran over to see what the ruckus was, but when he saw it was Anders laid out on the floor, he just grinned and said, "Somebody should have done that a long time ago."

I dug a dollar out of my pocket, laid it on the bar, and walked out.

After I got outside I started to wonder if I'd just gotten myself fired, but I didn't care. I'd have done it again. It was the first time I'd purposely punched another human being since Johnny McCurdle, and the result was just as satisfying, maybe more so.

As it turned out, either Colonel Hemingway detested his aide as much as everyone else, or Anders had been right and my "connections" made me too dangerous to can, because the next day all Hemingway said was it better not happen again.

And I think Georgia might have heard what happened, because when I saw her next she was, if not exactly friendly, at least not as frosty as she had been. She let me sit in on her classes, gave me a tour of the base, and a thorough run-down of how to get past the bureaucratic snafus that were peculiar to this operation, and generally did a great job of preparing me to take over in December. I wanted very much to ask her about my letter and why she'd never answered it, but I figured it would be best to wait for her to speak first. Obviously, she didn't feel the same about me as I did about her, or she would have said something, but I was determined to change her mind.

It had to happen; it was meant to be. If not, why would we have been brought together in Liberal, Kansas, of all places? I viewed our reunion not as coincidence, but as appointment with destiny. Georgia Welles was meant to be my girl.

I asked her out to dinner every day, and every day she said no. On Tuesday I asked if she'd join me for Thanksgiving dinner with the family. I don't know if I'd worn her down, or won her over, or if she was simply overcome by an unexpected wave of holiday spirit, but she finally said yes. I was so surprised that I actually asked her to repeat herself.

"I'm sorry. What was that?"

Her eyes smiled. "I said, 'Yes, I'd love to have dinner with you and your family.'"

After that I just grinned.

Seeing her sitting in the front seat of the Packard wearing a new dress and fussing nervously with her sleeve, I was grinning again.

✎ 39 ✎

Georgia

Dillon, Oklahoma—Thanksgiving Day, 1944

The land around Dillon is flat as a pancake, so I could see the Glennon farm a good mile before we turned into the driveway. It had a big barn flanked by a one-story frame house with a peaked roof and a good-sized porch that must have been a nice spot to spend an evening when the weather was fine. There were flower beds near the porch, filled with bare branches that looked like rose-bush canes. And next to the house, surrounded by a swath of pro-tective chicken-wire fencing, was an enormous dormant vegetable garden. It must have been something to see at the height of summer. As we got closer I noticed something else, something that was defi-nitely not to be found on most other farms.

"Morgan, is that a train caboose next to your house?"

"Sure is. That's where Aunt Ruby lives. It's all fixed up inside. Has a little sitting room and a wood stove for heating and every-thing. And over there," he said, pointing to a place just east of the barn, "is an old freight car that's been made into the biggest henhouse you've ever seen. The Glennon chicken and egg business is quite a going concern."

I laughed.

"I'm serious," he said, mocking offense. "My grandpa hauled home those train cars one day. We remodeled them together—the caboose so Ruby would have a place of her own and the freight car so I could start my own egg business. That was back in the Depression, and let me tell you, if it hadn't been for the chickens and Mama's quilts, I'm not sure we would have made it."

"Your grandfather must have been a smart man."

"He was," Morgan said quietly. "And a good one. You'd have liked him."

"And your mother's quilts, is she still making them?" ·

"Not like she did back then. During the Depression she turned out simple nine-patch designs on a sewing machine as fast and cheap as she could, just so we could scrape together enough to survive. Now she's gone back to what she really loves, making her special quilts, and all by hand. You've never seen anything like it. They look just like paintings and each one takes her months to finish." Morgan took a right onto the drive that led to the farmhouse. "Here we are!"

I cleared my throat and reached up to smooth my hair, thinking I should have worn a hat after all. Morgan looked at me, smiled, and reached over to pat my shoulder.

"Don't worry," he said, pulling up in front of the house and turning off the engine. "They're all going to love you."

I started to ask him how he could be so sure of that, but before I could say anything, a waving, smiling stream of people started pouring out of the front door and onto the porch.

I was introduced to Morgan's grandmother, Clare, first. Her hair was gray, and her face, with high, prominent cheekbones that made me wonder if there wasn't some Indian blood in the family, was lined and weathered, but her eyes were bright and intelligent, and her grip was impressively strong. Later, over dinner, she declared she could still lift a bale of hay and carry it from field to farm. I believed her.

Ruby was next. Morgan had told me about her, how she'd been his mother's best friend since grade school, how she'd come to live with them when her husband, like so many Oklahomans during the starving dust-bowl years, went west to look for work and how, when he'd been killed in a logging accident, Ruby had just stayed on and become one of the family. It was a tragic history, but you wouldn't have known it by looking at Ruby. She smiled easily and laughed often. She had a sharp, quick wit and was well informed on matters of local gossip, but there was nothing malicious about her humor. I liked her right away.

Standing next to Ruby was a broad-faced, sandy-haired man of medium height who I mistakenly took for Morgan's father, but he turned out to be Pete Norman, Ruby's "friend." Paul, I was informed, was still in the house, replacing a tube in the radio that had gone on the blink that morning. I shook Pete's hand and responded in kind to his shy, "Nice to meet you, ma'am."

Then we moved on to the final member of the reception line, a petite, green-eyed woman of about forty whose auburn hair showed not a streak of gray, Morgan's mother. She took my hand in hers and welcomed me. There was something calm and deep about her gaze, something that told you she had known sadness and survived. Her neck was long and slender, and she held her shoulders square. Morgan had told me about his mother's crippled leg beforehand, but it was still surprising to see how she tightly clutched a cane of polished wood in her left hand, and the effort and determination that went into every step she took. No wonder Morgan was so strong.

"I'm pleased to meet you, Mrs. Glennon. Thank you for having me."

"Actually," Morgan interrupted, "Mama is Mrs. Van Dyver. I forgot to tell you."

"Oh," I said awkwardly, embarrassed by my error and distracted, wondering where I'd heard the name before. "I didn't realize. I'm sorry."

"Everyone calls me Eva," she said kindly just as a tall, lanky man strode purposefully onto the porch and declared proudly, with a foreign accent, "Eva Van Dyver." Putting his arm around his wife's shoulders, he then leaned down to give her a quick peck on the lips and added. "Which makes me the luckiest man in Oklahoma. The radio's fixed. We can hear some music after dinner." Looking at my surprised face, he said jovially, "Georgia! How nice to see you again. I knew Morgan was bringing a friend to dinner, but I had no idea it was you."

"You've met before?" Ruby asked.

"Once, at the café in Liberal. Adjoining counter stools," he explained, giving no further details of our conversation, for which I was grateful.

"It's nice to see you again, too."

Paul clapped his hands together expectantly and said, "So, are we going to stand out here all day or go in and carve that delicious-smelling bird? I'm starving!"

Dinner was delicious, and Morgan's family couldn't have been nicer. It was the first time I'd ever sat down and shared a meal with a family, a real family.

Every head was still and bowed as Paul gave a simple, beautiful prayer of thanks. After he finished, everyone dug in, piling plates high with turkey, dressing, potatoes, green beans, and creamed onions, giving frequent and well-deserved compliments to the cooks, Ruby, Grandma Clare, and Eva, between bites.

"Well, it was Ruby did most of it," Grandma Clare said. "Eva and I lent a hand, but Ruby is the real cook in the family. Best in the county. Ruby, remember back when you were a little girl? You didn't have any more business being in the kitchen than a pig has in the henhouse. Remember when you made that pie for your daddy and you added salt in place of the sugar?"

Eva came to her friend's defense, saying Clare ought not to bring up that story after all these years, though she smiled broadly as she spoke, obviously still amused by the memory. "Besides, Mama, everybody has heard that story a million times."

"Georgia hasn't," said Grandma Clare.

"True enough," Ruby piped in good-naturedly. "So, just for the record, Georgia, I did make an apple pie with salt instead of sugar when I was eight years old. It took my daddy twenty minutes to make sure everybody in town heard the story and twenty years for me to live it down." Ruby laughed, asked Pete if he wanted more potatoes, and passed him the bowl.

"Well, honey," Pete said and patted Ruby's hand as she held out the bowl of potatoes, "it don't matter to me what kind of a cook you were when you were eight. All I know is I'd walk in from town through a tornado for one of your dinners now." This one speech was at least twice as long as anything Pete had said all evening. He looked in Ruby's eyes after he finished, and she blushed.

"Here! Here!" Paul lifted his water glass in a toast to Ruby and then addressed himself to Pete. "I'd snap her up quick if I were you, Pete. If any of the other fellows in town get a taste of Ruby's fried chicken, she'll be off the market."

Pete swallowed hard and reached up to loosen his necktie, which appeared to be bothering him. "Truth is," he said, clearing his throat, "I already have. Proposed to Ruby last night, and she said yes. So, Pastor, if you'll say the service, we'd like to be married in the spring." Pete was beaming as he spoke, but no one could really hear him because as soon as he uttered the word "proposed" the family was on their feet, hugging Ruby, slapping Pete on the back, and shouting congratulations to them both.

"That's great, Aunt Ruby!"

"Why didn't you tell us before?"

"Wonderful news!"

"Do you have a date in mind?"

Ruby, whose face and eyes were shining, took over where Pete left off, and Pete, who clearly wasn't much of a talker, seemed happy to let her do so. "I didn't want to say anything until we were all together. We don't really have a specific date in mind, just sometime in the spring, after Pete gets settled in his new business. Mr. Cheevers asked him to come in as a partner at the filling station," Ruby reported with pride. "He and Pete are going to add on an extra garage with a lift so they can take in more repair work. Pete's a real good mechanic. Mr. Cheevers is going to let us live rent-free in that little two-bedroom house he owns just down the street from the station, the one with the red roof, and let us buy that and the station from him, gradual, once the business starts to make some money. Eventually, Pete will own the whole thing!"

Eva's eyes were glistening with joyful tears, clearly delighted for Ruby's happiness, but she seemed taken aback by this last announcement. "You mean, you're going to move out?"

Ruby bit her lip, searching for words, but Paul came to the rescue. "It's less than five miles from here to town. You and Ruby can see each other every day. The caboose would be a little small for the two of them, don't you think?" He patted his wife's arm encouragingly. Eva pressed her lip together in a tight smile and nodded.

"Yes, of course. You're right. It's not that far. The most important thing is that you and Pete are happy together," Eva said and gave Ruby another squeeze, "and I know you will be."

Ruby smiled at her friend gratefully. "Well, if we do half as well as you and Paul, we'll be happier than about ninety-nine percent of the population."

"Good heavens!" Grandma Clare croaked. "Will you two stop that? We're supposed to be celebrating, and you're both about ready to burst into tears. Morgan," she commanded, "run into my room, would you please? In the bottom drawer of my dresser, under my blue sweater, you'll find a bottle of sherry. Bring that in here, and let's have a toast to Pete and Ruby."

Eva was shocked. "Mama, you've got a bottle of liquor hidden in your bedroom?"

"Oh, don't look at me like that, Eva. It's not like I've been drinking on the sly. You know I don't hold with that, but this is a special occasion. Pete's been coming around here for months, so I bought a little bottle just in case there was cause for celebration. I couldn't very well ask you or Paul to do it."

Paul let out a single hearty bark of a laugh. "The minister or his wife being seen buying spirits? In Dillon? Goodness, no! The gossip-mongers would certainly have a field day with that."

After the toast, everyone helped clear the table, then we took our desserts into the front room. Paul turned on the radio, looking for some music, but Grandma Clare said she wanted to listen to Abbott and Costello, so he put that on instead. Grandma Clare pulled her chair close so she could hear and then promptly dozed off. Ruby sat close to Pete on the sofa as they flipped through a copy of *Life* magazine. When Morgan went outside to get some more wood for the fire, Eva asked if I'd like to see her quilting room.

One whole wall was lined with shelves. Each shelf held yards and yards of different fabrics, grouped by color and shades, graduating from lights to darks, an eye-pleasing rainbow of cloth. Several of Eva's creations were mounted on the remaining walls: scenes of prairies, woodlands, seascapes, and mountaintops, with literally hundreds of tiny blocks of fabric, joined like myriads of tile fragments in a fantastic mosaic, creating the shapes and shadows that formed the images. Near the window, where it could catch the morning light, sat a long wooden quilting frame. The quilt stretched between the bars showed a large, stately oak tree blooming a glory of leaves, each slightly different in color and shape, with the lighter colored leaves dominating one area, giving the impression of after-noon sunlight filtering through the branches. Only half of the leaves had been quilted, outlined in hundreds of tiny, perfectly even stitches. That, I could see, was the final touch that made all the difference, turning the carefully sewn bits of fabric from a pretty picture into something much more, a reality you could step into, wrap yourself up in, full of life and depth and textures, a vision that invited your touch.

"Oh! They're beautiful!" I breathed. "Morgan told me about your quilts and how wonderful they are! But I never imagined anything so lovely. And they are all so different. Have you been to all these places?"

Eva laughed. "Oh no! We did go to San Diego to see Morgan, so I saw the ocean then, but mostly I've just got a good imagination."

"They are just amazing! I can't even begin to imagine how you do it."

"Well, I've had years of practice," she said, modestly. "It takes time and patience, of course, but it really isn't as hard as you'd think. Would you like to try it?"

And before I could answer, she had limped her way to the fabric-filled shelves, pulling out several shades of green and cream-colored cloth she thought would make a pretty nine-patch block. "You can make this one, and if you enjoy it, make more until you have enough for a quilt, or you can just do the one and make it into a pillow.

"You see how many I have." She smiled as she pointed to a chair in the corner that was indeed piled with a small mountain of throw pillows. "Those are all projects I started that didn't turn out quite like I'd pictured. After all that work, I might as well get something out of it. Anyway, they make nice gifts."

The next thing I knew, I was sitting at a scarred wooden worktable with Eva beside me, showing me how to hold a well-sharpened pencil at a sideways angle to trace a perfectly even line around a wooden template onto the green cloth. She was a patient teacher, kind and quick to praise, and motherly. How lucky Morgan had been to grow up in this wonderful family, at the knee of this caring, gentle woman, a mother so different from my own.

"My papa made these templates for me, years ago. I've got squares, triangles, diamonds; just about any shape you can think of in any size you'd ever need." Just then, Morgan poked his head in the door.

"There you are! I wondered what happened to you two. Better watch out for her, Georgia, or next thing you know you'll be buying yards and yards of fabric without the first idea what you plan to do with it, and you'll have so many pillows on your bed there won't be room for you to get in." He came up behind Eva's chair and leaned down to kiss the top of her head.

Eva reached her hand up and patted him affectionately on the cheek before shooing him off. "Now just go away for a little while, Morgan. I want Georgia to get started on this one block before you have to take her home. Don't worry. I'll give your girl back in a little while."

Your girl.

While Morgan drove, I held on to the paper sack filled with left-over turkey, dressing, and pie that Ruby and Grandma Clare had pressed on me, along with the unsewn pieces of the quilt block Morgan's mother said I could finish later, and thought about Morgan and his family and about what his mother had said, turning it over and over in my mind.

They were such a lovely family, like the families I'd seen in magazine advertisements, Norman Rockwell illustrations of families, healthy and clean-living, happily joined around the dinner table exchanging stories of the day, glad to be in each other's company, pure and pious and wonderfully normal—nothing like my family, assuming the word even applied to what Delia and I made up. Yet, when

Eva had shooed Morgan away, saying I was his girl, he'd laughed and left the room whistling.

Morgan was whistling still as he drove. Feeling my eyes on him, he turned to me and smiled again, beaming sunlight. And my heart ached inside me because now I knew for certain what, before, I had only suspected: I could never be Morgan Glennon's girl.

At my front door, I dodged his good-night kiss, turning my head quickly and thanking him for inviting me, my hand outstretched for a platonic farewell. He shook my hand, looking a bit confused, hurt even, but it was better this way. Better a small hurt now than to let things go on and risk the possibility of breaking his heart and the certainty of breaking my own. From now on, I resolved, our relationship would be strictly professional; it was for the best.

I shut the door, leaving Morgan to climb down the creaking wooden staircase to the waiting Packard as I snapped on the light switch and took a long look around my tiny apartment—rented room, rented furniture, not a picture on the walls, not a single object that spoke of permanence or intent, the room of someone who was running from something, a fugitive.

Well, I thought, *maybe that's what I am. How did that happen?*

For the first time, I actually welcomed the prospect of leaving this place. All I had to do was get through the next three weeks and then head . . . ? I'd been on the verge of thinking *Head home,* but I didn't know where home was. I never really had. Come December 20th, where was I to go?

I sighed, took a step toward the kitchen table with the intent of unloading the bag of leftovers, but felt something under my foot. It was an envelope. The landlady must have left it. I bent down to pick it up and noticed Delia's familiar, curlicue script on the outside. On the inside, I found a printed invitation with an ink smear on "i" in the word *cordially,* as if the cards had been made up quickly and mailed before they were dry.

You are cordially invited to the wedding of
Cordelia Carter Boudreaux
And
Colonel Nathan Bedford Prescott III
December 24, 1944
St. Margaret's Chapel
Reception to follow at the bride's home

And a note quickly dashed in Delia's own hand.

Georgia Darling,
Be my Maid of Honor?
Love,
Delia

⤜ 40 ⤛

Morgan

Liberal, Kansas—December 20, 1944

In my mind, I had resolved that when we said good-bye that day, the last, formal step in the handoff of responsibilities from Georgia to myself, I would simply shake her hand, say it had been nice to work with her, and walk away, proving I could be "professional," too.

Professional. It was a word I'd come to despise in the weeks since Thanksgiving, when, after what I'd thought had been a really great evening, Georgia resumed her distant, frosty demeanor just when I'd thought the ice had started to thaw. Every time I tried to ask her what had happened, or if I'd done something to offend her, she just looked at me and said in a flat voice, as though repeating a line she'd memorized from a play, "Nothing happened, Morgan. It was kind of you and your family to include me in your holiday celebrations, but I think it is best if we keep our relationship strictly professional."

And that was it. She wouldn't budge. No matter how hard I pushed or what I said, that was her answer—aloof, rehearsed, and humiliating. My initial confusion and hurt turned quickly to frustration and anger. Eventually, I decided that if that's the way she wanted it, fine. It wasn't like she was the only woman on the face of the earth. I'd get over her. Of course, it'd be a lot easier to do that if I didn't have to see her every day. I was looking forward to December 20th even more than Christmas.

As I said, the handoff was really a formality. I'd been teaching all Georgia's former students on my own for the last week and she'd really just been an observer, but we'd decided to meet about thirty minutes after my last class of the day, so she could give me the key to the room and her final student evaluations. I hadn't slept well the night before, so after I dismissed class, I headed over to the office to grab myself a cup of coffee. When I walked in I saw Colonel Hemingway talking to Georgia, whose packed suitcase was sitting next to her feet. Hemingway, was smiling as he spoke, obviously giving Georgia a hard time and looking like he was thoroughly enjoying himself.

"Well, I'm sorry, Mrs. Welles, but as of today, you are no longer on the Army Air Corps payroll, therefore the Army Air Corps is under no obligation to provide transportation for you, not across town and most certainly not to Chicago." Hemingway had a self-satisfied smirk on his face that he tried, unsuccessfully, to mask as he said, "I'm sorry for your troubles, but you should have planned ahead. There is simply nothing I can do for you."

"Sir," Georgia said, glaring daggers at Hemingway but keeping her voice low, "the army brought me to Liberal. Isn't it the army's responsibility to transport me back from Liberal? If I were a soldier who had finished his tour of duty, wouldn't the army send me home? You aren't going to tell me that Washington is planning on leaving all those boys stationed in Germany, or the Philippines, or Armpit, Alabama, stranded once the war is over, are you?"

Hemingway smiled indulgently. "Certainly not, but you've hit upon precisely my point. Those soldiers are *soldiers*. Something you, my dear, never were and never will be. So I'm afraid you'll have to arrange for your own ride home, Mrs. Welles. Now, if you'll excuse me." Still smirking, he turned triumphantly on his heel and walked out.

Georgia's shoulders drooped. "Great," she muttered to herself, sounding more tired and defeated than angry. "That's just great. Now what am I going to do?"

I was still sore at Georgia, but nobody deserved to be treated like that. "Georgia? Are you all right?" The sound of my voice startled her.

"Oh. Hi, Morgan. I'm fine. I'm just stuck, that's all. It seems that because the WASP was never militarized, the government feels no compunction to help get me home now that their need for my services has ended." Her sarcastic tone bubbled into frustration, and she shouted, "It's an airfield, for gosh sakes! How hard could it be for them to put me on the next plane that's headed toward Chicago?" She shook her head and sighed. "Well, I'm sure I'm not alone in this. As we speak, there are probably hundreds of stranded WASP who just received the same lecture and are trying to figure out what they do now."

"Can I give you a lift somewhere?"

"Yeah," she said with a wry smile, "How about Chicago?" That was one of the things I loved about Georgia; she always kept her sense of humor.

"Well, I was thinking more along the lines of the nearest train station."

She shook her head. "We're five days from Christmas; there aren't any seats available to Chicago, not on the train, not even on the bus. I checked. And my sister . . ." She put her hand to her eyes, rubbing them like she had a headache coming on, "I mean, my mother is getting married on Christmas Eve, and I'm supposed to stand up for her. There's no way I'll make it now. I guess I'll have to telephone and say I won't be there in time."

"Come on," I said, grabbing her suitcase and heading toward the door.

Georgia's forehead furrowed in confusion. "Where are we going? Morgan, you're sweet to want to help me, but I'm not going to impose myself on your family for Christmas. I told you before, I appreciated their kindness, but I'd prefer if we kept our relationship—"

"Georgia, will you just shut up! For once!" Her eyes grew wide at my outburst, and she started to answer me, but then changed her mind. "I've heard that speech two dozen times already and it's getting stale! In fact, it makes me mad as hell, and you know why?" She shook her head, silent.

"Because I'm a really nice guy and I'm crazy about you. And I think if you had a lick of sense, you'd see that. But!" I said loudly, giving an exaggerated shrug, "If you don't like me, then there's nothing I can do about it. Fine. Your loss. Mine, too, but I've accepted that. Just don't go giving me that speech again, all right? Every time you do, it makes me want to punch something! In fact, the only thing that makes me madder is listening to the high-handed load of bull Hemingway was giving you. Especially after the swell job you've done here. Now, shut up and let's go. Before I change my mind." I stomped off without looking to see if she was following, but the click of high heels on the linoleum told me she was right behind.

I walked as fast as I could. She was breathing heavy, trying to keep up and after a couple of minutes she shouted, "Morgan!"

"What!"

"Where the heck are you taking me?"

"Chicago!" I snarled and kept right on walking.

"Here," I said, "take the controls for a while. I need a break." Actually, I wasn't tired at all, but I knew this would be the last chance Georgia would have for a long time, maybe even forever, to handle a big craft.

"Thanks." She smiled as she took over the wheel. I leaned back and opened a bottle of Coke I'd brought along. Georgia's eyes scanned the horizon, and she adjusted her grip on the controls. I knew what she was doing, looking for that sweet spot, that place where you can feel every shift and shudder of the plane, like holding on to the reins of a horse just so, feeling the life and intent of the animal coming through the lines like electricity through a wire.

Georgia laughed to herself. "I still can't believe you just took this plane. This is government property, Morgan. You'll be lucky if there aren't a couple of MPs waiting for you when you land."

"Naw." I took another swig of my drink. "I just told Lowell, the head mechanic, that I was taking her up for a little shakedown. She just came out of the shop yesterday. I thought it'd be a good idea to make sure everything's working tip-top before I let the students take her up, that's all. Who'd object to that? I think it's darned nice of me, watching out for the welfare of my students this way. Especially during my personal time."

"Hemingway might have some objections if he hears I'm on board."

I grinned. "That's why I offered Lowell twenty bucks not to mention that part to anybody."

"Morgan, you're kidding! You paid him twenty—"

I held up my hand to stop her protest. "I said I offered him twenty, but after he heard about how Hemingway treated you, he wouldn't take it. Said you were a good pilot, never griped if you didn't get your pick of the planes, always had your repair sheets in order, and made your students do the same. He respects you. Lots of the guys do, you know. Not everybody's like Hemingway and that worm, Anders."

"I know that," Georgia said. "It took a while for some of the men to come around, but once they saw I could do my job as well as anybody, most of them treated me fairly. Don't get the idea that I'm leaving with hard feelings, Morgan, because I'm not. There are some things I think the military should have handled differently when it came to the WASP, but even so, this has been the best time of my life. It's been a privilege to serve, and I wouldn't have missed it for the world. I'm really going to miss it."

She was quiet for a moment, thinking. I watched her eyes move back and forth across the horizon, a wistful look on her face, as if logging the moment in her memory. I couldn't help but think how beautiful she was.

After a minute, her expression changed, and she returned to the present moment. Her lips bowed into a little smile, and her eyes sparkled. "Did you really knock out that little creep, Anders, because he'd said something nasty about me, or was that just a rumor?"

I didn't say anything. Just took another long drink from the bottle of Coke, swallowed, and grinned.

✺ 41 ✺

Georgia

Chicago, Illinois—December 24, 1944

It was a wedding only Delia could have arranged, with pink sweet-heart roses in the middle of winter, a hoop-skirted bridal gown (and though the hoops on the maid-of-honor dress were smaller, I still swore revenge), a red-velvet wedding cake under white frosting, punch made with ginger ale and Luzianne tea. It was just so entirely Delia, and, of course, that's what made the whole thing so perfect—right down to the groom.

I'd always thought that when Delia married, if Delia married, it would only be because she'd finally cornered some hapless mid-westerner into saying "I do" before he caught on to her moonlight-and-magnolias routine, but I was wrong. In the end, Delia had chosen carefully and, for her at least, well.

Colonel Nathan Bedford Prescott III, fifty-something, hand-some, tanned, and wearing a light-colored suit, who looked more like he was ready to take a stroll down the tree-lined boulevards of Charleston than the wind-swept, snow-banked sidewalks of Chicago, was not an actual colonel.

"It's an honorary title, of course," Delia tittered as she introduced me to her intended on the night I arrived.

"Of course," I murmured, trying to keep my face convincingly blank. "I'm pleased to meet you, Colonel. Congratulations." I reached out to shake his hand and was a little surprised when the colonel bowed formally, lifted my hand to his mouth and brushed it with his lips.

"The pleasure," he said in a southern baritone as smooth and golden as good Kentucky whiskey, "is entirely mine. Your mother has told me so many lovely things about you, Georgia."

"My mother?" Shocked, I stared at Delia and whispered out the side of my mouth, "You told him about . . . you know?"

"I did. I told him about you. About Florida and Earl. Everything. I love Nathan. If you love someone you should be honest with them, even if it means you might lose them. But"—she smiled—"I didn't lose him. Nathan was just thrilled to learn that he'd be your stepdaddy. Weren't you, Nathan?"

"Indeed, I was. Never having had children of my own, you can imagine how pleased I am to have so lovely and accomplished a young woman as yourself for my stepdaughter, Georgia. And it is with equal pleasure that I accept your kind congratulations."

I started to acknowledge his kindness, but the colonel continued without taking a breath. "When I arrived in the cold frontier to establish my business less than a year ago, I had not thought to find so fair a flower of the South in such a climate, and yet, there she stands! A hothouse rose! Fragrant and rare, a flower fully blown, blooming amidst the bare branches in the bleak midwinter! And better than all this, she has agreed to be mine! Oh, yes! I accept your congratulations with all joy and all humility, for surely there is no more fortunate man on the face of the earth than I." He ended his speech with another bow, this time to his bride, who sighed and held her hand to her breast.

"Oh, Nathan! I do love you so!" Apparently forgetting I was

even in the room, Delia moved forward, as if ready to embrace her groom, but I interrupted.

"So, Colonel, you have a business here in Chicago?"

"Yes," he replied politely, though I could see it took some effort for him to take his eyes off his beloved. "A school. The Prescott Institute for Illustration and Art. I am the founder and headmaster."

"Really?" I was a little taken aback to find that the colonel had an actual job. At first glance, I'd taken him for a snake-oil salesman. "So you're an artist? How interesting."

The colonel smiled gently and shook his head. "No, no. You misunderstand. I am the founder and headmaster of the institute. My role is administrative, seeing to the admissions, finances, facilities, hiring and firing of staff . . . that sort of thing. While not an artist myself, I certainly consider myself a patron of the arts."

"Nathan is a natural-born businessman," Delia reported proudly. "The institute only opened a few months ago, yet he has already enrolled thousands of students!"

"Thousands! You must have a large staff, not to mention a huge campus."

Delia beamed and said, "No! That's the beauty of it! Nathan runs the entire thing out of his apartment with just some help from a secretary to help with correspondence and such. But after the wedding, I'll quit Marshall Fields and take her job. Nathan is going to make me the dean of Student Affairs and Administration!"

"You don't have a campus, or a teaching staff?"

"No," he replied, without a trace of embarrassment. "Ours is a correspondence school. Our instructional methods were developed years ago by a friend of mine, Guillermo Puccini, a fine artist in the Italian tradition, who sold me the rights to his syllabus. Art, of course, is a timeless study, and the Prescott Institute for Illustration and Art teaches the classic methods, so we have no need for instructors, especially these so-called 'modern artists' with their wild ideas and nonexistent technique. Thus, we are able to maintain the purity of our curriculum," he explained with every appearance of sincerity.

"I correct all the lessons myself and grade them according to a standard system of points developed by Guillermo. Each lesson arrives monthly, in a simple, easy-to-follow format and is available to persons of talent across the country, whether they reside in the bustling borough of Brooklyn or the most isolated hamlets of the western plains, and at a cost that is less than a tenth of the tuition of a conventional art school."

My first instincts were right, I thought, smiling to myself. *He is a snake-oil salesman.*

Now that I thought about it, I remembered seeing advertisements for the Prescott Institute on the backs of matchbook covers and some of the less reputable magazines. The ads were littered with testimonials from satisfied alumni who purported to be making their living as professional artists, thanks to the instruction they'd received at Prescott. And the admission process was easy! All you had to do was complete a picture of a boy (guided by a system of grid lines to help you out), send it to the "Admissions Department" along with your two-dollar application fee, and the institute would score your drawing to see if you had "the talent it takes to become a professional artist or illustrator!"

I wanted to ask Colonel Prescott how many applicants got turned away, but I was pretty sure I knew the answer. In the eyes of the Prescott Institute, anyone who could pay the application fee had the talent to become a professional artist or illustrator. Still, Nathan didn't seem like a malicious con man, just a hopeless romantic. Like Delia coming to believe her invented southern-belle past, the colonel actually seemed to believe he really was providing a service. And maybe he was. For two dollars a month, he sold people a little piece of a dream. Well, maybe that was all right. Maybe, when they filled in the grid on the back of the matchbook application, that's what they'd been looking for in the first place.

But no matter how questionable my new stepfather's profession, when I saw the way he looked at Delia and the way she looked at him, I knew that some things were certain: Nathan and Delia were very much alike and very much in love.

The wedding itself was small, just fifty guests in attendance. There were a few people from the neighborhood, but most were friends of Delia and Nathan that I hardly knew. However, the ceremony was lovely, as was the reception at Delia's apartment.

Not really having anyone to talk with, I was more than happy to take charge of the punchbowl. Sister Mary Patrick, my old teacher from St. Margaret's, came to get a glass of punch, and we chatted for a bit.

"Ah," she sighed wistfully as she downed the last of her punch and peered at Delia and Nathan, who were standing across the room, surrounded by well-wishers. "They look so happy together. Your sister's a darlin' woman. It's happy I am to see she's found the right man at last."

"So am I," I said and meant it.

She wished me well and went off to visit with Father Kearney, who'd performed the ceremony. Before long, Delia broke away from her admirers and approached the punch table.

"Georgia, you're an angel to take care of this! But you haven't even had a piece of cake yet. Why don't you take a break and get something to eat?"

"Maybe later, Delia. I'm not all that hungry."

Delia frowned. "No, I've noticed that you haven't had much of an appetite since you got here. Is something wrong? You can tell me."

For an instant, I entertained the idea of telling Delia everything: about Morgan and our last flight together and how he'd hefted my bag out of the plane and reached to help me down, and how, when I'd taken his hand, it felt like an electric current was running up my arm. About how I'd leaned forward, coming inches from kissing him full on the lips and wrapping my arms around his shoulders, but had caught myself at the last second and given him a quick peck on the cheek instead, thanking him for the ride and walking away without looking back. Part of me wanted to tell Delia all of it, but I didn't. There was no point. It was too late now.

"I'm fine. Just a little tired maybe. I probably should go soon. I thought I'd sleep at Frannie's tonight."

"What are you talking about?" Delia said, looking offended. "You're going to stay here tonight, aren't you? It's Christmas. You should be with your family."

I rolled my eyes. "Delia, it's your wedding night. I'm sure you and Nathan would like your privacy. You don't need me hanging around."

"Don't be silly! Of course, you can stay here tonight. You can stay here every night. In fact, that's what I came over to speak to you about. Nathan and I have been talking. You know, we need a book-keeper for the institute. You could live here, at home, and work for Nathan. Now that you're finished with all this flying nonsense, I think it's just a perfect solution for everyone! We'll just be one big happy family—you, your daddy, and I!" Delia smiled and opened her hands wide, as if she were handing me a beautiful gift.

I took a deep breath and counted to ten silently.

"Delia," I said slowly, trying to keep my voice even and my emotions under control. "That's a sweet offer. Really. And Nathan seems like the perfect man for you, but he's not my daddy. As for this fly-ing 'nonsense,' I'm not done with it. I'll be going back to Waukegan tomorrow night to try and salvage what's left of my business."

"But that's silly, Georgia. Waukegan's not your home. You can't tell me that you ever thought of it that way."

"No," I admitted. "I never did. To tell you the truth, I'm not sure I've ever had a home, but if I did, it's in the air. That's what I'm going back to." She looked hurt, and I felt a stab of guilt. The last thing I wanted to do was hurt her feelings, especially not on her wedding day.

"Would it be all right if I came down to see you next weekend? Or maybe you and Nathan could come to Waukegan and see me. If the weather warms up, I can take you for an airplane ride." Delia smiled and nodded, and I gave her a kiss on the cheek. "Say good night to Nathan for me. And congratulations—to both of you."

42

Morgan

Dillon, Oklahoma—April 1944

The house was quiet. Mama sat at her quilt frame with her back to me, engrossed in her work. I stood just inside the door and watched her for a moment as she outlined the unfurled petals of a peony with tiny stitches, her needle rocking back and forth in rhythm with the tune she was humming. It took a minute for her to sense my presence.

"Morgan!" she exclaimed, looking over the tops of the reading glasses she'd recently begun wearing for close work. "This is a nice surprise! I wasn't expecting you until Sunday."

"I know. One of the guys let me borrow his car, so I thought I'd come out and see if I couldn't wrangle myself an invitation to dinner."

"Oh, I think we can probably make room for you," she teased. "We're having a nice lamb stew with some of the spring peas and new potatoes, but it'll be a while until dinner. It's Paul's day off. He went for a walk. Ruby drove into town to buy some trim for her wedding dress, and Grandma went with her. They won't be home for a couple of hours. Do you want a piece of pie to tide you over?"

"No, thanks. I had a big lunch."

Mama tipped her head to the side, sizing me up with her mother's eagle eye. "How are things?" she asked. "Anything happening at the base?"

"Nothing new. Actually, things are kind of winding down. We've got three classes in the pipeline to graduation, but there's a rumor they won't be sending any new trainees. Everybody expects the war to be over any day now, so there's not much point in training a new bunch of pilots. Guess I'll be out of a job before too long."

"Well, thank heaven for that. We've lost too many good boys in this fight," Mama said.

"Yes," I agreed. "Every time I see a new class graduate I'm proud, but I worry about what will happen to them in combat. Still, it seems funny to think of it being over. The only thing I've done in my adult life is fly for the military."

"Do you have any thoughts about what you'd like to do after the war?" she asked. Then, with a studied casualness that made me know this was what she'd been leading up to from the beginning she asked, "Do you hear anything from your friend, Georgia?"

I smiled. Mama always could read me like a book. "Not really. She sent me a note thanking me for flying her to Chicago. I wrote back, just a 'how are things' note, but she didn't answer for quite a while. Last week I got a letter from her. She didn't say so directly, but I get the feeling that things aren't going too well with her business. The fellow who was running it for her while she was flying sounds like he's a good mechanic, but not much of a businessman." I shrugged and walked over to Mama's quilt frame and took a look at her newest creation.

"This is a nice one," I commented, tracing one of the peonies with my finger. "Who's it for?"

"A lady in San Francisco."

"San Francisco? That's a long way. How did she hear about you?"

"I don't know. A friend of a friend, I suppose. Most of my business comes from referrals. So," she said, returning to the subject that interested her most, "are you going to write back?"

Mama hit upon the very question that had been bothering me from the moment I'd read Georgia's letter. "Part of me wants to, but, you know, Mama, every time I try to get close to her, she backs away. I sent her those letters while I was in the hospital, and nothing. Then, out of the blue we end up working at the same base, side by side. I figured it had to be some kind of a sign, so I swallowed my pride and tried again. And just when I think I'm getting somewhere with her, just when she's warming up to me—boom! She slams the door again! We had a nice time flying to Chicago. I thought maybe that would soften her up, but her letter read like a note thanking her Aunt Tilly for the lovely bath powder she'd sent for Christmas!"

Thinking about it still made me mad. I unclenched my jaw and groaned. "I don't know, Mama. I'm miserable without her, but maybe it would just be better to leave it. A fellow gets awfully tired of rejection, you know what I mean?"

Mama picked up her needle and started sewing again, keeping her eyes on her work as she spoke. "I don't doubt it, Morgan. Think of Paul and what I put him through all those years. I certainly led him a dance." She shook her head and sighed, as if she wasn't quite able to believe the foolishness of her own past.

"And, you know, all that time, I really was in love with him, but I just couldn't admit it, not to myself or anyone. It was too dangerous. Having fallen in love once before only to be abandoned was so painful that I just wasn't willing to risk it happening again, and I had really come to believe that no one really could love me—that I wasn't worthy of love."

I shook my head, wondering how Mama, my dear, wonderful Mama, could ever have thought that about herself. Women were so hard to understand. "So, do you think that's what happened to Georgia? Maybe she got hurt before and is afraid of it happening again?"

"Morgan, I couldn't begin to guess. But I do know that loving and allowing yourself to be loved takes a great deal of courage and trust. That isn't easy for some people. It wasn't for me, so I pushed Paul away again and again, but now . . ." she paused for a moment and looked out at the new leaves and swelling buds of the rose-bushes Paul had planted outside the window of her sewing studio. She smiled to herself. "Now, I thank the good Lord for making Paul so stubborn. He just wouldn't give up."

"I couldn't." The sound of Paul's voice startled us both. "I didn't have a choice."

He walked up behind Mama's chair. She turned to greet him, and he leaned down to kiss her cheek before continuing. "No matter how many times I would tell myself that it was hopeless, that I'd had enough, I just couldn't get your mother off my mind. Waking or sleeping, there she was."

I know what that's like, I thought.

"And, though Saint Paul was really talking more about brotherly love, or charity, the words from his letter to the Corinthians kept playing in my mind, how love 'beareth all things, believeth all things, hopeth all things, endureth all things.' Finally, I decided that if I was truly in love," he said, locking eyes with Mama, "then I had no business giving up, because if I did, I was certain to lose out on one of life's greatest and most precious gifts."

Mama put down her needle and reached out to hold his hand, her eyes shining with love. He squeezed her hand, then turned to me.

"So the question you have to answer, Morgan, isn't whether or not you'll be successful in your suit, but are you in love? If you are, then your way is clear. You have to bear, believe, hope, and endure all things. If you're really in love, then there simply is no other choice."

~ 43 ~

Georgia

Waukegan, Illinois—May 1945

"Mrs. Welles, I really wish I could help you. If I needed another flight instructor, I'm sure I couldn't find one better than you." Mr. Rawlings moved an unlit cigar from one side of his mouth to the other and resumed chewing on its bedraggled end. "But I'm a businessman and a father; I'm interested in buying Welles Flight School to make a profit and provide my sons with a future."

Mr. Rawlings owned a company that made radios, and he lived in a big house on Chicago's "gold coast." Wealthy before Pearl Harbor, he'd become even wealthier through government contracts during the war. His sons, Skip and Joe, Jr., both pilots, were stationed in Europe and due to return home soon.

Mr. Rawlings was looking to buy a flight school and install Joe and Skip as instructors. Welles Flight School was perfect for his purposes, both because it was near his home in Chicago and because I was at the end of my financial rope and he knew it.

I'd been trying to hold out, believing that business would rebound after the war, but I owed money everywhere. Selling the flight school was my only hope of avoiding bankruptcy. I'd come to tell him I'd only sell if he'd let me stay on as an instructor and Stubbs as mechanic. I was bluffing, but I hoped Rawlings wouldn't realize that.

"Over time," he said, chomping on his cigar butt and trying to appear sympathetic, "I believe the flight school will be big enough to need three full-time instructors, but that won't be for quite some time. Who knows for how long? Not only do I have to pay off the debts that you've already accrued"—he frowned and leaned toward me, speaking in a low, disapproving voice, as if to say that I had no one but myself to blame for my troubles—"but I have to carry the salaries of my own boys. It could be months before I see a profit. Maybe years. Mrs. Welles, much as I'd like to, I simply cannot afford to take on any additional employees."

I looked at him unblinking, hoping he might mistake my stare for steely resolve and relent but also to give myself time to think. What could I do? If I sold the company to Rawlings, I might never be able to work in aviation again. I'd put in for every pilot job within five hundred miles, using the name G. C. Welles on the applications, with no success. There were plenty of pilots looking for work, and the few companies that did indicate an interest in hiring me, changed their minds once they learned that G. C. Welles was a woman. I didn't want to sell to Rawlings and potentially ground myself forever, not to mention see the demise of the business that Roger had entrusted to me, which Rawlings had already informed me would be renamed Rawlings Brothers Flight Instruction, but what else could I do? I asked myself again and blinked.

Rawlings smiled, knowing he'd won. He put both hands on his desk and pushed the sales contract toward me.

"Mrs. Welles, you've run out of time and options." He held out a pen. "Sign."

* * *

Stubbs Peterson was in the office, pacing, smoking cigarettes, and waiting for me to return from my appointment with Mr. Rawlings. It was easy to see how Stubbs had earned his nickname. He was built like a fireplug, short and stubby, not even as tall as I was. It had been a while since he'd seen fifty, but he crossed the room, back and forth, like he was running a race. Judging by the smell of smoke, he must have gone through a whole carton of Chesterfields while he waited.

"For heaven's sake, Stubbs," I complained, coughing and fanning my hand in front of my smoke-teared eyes. "Couldn't you have opened a window or something?"

He ignored the question. "Well? Did he go for it?"

"No."

Stubbs frowned and started pacing faster, berating himself as he did. "It's my fault. All my fault. I should have done something."

"Stubbs, don't say that. You did the best you could, the best anyone could."

"No. It's my fault. When you got back, the place was in such a mess. Look how long it took you to get the files back in order."

"Sure, they were a mess, but no worse than they were when I first came to work for Roger," I said and rubbed my eyes, this time from fatigue instead of smoke. I felt a terrible headache coming on. "You're no bookkeeper, Stubbs, neither was Roger, but that isn't why the business failed. We just had more expenses than income, that's all." Exhausted, I flopped into my desk chair. "If anyone is to blame, it's me."

But Stubbs wasn't listening. "I should have done something."

"Stubbs, come on. What more could you have done? There was no money coming in. When's the last time you took a paycheck? Two months? Three?"

He didn't say anything, just looked at me and shrugged noncommittally.

"Let yourself off the hook. We did everything we knew how to do. We just got beat, that's all. Cheer up. It could have been a lot worse. I'm not crazy about Mr. Rawlings, but thank heaven he came along." I pulled a fat envelope from the pocket of my jacket. "There's twelve thousand dollars in here. Considering how much I owe, it's a pretty decent price. Oh!" I said, brightening. "I almost forgot. At the last minute, Rawlings decided to let me keep one of the trainers."

Stubbs stopped pacing for a moment. "Really? Why'd he do that?"

"Because at the last minute, I said if he didn't let me keep one of the planes, then I wasn't signing." I smiled at the memory of my own stubbornness. At first Rawlings had thought I was bluffing again, but I'd meant it. I'd have let the bank take everything before I was going to sign those papers and let Rawlings Brothers leave me without so much as a glider to call my own. "Once he saw I wasn't kidding, he said I could keep one trainer for myself, the PT-20."

"What? That old Ryan trainer? It's a piece of junk! Do you have any idea how many hours are on that engine? It needs to be completely rebuilt. It was the first plane Roger bought."

"I know," I said quietly. "That's why I asked for it."

Stubbs sighed and shook his head. "Well, you can't fly that thing."

"It runs, doesn't it?"

He rolled his eyes. "Yeah, for the moment, but it needs a whole new engine."

"Fine!" I hissed through clenched teeth, irritated that he wouldn't let me enjoy my one small victory. "I'll take my half of the money and buy a new engine."

Stubbs eyes grew wide, and he sucked hard on his cigarette. "Half? Georgia, I'm not taking half that money. This was your business, yours and Roger's, and I'm not taking half of what you got for it. Wouldn't feel right about it. You and Roger were always—"

"Stubbs!" I shouted. He froze and stared at me. I lowered my voice.

"I'm tired. I've lost my business, and I've got a headache. I know you mean well, but could we maybe fight about this tomorrow? What's done is done, and we'll just have to make the best of it."

"Sorry, Georgia," he mumbled, chastened. "Sure. We can talk tomorrow."

"Thanks."

"Can I do anything for you? Get you some aspirin, or something to eat?" He looked at his wristwatch. "The Soaring Wings is still open. I could run over and ask Thurman to make you up a grilled cheese."

"Yeah. That would be great." I wasn't really hungry, but I knew Stubbs needed something to do. Running to the café would give him a mission and me some time alone.

"Okay," he said. "I'll be back as quick as I can."

"That's all right. Take your time. I need a little time to get my desk cleaned off, anyway." He nodded and walked toward the door, lighting up a fresh Chesterfield as he went. I started shuffling through the papers on my desk.

"Say, Stubbs, did the mail come yet?"

"Yeah," he called over his shoulder, "it's right there, under that stack of past-due notices."

I pushed the pile of bills aside and saw it, a dirty, ragged envelope, fat with multiple pieces of stationery, addressed to me, and covered with FORWARD TO ADDRESSEE stamps in a rainbow of colors. It must have been lost in a morass of military mailbags, chasing me as I moved from one air base to the next for months on end.

The letter was postmarked August 11, 1944. And it was from Morgan.

Dear Georgia,

I'm writing you from a hospital in New Guinea. I had to ditch the plane after basically being run off the map during a dogfight and got myself a little banged up in the process. Nothing to worry about; they had to take a couple of toes, but the doctors say I should be fine in a few weeks.

I'm not writing to give you my medical update but because I wanted to tell you something. After bailing out, I had about a week to sit around, wait for rescue, and think. Many of my thoughts were of you, as they have been ever since San Diego. I've tried to deny it for a long time, but I can't anymore and I don't want to. I love you, Georgia. That's all there is to it. I know we hardly know each other. The collective hours we've spent in each other's company add up to days, not months or weeks. I know almost nothing about your family, or where you come from. Heck, I don't even know what your favorite color is. And still, I love you.

I know you were married to a pilot who was killed in combat. Maybe that's why you're so hesitant about letting me get closer to you, but I don't know for sure. You never told me. Just like I never told you why, when we were so close to coming together that night in San Diego, I put a halt to things. I know you were hurt and embarrassed. I should have explained to you right then why I backed away, but I couldn't do so without letting you in on my family secrets.

Even now, I'm nervous about telling you the whole truth—hearing it might convince you that you should have nothing to do with me, but I've decided to tell you anyway. Partly because, when I was out on that island and thinking I might die there, I promised myself that if I did live, I would stop living my life in the shadows of secrets that veiled my family since before I was born, but mostly because I love you and if you love

someone you should be honest with them, even if being honest
means you might lose them.

I stopped for a moment and held the pages of the letter to my
breast. Who'd ever have thought it? Morgan Glennon quoting
Cordelia Carter Boudreaux Prescott.

So here goes. I'm a bastard. My mother met my father when
she was seventeen years old. He was a pilot, a barnstormer
who stopped in our town for just a few days. She didn't even
know his real name. After he left, my mother found out she
was going to have a baby, me. When you just write it out like
that, it looks bad, I know. You'll probably think my mother
was the worst sort of woman and that she held herself very
cheaply indeed, but you'd be wrong. Mama was young, and in-
nocent, too trusting, and too in love. Maybe my father was too,
in fact, now I think he probably was, but he wasn't brave, at
least not then, and he wasn't wise. He left her alone without
thinking about the consequences of his actions and how Mama
might have to pay for them. And later, when he found out
about me, he walked away a second time, because he was
afraid of what might happen if people found out. He left my
mother to pay the price for loving him. And she did pay, for her
whole life. So did I.

That's why I backed off that night in San Diego, not be-
cause I didn't love you, but because I did and still do. Knowing
that, I couldn't put you in a position to have to pay for my care-
lessness, especially when I was about to ship out. No matter
how much I wanted you, Georgia, I couldn't do that to you. It
would have been wrong, morally and practically. Faith goes
deep in me. I know that lots of people look at the Bible as a big
bunch of rules that are designed to keep people from having
fun and for a while, I guess I felt the same. But the older I get,

the more I see God's laws our best chance for living happily and well in a fallen world, a guide given for our own protection and out of love. Just like I feel about you. Because I loved you, I wanted to protect you from the kind of pain and payment that was exacted from my mother.

But there's more, the secret so big that my own mother never told me. My father isn't just some nameless pilot; he is Charles Lindbergh. I didn't know it until just recently. When I was a kid, Lindbergh was my idol, but I never dreamed there was any connection between us. He was sent to the Pacific to teach pilots how to stretch out their fuel and he ended up on my base. We actually flew together and he told me he was my father. That was the night before I found myself stranded on that island.

I don't have enough paper or time to explain all the things that went through my mind while I was hoping for rescue. At first, I was mad, at Lindbergh, at Mama, at the whole world, and there is probably some of that still in me. I imagine it will take a while for me to work all this out in my mind, but the more I waited and the closer I got to death, the closer I moved toward forgiveness. From the first minute they met, my parents made terrible mistakes, but having come so close to doing the same myself, I can't exactly throw stones. While I can't help but wish I'd known about my own past sooner, I see now that Mama was doing what she thought was right at the time. As for my father, he should have owned up to his responsibilities years ago, but at least it is to his credit that he finally tried to do so. I'm glad, at last, to know my father. Even though he's never been a real part of my life and I don't expect that will change in the future, I can see that some parts of my personality, good and bad, I've inherited from him. On the good side, the love of flight comes quickly to mind and I'm sure there are other things too. On the bad side, there is this tendency to hide feelings and play it safe, leaving those I care about most in the dark.

And, like him, I'm trying to make up for that. Maybe it is too late. Maybe you can't forgive me. Maybe you'll find the truth of my family history so shocking that you can't love me. Or maybe you never loved me to begin with. It's a chance I had to take.

I'll be in the hospital a few weeks. I'm not sure where they will send me next, but they'll forward my mail. I really hope to hear from you, Georgia. And if I don't? I guess that means one of the maybes was true.

Love,
Morgan

"I love you, too, Morgan." I whispered. I read the closing again and wiped tears from my eyes. "I just pray I haven't figured it out too late."

44

Georgia

Waukegan, Illinois—May 1945

Stubbs squared his shoulders and planted his feet, looking as imposing and resolute as it is possible for a five-foot-four-inch man to look. "I don't care if you are the boss, Georgia! I am not letting you fly that rattletrap of a trainer all the way to Oklahoma. You'll get yourself killed!"

"Not if you go and tune that engine like I told you to, I won't!"

We stood toe to toe for a long minute. This time I didn't blink.

"Fine!" Stubbs grumbled. "But it'll take me three or four hours. Maybe"—he sneered—"you'll have come to your senses by then and we can forget the whole thing."

I laughed. "Stubbs, I finally *have* come to my senses. That's why I'm flying to Oklahoma in that rattletrap of a trainer, and I'm doing it in one hour. Do you hear me? One!"

His tone changed from sniping to pleading. "Georgia, be reasonable. I can't have it ready in an hour, not even close. You've got to—"

"One hour!" I turned on my heel and strode off toward the office to pack, wondering if the overnight kit Roger used to keep for emergencies and late nights was still in the bottom drawer of the file cabinet.

It was, but I hadn't even opened it when I heard the sound of engine noise. I walked to the window of the office and looked out just in time to see a plane, a brightly painted Stearman Katydet trainer, older than my Ryan but in much better condition, come in for a landing. And somehow I knew, even before he landed, Morgan was flying it.

And suddenly he was on the ground and I was in his arms, kissing him and crying. "How did you know? After all this time. How did you know?"

And he was grinning and confused but kissing me anyway. "How did I know what?"

"That I was coming to find you today! If you'd come an hour later you'd have missed me because I'd have been on my way to Oklahoma." I laughed and cried all at the same time. "I got your letter . . ."

"My letter?"

"The one you wrote from the hospital in New Guinea. The post office must have lost it. I only got it today, but as soon as I read it, I knew I had to go to you! Oh, Morgan! I love you! I always did, but I was just so afraid, and after I met your family . . . Well, I just thought they were so perfect. Your dad's a minister and your mother is so sweet. I just thought they'd never be able to accept someone like me and . . ." But before I could explain more, he kissed me again, sweet and soft on the mouth, and I kissed him back. Words could wait. I didn't need to talk or explain anything, not just then.

There were problems to be solved, I knew, apologies to be offered and accepted, plans made, and arrangements to be executed, but there was no hurry. Nothing in our past, present, or future would ever come between us again. We had time, time to share our stories, to share our hopes and our fears, our disappointments and our dreams.

Morgan and I had all the time in the world.

Epilogue

Morgan

Hana, Hawaii—August 26, 1975

When you are young, the old people nod sagely and tell you not to be in such a hurry, that time flies quickly enough without you searching for a tailwind, and you nod back and listen politely even though you don't believe them. But, of course, it is true. Life speeds by in an instant, rushing like wind between your open fingers. If you've been fortunate enough to find your happiness, it goes even faster.

It's been more than thirty-one years since I woke in my bed in Liberal, Kansas, decided that my mother was right, that I couldn't give up on love, and flew all the way to Waukegan in search of it. It's thirty years to the month since Georgia and I were married, and one year to the day since my father died.

We'd wanted to come to Hawaii for years and years, but somehow we never found the time. You know how it is—business is too busy or too slow, the children are too young or too old—in the busyness of life, you can always find some reason or other for putting off the things you'd really love to do. Not that I'm complaining. Georgia and I have built a wonderful life together. Our children, Janet, the oldest, and the twins, Carter and Clare, are all grown now and I couldn't be prouder of them.

Clare is in Arizona, working on her masters degree in aerospace engineering. She wants to design airplanes someday. Isn't that something? Janet and Carter still live in Oklahoma. They both fell in love young, married, and have given us three wonderful grandkids. All the kids learned to fly a plane before they could drive a car. Janet and Carter are instructors and help us run the business, which is lucky for us. I don't see how we could manage it otherwise.

At the end of the war, we didn't have much. For the first two years of our marriage, until Janet came along, Georgia and I lived in Ruby's old caboose in the backyard. The quarters were tight, but we were so happy we didn't care. And it was nice to be so close to Mama and Paul. Mama and Georgia got to be real close, and, just as I'd feared, Mama turned Georgia into a quilter. There's a bedroom in our house that's supposed to be for guests, but it's so filled up with fabric and sewing machines and quilt batting that you can't get to the bed. We bought the place in '47, and we've lived there ever since, but, like I said, at first we didn't have much. We sank every penny into the school.

Georgia and Stubbs Peterson had six thousand dollars each, and I had the same, money I'd saved from my service pay plus the proceeds of an account my father had opened for me years before but Mama had never touched. When we decided to pool our money and open a flight school with nothing but our collected savings and those two trainers, Georgia's Ryan and my Stearman, none of us could have imagined that one day we'd eventually own the biggest private airfield in all of western Kansas and Oklahoma, but we do. Georgia and I fly every single day of our lives, sometimes together and sometimes separately, and every single flight is just as awe-inspiring as the first, like being born, opening your eyes, and seeing the world for the very first time. As I've grown older, many of life's pleasures have faded for me, but flying? Never.

Over the years we've helped hundreds of would-be pilots, male and female, find their wings. The first woman to graduate from Welles Flight School was Georgia's best friend from grade school, Fran. Lately, we've had almost as many women coming through the door as men. Recently the government has been making noise about finally granting the WASP the full military status and benefits that should have been theirs to begin with, and all kinds of reporters have been showing up on our doorstep, wanting to interview Georgia. The stories have been run in newspapers all over the country, and now women from everywhere have been deciding they want to learn how to fly and insisting that Georgia be their instructor. I can't blame them for that. They couldn't ask for a better teacher.

Our children know where and what they come from. We've told them about Roger, about Delia and Earl and Nathan, and about Mama and Lindbergh, too. Not that we go around sharing our private business with the whole world, but we don't keep secrets anymore, not about the family or from the family. The good, the bad, the truth; it's all part of who we are.

When we opened the school back in '45, we decided to call it Welles Flight School in honor of Georgia's late husband. After Georgia told me about him, I thought it was only right. I never met him, but he was a good man and should be remembered. And though I've no reason to suppose it's true, I can't help but wonder if old Roger hasn't been up there watching out for all of us in some way, or at least for Georgia. She was born with wings in her heart, just like I was. Roger helped her find them, just like my parents helped me. Every one of us stands on the shoulders of those who have gone before. I'm grateful.

I always meant to tell my father that, but the years went by and I never did. When I heard he'd moved to Hawaii a few years back, I started talking to Georgia about going there, maybe to celebrate our wedding anniversary, and bringing the whole family along. She agreed right off, said she'd heard it was beautiful there, but talk of sightseeing aside, she knew why I really wanted to go. I wanted to see him one more time, to introduce him to his grandchildren, to let him know that, even though we'd gotten off to a rocky start, we'd turned out all right in the end. I wasn't quite sure how I'd say it, though.

Maybe that's why every year, when Georgia would ask if we were going to Hawaii for our anniversary, I'd come up with some reason why we couldn't, not just yet.

Then, a year ago today, I sat down at the kitchen table to drink my coffee, opened the paper, and read that he was gone. I started crying and I couldn't stop. Georgia didn't say anything at first, just put her arms around me.

When I finally found breath enough to speak, I said, "Somehow I always thought I'd see him again. I thought there'd be time, and that I'd finally figure out what I meant to say. Now it's too late."

Georgia reached up and brushed her hand over my head, then traced her finger along the outline of my hair where it is beginning to recede, just like his did. She smiled, and the understanding and love of a lifetime together showed in her eyes. "Morgan, that's not true. You of all people should know—it's never too late to say you love someone."

So here I am, driving a rented Chrysler sedan along the narrow, impossibly winding road from Lahaina to Hana with Mama sitting beside me. I'd asked Georgia and Paul and everyone else if they wanted to go along, but they all claimed a sudden interest in taking a ride on a glass-bottomed boat. I guess they knew it was something Mama and I needed to do on our own.

* * *

Mama is in her seventies now, but her eyes are still sharp. She spots the sign before I do. "There," she points out the window. "Mile marker forty-one."

I turn down the road that I've been told leads to the Palapala Ho'omau church, and there it is. A simple white church constructed of limestone coral. It's smaller than I had imagined. I park the car and go to open Mama's door and help her out. The terrain is uneven, so I make sure she has a good grip on her cane before I hand her the big black bag she insists on carrying herself.

There are no other visitors today. The only sound is the chirping of the brilliantly feathered birds that flutter through the trees like so many bright guardian angels and the soft shuffle of our feet as we walk slowly down the path.

It takes me some time to locate the correct grave. The headstone is simple and dignified, modest and not at all out of place among the rest. A blanket of stones of uneven sizes but with rounded edges and shallow-cratered indentation, as if they had been tumbled together in the surf, surrounds the headstone. Mama and I stand at the foot of the grave, not saying anything.

Our heads are bowed, as if praying, but I wonder if she is having better luck than I am when it comes to finding words. There is so much I want to say and so much I feel, but the only sentence I can conjure is, *I'm here.* I hope that is enough.

After a few minutes, Mama lifts her head. I can see the tears in her eyes. She opens the black bag and pulls out the quilt, the one she stitched for me all those years ago, with Mama and me standing in shadow on the earth and the fluttering edges of an aviator's scarf, the spirit of my father, looking on from a distance. She unfolds the quilt and lays it over the grave like she is tucking a child to sleep. I help her.

We stand again and see, and think, and feel, and say our farewells.

There is nothing on the headstone to indicate that the man who lies under it was one of the most famous men of his time, that he flew across oceans and made the world smaller, that during his lifetime, he was feted and hated with passion and vehemence by people all over the world. If you did not know his story, you would not have known any of that by looking at this stone. He designed it himself. I suppose that was how he wanted it. Before many generations pass, all that will be known of the man who lies here is his name, Charles A. Lindbergh, that he was born in Michigan in 1902 and died in Maui in 1974. And, eventually, worn by weather and time, the engraving on the stone will fade, and even this small biography will be lost to the living. Other than this, the only clue the headstone gives about the identity of the man below, of his life and loves, is a fragment of a psalm. I read it aloud: "If I take the wings of the morning and dwell in the uttermost parts of the sea . . ."

Mama, the minister's wife, completes what the stone has left unfinished, "Even there shall thy hand lead me, and thy right hand shall hold me."

"Do you believe that, Mama?"

She smiles through her tears and nods. "Yes, Morgan. I do."

I reach out to squeeze her hand. "So do I."

A CHAT WITH MARIE BOSTWICK

When my first novel, *Fields of Gold,* was purchased, my editor asked if I wanted to write a sequel. At the time the answer was no.

If you haven't read it first, (and don't worry if you haven't—I've worked hard to make sure you can read the books in any order and still keep up with the story), *Fields of Gold* focused on Morgan's mother, Eva Glennon, and was told in her voice. I spent four years writing about Eva and in that time, came to feel very close to her, even a bit protective of her. By the end of the story she was in the land of "happily ever after," which was just where I wanted her to be. But, at least in terms of fiction writing, happily ever after doesn't make for very interesting reading. There didn't seem to be much more to say about Eva's life, so I decided to leave her in peace and move on to another character and another story.

But one day, many months later, the galleys for *Fields of Gold* arrived . . . After I quit crying for joy, still slightly disbelieving that my dream was actually coming true and that my book was really going to be published, I sat down to read the story for the first time in over a year. That's when I realized that while I knew everything about Eva, I had questions about the other characters, especially Morgan. What had it been like for him to grow up in such a small town with the label of illegitimacy pinned to his chest? What had been said in that first face-to-face meeting with his father? Was there a happily ever after in his future? I simply didn't know.

And then, after *Fields of Gold* was released, I started getting emails from some of you wondering the same thing. As much as I wanted to answer those questions and was beginning to formulate some thoughts on the subject, I didn't feel I had enough upon which to base an entire novel. So I started working on a completely different story for my third book but questions about Morgan kept interrupting my train of thought. One day, as I was walking to nowhere on the treadmill in my basement, a place where some of my best ideas seem to form, the character of Georgia Carter became suddenly very clear. Morgan couldn't carry the story alone, nor could Georgia, but together? Oh, yes! Though a third of the way through the other project, there was no doubt in my mind that I had to abandon it and get to work on Morgan and Georgia's story that very day.

If you've read my other historical fiction titles, you know that while I make no claims to being a historian, I do a great deal of research before writing and try to stay as close to the facts as possible. However, if need be, I do alter the historical record, or at least squeeze it a bit, in the interest of keeping the story moving while maintaining the sense of history and believability.

My research for *On Wings of the Morning* began by reading some excellent books about the Women's Air Service Pilots (WASP). As I've said, I try hard to stay true to the historic record, but this is a work of fiction so if you're interested in the real, in-depth history of the WASP, I'd highly recommend the following nonfiction titles:

Those Wonderful Women in Their Flying Machines: The Unknown Heroines of World War II by Sally Van Wagenen Keil
Yankee Doodle Gals: Women Pilots of World War II by Amy Nathan
Clipped Wings: The Rise and Fall of the Women's Airforce Service Pilots (WASPs) of World War II by Molly Merryman

The first two titles are accurate and affectionate accounts of the WASP, filled with anecdotes as well as information. The third is a more scholarly work, loaded with resources and documents that give a thorough analysis of the social mores of the day and sexism, which the women of the WASP faced and that ultimately led to its demise. The WASP didn't suddenly disband just because there was nothing left for them to do, but because their continued existence was threatening to a particular group of male pilots and those within the military, as Ms. Merryman's book convincingly documents. This particular title heavily influenced the tone and plot of my fictional account of the WASP. All three books are expertly researched, worthwhile reading.

Additionally, the WASP have a terrific web site at www.wings acrossamerica.org with all kinds of documents, photos, interactive games, and videos of interviews with actual WASP pilots. This site has undergone considerable upgrading since I first began referring to it. It is well worth checking out and, if you can, supporting financially so the inspiring stories of the WASP can be recorded and preserved for future generations. One of the things that so bothered me while researching this book was that until very recently, I'd had no idea that the WASP even existed, let alone the extent of their influence and sacrifice in winning the war. Of the many injustices and slights heaped upon these brave women, this is the unkindest cut of all—that so few know about who they were and what they did for our nation. Hopefully, this book will serve, at least in some small way, to help right that wrong and fuel increased interest in the story of the amazing women of the WASP. Theirs is a story that needs to be told.

Georgia and her WASP friends, Pam, Donna Lee, and Fanny, are completely fictional, but their stories are representative of the collective stories of the WASP and the adventures, challenges, and dangers they faced. Like Georgia and her friends, the WASP came from a wide range of educational, economic, vocational, and geographic backgrounds. They volunteered to fly for the WASP for different reasons, but they all shared a deep sense of patriotism, adventure, and the longing for flight. The figures I cite regarding the numbers of missions flown, aircraft delivered, and casualties suffered by the WASP are accurate and show how greatly the WASP contributed to the war effort.

However, in order to make the dates of Georgia's history mesh with the dates of Morgan's history already set forth in *Fields of Gold,* I had to compress time a bit. For example, a picture of Shirley Slade (a real life WASP) actually appeared on the cover of *Life* magazine in July of 1943, but to make the story work, I had to change that date to May of the same year. Likewise, when it came to training dates and locations, I had to take similar liberties with dates but the basic story of what the WASP learned in their training, where they trained, and the conditions under which they trained (there really was a sudden increase in the number of male pilots requesting "emergency" landings at Avenger Field after word got out that the WASP were in residence) should give you a sense of what it took for a young woman to become a WASP.

Morgan Glennon is a completely fictional character as are Eva, Paul, and the other inhabitants of Dillon, Oklahoma, a town that, if it really existed, would be located about ten miles south of Liberal, Kansas, just across the Oklahoma state line. Long before he made his historic flight to Paris, in 1922 and 1923 Charles Lindbergh did barnstorm in Texas and Oklahoma. It is that period of his life, when he was a young, still-unknown pilot barnstorming his way through the Plains and, I imagine, causing the hearts of many a small town girl to beat just a bit faster, that served as the jumping off place for his romance with Eva. However, there is no evidence that he had any relationships with young women at that time. His relationship with Eva Glennon and Morgan's eventual birth are complete inventions on my part.

However, many of the other facts concerning Charles Lindbergh are true. Though he was vehemently opposed to America's entry into World War II, Lindbergh did volunteer to serve in the military after war was declared. When he was denied a commission, Lindbergh served as an adviser to companies building military aircraft. In that capacity, he went to the Pacific and flew alongside military pilots, most famously the 475th Fighter Group. Though a civilian, and an aging one at that, during his tour Lindbergh flew combat missions, shot enemy aircraft, and taught pilots the fuel mixing techniques described in the story that allowed them to significantly expand their flight range and gave them a valuable element of surprise when facing the enemy. Though his confrontation with Morgan is entirely fictional the exchange between the two men gives a sense of the complex and sometimes contradictory nature of Lindbergh's personal life and achievements. Even now, four decades after his death, people are still arguing about Charles Lindbergh and if he was a hero, villain, or something in between. For more information about the real Charles Lindbergh, I recommend the excellent biography, *Lindbergh* by Scott Berg. Also, if you'd like more information about Lindbergh's adventures with the 475th Fighter Group, I urge to visit their web site, www.475thfghf.org.

I hope the above has answered any questions you might have about this story. If not, I hope you'll visit my web site, www.mariebostwick. com and send me an email . Actually, I hope you'll do that even if you don't have questions. The web site is full of information about my books, appearance schedule, reader's contests, and the like. Additionally, there are downloadable copies of discussion questions for each of my books as well as a contact form where you can send questions, comments, or invitations to have me speak at your bookstore or community organization. I love to hear from my reading friends and do my best to answer all inquiries as quickly and thoroughly as time, tide, and deadlines allow.

Besides writing, connecting with readers is one of the things I enjoy doing most. If you have a book group with ten or more people, a speakerphone, and would like me to participate in one of your discussions, please drop by my web site, *www.mariebostwick.com*, and click on the "Book Club Invitations" tab to make your request. If you invite me, I'll be there!

Thank you for reading *On Wings of the Morning*. Time is the most precious, finite commodity that we have, and I am honored that you chose to spend some of yours with Morgan, Georgia, and their friends. I hope you enjoyed reading this story as much as I enjoyed writing it.

Until we meet again.

Blessings,

Marie Bostwick

If you enjoyed On Wings of the Morning, *don't miss Marie Bostwick's delightful and heartwarming holiday story, "A High-Kicking Christmas," about a burned-out Rockette who finds herself in small-town Vermont putting on a Christmas pageant and discovers that the handsome young pastor she's working with lights up her life even more than Broadway ever did!*

Comfort and Joy, *also features stories by* #1 New York Times *bestselling author Fern Michaels, and rising stars Cathy Lamb and Deborah J. Wolf.*

A Zebra paperback, on sale now!